P9-DOF-730

SAINT
ANYTHING

SAINT
ANYTHING

CHAPTER

1

"WOULD THE defendant please rise."

This wasn't an actual question, even though it sounded like one. I'd noticed that the first time we'd all been assembled here, in this way. Instead, it was a command, an order. The "please" was just for show.

My brother stood up. Beside me, my mom tensed, sucking in a breath. Like the way they tell you to inhale before an X-ray so they can see more, get it all. My father stared straight forward, as always, his face impossible to read.

The judge was talking again, but I couldn't seem to listen. Instead, I looked over to the tall windows, the trees blowing back and forth outside. It was early August; school started in three weeks. It felt like I had spent the entire summer in this very room, maybe in this same seat, but I knew that wasn't the case. Time just seemed to stop here. But maybe, for people like Peyton, that was exactly the point.

It was only when my mother gasped, bending forward to grab the bench in front of us, that I realized the sentence had been announced. I looked up at my brother. He'd been known for his fearlessness all the way back to when we were kids playing in the woods behind our house. But the day those older boys had challenged him to walk across that wide, gaping sinkhole on a skinny branch and he did it, his ears had been bright red. He was scared. Then and now.

There was a bang of the gavel, and we were dismissed. The attorneys turned to my brother, one leaning in close to speak while the other put a hand on his back. People were getting up, filing out, and I could feel their eyes on us as I swallowed hard and focused on my hands in my lap. Beside me, my mother was sobbing.

"Sydney?" Ames said. "You okay?"

I couldn't answer, so I just nodded.

"Let's go," my father said, getting to his feet. He took my mom's arm, then gestured for me to walk ahead of them, up to where the lawyers and Peyton were.

"I have to go to the ladies' room," I said.

My mom, her eyes red, just looked at me. As if this, after all that had happened, was the thing that she simply could not bear.

"It's okay," Ames said. "I'll take her."

My father nodded, clapping him on the shoulder as we passed. Out in the courthouse lobby, I could see people pushing the doors open, out into the light outside, and I wished more than anything that I was among them.

Ames put his arm around me as we walked. "I'll wait for you here," he said when we reached the ladies' room. "Okay?"

Inside, the light was bright, unforgiving, as I walked to the sinks and looked at myself in the mirror there. My face was pale, my eyes dark, flat, and empty.

A stall door behind me opened and a girl came out. She was about my height, but smaller, slighter. As she stepped up beside me, I saw she had blonde hair, plaited in a messy braid that hung over one shoulder, a few wisps framing her face, and she wore a summer dress, cowboy boots, and a denim jacket. I felt her look at me as I washed my hands once, then twice, before grabbing a towel and turning to the door.

I pushed it open, and there was Ames, directly across the hallway, leaning against the wall with his arms folded over his chest. When he saw me, he stood up taller, taking a step forward. I hesitated, stopping, and the girl, also leaving, bumped into my back.

"Oh! Sorry!" she said.

"No," I told her, turning around. "It was . . . my fault."

She looked at me for a second, then past my shoulder, at Ames. I watched her green eyes take him in, this stranger, for a long moment before turning her attention back to me. I had never seen her before. But with a single look at her face, I knew exactly what she was thinking.

You okay?

I was used to being invisible. People rarely saw me, and if they did, they never looked close. I wasn't shiny and charming like my brother, stunning and graceful like my mother, or smart and dynamic like my friends. That's the thing, though. You always think you want to be noticed. Until you are.

The girl was still watching me, waiting for an answer to the question she hadn't even said aloud. And maybe I would have answered it. But then I felt a hand on my elbow. Ames.

"Sydney? You ready?"

I didn't reply to this, either. Somehow we were heading toward the lobby, where my parents were now standing with the lawyers. As we walked, I kept glancing behind me, trying to see that girl, but could not in the shifting crowd of people pressing into the courtroom. Once we were clear of them, though, I looked back one last time and was surprised to find her right where I'd left her. Her eyes were still on me, like she'd never lost sight of me at all.

For all the invisible girls
and for my readers, for seeing me

SAINT
ANYTHING

a novel

SARAH DESSEN

Viking

An Imprint of Penguin Group (USA)

VIKING
Published by the Penguin Group
Penguin Group (USA) LLC
375 Hudson Street
New York, New York 10014

USA * Canada * UK * Ireland * Australia * New Zealand * India * South Africa * China

penguin.com
A Penguin Random House Company

First published in the United States of America by Viking,
an imprint of Penguin Young Readers Group, 2015

LIBRARY OF CONGRESS CATALOGING-IN-PUBLICATION DATA
Dessen, Sarah.
Saint Anything / Sarah Dessen.
pages cm
Summary: Sydney's charismatic older brother, Peyton, has always been the center of
attention in the family but when he is sent to jail, Sydney struggles to find her place
at home and the world until she meets the Chathams, including gentle,
protective Mac, who makes her feel seen for the first time.
ISBN 978-0-451-47470-4 (hardback)
[1. Family problems—Fiction. 2. Brothers and sisters—Fiction.
3. Self-perception—Fiction. 4. Friendship—Fiction. 5. Family life—Fiction.
6. Dating (Social customs)—Fiction.] I. Title.
PZ7.D455Sai 2015   [Fic]—dc23   2014039813

Printed in U.S.A.

1   3   5   7   9   10   8   6   4   2

Designed by Nancy Brennan   Set in Berling LT

CHAPTER

2

THE FIRST thing you saw when you walked into our house
was a portrait of my brother. It hung directly across from
the huge glass door, right above a wood credenza and the
Chinese vase where my father stored his umbrellas. You'd be
forgiven if you never noticed either of these things, though.
Once you saw Peyton, you couldn't take your eyes off him.

Though we shared the same looks (dark hair, olive skin,
brown, almost black, eyes) he somehow carried them totally
differently. I was average, kind of cute. But Peyton—the second in our house, with my father Peyton the first—was gorgeous. I'd heard him compared to everything from movie
idols of long before my time to fictional characters tromping
across Scottish moors. I was pretty sure my brother was unaware as a child of the attention he received in supermarkets
or post office lines. I wondered how it had felt when he'd suddenly understood the effect his looks had on people, women
especially. Like discovering a superpower, both thrilling and
daunting, all at once.

Before all that, though, he was just my brother. Three
years older, blue King Combat sheets on his bed in contrast

to my pink Fairy Foo ones. I basically worshipped him. How could I not? He was the king of Truth or Dare (he always went with the latter, naturally), the fastest runner in the neighborhood, and the only person I'd ever seen who could stand, balanced, on the handlebars of a rolling bicycle.

But his greatest talent, to me, was disappearing.

We played a lot of hide-and-seek as kids, and Peyton took it *seriously*. Ducking behind the first chair spotted in a room, or choosing the obvious broom closet? Those were for amateurs. My brother would fold himself beneath the cabinet under the bathroom sink, flatten completely under a bedspread, climb up the shower stall to spread across the ceiling, somehow holding himself there. Whenever I asked him for his secrets, he'd just smile. "You just have to find the invisible place," he told me. Only he could see it, though.

We practiced wrestling moves in front of cartoons on weekend mornings, fought over whom the dog loved more (just guess), and spent the hours after school we weren't in activities (soccer for him, gymnastics for me) exploring the undeveloped green space behind our neighborhood. This is how my brother still appears to me whenever I think of him: walking ahead of me on a crisp day, a stick in his hand, through the dappled fall colors of the woods. Even when I was nervous we'd get lost, Peyton never was. That fearlessness again. A flat landscape never appealed to him. He always needed something to push up against. When things got bad with Peyton, I always wished we were back there, still walking. Like we hadn't reached where we were going yet, and there was still a chance it might be somewhere else.

I was in sixth grade when things began to change. Until then, we had both been on the lower campus of Perkins Day, the private school we'd attended since kindergarten. That year, though, he moved to Upper School. Within a couple of weeks, he'd started hanging out with a bunch of juniors and seniors. They treated him like a mascot, daring him to do stupid stuff like lifting Popsicles from the cafeteria line or climbing into a car trunk to sneak off campus for lunch. This was when Peyton's legend began in earnest. He was bigger than life, bigger than *our* lives.

Meanwhile, when I didn't have gymnastics, I was now riding the bus home solo, then eating my snack alone at the kitchen island. I had my own friends, of course, but most of them were highly scheduled, never around on weekday afternoons due to various activities. This was typical of our neighborhood, the Arbors, where the average household could support any extracurricular activity from Mandarin lessons to Irish dancing and everything in between. Financially, my family was about average for the area. My father, who started his career in the military before going to law school, had made his money in corporate conflict resolution. He was the guy called when a company had a problem—threat of a lawsuit, serious issues between employees, questionable practices about to be brought to light—and needed it worked out. It was no wonder I grew up believing there was no problem my father couldn't solve. For much of my life, I'd never seen any proof otherwise.

If Dad was the general, my mom was the chief operating officer. Unlike some parents, who approached parenting as a tag-team sport, in our family the duties were very clearly divided. My father handled the bills, house, and yard upkeep, and my mom dealt with everything else. Julie Stanford was That Mother, the one who read every parenting book and stocked her minivan with enough snacks and sports equipment for every kid in the neighborhood. Like my dad, if my mom did something, she did it right. Which was why it was all the more surprising when, eventually, things went wrong anyway.

The trouble with Peyton started in the winter of his tenth grade year. One afternoon I was watching TV in the living room with a bowl of popcorn when the doorbell rang. When I looked outside, I saw a police car in the driveway.

"Mom?" I called upstairs. She was in her office, which was basically command central for our entire house. My dad called it the War Room. "Someone's here."

I don't know why I didn't tell her it was the police. It just seemed saying it might make it real, and I wasn't sure what was out there yet.

"Sydney, you are perfectly capable of answering the door," she replied, but sure enough, a beat later I heard her coming down the stairs.

I kept my eyes on the TV, where the characters from my favorite reality show, *Big New York*, were in the midst of yet another dinner party catfight. The Big franchise had been part of my afternoon ritual since Peyton had started high school, the guiltiest of guilty pleasures. Rich women being petty and pretty, I'd heard it described, and that summed it up. There were about six different shows—*Dallas, Los Angeles,* and *Chicago* among them—enough so that I could easily watch two every day to fill the time between when I got home and dinner. I was so involved in the show, it was like they were my friends, and I often found myself talking back to the TV as if they could hear me, or thinking about their issues and problems even when I wasn't watching. It was a weird kind of loneliness, feeling that some of my closest friends didn't actually know I existed. But without them, the house felt so empty, even with my mom there, which made *me* feel empty in a way I'd grown to dread the moment I stepped off the bus after school. My own life felt flat and sad too much of the time; it was reassuring, somehow, to lose myself in someone else's.

So I was watching Rosalie, the former actress, accuse Ayre, the model, of being a bully, when everything in our family's life shifted. One minute the door was shut and things were fine. The next, it was open and there was Peyton, a police officer beside him.

"Ma'am," the cop said as my mother stepped back, putting a hand to her chest. "Is this your son?"

This was what I would remember later. This one question, the answer a no-brainer, and yet still one my parents, and Mom especially, would grapple with from that point on. Starting that day, when Peyton got caught smoking pot in the Perkins Day parking lot with his friends, my brother began a transformation into someone we didn't always recognize. There would be other visits from the authorities, trips to the police station, and, eventually, court dates and rehab stays. But it was this first one that stayed in my mind, crisp in detail. The bowl of popcorn, warm in my lap. Rosalie's sharp voice. And my mom, stepping back to let my brother inside. As the cop led him down the hallway to the kitchen, my brother looked at me. His ears were bright red.

Because he hadn't had any pot on his person, Perkins Day decided to handle the infraction itself, with a suspension and volunteer hours doing tutoring at the Lower School. The story—especially the part about how Peyton was the only one who ran, forcing the cops to chase him down—made the rounds, with how far he'd gotten (a block, five, a mile) growing with each telling. My mom cried. My dad, furious, grounded him for a full month. Things didn't go back to the way they had been, though. Peyton came home and went to his room, staying there until dinner. He served his time, swore he'd learned his lesson. Three months later, he got busted for breaking and entering.

There's a weird thing that happens when something goes from a one-time thing to a habit. Like the problem is no longer just a temporary houseguest but has actually moved in.

After that, we fell into a routine. My brother accepted his punishment and my parents slowly relaxed, accepting as fact their various theories about why this would never happen again. Then Peyton would get busted—for drugs, shoplifting, reckless driving—and we'd all go back down the rabbit hole of charges, lawyers, court, and sentences.

After his first shoplifting arrest, when the cops found pot during his pat-down, Peyton went to rehab. He returned with a thirty-day chip on his key chain and interest in playing guitar thanks to his roommate at Evergreen Care Center. My parents paid for lessons and made plans to outfit part of the basement as a small studio so he could record his original compositions. The work was halfway done when the school found a small amount of pills in his locker.

He got suspended for three weeks, during which time he was supposed to be staying home, getting tutored and preparing for his court date. Two days before he was due to go back to school, I was awakened out of a deep sleep by the rumbling of the garage door opening. I looked out the window to see my dad's car backing onto our street. My clock said three fifteen a.m.

I got up and went out into the hallway, which was dark and quiet, then padded down the stairs. A light was on in the kitchen. There I found my mother, in her pajamas and a U sweatshirt, making a pot of coffee. When she saw me, she just shook her head.

"Go back to sleep," she told me. "I'll fill you in tomorrow."

By the next morning, my brother had been bailed out, charged yet again with breaking and entering, this time with added counts of trespassing and resisting arrest. The previous evening, after my parents had gone to bed, he'd snuck out of his room, walked up our road, then climbed the fence around the Villa, the biggest house in the Arbors. He found an unlocked window and wriggled through, then poked around for only a few minutes before the cops arrived, alerted by the silent alarm. When they came in, he bolted out the back door. They tackled him on the pool deck, leaving huge, bloody scrapes across his face. Amazingly, my mother seemed more upset about this than anything else.

"It just seems like we might have a case," she said to my dad later that morning. She was dressed now, all business: they had a meeting with Peyton's lawyer at nine a.m. sharp. "I mean, did you see those wounds? What about police brutality?"

"Julie, he was running from them," my dad replied in a tired voice.

"Yes, I understand that. But I also understand that he is still a minor, and force was not necessary. There was a *fence*. It's not like he was going anywhere."

But he was, I thought, although I knew better than to say this aloud. The more Peyton got into trouble, the more my mom seemed desperate to blame anyone and everyone else. The school was out to get him. The cops were too rough. But my brother was no innocent: all you had to do was look at the facts. Although sometimes, I felt like I was the only one who could see them.

By the next day at school, word had spread, and I was getting side-eyed all over the hallways. It was decided that Peyton would withdraw from Perkins Day and finish high school elsewhere, although opinions differed on whether it was the school or my parents who made this choice.

I was lucky to have my friends, who rallied around me, letting people know that I was not my brother, despite our shared looks and last name. Jenn, whom I'd known since our days at Trinity Church Preschool, was especially protective. Her dad had had his own tangles with the law, back in college.

"He was always honest about it, that it was just experimentation," she told me as we sat in the cafeteria at lunch. "He paid his debt to society, and now look, he's a CEO, totally successful. Peyton will be, too. This, too, shall pass."

Jenn always sounded like this, older than she was, mostly because her parents had had her in their forties and treated her like a little adult. She even looked like a grown-up, with her sensible haircut, glasses, and comfortable footwear. At times it was strange, like she'd skipped childhood altogether, even when she was in it. But now, I was reassured. I wanted to believe her. To believe anything.

Peyton received three months in jail and a fine. That was the first time we were all in court together. His lawyer, Sawyer Ambrose, whose ads were on bus stops all over town (NEED A LAWYER? CALL ON SAWYER!), maintained that it was crucial for the jury to see us sitting behind my brother like the loyal, tight family we were.

Also present was my brother's new best friend, a guy he'd met in the Narcotics Anonymous group he was required to attend. Ames was a year older than Peyton, tall with shaggy hair and a loping walk, and had gotten busted for dealing pot a year earlier. He'd served six months and stayed out of trouble ever since, setting the kind of example everyone agreed my brother needed. They drank a lot of coffee drinks together, played video games, and studied, Peyton with his books from the alternative school where he'd landed, Ames for the classes he was taking in hospitality management at Lakeview Tech. They planned that Peyton would do the same once he got his diploma, and together they'd go work at one resort or another. My mom loved this idea, and already had all the paperwork necessary to make it happen: it sat in its own labeled envelope on her desk. There was just the little matter of the jail thing to get out of the way first.

My brother ended up serving seven weeks at the county lockup. I was not permitted to see him, but my mother visited every time it was allowed. Meanwhile, Ames remained; it seemed like he was always parked at our kitchen table with a coffee drink, ducking out occasionally to the garage to smoke cigarettes, using a sand-bucket ashtray my mom (who abhorred the habit) put out there just for him. Sometimes he showed up with his girlfriend, Marla, a manicurist with blonde hair, big blue eyes, and a shyness so prevalent she rarely spoke. If you addressed her, she got super nervous, like a small dog too tightly wound and always shaking.

I knew Ames was a comfort to my mom. But something about him made me uneasy. Like how I'd catch him watching me over the rim of his coffee cup, following my movements with his dark eyes. Or how he always found a way to touch me—squeezing my shoulder, brushing against my arm—when he said hello. It wasn't like he'd ever done anything to me, so I felt like it had to be my problem. Plus, he had a girlfriend. All he wanted, he told me again and again, was to take care of me the way Peyton would.

"It was the one thing he asked me the day he went in," he told me soon after my brother was gone. We were in the kitchen, and my mom had stepped out to take a phone call, leaving us alone. "He said, 'Look out for Sydney, man. I'm counting on you.'"

I wasn't sure what to say to this. First of all, it didn't sound like Peyton, who'd barely given me the time of day in the months before he'd gone away. Plus, even before that, he'd never been the protective type. But Ames knew my brother well, and the truth was that I no longer did. So I had to take his word for it.

"Well," I said, feeling like I should offer something, "um, thanks."

"No problem." He gave me another one of those long looks. "It's the least I can do."

When Peyton was released, he was still quiet, but more engaged, helping out more around the house and being present in a way he hadn't been in the previous months. Sometimes, after he got home from school, he'd even watch TV with me. He could only stand *Big New York* or *Miami* for short periods, though, before getting disgusted with every single character.

"That's Ayre," I'd try to explain as the gaunt, heavily nipped-and-tucked one-time Playmate had yet another meltdown. "She and Rosalie, the actress? They're, like, always at each other."

Peyton said nothing, only rolling his eyes. He had little patience for anything, I was noticing.

"You pick something," I'd say, pushing the remote at him. "Seriously, I don't care what we watch."

But it never worked. It was like he could alight next to me for just so long before having to move on to checking e-mail, strumming his guitar, or getting something to eat. His fidgeting kept increasing, and it made me nervous. I saw my mom notice it as well. Like some kind of internal energy had lost its outlet and was just building up, day after day, until he found a new one.

He got his diploma in June, in a small ceremony with only eight classmates, most of whom had also been kicked out of their previous schools. We all attended, Ames and Marla included, and went out to dinner afterward at Luna Blu, one of our favorite restaurants. There, over their famous fried pickle appetizer, we toasted my brother with our soft drinks before my parents presented him with his graduation gift: two round-trip tickets to Jacksonville, Florida, so he and Ames could check out a well-known hospitality course there. My mom had even made them an appointment with the school's director, as well as set up a private tour. Of course.

"This is great," my brother said, looking down at the tickets. "Seriously. Thanks, Mom and Dad."

My mother smiled, tears pricking her eyes, as my dad reached over, clapping Peyton on the shoulder. We were sitting outside on the patio, tiny fairy lights strung up overhead, and we'd just had a great meal together. The moment seemed so far away from the year we'd had, like everything in the fall and before it was just a bad dream. The next day, my mom sat down with me to talk about my hopes for college. Finally, I was the project. It was my turn.

That fall, I started tenth grade at Perkins Day. My own transition to Upper School the year before had been as unremarkable as my brother's had been eventful. Jenn and I made friends with a new girl, Meredith, who'd moved to Lakeview to train at the U's gymnastics facility. She was small and all muscle, with the best posture I'd ever seen, not to mention the perkiest ponytail. She'd been training for competition since she was six. I'd never met anyone so driven and disciplined, and she basically spent every hour she wasn't at school in the gym. Together, we three formed an easy friendship, as we all felt a little older than our classmates: Jenn because of her upbringing, Meredith because of her sport, and me because of everything that had happened in the last year. My brother's legend, for better or worse, still preceded me. But my choice of friends—and the fact that we avoided all parties and illegal extracurriculars even as our classmates experimented—made it clear we were very different.

With Peyton working as a valet at a local hotel and taking his hospitality classes with Ames at Lakeview Tech, my dad doing more traveling, and my mom returning to her volunteer projects, I often had the house entirely to myself after school. I started to feel that sadness again, creeping up each afternoon as the sun went down. I tried to fill it with *Big*

New York or *Miami*, watching back-to-back-to-back episodes until my eyes were bleary. Even so, I always felt a rush of relief when I heard the garage door opening, signaling someone's return and the shift to dinner and nighttime, when I wouldn't be by myself anymore.

Then, the day after Valentine's Day, my brother left his job at the regular time, a little after ten p.m. Instead of coming home, however, he went to visit an old friend from Perkins Day. There, he drank several beers, took a few shots, and ignored the repeated calls from my mother until his voice mail was full. At two a.m., he left his friend's apartment, got into his car, and headed home. At the same time, a fifteen-year-old boy named David Ibarra got onto his bike to ride the short distance back to his house from his cousin's, where he'd fallen asleep on the couch while playing video games. He was taking a right from Dombey Street onto Pike Avenue when my brother hit him head-on.

I was awakened that day by the sound of my mother screaming. It was a primal, awful sound, one I had never heard before. For the first time I understood what it really meant to feel your blood run cold. I ran out of my room and down the stairs, then stopped just outside the kitchen, suddenly realizing I wasn't sure I was ready for what was happening in there. But then my mom was wailing, and I made myself go in.

She was on her knees, her head bowed, my father crouching in front of her, his hands gripping her shoulders. The sound she was making was so awful, worse than an animal in pain. My first thought was that my brother was dead.

"Julie," my dad was saying. "Breathe, honey. Breathe."

My mom shook her head. Her face was white. Seeing my strong, capable mother this way was one of the scariest things I'd ever endured. I just wanted it to stop. So I made myself speak.

"Mom?"

My father turned, seeing me. "Sydney, go upstairs. I'll be there in a minute."

I went. I didn't know what else to do. Then I sat on my bed and waited. Right then, it felt like time *did* stop, in that five minutes or fifteen, or however long it was.

Finally, my father appeared in the doorway. The first thing I noticed was how wrinkled his shirt was, twisted in places, like someone had been grabbing at it. Later, I'd remember this more than anything else. That plaid print, all disjointed.

"There's been an accident," he said. His voice sounded raw. "Your brother hurt someone."

Later, I'd think back to these words and realize how telling they really were. *Your brother hurt someone.* It was like a metaphor, with a literal meaning and so many others. David Ibarra was the victim here. But he was not the only one hurt.

Peyton was at the police station, where they'd taken him after a Breathalyzer test had confirmed his blood alcohol level was twice the legal limit. But the DUI was the least of his problems. As he was still on probation, there would be no leniency this time and no bail, at least at first. My father called Sawyer Ambrose, then changed his shirt and left to meet him at the station. My mom went to her room and shut the door. I went to school, because I didn't know what else to do.

"Are you sure you're okay?" Jenn asked me at my locker right after homeroom. "You seem weird."

"I'm fine," I told her, shoving a book in my bag. "Just tired."

I didn't know why I wasn't telling her. It was like this was too big; I didn't want to give it any air to breathe. Plus, people would know soon enough.

I started getting texts that evening, around dinnertime. First Jenn, then Meredith, then a few other friends. I turned my phone off, picturing the word spreading, like drops of food coloring slowly taking over a glass of water. My mother was still in her room, my dad gone, so I made myself some macaroni and cheese, which I ate at the kitchen counter, standing up. Then I went to my room, where I lay on the bed, staring at the ceiling, until I heard the familiar sound of the garage door opening. This time, though, it didn't make me feel better.

A few minutes later, I heard a knock on my door, and then my dad came in. He looked so tired, with bags under his eyes, like he'd aged ten years since I'd seen him last.

"I'm worried about Mom," I blurted out before he could say anything. I hadn't even been planning to say this; it was like someone else spoke in my voice.

"I know. She'll be okay. Did you eat?"

"Yeah."

He looked at me for a minute, then crossed the room, sitting down on the edge of my bed. My dad was not the touchy-feely type, never had been. He was a shoulder-clapper, a master of the quick, three-back-pat hug. It was my mom who was always pulling me into her lap, brushing a hand over my hair, squeezing me tight. But now, on this weirdest and scariest of days, my father wrapped his arms around me. I hugged him back, holding on for dear life, and we stayed like that for what felt like a long time.

There was so much ahead of us, both awfully familiar and, even worse, brand-new. My brother would never be the same. I'd never have another day when I didn't think of David Ibarra at least once. My mom would fight on, but she had lost something. I'd never again be able to look at her and not see it missing. So many nevers. But in that moment, I just held my dad and squeezed my eyes shut, trying to make time stop again. It didn't.

CHAPTER

3

〜⁊⊱〜

"NERVOUS?"

I looked over at my mom, who was sitting at the kitchen table, a bagel she wouldn't eat in front of her. It was sweet of her to make an effort.

"Not really," I said, zipping my backpack shut. This wasn't true: I'd already checked twice that I had my parking permit and class schedule, and yet I still kept having to make sure. But I didn't want her to worry. About me, anyway.

"It's a big change, a new school," she said.

In the silence that followed, this sentence hovered between us, like an empty hook waiting for something to be hung on it. Ever since I'd decided in early June to leave Perkins Day and enroll at Jackson High School, my mom had been giving me opportunities to explain why. I thought I had. I'd been at Perkins Day my whole life. I needed something different, especially after the last year. And then, the reason I didn't talk about: the money.

Peyton's latest defense had not been cheap, and the bills from it, along with all the others from Sawyer Ambrose, were piling up. Though it wasn't discussed outright, I knew things were tighter than they'd ever been. We'd let our house-keeper go and sold one of our cars, as well as a beach house we rarely used in Colby, our favorite coastal town. Nobody had said anything about my school expenses, but with college coming up in two years, I figured it was the least I could do. Plus, I was ready to be anonymous.

My mom and I had gone to Jackson to enroll me two days after my brother was sentenced. She was still like a walking ghost, drinking cup after cup of coffee each day and barely eating. My dad had resumed traveling, taking one out-of-town consulting gig after another, so that left just us at the house—at least when she wasn't making the three-hour round-trip to Lincoln Correctional Facility twice a week and every other weekend. Still, she had rallied for our appointment with the school counselor, putting on makeup and arranging my transcripts in a folder labeled with my name. When we pulled into a visitor's spot, she cut the engine, then peered up at the main building.

"It's big," she observed. Then she looked at me, as if I might change my mind, but I was already opening my door.

Inside, it smelled like cleaning fluid and gym mats, a weird thing, as the PE building was on the other side of the center courtyard. At Perkins Day's Upper School—which had just done a huge remodel, funded by an alumnus who founded the social networking site Ume.com—everything was new or close to it. Jackson, in contrast, felt more like a patchwork quilt, the campus made up of old buildings with added newish wings, plus the occasional trailer here and there. The day we visited, no one was there but a few teachers and other staff, which made the halls seem even wider, the grounds that much bigger. In the guidance office, which reeked of cinnamon air freshener, there was no one at the main desk, so we took seats on a saggy couch.

My mom crossed her legs, then looked over at a metal bookshelf on her right, which held a box of mismatched clothing items marked LOST AND FOUND, a stack of pamphlets about eating disorders, and a box of tissues, which was empty. I could tell by her face that if she hadn't already been depressed, this scenario would have done the trick.

"It's okay, Mom," I said. "This is what I want."

"Oh, Sydney," she replied, and then, just like that, she was crying. This was part of the new Julie as well. She'd always been an easy crier, but over things like weddings and sappy movies. Normal stuff. These sudden sobby waterworks were another thing entirely, and I never knew what to do when they happened. This time, I couldn't even offer her a tissue.

Now, back in the kitchen, I checked my backpack again, then wondered if I should change. At Perkins Day we wore uniforms, so I wasn't used to dressing for school. After trying multiple options, I'd gone with jeans and my favorite shirt, a white button-down with a pattern of tiny purple toadstools, as well as the silver hoop earrings I'd gotten for my sixteenth birthday. But I would have worn camouflage if I thought it would help me disappear into the crowd.

"You look great," my mom said, as if reading my mind. "But you'd better go. Don't want to be late the first day."

I nodded, slid my backpack over one shoulder, then

walked over to where she was sitting. The bagel had one bite out of it now. Progress.

"I love you," I said, bending over and kissing her cheek.

She reached down, taking my hand and squeezing it, a little bit too tight. "I love you, too. Have a good day."

I nodded, then went out into the garage and got into my car. As I backed down the driveway, I looked in the kitchen window to see her still sitting there. I thought she might be watching me as well, but she wasn't. Instead, she was looking at the opposite wall, her mug now in her hands. She didn't drink or put it down, just kept it there, right at her heart, and something about this made me so sad, I couldn't wait to be gone.

* * *

School let out at three fifteen. Ten minutes after the bell, I was the only car left in the lower lot. For once, it felt good to be alone.

The school was just *so* big. The hallways that had seemed so wide three weeks earlier were, when I stepped inside that first day, totally packed with people: you couldn't take a step without bumping someone, or at least their arm or elbow. I'd expected that, though. It was the noise that was the real surprise. There was the shrillness of the bells: long, earsplitting tones. The jackhammers of the construction crew replacing one of the many broken sidewalks. And, always, people yelling: in the hallways, across the courtyard, outside the classroom door, at a volume that startled you even with the door solidly shut. It defied logic that in a place so cramped, you'd worry you might not be heard. But everyone did. Apparently.

I'd had only one true interaction all day, with a very perky girl named Deb who was, in her words, a "self-appointed Jackson ambassador!" She'd appeared at my homeroom with a gift bag holding a school calendar, a Jackson football pencil, and some home-baked cookies, as well as her personal business card if I had any questions or concerns. When she left, everyone stared at me as if I were even *more* of a freak. Great.

Now that I was alone, though, I wondered what to do with myself. I couldn't go home yet, as there were still a good two hours until dinner, the same stretch of time I'd dreaded even before my brother was sent away. Suddenly, I felt so helpless. If I hated the crowds but also my own company, where did *that* leave me? It was the saddest I'd felt in a long time. I started my car, like if I drove off I could leave the sadness there.

A block from school, I was at a light when I looked across the street and saw a little strip mall. There was a nail salon, a liquor store, a weight-loss company, and, in the corner, a pizza place.

After school meant pizza to me as much as or even more so than my popcorn-and-*Big* routine. Just one block from Perkins, there was also a small shopping center, and the Italian place there, Antonella's, served as the de facto clubhouse for the entire school. They had gourmet brick-fired pizzas, a coffee bar, gelato, and the sweetest fountain Cokes I'd ever tasted. Meredith always went straight to the U for practice, but Jenn and I hit Antonella's at least once a week, splitting a ham, pineapple, and broccoli pizza and ostensibly doing our homework. Mostly, though, we gossiped and spied on the more popular kids, who always sat at the long, family-style tables by the window, flirting and blowing straw wrappers at one another.

Everything today had been new. With pizza, I could finally have something familiar. Before I could overthink it, I put on my blinker, switched lanes, and turned into the parking lot.

I knew the minute I stepped in that this place was very different. Seaside Pizza was small and narrow, lit not with modern light fixtures like Antonella's but with yellow fluorescents, some of which didn't work. The seating consisted of worn leather booths and a few tables, and the walls were covered in a dark paneling and lined with black-and-white photographs of beaches and boardwalks. There was a tall glass counter, behind which sat a row of different kinds of pizzas and a wide, beat-up oven with the word HOT painted in faded letters across its front. A TV playing a sports talk show hung from the ceiling above the drink machine, next to which was a tall, tilting pile of plastic menus. Overhead, music was playing. I could have sworn I heard what sounded like a banjo.

Once inside, I let the door shut behind me but kept my hand on the glass as I realized that this, too, was probably a mistake. Clearly, this was not a popular place with Jackson students, or anyone, for that matter: I was the only one there.

I turned around to leave, only to find that there was now a guy on the other side of the door. He was tall with shoulder-

length brown hair, wearing a white T-shirt, jeans, and a
backpack. He waited for me to take a step away from the
door, then another, before slowly pushing it open between us
and coming in.

I felt like I couldn't dart out without seeming like a freak,
so I turned back to the counter, taking down a menu from the
pile. I figured I'd pretend to study it for a second, then slip
away while he was ordering. When I glanced up a beat later,
though, I saw he was behind the counter, tying on an apron.
Crap. He *worked* there. And now he was looking at me.

"Can I help you?" he asked. His T-shirt, I saw now, said
ANGER MANAGEMENT: THE SHOW. WCOM RADIO.

"Um," I said, looking back down at the menu. It was
sticky in my hands, and I made out none of the words even as
I read it. Panicked, I glanced at the row of pizza slices under
the glass counter. "Slice of pepperoni. And a drink."

"You got it," he replied, grabbing a metal pizza pan from
behind him. He moved the slices around with some tongs for
a second before drawing out one that was huge and plunk-
ing it on the pan, which he slid into the oven. Back at the
register, he shook a lock of hair out of his eyes and hit a few
buttons. "Three forty-two."

I fumbled for my wallet, sliding him a five. As he made
change, I noticed there was a cup next to the register filled
with YumYum lollipops. TAKE ONE! said a sign in pink marker
behind it. I'd loved them as a kid, hadn't had one in years. I
started picking through them, past the plentiful green apple,
watermelon, and cherry ones, looking for my favorite.

"Dollar fifty-eight's your change," the guy said, holding it out in his hand. As I took it, as well as the empty cup he'd set on the counter, he said, "If you're looking for cotton candy or bubble gum, I'll save you the time. There aren't any."

I raised my eyebrows. "They're popular?"

"To put it mildly."

Just then, the door banged open behind me and someone rushed past, their footsteps slapping the floor. I turned just in time to see a blonde girl disappearing into a back room marked PRIVATE before the door shut behind her.

The guy narrowed his eyes at the door, then looked back at me. "Your slice will be up in a minute. We'll bring it out."

I nodded, then walked over to fill my cup and grab some napkins. I sat down at a table, then studied my phone just for something to do. A few minutes later, I heard the oven opening and closing, and he came out a set of swinging doors with my pizza, now on a paper plate, and slid it in front of me.

"Thanks."

"Sure thing," he replied, and then I listened to him walk to the PRIVATE door and knock on it.

"Go away," a girl's voice said. A minute later, though, I heard it open.

Alone again, I took a bite of my pizza, even though I wasn't really hungry. Then I took another. At about that point, I had to resist stuffing the entire thing into my mouth. I mean, pepperoni pizza is pepperoni pizza. It's, like, the most generic of slices. But this one was *so good*. The crust was both spongy and crispy—somehow—and the sauce had this certain bit of tanginess, not sweet but almost savory. And the cheese: there weren't even words. Oh, my God.

I was so involved in devouring my slice that at first I didn't even notice someone else had come from behind the counter. Then I heard a voice.

"Everything good?"

I looked up to see a man about my dad's age, maybe a bit younger. He had dark hair, streaked with a bit of white, and was wearing an apron.

"It's great," I said. My mouth was half full. I swallowed, then added, "Probably the best I've ever had."

He smiled at this, clearly pleased, then reached over the register, picking up the cup of YumYums. "Did you get a lollipop? It's the perfect chaser. But don't waste your time looking for cotton candy or bubble gum. We ain't got 'em."

"I did hear they were popular."

At this, he made a face, shaking his head, just as I heard the back door open. A moment later, the younger guy walked back past me, the blonde girl behind him. She was holding a lollipop. A pink one.

"You leave the counter unattended now?" the man asked, picking up the tongs and moving some slices around. "Nobody told me we're working on the honor system."

"Don't yell at him," the girl said. She was wearing a sundress and flip-flops, a bunch of silver bangles on one arm. "He was checking on me."

The older man opened the oven, looked inside, then banged it shut again. "You need checking?"

"Today I did." She pulled out a chair at a table opposite the register, sitting down. "Daniel just dumped me."

He stopped moving, turning to look at her. "What? Are you serious?"

The girl nodded slowly. She'd put the lollipop back in her mouth. After a moment, she reached over to the nearby napkin dispenser, took one out, and dabbed her eyes.

"Never liked that kid," the man said, turning back to the oven.

"Yes, you did," the younger guy said, his voice low.

"I didn't. He was too pretty. All that hair. You can't trust a guy with hair like that."

"Dad, it's okay," the girl said, still dabbing. She pulled the lollipop from her mouth. "It's his senior year, he didn't want to be tied down, blah blah blah."

"Blah my ass," her father said. Then he glanced at me. "Sorry."

Caught watching, I felt my face flush and went back to my pizza, or what was left of it.

"What sucks, though," the girl continued, pulling out another napkin, "is that those are the same reasons that Jake gave for dumping me when the summer *started*. 'It's summer! I don't want to be tied down!' I mean, honestly. I can't deal with this seasonal abandonment. It's just too harsh."

"That hair," the man muttered. "I always hated that hair."

The front door opened then, and a couple of guys came in, both of them carrying skateboards. During the ensuing transaction, I finished my slice and tried not to look at the blonde girl, who had pulled one leg up under her and now sat with her chin propped in her hand, eating her lollipop and staring out the window.

The skaters found a table, and soon enough the younger guy came out and delivered their food to them. On his way back behind the counter, he flicked the girl's shoulder, then said something I couldn't make out. She looked up at him, nodding, and he moved on.

I glanced at my watch. If I left now, I'd still have at least an hour before dinner. Just thinking this, I felt like I was suddenly wearing something heavy. It wasn't like Seaside Pizza was so ideal, either. But it wasn't those same four walls, resonating with their emptiness. I got up and refilled my drink.

"You should take a lollipop," the girl told me, her eyes still on the window, as I started back to my table. "They're complimentary."

Clearly, resistance was futile: this was expected. So I went back to the cup and started to poke around. I was actually waiting for the girl to warn me about the shortage of pink flavors, but she didn't. But after I'd been at it for a moment, she did speak up.

"What flavor you looking for?"

I glanced over at her. Behind the counter, her father was spreading sauce across a circle of dough, while the guy my age counted bills at the register. "Root beer," I told her.

She just looked at me. *"Seriously?"*

Clearly, she was shocked. Which surprised me enough

that I couldn't even formulate a response. But then she was talking again.

"*Nobody*," she said, "likes root beer YumYums. They are always the ones left when everything else, even the really lousy flavors, like mystery and blue raspberry, are gone."

"What's wrong with blue raspberry?" the man asked.

"It's blue," she told him flatly, then turned her attention back to me. "Are you being totally honest right now? They *really* are your top pick?"

Everyone was looking at me now. I swallowed. "Well . . . yeah."

In response, she pushed her chair out, getting to her feet. Then, before I even knew what was happening, she was walking toward me. I thought maybe I was about to get into a confrontation about candy preferences, which would have been a first, but then she passed by. I turned to see her head to the same back door, then open it and go inside.

I looked at the man behind the counter, but he just shrugged, sprinkling cheese over the sauce on his pizza in progress. Noises were coming from the back room now—drawers opening and closing, cabinets slamming—but I couldn't see anything. Then it got quiet, and she emerged, a plastic bag in her hand. She walked right up to me, until we were only inches apart, and held it out.

"Here," she said. "For you."

I took it. Inside were at least fifty root beer YumYum lollipops, maybe even more. I just stared at them for a minute, speechless, before I looked up at her.

"I might hate them, but they're still candy," she explained. "I couldn't just throw them away."

I looked down at the bag again: it was actually heavy in my hands. "Thank you," I said.

"You're welcome." She smiled, then stuck out her hand. "I'm Layla."

"Sydney."

We shook. Then there was a pause. When I looked up at her again, she raised her eyebrows.

"Oh," I said quickly, pulling one out and unwrapping it. I stuck it in my mouth, and just like that, I was ten again, walking back from the Quik-Zip with Peyton after spending my allowance on candy. He always got chocolate: with peanuts, with almonds, with caramel. But I liked sugar straight, and time to savor it. In every bag of YumYums there were at least two root beers: I always ate one right away, then kept the other for after the rest were gone. I thought of my brother up at Lincoln and wondered if they ever got chocolate there. It occurred to me I should tell my mom to bring him some.

Just then, a phone rang behind the counter. The younger guy answered it.

"Seaside Pizza, this is Mac." He grabbed a pad, then pulled a pencil out from behind his ear. "Uh-huh. Yep. That's a buck extra. Sure. What's the address?"

As he wrote, the older man looked over his shoulder, read the order, then grabbed a ball of dough and began flipping it in his hands. "Delivery's close enough for you to get dropped at the house," he said to Layla. "Call your mom and see if she needs anything."

"Okay," she said over her shoulder. Then she looked back at me. "You go to Jackson?"

I nodded. "Just started today."

She made a face. "Ugh. How was it?"

"Not so great," I replied, then nodded at the bag. "But this helps."

"It always does," she said. Then she waved, turned on her heel, and began walking toward that back door again. I returned to my table with all my YumYums and gathered up my trash and backpack.

"Tell her to meet me outside," the younger guy was telling the older one as I headed for the door. "Starter's been stubborn lately. Might have to mess with it."

"Don't forget the sign this time!"

We ended up leaving together, just as we'd come in. As I crossed the lot to my car, he jogged up to an older model truck. I watched as he reached into the bed, pulling out a magnetic sign and slapping it on the driver's side door. SEASIDE PIZZA, it said, BEST AROUND. A phone number was printed below.

It was late enough now that I could leave and get home right around dinnertime. But I stayed until Layla emerged, carrying one of those square pizza warmers. A couple of cars were between us at the first stoplight, but I remained behind them turn for turn for a few blocks until eventually the traffic split us. Only then did I open another lollipop, which I savored all the way home.

CHAPTER
4
〜〜

OVER THE next two days, things didn't really improve at school. But they didn't get worse, either. I figured out the fastest way to my classes, discovered it was actually easier to find a spot in the upper parking lot, and had two conversations with classmates (although one was mandatory, as we were thrown into a group project together; still, it was something).

I didn't go back to Seaside Pizza again, as I was too worried I'd look like a freak, a stalker, or both. Instead, the next day, I met Jenn at Frazier Bakery to catch up and do homework. The following day, I went home after school, thinking it might not be so bad. Then I saw Ames's car in the driveway.

"Sydney? Is that you?"

I put my bag on the stairs, then took a breath before walking into the kitchen. Sure enough, there he was with my mom at the table, drinking coffee. A plate of cookies sat between them. When my mom saw me, she pushed them in my direction.

"Hello, stranger," said Ames as I walked to the fridge, taking out a bottled water. "Long time, no see."

Although he was smiling as he said this, it still kind of gave me the creeps. But my mom was already pulling out a chair, assuming I would join them, so I did.

"How was school?" she asked. Turning to him, she added, "She just started at Jackson this week."

"Really?" He grinned. "My old stomping grounds. Does it still smell like Lysol everywhere?"

"You went to Jackson?" my mom asked. "I didn't know that!"

"Sophomore and junior year." Ames sat back, stretching his legs. "Then I was asked to leave. Politely."

"Sounds like someone else I know," my mom said, taking a sip from her mug.

"You liking it?" Ames asked me.

I nodded. "Yeah. It's fine."

This had been my default answer whenever I was asked any variation of this question. Only once had I told the truth, and that was to Layla, a total stranger. I still wasn't sure why.

Just then, I heard a buzzing noise: my mom's phone, over on the counter. She got up, glanced at it, then sighed. "I totally forgot I'd committed to this Children's Hospital event last spring. Now they keep nagging me about meetings and budgets."

"Remember what we were talking about, Julie," Ames said. "First things first."

She gave him a grateful look. "I know. But I should at least bow out gracefully. I'll be right back."

With that, she was gone, padding up the stairs to the War Room. Which left me with Ames.

"So," he said, leaning forward. "Now that it's just us, tell me the truth. How are you really?"

He always smelled like cigarettes, even if he hadn't just smoked one. I eased back a bit. "Okay. It's a change, but I wanted to do it."

"Bet it's been hard to follow in Peyton's less-than-ideal footsteps. My little bro felt the same way."

I nodded, picking up a cookie and taking a bite. I wished my mom would hurry up and come back downstairs.

"You know," he continued, "if you ever need to talk, I'm here. About Peyton. About anything. Okay?"

No thanks, I thought. But out loud I said, "Okay."

By the next day at lunch, I was already dreading the final bell. I had no idea how often Ames came over in the afternoons, but I was certain I did not want to see him, much less talk to him, especially if my mom wasn't around. Thinking this, though, I immediately felt a pang of guilt. He hadn't done anything except creep me out. And that wasn't a punishable offense.

I knew I could say something to my mom. But she had so much on her mind, and Ames was Peyton's best friend. He'd been supportive during this last crisis, and every one since he'd been in the picture. Even when my dad was sick of hearing about Lincoln and the warden and Peyton's appeal, Ames listened. I didn't want her to lose him, too. Especially since I had nothing specific to point to, just a feeling. Everybody has those.

There had been a time when I told my mom everything.

Even after Jenn came into the picture, and then Meredith, I'd always considered her my best friend. We just saw things the same way. Until we didn't.

It started with Peyton's initial busts, how surprised I'd been to hear her defend him, even when he did the indefensible. No matter the offense, she could find some reason it was not entirely my brother's fault. And then there was David Ibarra.

In those first days after the accident, as my parents dealt with bail and lawyers, all I could think of was this kid, just a little younger than me, lying in a hospital bed. I knew from the reports I both came across and sought out that he was paralyzed and not expected to walk again, but there were not that many more details, at least initially. I had so many questions. I couldn't help but ask them.

"Shouldn't we apologize?" I said one day. "Like, in the paper, or make a statement?"

She gave me a heavy, sad look. "It's an awful thing that happened, Sydney. But the law is complicated. It's best if we just try to focus on moving forward."

The first time I heard this, it made me think. By the fourth or fifth, I saw it for the party line it was. I looked at David Ibarra and saw shame and regret; my mother saw only Peyton. From that point on, I was convinced that no matter what we looked at, our views would never be the same.

My fourth day at Jackson, I was sitting at lunch with a turkey sub, flipping through my math textbook, when I felt somebody slide onto the wall a bit down from me. I heard some clicking noises, followed by the plucking of guitar strings. When I glanced over, I saw a guy in black glasses, jeans, and a vintage-looking button-down shirt, a guitar in his lap, strumming away.

He wasn't playing a song as far as I could tell. It was more bits and pieces: a chord here, a short melody there. Every once in a while, he'd hum for a second, or sing a phrase, sometimes pausing to jot in a notebook beside him. I went back to my textbook. A few minutes later, though, I heard a voice.

"Oh, Eric. Really?"

I looked up, and there was Layla. She had on shorts, an oversize floral-print T-shirt, and strappy sandals, her blonde hair loose over her shoulders. As I watched, she put her hands on her hips, cocking her head to one side.

"What?" the guy said. "I'm practicing."

"Oh please, you are not," she replied. "You're running your tired game on this poor girl, and it's not going to work because I already warned her about you."

He stopped playing. "Warned her? What am I, a predator now?"

"Just slide over."

He did, looking displeased, and she plopped down between us, turning to face me. "I've been looking for you. I should have known Eric would find you first, though. He's got a nose for new blood."

"Okay, you *really* need to stop now," Eric said.

Layla flipped her hand at him, as if he were a gnat circling. To me she said, "I'm not saying I believe you are a girl who would fall for this act; I wouldn't insult you that way. But I was. So I've made it my mission to spare others my experience."

"We," the guy said, doing one big strum for emphasis, "have been broken up for over a year. I think you can stop now."

She turned to look at him, again tilting her head to the side. Then she reached out and brushed his hair back from his forehead. "You need a haircut. Shaggy Hipster doesn't suit you."

"Don't touch me," he grumbled, but it was good-natured, I could tell. He went back to playing, leaning over the guitar, and she smiled, then turned back to me.

"Eric's in a band with my brother," she told me. "They're pretty awful, actually."

"Her brother," Eric corrected her, "plays drums in *my* band. And we're in transition."

"They can't keep a guitar player." She nodded in his direction. "Too much ego in the room."

"Someone has to be the leader!" Eric said.

Layla smiled again. "Anyway. They're playing Friday night, at Bendo? That club on Overland? It's all ages. Free pizza if you get there early. You should come."

I was shocked at this invitation. We'd met only once; she owed me nothing. And yet I knew, immediately, that I would go.

"Sure," I said. "That sounds great."

"Perfect." She got to her feet, tucking her hair behind her ears. "Oh, and one more thing. If you want company at lunch, we sit over there."

She pointed to the right of the main building, where there was a circle of benches around a spindly tree. On one of them, I saw the guy from the pizza place—her brother, I now understood—peeling an orange, a textbook open beside him.

"Oh," I said. "Okay."

"No pressure," she added quickly. "Just, you know, if you want."

I nodded, and then she was walking away, sliding her hands in her pockets. As I watched her go, Eric cleared his throat.

"Our band is not that bad," he told me. "She just has high standards."

I didn't know what to say to this, so probably it was good that the bell rang then. He put away his guitar, I packed up my stuff, and then we nodded at each other before heading in our separate directions. All afternoon, though, during two lectures and a lab, I kept thinking about what he'd said. High standards, but she'd invited me anyway. Maybe she'd regret it. But I really hoped not.

* * *

"I don't know." Jenn wrinkled her nose, the way she always did when she was suspicious. "Isn't that a nightclub?"

"It's a music venue," I said. "And this is an all-ages show."

She picked up her pencil, twirling it between her thumb and index finger. "I thought we were going to Mer's meet on Friday."

"That's at four. This is three hours later."

She wasn't going to go. I'd known it the minute I brought it up. We were not clubgoers, never had been. But our "we" had already changed. My part of it, anyway.

I looked across Frazier Bakery, where we always went after school when we weren't in the mood for Antonella's. A sandwich, salad, and pastry place, it was that weird mix of chain restaurant and forced homeyness: needlepoint samplers, perfectly worn leather chairs by a fake fireplace, your food served on wax paper patterned with red and white checks, silverware tied with a bow. That day, I'd been talked into a specialized coffee drink by the very cute guy working the counter—DAVE! his name tag read—something he swore would change my life. Apparently, this meant I'd be way hyped up and keep having to pee. Not exactly what I'd expected.

"Just meet me there for an hour," I said, taking another sip anyway. "If you hate it, you can leave."

"Why is this so important?" she asked me, putting her pencil back down. "You've never been into clubbing before."

"It's not clubbing. It's a band, playing a show."

She adjusted her glasses, then looked down at the textbook in front of her. "It's just not my thing, Sydney. Sorry."

I knew Jenn well. Once she made up her mind, she didn't waver. "Okay. That's fine."

She smiled at me, and then we both went back to work. The adult contemporary music overhead, Jenn's blueberry scone and my piece of carrot cake, our booth by the window: it was all as familiar as my own face. But I found I couldn't concentrate on my calculus, as much as I tried. I just sat there and listened to her pencil scrape the page until it was time to go.

So I was alone when I walked into Bendo the following evening and got my hand stamped by a bulky guy with a neck tattoo. I'd had a meeting for my English group project at lunch, so I was going in with only my casual invitation and a fair amount of trepidation. Not to mention a lie.

"You're going out?" my mother asked me when I came downstairs after dinner, having changed my outfit twice before going back to my first choice. She looked at her watch. "I didn't realize you had plans."

"Just meeting Jenn and Meredith at Frazier for dessert," I said. "I'll be back by ten."

She looked at my dad, who was sitting next to her on the couch, as if he might object to this. When he didn't, instead keeping his eyes on the twenty-four-hour local news channel and a report about school redistricting, she said, "Maybe make it nine thirty."

I felt a flicker of irritation. Unlike Peyton, I'd never done a thing to warrant suspicion. Even though I was, at that moment, lying, I still resented it. "Seriously? Mom, I'm a junior."

Now they both looked at me. My mom raised her eyebrows at my dad, who said, "Do I need to remind you that we make the rules?"

"Come on," I said. "I've had a ten o'clock curfew since I got my license."

"Your mother wants you home earlier," he replied, turning back to the TV. "Do it tonight, and then we'll talk."

Now my flicker was a full flame. I looked at my mom. "Really?"

She didn't say anything, just went back to the magazine in her lap. I stood there a minute, then another. Then I turned on my heel and left. I couldn't remember the last time I'd been angry with my mom. All I'd felt lately was pity and sadness, along with an overwhelming need to protect her. This feeling was new, and it made me uneasy. Like more was changing than I was ready for.

Once inside Bendo, I had no idea what to do with myself. It was a big space, with painted black walls and a bar running down one side. Up front was the stage, where a drum set, microphones, and amps were set up. I'd expected it to be crowded, so I could lose myself quickly, but there was only a handful of people there, most of them gathered around a row of pizza boxes that lined one end of the bar. I felt like it was so obvious I didn't belong there that I should leave before I embarrassed myself.

"Hey. You came."

I turned around, and there was Eric, the guitar guy. He was in jeans and a plaid shirt that looked like it came from a thrift shop, this time with a tuner in the front pocket. It looked like he'd gotten a haircut.

"I was intrigued," I said.

He smiled, as if this pleased him. "We're trying some new stuff tonight we've been working on. It's a bit meta, so I'm hoping the crowd can keep up."

I nodded, not sure what to say to this. Turned out I shouldn't have worried, as he kept talking.

"We've been through a lot of evolution as a band lately, which I think is necessary. Music isn't stagnant, right? So you can't be, either. Last year, we were really focused on a more rockabilly-slash-bluegrass-slash-metal sound. I mean, *nobody* was doing what we were doing. But then, of course, everyone started copying our sound and approach, so I had to think out of the box again. I'm telling you, it's a lot of work, fronting a *good* band. Anyone can lead a crappy, unoriginal one. Most people do just that. But I—"

Suddenly, I felt a hand grip my arm and begin to pull me away from him. I stumbled over my own feet, startled, before I realized it was Layla. She was wearing a blue dress and flip-flops, her eyes lined in a dramatic cat's eye.

"I'm doing this for your own good," she announced as I looked back apologetically at Eric. "You do not want to get sucked into band discussions with him. You'll never escape."

With this, she deposited me at a bar stool, then climbed onto the one beside it. A moment later, Eric joined us, looking disgruntled.

"I was *talking*," he said to her.

"You're always talking," she replied. "And she's *my* friend. I invited her."

I felt myself blink. Now we were friends? Eric glared at her, then helped himself to a piece of pizza, leaning back against the bar.

"You been here before?" Layla asked me. I shook my head.

"It's a pretty good place, other than the fact that everything is always sticky. You want a slice?"

Before I could answer, she'd grabbed two paper plates from a nearby stack and put a slice on each. As she slid mine toward me, she said, "Pizza is key to this band's popularity. The thinking is if you feed them, they will come."

"They come for the *music*," Eric said.

"Keep telling yourself that." She smiled at me, then took a big bite, glancing up to the stage, where her brother was now behind the drum kit, adjusting something. "So how was the first week at Jackson? Be honest."

I swallowed the bite I'd been chewing. It was delicious, even better than I remembered. "Not so great."

"You just move here?"

"No. I transferred from Perkins Day."

At this, she and Eric glanced at each other. "Wow," he said. "That's big money."

"And a really good school," she added, shooting him a look. "Why'd you switch?"

From the stage, there was a cymbal crash, followed by some feedback. I said, "I just needed a change."

Layla studied my face for a second. "I hear that. Change is good."

"Yeah," I replied. "I'm hoping so, anyway."

She looked past me then, suddenly distracted. Following her gaze, I saw a girl a few years older than us coming in, dressed in jeans and a T-shirt, her hair in a high ponytail, pushing a wheelchair. Seated in it was a woman in a velour tracksuit. She was the oldest person in the club by at least twenty years.

Like always when I saw a wheelchair, I thought of David Ibarra. It was just one of the triggers capable of bringing his face—which I knew well from all the newspaper photos and online stories I'd sought out in the days and then months after everything happened—and then everything else rushing back. See also: the sound of squealing brakes; anyone riding a bike on the street; and, to be honest, the sound of my own breath. He was always only a beat from my consciousness. Despite my mom's party line, my knowledge of him and the need to recall it regularly was like my penance for what Peyton had done, the sentence *I'd* been given.

The fact that he'd been just days past his fifteenth birthday when the accident happened. A soccer player, a forward. The fact that the impact crushed his spine, leaving him able to use his arms and upper body, but wheelchair dependent. I could list the fund-raisers that had been held to purchase him a high-tech chair—community yard sales, a benefit concert—as well as the civic organizations that pitched in to make his parents' home fully accessible with ramps, wider doors, and new hardware. I sought this out because I felt like I should, as if it might lessen the guilt. But it never did.

"They're here," Layla said now to Eric, jerking me back to the present. "Come on."

They both got up, crossing over to meet the lady in the wheelchair just as the girl pushing her reached the center of the club. I wasn't sure what to do, so I stayed put, watching as Eric pulled a table into place and Layla took over the wheelchair, pushing the woman carefully up against it. A moment later, her brother appeared, carrying a can of Pepsi and a glass of ice. He fixed the drink, then put it on the table as the older girl sat down.

Layla looked at me, motioning for me to come over, as if all of this was just the most natural thing ever. And maybe it was, because I went. When I got to the table, she said, "Hey, Mom. This is Sydney. Remember, I told you about her?"

Her mom looked up at me. She had a round, kind face and blonde hair that had clearly been styled for the occasion, and was wearing red lipstick. She stuck out her hand. "Tricia Chatham. So nice to meet you."

"You too," I said.

"You want some pizza?" Layla asked. "It's still hot."

"Oh, no, honey. I brought my own snacks. Rosie, can you get my bag?"

At this, the older girl reached behind the chair, unlooping one of those big, colorful, quilted purses from the handle. This one was pink with roses. She unzipped it, then put it on the table, and her mom reached in, rummaging around for a second before pulling out a can of cheese puffs. Without prompting, Layla's brother took it, popping the top, then handed it back to her.

"That's Mac," Layla said, pointing at him. "And this is my sister, Rosie."

I said hi, and Rosie nodded. I noticed that all three women

had the same light hair and green eyes, but distributed differently: stretched wide on the mom, pinched tight on Rosie,
and on Layla, just right. Mac had clearly gotten his dark hair
and eyes from their dad.

"When's the music starting?" their mom asked, taking out
a handful of cheese puffs. "Some of us have TV to get back to."

"Mom, we set the DVR," Rosie said.

"So you say." She ate a puff, then looked at me. "I don't
trust technology. Especially when it comes to my shows."

"She really likes her TV," Layla explained to me. Then
she turned to Eric, raising her eyebrows.

"Right," he said, nodding. "We'll get ready."

He and Mac walked off toward the stage. Meanwhile,
Layla grabbed two more chairs, pulling them next to the
table, then gestured for me to take one before sitting down
herself.

"So, Sydney," her mom said, taking out another handful
of puffs. "What's your story?"

"Mom," Rosie said, rolling her eyes. She was sitting very
straight, legs tightly crossed. "God."

"What? Is that rude?"

"If you have to ask, the answer is probably yes," Rosie
replied.

Her mom waved this off, still looking at me. I said, "Um,
I just transferred to Jackson. But I've lived in Lakeview since
I was three."

"She used to go to Perkins Day," Layla added. Rosie and
Mrs. Chatham exchanged a look. "She needed a change."

"Don't we all," Rosie said in a low voice.

"Perkins Day is an excellent school," Mrs. Chatham said. "Highest test grades in the county."

"Mom used to work in school administration," Layla explained to me. "She was an assistant principal."

"Ten years," Mrs. Chatham said. She offered me the can of puffs, which I declined, then held it out to Layla, who took one. "Still be there, if I hadn't gotten sick. I loved it."

"She has MS," Layla said. "With other complications. It's the worst."

"Agreed." Mrs. Chatham offered Rosie the can. She shook her head. "But you take what you get in this world. What else can you do?"

In reply, there was a burst of feedback from the stage, and we all winced. Rosie said, "Great. I already have a headache."

"Now, now," Mrs. Chatham said. "They've been working on some new stuff. It's apparently very meta."

I smiled at this, and she caught me and grinned back. I'd had a hunch before; now it was sealed. I was so, so glad I'd come.

Eric, now behind the microphone with his guitar, tapped it with a finger. "One, two, three," he said, then played a few chords. Another guitar player, tall and skinny with an Adam's apple you could see from a distance, climbed up on stage. "One, two."

Layla rolled her eyes at me. "They already did sound check. I swear, he is such a diva."

I looked back at Eric, who had turned to say something to Mac. "So you guys dated?"

"In my salad days, when I was green in judgment," she replied. I looked at her. "That's Shakespeare. Come on, Perkins Day, keep up!"

I felt myself blush. "Sorry."

"I'm kidding." She reached over, grabbed my arm, and shook it. "And yes. We dated. In my defense, I was a sophomore and stupid."

Eric was back at the microphone, counting again. "He doesn't seem that bad."

"He's not *bad*." She reached up, pulling her hair back. "He's just got a huge ego that, left unchecked, is a threat to society. So I try to do my part."

"One, two," Eric repeated, tapping the microphone. "One—"

"We hear you!" Layla yelled. "Just start."

Mrs. Chatham hushed her, but it worked: after announcing themselves as "the new and improved renowned local band Hey Dude," they began playing. I was no musical expert—and certainly did not have high standards—but I thought they sounded good. A bit loud, but we were sitting close. At first, I couldn't make out what Eric was singing, although the melody was familiar. As soon as the chorus began, though, I realized I actually knew it by heart.

She's a prom queen, with a gold crown,
and I'm watching as she passes by . . .

I leaned over to Layla. "Is this—"

"Logan Oxford," she finished for me. "Remember him? In sixth grade, I had his poster on my wall!"

I'd had a notebook with his picture on the cover. As well as every song he ever recorded, a copy of his documentary/ concert movie *This One's for You*, and, although I was hugely embarrassed to admit it now, the kind of crush that made me imagine scenarios where we were married. Oh, the shame. And now it was all flooding back in this big, sticky club. I wished Jenn had come. She was even more nuts for him than I was.

"I don't get it," Rosie yelled across to us. "They're playing retro top forty now?"

"I believe," Mrs. Chatham said, picking up her Pepsi, "that it is supposed to be an ironic take on the universality of the early teen experience. But I *might* have that wrong. I will admit to tuning out at some point."

"I loved Logan Oxford," Layla sighed, eating another cheese puff. "Remember his hair? And that dimple, when he smiled?"

I did. Rosie said, "Didn't he just get busted for drugs?"

"Look who's talking."

I felt myself blink. But Rosie, hardly bothered, just shot her the finger.

"Ladies," Mrs. Chatham said. "Let's be ladies, please."

To say I was taken aback was a huge understatement. Who *were* these people?

Hey Dude was wrapping up "Prom Queen" now and, after

a bit of a bumpy transition, launched into "You+Me+Tonight."
My inner thirteen-year-old was swooning as I looked over
at Layla, who was singing along. She said, "Remember this
video? Where he was in that convertible, driving through the
desert all alone?"

"And the lights appear far in the distance, and then suddenly he's on that busy street?" I added.

"Yes!"

"I wanted a car just like that for *years*," I said.

She sighed, propping her chin in her hands. "I still do."

The music just kept going, bringing every one of my
awkward early teen memories with them. After another Logan Oxford song, they played one by STAR7 ("Baby, take
me back, I'll do better now, I swear") and then a medley by
Brotown, one of which I distinctly remembered slow dancing to for the first time. There were a few shrieks of feedback, and Eric kept getting too close to the microphone and
muffling his own voice, but by the time they were done, a
decent crowd had gathered at the base of the stage, most of
them girls. When two brunettes ran past our table, singing
along loudly and giggling, Layla narrowed her eyes.

"Uh-oh," she said. "Eric might have *groupies*. Can you
even imagine?"

"No," Rosie said flatly.

He could, though. It was clear in the way he brightened,
leaning into the microphone too close again before winding
up the final chords with a flourish. The applause was actually loud, with a fair amount of whoops and whistles, and
Mrs. Chatham looked around, smiling.

"Well, listen to that," she said. "They might actually be on to something."

Eric was waving to the crowd now, soaking it up, as Mac and the other guitar player left the stage. The brunettes pushed forward, getting Eric's attention, and he crouched down, cupping his ear as one of them spoke. This time, Layla said nothing.

"Excuse me," I heard a voice say from behind us. It was a tall girl with red hair, dressed in a tight black T-shirt and white jeans. "But, um, are you Rosie Chatham?"

Rosie looked at her. "Yeah."

"I'm Heather Banks. I used to train at Lakewood Rink when you were there?"

The expression on Rosie's face was not exactly welcoming. Mrs. Chatham said, "How wonderful! Were you working with Arthur?"

"No, Wendy Loomis. And I was just taking lessons, not competing." She looked at Rosie again. "I just have to tell you . . . you were amazing. Where are you skating now?"

"I'm not."

"Oh." Heather blushed. "I didn't realize. I'm—"

"She got injured," Mrs. Chatham told her. "Knee issues. But *before* that, she did two years with the Mariposa touring show."

"Wow! That's amazing! So you were, like, one of the characters?"

"I need something to drink," Rosie announced, pushing out her chair. Then, as we all watched, she just walked away, leaving the poor girl standing there, watching her go.

"It's a sensitive issue," Mrs. Chatham said in the awkward silence that followed. "You understand, I'm sure."

"Oh, totally!" Heather said. "I, um, just wanted to say hello. You all have a good night."

"You too, honey," Mrs. Chatham replied. Once the girl was gone, she looked over at the bar, where Rosie was talking to Mac. Now that I looked at her, I realized she did have a skater's body: small, muscular, and compact. She kind of reminded me of Meredith, although older and with a rougher look to her.

"Rosie has issues," Layla explained to me.

"*Everyone* has issues," her mother said. "Now, go see if she's okay."

Making a face, Layla got to her feet, leaving the table. I wondered if I should follow her, but that meant leaving Mrs. Chatham alone. So I stayed put. After a moment of silence, she said, "It's good that you came."

I wasn't sure if this was her reading my mind or she meant from her point of view. I said, "I was nervous. Not knowing anyone and everything."

"But now you do." She smiled at me. "And I'm glad to see Layla making a new friend. She's had a tough time lately."

"I heard she and her boyfriend just broke up?"

"Second one in three months." She shook her head. "Boys this age, they can be brutal. But they're not all bad. At least, that's what I keep telling her."

Just then, Mac appeared, carrying a fresh can of Pepsi. He was in jeans and a faded SEASIDE PIZZA T-shirt, and looked like he'd broken a sweat playing. Not that I was looking closely or anything.

"That's my boy," said his mom as he popped the tab and refilled her glass. "Thank you."

"You need anything else?"

"Not a thing. Sit down."

He did, right next to me, which was slightly unnerving. At the pizza place, there had been distance between us most of the time: the door, the counter, or him standing while I sat. Proximity let me notice things I had not before, like his long lashes and the slight freckling across his nose, as well as the thin silver chain I could just see peeking out from the neck of his T-shirt.

"Cheese puff?" Mrs. Chatham asked Mac, holding out the can.

"Really, Mom?"

"What? It's calcium!"

Mac rolled his eyes, looking up at the stage. To me Mrs. Chatham said, "He's so healthy these days. It's no fun whatsoever."

"Neither is early-onset diabetes," he told her.

His mother sighed, then held the can out to me. When I hesitated, she said, "See what you've done? She can't even bring herself to take one. You've given the girl a complex."

Mac looked at me. "Sorry."

"It's fine." I felt my face get hot. Which made sense, as he was better looking than Logan Oxford at his peak and Dave! at Frazier combined. "I'm not, um, much of a puff fan anyway."

God, I was an idiot. I didn't even know what I was saying. Thank God Layla picked that moment to return to the table.

"Eric's looking for you," she informed her brother. "He has, and I quote, 'notes and feedback for you vis-à-vis your performance.'"

"Great," Mac said flatly, getting to his feet. The silver chain disappeared again, out of sight. "Mom, you staying for the next set?"

"Oh, honey, I'm pretty tired," Mrs. Chatham said. "And my show comes on at ten, so . . ."

"I *told* you," said Rosie, who had rejoined us. "I set the DVR."

Hearing this, I suddenly remembered that I was also supposed to be somewhere at a certain time. I looked at my watch: it was just after nine. "I should go, too, actually."

"Let me guess," Layla said. "You're addicted to *Status: Mystery*, too, and do not trust entirely reliable technology to function properly in your absence."

Rosie snorted. I said, "Um, not exactly. Usually I can stay out later, but there's been some stuff going on. My mom kind of wants me to stick close. So I told her I'd be home early tonight."

It wasn't until I finished this monologue that I realized how long and unnecessary it was. I had no idea why I'd felt the need to explain myself quite so much to people I had only just met, and by the way they stood there looking at me when I concluded, they didn't, either. Whoops.

"Well, you go, then," said Mrs. Chatham finally, saving me.

"But don't be a stranger, okay? Come by the house anytime."

I nodded, then got to my feet. "Thanks."

"We'll walk you out," Layla said, nodding at Mac. "This parking lot can be a little sketchy. Back in a sec, Mom."

Mrs. Chatham waved, and I followed Layla through the increased crowd toward the door, Mac behind me. Sandwiched between them, I could see people appraising us as we made our way outside, and I was sure I looked like the mismatched piece, the part that did not belong. But that was not a new feeling. And at least here, with them, it made sense.

"Where'd you park?" Layla asked once we were in the lot. I pointed. As we walked over, passing a few people grouped around their own vehicles, she said, "Wow. Nice ride. Is that a sport package?"

I looked at my car, which was a BMW that had been my mom's before she decided she wanted a hybrid SUV. "Maybe," I said, feeling wholly ignorant. "I'm not—"

"It's an '07," Mac said, glancing inside. "Automatic. So I'm betting not."

"Looks like it does have some upgrade, though. See the wheels?" Layla let out a low whistle. "Those are *sweet*."

I must have looked as clueless as I felt, because a second later, Mac looked at me and said, "Oh. Sorry. Our dad's just really into cars."

"In our house, you get a mandatory education on the topic, like it or not," Layla added. "And once you know all that stuff, you can't *not* notice. Believe me. I've tried."

"Hey, *dude*!" I heard someone yell. We all turned to see Eric at the club's entrance, looking annoyed. "If you're not too busy, I could use my drummer?"

"He's not yours," Layla hollered back. "A band is a collaboration, last I checked."

"Whatever." Eric threw up his hands, then turned to go inside. "We're on in five. If he feels like joining us."

Layla laughed, and Mac shot her a look. "I'm sorry, I'm sorry. It's just so easy to set him off. And you have to admit, he is pretty insufferable when he gets in his diva mode."

"True," Mac replied. "But you're not exactly helping."

It was nine fifteen now. I really had to go. I unlocked my car, the lights flashing, then stepped forward to open my door. "Thanks for the invite," I said to Layla. "It was really fun."

"Good," she said. "And Mom's right. You should come out to the house sometime. I'll teach you about your car. Even if you don't want to learn."

I smiled. "Sounds good."

"See you at school, Sydney."

She waggled her fingers at me, then took a few quick steps to fall in beside Mac, who was already heading toward the club. The lot was much fuller than when I'd gotten there, with more cars still arriving. For some people, the night hadn't even really started yet. Hard to believe, when it had already been my most eventful in, well, ages. I watched the Chathams walk across the lot, keeping my eyes on them until they folded into the crowd by the doors.

Then I raced home, praying for green lights, pulling into the garage at 9:35. I went inside with my apologies ready, only to find the downstairs empty. My mom was already in bed, my dad shut away in his office on a call. I'd done the right thing. I always did. It just would have been nice if someone had noticed.

CHAPTER
5

〜〜

THE FLYER was sitting on the table when I came down for
breakfast Monday morning. I saw it as soon as I walked in the
kitchen, but it wasn't until I got up close that I could read
what it said.

FAMILY DAY: SATURDAY, SEPTEMBER 20TH,
1–5PM. INFO EXT. 2002 OR
warden@lincolncorrection.us.

"What's this?" I said to my mom, who was at the stove,
pushing some bacon around in a pan.

She glanced over her shoulder. "It's coming up at Lincoln
in a few weeks."

"But Peyton doesn't want me there," I said. "Right?"

"It's not that he doesn't want you. It's just . . ." She trailed
off, sighing. "I'm hoping this opportunity might change his
mind."

When my brother was first sent to prison, he had to submit forms for each person he wanted to visit him. My mom
and dad were no-brainers, of course, as was Ames, and my

mom assumed I'd be as well. But despite the fact that minors and children were allowed—even encouraged, as Lincoln believed connection with family was very important for inmates—Peyton said no, he didn't want me to see him there. And I was so, so glad.

My mother, however, was convinced he'd feel differently eventually. She wanted me to be part of this, just as she wanted me to talk to Peyton when he called collect and write him letters, both things that I resisted. I knew this made me a terrible sister. But I hadn't known what to say to my brother when he was sitting across this very same breakfast table, much less locked away in a prison in another state. It came naturally to both my mom and Ames to still be fully on Team Peyton, despite what he'd done to David Ibarra, not to mention our family. It wasn't that easy for me.

I'd spoken to him only twice since he'd been sent away, both times when I was the only one home to answer the phone. Letting it ring until it went to voice mail was not an option. It was not easy for Peyton to get access to a phone. If he did, we were to accept the call and stay on as long as he was allowed to talk. Period.

I'd learned this the hard way one afternoon when my mom was at the grocery store. I answered, said yes to the call, then waited through a series of clicks and beeps. Finally, my brother spoke.

"Sydney?"

It was the first time I'd heard his voice in over a month. He sounded far away, like he was standing back from the receiver. Also, there was a steady buzz on the line, which made it hard to make him out. "Hey," I said. "Mom's not here."

I regretted this the minute I said it. In my defense, though, she was the one he usually spoke with. If my dad answered, the conversations were always shorter and more about legal issues than anything else.

"Oh." There was a pause. Then, "How are you?"

"I'm okay. You?"

I winced. You don't ask someone in prison how they're doing. Just assume the answer is "not so good." But Peyton replied anyway.

"I'm all right. It's boring here more than anything else."

I knew he was just making conversation. But all I could think of was David Ibarra in his wheelchair. That had to be boring, too.

"You should write me a letter," he said then. "Fill me in on what's going on with you."

This conversation was hard enough. Now he wanted me to put words on a page? My mom had said that mail could be a huge element in a prisoner's mental health, which was why she'd recruited many in our family and several close friends to send letters and postcards. She'd even provided stamps and addressed envelopes, a stack of which sat untouched on the desk in my room. Every time I even thought about pulling out a piece of paper to try, all I could imagine was filling that empty white space with all the words I could never, ever say. Silence was safer.

I'd ended the call soon after, telling him I'd let my mom know he'd phoned. When she walked in ten minutes later and I passed along the message, she went ballistic.

"You didn't wait until he was *told* to hang up?" she demanded, dropping one of her cloth shopping bags with a clunk on the island. "You just hung up on him?"

"No," I said. "I said good-bye. We both did."

"But he *could* have talked longer? No one was *stopping* him?"

I suddenly felt like I might start crying. "I'm . . . I'm sorry."

My mom bit her lip, then looked at me for a long moment. Finally, she sighed, reaching out to put both her hands on my shoulders. "Sydney. I cannot emphasize enough how important it is for your brother to have contact with the outside world. Even if you only talk about the weather. Or what you ate for lunch. Just talk. Keep him talking until his time on the phone is up. It's critical. Do you understand me?"

I nodded, not sure I could speak without sobbing. When she turned around to unload the groceries, I had to take several deep breaths before I was calm enough to help her.

The second time I'd talked to Peyton was when I came home from having coffee with Jenn and found Ames on the phone with him.

"Your gorgeous sister just walked in," he said into the receiver, then waved me over with his free hand. "Yep. Oh, don't worry. I'm keeping the boys away from her. They'd better think twice before they come around *our* girl."

I felt my face get hot, the way it always did when he said stuff like this. Oblivious, he grinned at me, pulling out the chair right beside him.

"Yeah, she's right here, I'll put her on. Uh-huh. Be there in a few days with vending machine money in hand. Right. Here she is."

He handed the phone out to me, and I took it. The mouthpiece was hot from his breath. I tried to hold it away from my own lips as I said, "Hey, Peyton."

"Hey," he said. "How's it going?"

"Okay." I looked at Ames, who was watching me. "Did you, um, get to talk to Mom yet?"

"Yeah. She answered when I called."

"Oh, right," I said. "Well—"

A loud tone sounded on the line, followed by a recording announcing that the call would terminate in thirty seconds. "I'd better go," my brother said. "Tell Mom I love her, okay?"

"Sure," I said.

"Bye, Sydney."

I didn't reply, and then the line went dead. Still, I sat there a second, letting the dial tone fill my ear, before I hit the END button. "Time's up."

"Always comes too quickly," Ames said. He smiled at me. "He sounds good, right?"

I nodded, although to me he hadn't really sounded like anything. Not even Peyton.

But that was the phone; Family Day would be face-to-face. Now, in the kitchen, I sat down, picking up my fork while Mom slid into a seat across from me. I'd been starving since I smelled the bacon cooking, but now the last thing I wanted to do was eat.

"Is Dad going to this thing?"

"If he's in town," she said, taking a tiny nibble of her toast, then chasing it with coffee. "Otherwise, it'll just be you, me, and Ames."

I put my fork back down. "I don't know," I said. "I'm worried I might freak out or something."

She looked at me. "Freak out?"

I shrugged. "It's just kind of scary."

"It is," she agreed. She took another sip. When she spoke again, her voice had a hard edge to it. "It's very scary. Especially for your brother, who is locked away, alone, with no support system other than us, his family."

"Mom," I said.

"If he can deal with *that* for seventeen months," she continued, "I think you can handle being slightly uncomfortable for a couple of hours. Don't you agree?"

"Yes," I said softly. She was still glaring at me, so I repeated it, more loudly this time. "Yes."

That was the last we spoke of it. By the time I left ten minutes later, she was back to normal, checking that I had lunch money and waving to me from the front window as I pulled out of the driveway. As far as she was concerned, the matter was handled.

I, however, was still shaken. At school, I cut the engine and just sat in my car, watching everyone else head to homeroom until the bell rang and I had no choice but to join them.

Jenn called as I was walking to lunch, as had become our routine. She and Meredith would put me on speakerphone, so it was kind of like I was there as they caught me up on what was going on at Perkins. There was something soothing about their voices that balanced out the constant cacophony of Jackson. Today, though, it was Jenn who heard something.

"Are you okay?" she asked me after Meredith caught me up on the meet she'd had that weekend.

"Yeah. Why?"

"You just don't sound like yourself," she said. "Everything all right?"

"Yeah," I said. I had a flash of that flyer on the table. "It's just really noisy here. Like always."

As if to punctuate this point, there was a burst of laughter just behind me. "Good Lord," Meredith said. "How do you even concentrate?"

"I'm just walking to lunch," I told her. "It's not that mentally challenging."

They were both quiet for a moment. Now I was turning on everyone.

"Sorry," I said. "Look, let me call you guys back in a bit, okay? I'll just get somewhere quiet."

"Okay," Jenn replied. "Talk to you later."

Meredith didn't say anything. She was incredibly physically tough, but always the first to get flustered at raised voices or confrontation. "Bye, Mer," I said, trying.

"Bye," she replied, but now it was she who was clearly not okay. Before I could speak again, though, they were gone.

I sighed as I stepped out into the courtyard. As I walked to the food trucks, I glanced over at the grassy spot where Layla ate, but the benches there were empty. I got a grilled cheese and a drink, then sat down on the wall, dropping my bag at my feet. Then I did something I hadn't allowed myself to do in weeks: I pulled out my phone, opened the browser, and typed in two words.

David Ibarra

There was a time I'd done this almost daily. I'd spent hours following the Internet presence of this boy I'd never met. I'd learned that his nickname was Brother because, according to one of the many articles after the accident, he treated everyone like family. His name popped up on several video game forums, so I knew he was really good at Warworld. The sports archive of the local paper had all his rec soccer stats: strong on defense, not so much on scoring. And while his Ume.com profile was private, there was an open page dedicated to him called Friends of Brother, which appeared to be maintained by his sister. That was where I'd gotten most of the info on his recovery and various fund-raisers to help with his medical bills. It was also a source for page after page of comments from his friends and family.

So proud of you for your continuing strength and courage! We love you.

Won't be able to make the spaghetti dinner, but we're sending a contribution. You're our hero, Brother.

Sending good wishes from here in the Lone
Star State! Can't wait to see you at the reunion.
Stay strong.

So many times I'd imagined leaving a comment of my own, although I knew I never could. My last name was the last thing they wanted on that page, even with an apology following it. But that didn't stop me from crafting what I'd write. Sometimes, on really bad days, I'd go so far as to imagine myself going to him in person and saying everything I carried so heavily in my heart. Would he listen, and maybe somehow understand? In the next beat, though, it would hit me like a slap how pathetic I was for even thinking this. Like there was anything I could say that would give him that night—and his legs—back.

The hardest thing, though, was the summary of the Ume.com page, posted at the very top. I could wade through a hundred comments of love and good wishes. These few sentences, though, hit me like a punch to the gut, every single time.

In February 2014, David Ibarra was hit by a
drunk driver while riding his bike home from his
cousin's house, leaving him partially paralyzed.
This page is dedicated to his story. Please leave a
comment! And thank you for your support.

Now, on the wall, I read these familiar words once, then twice. Like it was some sort of mantra, a spell to cancel out what had happened that morning with my mom. I'd always remember the truth. Just to be sure, though, I made a point of bringing it front and center, right there before my eyes

There had been no shortage of bad moments in those early weeks after Peyton's accident. But one had really stuck with me. It was a passing remark I'd overheard as I came down the stairs one day. My parents were in the kitchen.

"What was a fifteen-year-old doing out riding his bike at two in the morning, anyway?"

Silence. Then my dad. "Julie."

"I know, I know. But I just wonder."

I just wonder. That was the moment I realized my mom would never be able to really hold Peyton responsible for what he'd done. Their bond was too tight, too tangled, for her to see reason. Like anyone deserved to be hit by a car and paralyzed. Like he was asking for it. For days afterward, I had trouble even looking at her.

In February 2014, David Ibarra was hit by a drunk driver while riding his bike home from his cousin's house, leaving him partially paralyzed. This page is dedicated to his story. Please leave a comment! And thank you for your support.

I just wonder.

"Hey."

As I looked up, startled, I had this fleeting thought that I would see David Ibarra in front of me. But it was Layla. When she saw my face, her eyes widened.

"What's wrong?"

I swallowed, hard. And then, somehow, I was talking. "My brother's in prison for drunk driving. He left a kid paralyzed. And I hate him for it."

As I spoke, I realized I'd held these words in for so long and so tightly that I *felt* the space they left empty once released. It was vast enough that I could think of nothing to follow them.

Layla looked at me for a long moment. Then she sat down beside me and said, "So there's this thing about me."

I don't know what reply I'd been expecting from her, but it wasn't this. I said, "I'm sorry?"

"I never forget a face. Like, never. I wish I could sometimes." She swallowed, then turned to look at me. "I saw you, in the courthouse. A few weeks back? You were coming out of the bathroom."

Until that moment, I had totally forgotten everything about that day except Peyton being sentenced. But as she said this, the rest of the details came rushing back. Ames taking me to the bathroom and waiting outside. Washing my hands, dreading rejoining him. And a girl who met my eyes and didn't look away.

"That was you?" She nodded. "I'd forgotten."

"I know. Anyone else would have. But I recognized you the minute I saw you at Seaside."

"You didn't say anything."

"Because it tends to creep people out." She sighed. "I mean, for everyone else, you see a stranger and then forget them. Faces only stick for a reason. But with me, it's like a photograph, filed away in my mind."

"That's nuts," I said.

"I know. Mac always says I should join the circus, or run a scheme or something, so I'm at least putting my power to use."

We were quiet another moment. Finally I said, "Why were you there?"

"At the courthouse?" I nodded. "I was with Rosie. She's had to check in with the judge about her progress every couple of months since she got busted."

I had a flash of the crack her sister had made about Logan Oxford and Layla's equally snide reply. "Was it drugs?"

"Yep." She sat back, turning up her face to the sun. "After her knee injury, she got a bit too fond of the Vicodin they gave her. Tried to pass off some fake prescriptions. Totally moronic. Got arrested, like, instantly."

"Did she go to jail?"

Layla shook her head. "Rehab. Then they put an anklet on her. She just got it off a couple of weeks ago."

"Really."

"Yeah. You think she's grumpy now, imagine her stuck in the house for six months." She sighed. "It's her own stupid fault, though. *So* infuriating. She had everything going for her and just blew it."

"That's like my brother." It was new to be talking to someone I didn't know well about this, but easier than I would have thought. "He had so many chances. But he kept getting into trouble anyway. And then the accident . . ."

I trailed off, not sure how much further I wanted to go into this. Layla didn't say anything. In the silence, I realized I did want to keep talking. Really badly, actually.

"He'd been sober for over a year. Doing really well. And then one night, for no reason that we can figure out, he got drunk and behind the wheel. Hit a kid riding his bike. The kid is in a wheelchair now. Forever."

Layla winced. "Wow. That's awful."

It was. It was really, really awful. And not just for Peyton, my mom and dad, or even me.

"His name is David Ibarra." I looked down at my hands. "I think about him all the time."

"Of course you do." She said this simply, flatly. "Anyone would."

"It's like you with the faces. I can't stop." I took in a breath. "And my mom, it's like she can't see what Peyton did for what it is. She just worries about him and how he's doing, and my dad doesn't talk about anything, and now she wants me to visit him. And I don't want to. At all. We got in a fight about it this morning."

Saying this, I realized one reason I'd never spoken to Jenn or Meredith this way. Layla might have known my face, but she was still a blank slate when it came to Peyton, not already in possession of some bias or feeling toward him. Unlike everyone else in my world.

"If you don't want to go, you shouldn't," she said. "Just tell your mom you're not in that place yet."

"I don't know if I ever will be. I mean, I've always loved my brother," I said. "But I really hate him right now."

Across the courtyard, someone laughed. Two girls in field hockey uniforms passed by, one on the phone, the other opening a piece of gum. Happy, normal lives going on in happy, normal ways, in a world that was anything but. Once you realized this, experienced something that made it crystal clear, you couldn't forget it. Like a face. Or a name. However you first learn that truth, once it's with you, it never really goes away.

CHAPTER

6

FOR THE first couple of days after I told Layla about Peyton, I kept waiting to regret it. It was strange, telling the story from the beginning instead of catching someone up on only the latest awful chapter. Like finally I was in a place quiet and safe enough to hear it, too. Just the facts, laid out like cards on a table. This happened, then this, then this. The end.

Even so, I'd thought it would change everything. This wasn't unrealistic. Peyton's crimes and convictions had skewed the view people had of my entire family. People in the neighborhood either stared or made a point of not looking at us; conversations at the pool or by the community bulletin board stopped when we came into earshot. It was like stepping into a fun house hall of mirrors, only to find you had to stay there. I was the sister of the neighborhood delinquent, drug addict, and now drunk driver. It didn't matter that I'd done none of these things. With shame, like horseshoes, proximity counts.

But not, apparently, with Layla. Instead of keeping me at arm's length, she looped me more tightly into her world, which I soon learned was jam-packed as it was. If I was the invisible girl, Layla was the shining star around which her family and friends revolved. We didn't form a friendship as much as I got sucked into her orbit. And once there, I understood why everyone else was.

"Everyone, this is Sydney," she'd announced the day after our talk, when I finally gathered up the courage to accept her invitation to join her and her friends at lunch. "She transferred from Perkins Day, drives a sweet car, and likes root beer YumYums."

I blinked, startled at being summarized in this fashion. But it was better than any of the other labels I could think of, so I took a seat on one of three benches I now knew they staked out each day. Mac was on another, eating from a plastic ziplock bag full of grapes, while Eric, wearing a fedora, strummed his guitar, facing the courtyard.

"We've already met, remember?" Mac said.

"She's met you guys," she responded. "But not Irv."

"Who's Irv?" I asked.

Just then, a shadow came over me. Not a metaphorical or symbolic one, but a real, actual shadow, as in something large had blocked out the sun. I went from squinting to sitting in shade in a matter of seconds. I looked behind me, expecting to see—what? A sudden skyscraper? A wall? Instead, it was the human equivalent: the biggest, broadest, thickest black guy I had ever seen. He was wearing dress pants, a shirt and tie with a Jackson High football jersey over it, and sunglasses. As I stared at him, he held out a huge hand.

"Irving Fearrington," he said. "Pleasure to meet you."

My hand looked like a toy wrapped in his. I had the fleeting thought that he could rip my entire arm out of my socket and eat it and I would not be surprised. Somehow, despite this, I managed to say, "Hi."

"Whatcha got for lunch today, Irv?" Layla said as he lowered his huge girth onto the last open bench. "Anything good?"

"Dunno yet." He unzipped his backpack—God, his wrists were thicker than my *legs*—and pulled out a large insulated cooler. As he opened it, I saw it was packed with plastic bags, which he began unloading. One had what looked like chicken legs. Another, some kind of grain. On and on, they kept coming: edamame, a stack of hamburger patties, hard-boiled eggs. And finally, at the very end, there was a bag packed with cookies.

"Score!" Layla said, seeing this. Irv grinned, suddenly looking much less intimidating. Like he might pull *out* your arm, but not eat it. "Toss those over."

"I don't think so." He wagged a huge finger at her. "You know the rules. Protein first."

"Irving. For God's sake. I already have one diet nag in my life."

"I didn't say a word," Mac said, eating another grape.

"Protein," Irv repeated, waving his hand at his substantial meal. "Your choice."

"Fine. Give me a couple of eggs."

He handed over the bag, and she opened it, taking out two, then passed it back. Irving held it to me. "Egg? Whites are the perfect protein."

"Um, no, thanks," I said, holding up the grilled cheese I'd gotten. "I'm good."

"Lucky you," Layla grumbled, peeling an egg. "If I showed up with one of those, these two would never let me hear the end of it."

"But you *wouldn't* show up with that," Mac said. "You'd just get fries and call it lunch. And fries aren't a meal."

"Fine, Grandma. Just shut up and eat your grapes, would you?"

In response, he threw one at her. It went wide, though, and hit me square in the face. As it bounced off, rolling into the grass, I saw his eyes widen, horrified.

"*Nice*, Macaulay Chatham," his sister said. "Is that part of your game now? Throwing food at pretty girls to get their attention?"

I was pretty now? And then we were both blushing.

"I wasn't aiming at her," he said, clearly embarrassed. To me he said, "Sorry."

"It's fine," I said.

"Although I *can* see that as the beginning to a great love story," Layla said.

"Here we go," Irv groaned, eating half a hamburger patty in one bite.

This Layla ignored, pulling a knee up to her chest. "Seriously. Can't you just see it? 'He threw a grape at me on a sunny day, and I just *knew* it was love.'"

"That," Mac said, spitting out a seed, "is the stupidest one yet."

"Which is really saying something," Irv added.

She made a face, wrinkling her nose, then said to me, "These boys have no sense of romance. I, on the other hand, am a connoisseur."

"You call yourself a connoisseur of everything," her brother pointed out.

"Not everything. Just candy, French fries, and love." She smiled at me. "All the important stuff. Seriously, though, I know the start to a good love story when I hear it. I should. I've read hundreds of them."

I raised my eyebrows. "Really?" On his bench, Mac sighed audibly.

"Oh, yeah. It's, like, my thing." She peeled the second egg. "Romance and instruction manuals."

"But not romance instruction manuals," Eric, who I hadn't even thought was listening, added.

"Seriously, though," Layla continued, "I *love* reading about how to do things. Even if it's something that, like, I will never do in a million years, like weave a rug or grout a floor."

"Wow," I said.

"I know. I'm, like, a process addict or something." She ate the egg, chewing thoughtfully, then swallowed and added, "Or, you know, a connoisseur."

Truth: I was having trouble keeping up. Not just with this conversation, but the people actually having it. I'd spent so much time alone lately that I'd forgotten what it was like to be relaxed in another person's company. I liked it.

After that first lunch, I began eating with them every day. Once the bell rang, I'd get something to eat from the food trucks, then cross the grass to either join whoever was already there or stake out the benches until they arrived. Foodwise, every day it was the same. Mac and Irving brought their lunches. Eric was partial to a fruit punch and buttery grilled cheese from the cafeteria. And Layla looked for fries.

She hadn't been kidding about the connoisseur thing. This girl took her frites seriously. It wasn't enough for them to be potatoes and fried, all that most people, myself included, really cared about. Oh, no. There were specifications. Required seasonings. Rules about everything from temperature and packaging to whether the ketchup was from a packet or a bottle. (This last one had subrules and addendums, as well.) Going to look for fries with Layla was like tagging along with my mom while she perused office supplies, requiring both patience and a substantial time commitment. By the time Layla got what she wanted, I was often finished with my entire lunch, if not already hungry again.

"What's most important is the shape," she explained to me the first time I joined her on this quest. "They should be long, not stubby. Decent width, but not thicker than a finger. Only the most basic seasoning, nothing crazy. And served hot."

"But not too hot?" I asked as she leaned into the window of the DoubleBurger truck and sniffed.

"No such thing," she replied. "Hot fries cool down. Cold fries never warm up. Let's keep walking; I'm not liking the grease smell here today."

The guy behind the counter just looked at her as she

turned, continuing on. I gave him an apologetic shrug and followed. "What about fast food ones?" I asked. "They're pretty much all the same, right?"

She stopped dead in her tracks. I almost crashed into her. "Sydney," she said, turning to face me. "That is *not true*. The next time I do a Trifecta, you're coming. I'll show you how wrong you are."

"A Trifecta?"

"That's when I get fries from the Big Three," she explained. She held up her fingers, counting off. "Littles, Bradbury Burger, and Pamlico Grill. None of them are perfect. But if you mix them together, it's like the paradise of fries. It's time-consuming, so I only do it on special occasions or when I'm super depressed."

Hearing this, I had that feeling again, like the conversation was a pack of wild horses pounding out ahead of me, leaving nothing but dust behind. Trifecta? Depression? Grease smell? She was already talking again.

"These trucks aren't the best for fries, because mobile fryers just taste different from ones in brick-and-mortar stores. But they do have some cool flavors you can't get in the traditional places. There's one place that I really like . . . Oh, they're here today! Come on."

In my pocket, I felt my phone buzz. I pulled it out and glanced at the screen. JENN, it said, with a picture of her from her last birthday party, a cheap plastic tiara on her head. I reached for the IGNORE button, feeling a pang of guilt. But not enough to not press it. I'd call her later.

Layla, meanwhile, had walked up to a truck I'd never

tried before called Bim Bim Slim's, which sold some kind of Asian-Creole fusion. The smells coming from it were like nothing I'd ever experienced before. She didn't even glance at the menu.

"Regular bim fry," she told the guy. "Actually, make it two orders. No sauce. Just extra ketchup packets."

"You got it."

Moments later, he handed over a white bag that smelled heavenly and was already sprouting grease stains. Layla smiled, satisfied. "Perfect. Come on."

Back at the benches, she nudged Eric off his seat—"Move, I need to set up!"—then sat down, opening the bag and putting her face over the opening. As we all watched, she took a deep breath, eyes closed. Then silence.

"Are we waiting for something?" I whispered to Irv, who was gnawing on a turkey leg.

"The verdict," he replied, voice equally low.

Finally, Layla opened her eyes. "Okay. These will do."

What followed was an intricate multistep process that began with the flattening and placement of the bag to turn it into a proper eating surface and ended with three identically sized pools of ketchup, each on its own napkin. To one, she added pepper. The next, salt. And the third, some unidentified substance she pulled from her purse, housed in a test tube.

"I know just what you're thinking," Irv said to me. "This has all been a little intense, but now it's getting weird. I felt the same way my first time."

"That's because it *is* weird to carry your own personalized spice blend around," Mac said, his eyes still on his history textbook. He was always studying at lunch, I'd noticed, but still listening to everything as well.

Layla ignored them, picking up a fry and dipping an end in one of the ketchups. She took a bite, chewing thoughtfully, then repeated the process with the other two options. When the fry was gone, she wiped her fingers on a napkin, then looked at me.

"Okay. Try one."

"Me?" I had assumed this was an individual sport.

She nodded, gesturing for me to come over. I did, taking a seat next to one of the ketchup stations, and she pushed the bag/plate toward me. "Take one from the middle. Those are the best. I always eat from the inside out."

I did as I was told, selecting a thick-but-not-overly-so one. Then I realized that, although I'd been eating fries since before I could talk, this was the first time I'd not been sure how to do it. This was made more awkward by the fact I had an audience.

"One, two, three," Layla said, pointing at each of the ketchups. "Triple dunk. Then eat half, flip it over, and repeat with other side. That way you avoid the double dip."

"What's in that last one?" I asked, still hesitant.

"My own creation. Don't worry, it's not spicy or gross. I promise."

In every friendship, at some point comes a test. Never before in my experience, however, had it involved food. *First time for everything*, I thought, and followed directions.

I'm not sure what I'd been anticipating. A good fry? Some tangy sauce? It was not, however, the perfection that subsequently unfolded inside my mouth. Considering the intricacy of preparation, maybe this is what I should have been expecting. But the crispness of the outer shell, the mushy, hot softness of the potato within, suddenly tinged with the sweetness of the ketchup mix, was a total surprise. Wow.

"See?" Layla said, smiling at me. "Great, right?"

"It's amazing," I said, already turning it over and prepping the next bite.

She clapped her hands, clearly thrilled. "I love a new convert to my process."

"Welcome to the illness," Mac said.

"Oh, don't listen to him, he used to eat his weight in these things. And he was *barbaric* about it. Just dumped them out, covered them in ketchup, and dove in." She shuddered. "Ugh."

I glanced over at Mac, who was eating an apple. He saw me and rolled his eyes, and I quickly looked away. In the next beat, like always, I regretted this, but there was something about him that made me so *nervous*. From someone that good-looking, even the smallest bit of attention was like the brightest of lights focused on me.

I knew this reaction well, because I'd seen it from the other side in girls when they were around my brother. He and Mac had the same dark, intense looks, that identical way of drawing attention just by existing. But while Peyton had long been aware of it, I had the feeling Mac wasn't.

He didn't carry himself like he knew he was attractive. And sometimes, when he did catch me watching him, he seemed surprised.

But I shouldn't have even been thinking like this, and not just because Mac would never be interested in me in the first place. I'd only been hanging out with Layla for a week or so, but certain rules, spoken and unsaid, were already clear. You weren't barbaric with fries. You didn't take the bubble gum or cotton candy YumYums. And you never even thought about dating her brother. Just ask Kimmie Crandall.

I'd first heard this name during a typical fast-paced lunch conversation. It began with a discussion about milk and how people either really liked it or really didn't: there was no in between. Then it shifted to other things that people hated, which segued into a speed round during which Layla, Eric, and Irv tried to come up with the most awful combination ever.

"Someone you truly dislike eating with their mouth open," Eric offered. "And something gross. Like egg salad."

"What's wrong with egg salad?" Irv asked.

"Just play the game," Layla told him.

Irv thought for a second. "Someone you truly dislike eating egg salad with their mouth open while wearing a sweater that smells like wet dog."

My turn. "Um," I said. "Someone you truly dislike eating egg salad openmouthed in a wet-dog sweater while telling a boring story with no point."

"Nice," Layla said appreciatively. "I hate that. You're up, Mac."

Mac, who was continuing his run of various fruits at lunch with a handful of blackberries, said, "Everything you guys said plus golf."

Layla sighed. "You're supposed to repeat the whole sentence. God, you *never* play right."

"Then exclude me. I'll be fine, I promise," he said, turning another page in his chem textbook.

"Party pooper," Irv said. Mac threw a blackberry at him, this time connecting. "Watch it, fatty."

"Nice mouth," Mac replied, but he hardly seemed bothered. Not to mention fat. There was a lot I wasn't privy to yet, clearly.

Layla sat up straight, holding up her hands. "Okay. This: Kimmie Crandall, eating egg salad with her mouth full, wearing a sweater that smells like wet dog, while telling a boring story with no point about golf."

"Sold!" Eric said. "You win!"

"Hands down," Irv agreed. "Still the champion."

Mac turned to look across the courtyard, adding nothing to this. I said, "Who's Kimmie Crandall?"

Silence. Then Layla said, "Mac's ex-girlfriend. And my former best friend."

"Oh." That explained the quiet. "Sorry."

"Don't be. We're both *much* better off without her."

Mac got up then, balling his lunch stuff up and starting over to the trash cans. As he walked away, Irv said, "Still too soon?"

"It's been three months." Layla sat back. "There has to be a statute of limitations on pretending someone doesn't exist."

"Maybe it's different when that person was your girl-friend," Eric said.

"She broke the friendship code. That means I can make fun of her whenever I want." Turning to me, she said, "She totally started hanging out with me just to get to Mac. I was friendless and desperate and couldn't see. Then she hooked him in, stomped on his heart, and proceeded to talk smack about us to anyone who would listen."

"That's awful," I said, looking at Mac. He was walking back toward us now, running a hand through his hair. "Does she go here?"

She shook her head. "The Fountain School. She was a mean hippie. Who even knew such a thing existed? Bitch."

This was the harshest thing I'd ever heard her say, and it stunned me into silence for a second. Obviously, for all the nagging and fruit throwing, there was a loyalty there that ran deep. Once I was aware of it, I saw proof of it again and again. I couldn't really relate, as by the time Peyton got into dating, he was already slipping away from us. I could, how-ever, take note. So I did.

❊ ❊ ❊

Two nights later, it was my mom who had something waiting by her plate. Instead of a flyer, it was a brochure. All I could see from my seat was a picture of a beach.

"What's this?" she said as she came in carrying a platter of roasted chicken. She set it down, but did not pick up the paper. Like it was so not for her, she shouldn't even touch it.

"Hotel St. Clair," my father told her, reaching for the chicken. My dad was always hungry. He was a constant nibbler, known for standing in front of the fridge for long periods, grazing, and always jumped on food as soon as it arrived. "In the St. Ivy Islands."

"Why is it by my plate?"

"Because," my dad said, serving himself a large helping, "I have a conference there next week, and I want you to come with me."

Immediately, my mom's face said *NO*. Or maybe *NO!* The little crease appeared between her eyes that Peyton had, in her earshot, once not-so-smartly referred to as Anger Canyon. "A trip? Now? Oh, I don't think so."

"Give me one reason why."

She sighed, then sat down, pushing the folded paper aside to pick up her napkin. "Next weekend is visitation at Lincoln."

"Julie, you go often enough to miss one day."

"He counts on me to be there, Peyton."

"We'll make sure Ames visits, then."

She shook her head. "And Sydney just started a new school. . . . It's just not a good idea."

My dad looked at me. His expression made it clear I should say *I'm fine*. So I did.

"Honey, you can't just stay here by yourself," she told me, sounding tired.

"I already talked to Jenn's parents. They'd love to have her."

I blinked, surprised. It was true I hadn't talked to Jenn

in a few days, but I was still surprised she hadn't mentioned anything about this. She might not, I realized, even know. When my dad wanted something, he went for it.

"Julie," he said now, "you need this. *We* need this. It's two days on a beautiful beach, and everything's taken care of. Just say yes."

The *NO* was still on her face. Even so, she said, "I'll think about it."

My dad didn't say anything, his expression measured, as he felt out how hard to push the issue. "Okay," he said. "Do that."

And with that, the subject was dropped. But clearly not forgotten, as I heard them talking about it twice more that evening: once as they watched the news while I very quietly loaded the dishwasher, and again from upstairs, as I was getting ready for bed. The next morning, as I passed the War Room, I saw she'd pulled her file labeled TRAVEL onto the desk, the one that contained packing lists, intricate clothes-folding diagrams, and all her guidebooks. If they went, it would be her first trip in over a year, and I wanted her to have that. Plus, a whole weekend with Jenn might help to bridge the distance that I'd recently felt creeping into our increasingly rare conversations, both on the phone and face-to-face. Maybe this would be good for all of us. But the morning they were supposed to leave, we got a phone call.

"Jenn's sick," my mom reported when I came downstairs for school. My dad was leaning against the fridge with his coffee. "Stomach bug. They all have it."

"Ugh," I said.

"Exactly. So you can't stay there this weekend." She looked at my dad. "What now?"

"Meredith?"

"She's away at a meet," I told them. "Left yesterday."

My mom sighed. "Well, that's that. Peyton, you go ahead, and I'll stay here. It's probably better this way, anyway."

"No, no, hold on," my dad said. "Let me think."

"I'm seventeen," I told them. "I can stay alone for a weekend."

"*That's* not happening," my mom told me. "I think we all know well what a lack of supervision can lead to."

Hearing this, I felt stung. I'd never done anything, not even skipped school. The last thing I deserved was to have the same old assumptions applied, but clearly, this wasn't about me.

"Hold on," my dad said, pulling out his phone and typing something as I got down a bowl and poured my cereal. I was just about to add milk when he said, "Done. It's taken care of."

I looked at him. Now I was an It. Nice. "How?"

He replied to my mom, not me. "Ames and Marla. They'll be here at four, stay the whole weekend. He says it's not a problem at all."

"Oh, they don't need to do that," I said quickly. "I'm fine. I mean, I'll be fine."

"Ames and Marla?" My mom wrinkled her brow. "Oh, I hate to impose on them that way. He's already going to Lincoln tomorrow."

"He's happy to do it, he says. And Marla's got the whole weekend off."

Oh, great. I'd heard Marla say a total of about ten words in the months I'd known her. Having her here would be no different, really, than Ames and I alone. I said, "Um, I actually have this new friend, Layla. I'm sure I could stay with her."

They both looked at me. "A new friend? You haven't mentioned that."

"Well, I just met her. But—"

"I'm not sending you to stay with a family I don't know at all, Sydney," my mom said, shaking her head. "That could even be worse than staying by yourself."

"Then I'll just do that."

"Ames and Marla are coming," my dad said. His tone made it clear this negotiation was over. "Now, Sydney, eat your breakfast. You're going to be late."

Helpless, I sat down at the table as my dad walked over and kissed my mom on the forehead, then said something quietly to her that I couldn't hear. She smiled, reluctantly, and I realized how long it had been since I'd seen her anything but barely coping or outright sad. And what would I tell her, anyway? That this person whom you count on and totally adore gives me the creeps—for no reason I could specifically say—and his girlfriend wouldn't help matters? I'd sound crazy. Maybe I was.

"Sydney?" she asked me suddenly. I looked up. "Everything okay?"

I met her eyes, saying nothing but wishing she would. That somehow, in the midst of all her grief and distraction, she might be able to finally see me, if not hear the words I couldn't speak aloud.

A beat passed, then another. She was starting to look worried, the canyon finding its way onto her face again. From the open doorway, my dad was watching me, too.

"Yeah," I told them. "I'm fine."

CHAPTER 7

THIS TIME at Seaside, I was sure of it. The music playing was bluegrass.

"You want another slice?"

I shook my head. Layla slid out from the booth where we were sitting, taking her plate with her. As she ducked behind the counter, grabbing a second piece to heat up, I walked over to the jukebox. It was the vintage kind, with actual typed titles and a slot to put in coins. Each selection was a quarter. The song currently playing was called "Rope Swing."

"We call that thing the Dinosaur," Layla said from behind me. A moment later, she was leaning on the glass. "My dad bought it at a flea market when he took over this place from my grandfather."

"So pizza runs in the family," I said.

"Not exactly. My mom's the Italian one. Daddy's family is from the mountains," she said. "But when he married in, it was understood he'd take over Seaside eventually. He wanted to make it more his own, though; hence the Dinosaur. That's when the music rule started."

"Music rule?"

"Nothing but bluegrass during business hours." She shook her head. "We have tried everything to talk reason into him. I mean, this place is called Seaside Pizza. Bluegrass is mountain music. It's totally incongruous."

"It's pretty, though," I said as "Rope Swing" went into another chorus.

"Oh, it's great. I mean, it's the first thing I learned to play. It's just not exactly what teenagers want to listen to after school. And since we're always trying to get more business, it's kind of ridiculous."

"You play music?"

She nodded, still looking at the song choices. "It's the only thing my dad's into other than cars and work. He taught me the banjo when I was seven."

"You play *banjo*?"

"You say it like I said I do brain surgery or castrate elephants," she said, and laughed.

"It's just pretty impressive."

She shrugged. "I like singing better. But Rosie's the one with the voice."

With this, she turned on her heel, going back behind the counter. Mac was back there as well, working some dough in his hands with one of his textbooks open on the counter in front of him, while his dad chopped peppers, facing the window. It was only my third time or so after school at Seaside, but I'd already learned enough of the routine to feel comfortable there. Which was why I'd made a point of coming today. I planned to stay as long as I possibly could.

I'd gone to school at seven forty-five that morning. At

lunch, I checked my voice mail to find a message my mom
had left as she and my dad drove to the airport an hour or so
earlier. She told me their flight was on time, that she'd have
her phone with her all weekend, and I should call if I needed
anything at all. But I didn't know what I needed, only what I
absolutely did not: to be stuck with Ames (and silent, shrink-
ing Marla) for the entire weekend.

I'd had a pit in my stomach all day, trying to figure out
how to be gone as long as possible. There was school, at least,
and then I'd go meet Layla at Seaside, where she went every
day after the final bell until deliveries starting coming in and
Mac could drop her at home. I could stay until at least six
or so, getting home with only a couple of hours left before
I could reasonably go to bed. Saturday, I planned to slip out
early and stay gone all day, using an excuse I hadn't formu-
lated yet. That was as far as I'd gotten.

I slid back into the booth opposite Layla, who was now
digging into her second slice. Unlike fries, her pizza she consumed in a somewhat normal way, folding it in half like a
taco and proceeding from tip to crust. For such a small, lithe
person, she could eat a lot, I was noticing. In contrast, I'd
never seen Mac sample a single thing at Seaside, which had
to require a huge amount of self-control. The only reason
I'd turned down a second slice was that dread was taking up
much of my stomach.

As I thought this, my phone beeped. I pulled it out of my
purse. The text was from Ames, whose number my mom
had insisted I add to my contacts before leaving for school
that morning.

Just got here. What's your ETA? Cooking you dinner!

"What's up?"

I looked up at Layla. She was dabbing her mouth with a napkin, half the slice already devoured. "Nothing. Just a text from . . . My parents are out of town."

"So they're checking in?"

"Yeah."

She went back to eating, and I wondered why I didn't tell her what was going on. Nothing had surprised her so far; this probably wouldn't, either. But I liked Layla, and felt lucky that learning about Peyton hadn't changed how she felt about me. Adding on another layer of weirdness, though, might do just that.

An hour or so, I wrote back. You don't have to cook.

I hit SEND. In seconds, he'd replied.

I want to.

I stuffed my phone back in my bag, turning off the ringer. As I did, I felt a rush of new anger toward my brother. There had been so many ripple effects of his bad choices, but this one was mine alone to deal with. Thanks a lot.

I swallowed, then looked over at the register. Mac was tossing the crust now, using both hands to shape and thin it. I watched him, drawing something like comfort from the repetitive movements, and then he suddenly looked at me. For once I stared back, if only for a second, before turning away.

At five thirty, the phone started ringing and business started to pick up. The bluegrass, which apparently played nonstop whether anyone inserted coins or not, went from clearly audible to faint to silenced as more people came in. By quarter of six, when Layla and I gathered up our stuff and vacated the booth, there was a line at the counter, the evening shift guys had come on, and Mac was zipping pizza boxes into warmers, getting ready for deliveries.

"I guess you're going?" I said to Layla as he headed to the truck, parked outside at the curb.

She glanced at the counter, where her dad was making change for someone. "Looks pretty busy, so I'll probably stick around until Mac's heading in my direction."

"I can take you home," I offered.

"Nah, my dad probably wants me to take orders. But thanks. I *do* want to ride in your car sometime. I bet it's amazing."

I was so desperate to avoid what awaited me, I almost offered the car to her, just to stall. But she was already heading back behind the counter. "I'll see you Monday, okay?"

"Yeah," I said, pulling my bag over my shoulder. "See you then."

As I pushed out the door to the parking lot, Mac was piling the warmers into the truck. As I crossed in front of him, he called out, "Be safe."

I turned, looking back at him. This was what you said to

someone getting into a car or leaving for the night. It carried no great meaning or symbolic importance. But even so, hearing him say it, I felt tears prick my eyes.

"Thanks," I replied. "You too."

He nodded, then went back to what he was doing. I got into my car, buckled up, and started the engine. Like the first time I'd come to Seaside, I ended up behind him at the light, and for two blocks, then three. At the next intersection, he put on his right blinker and turned. As he did, he waved to me out his window. Just a flutter of fingers, an acknowledgment. I was on my own now.

❧ ❧ ❧

When I walked in my house, the first thing I saw were the candles. They were the ones my mom only pulled out for special occasions, like Christmas and Thanksgiving, kept stored in the sideboard behind the liquor. If you didn't know this, you'd have to search for them. They sat on the table, not yet lit.

"Hey there," Ames said, appearing in the kitchen doorway. He was wearing a button-down shirt, jeans, and sneakers, and holding one of our wooden spoons. "How was school?"

It was all just so *weird*, the juxtaposition of this question, which my mom asked me every day, and the candles, which indicated something almost romantic.

"Where's Marla?" I asked. It wasn't like she had a presence that filled a room or anything, but I could just feel there were only two of us there.

"Sick," he replied. "Stomach flu. Poor kid. Sucks, right?"

By the way he turned, walking back into the kitchen, I could tell he expected me to follow him. But I stayed where I was, feeling my face grow flushed. Marla wasn't coming? At all?

"You didn't have to cook," I said.

"I know. But you haven't lived until you've had my spaghetti with meat sauce. I'd be doing you a disservice not letting you experience it."

"I'm actually not that hungry," I said.

At this, he turned, a flicker of irritation on his face. As quickly as it appeared, though, it was gone. "Just have a taste, then. You won't regret it, I promise."

Everywhere I turned, I was stuck. I wasn't prone to panicking, but suddenly I could feel my heart beating. "I'm, um, going to go put my stuff away."

"Okay," he said. "Don't be too long. I want to catch up. It's been a while."

I took the stairs two at a time, like someone was chasing me, then ducked into my room, shutting the door behind me. I sat down on my bed, pulling out my phone, and tried to think. A moment later, I heard music drifting upstairs, and somehow, I knew he'd now lit the candles. That was when I looked up a number and dialed it.

A man answered. "Seaside Pizza. Can you hold?"

I'd been expecting Layla. Now I didn't know what to do. "Yes."

A click, and then silence. I thought about hanging up,

but before I could, he was back. "Thanks for holding. Can I help you?"

Shit. "Um . . . I want to place a delivery order?"

I could hear talking in the background, but none were a girl's voice. "Go ahead."

"Large half pepperoni, half deluxe," I said.

"Anything else?"

"No."

"Address?"

I took a breath. "It's 4102 Incline—"

There was a clanging noise in the background. "Sorry, can you hold another minute?"

"Sure," I said. Downstairs, the song had changed, and I could smell garlic, wafting up under my closed door.

"Sorry about that," a voice said on the other end of the line. It was a girl. Oh, my God. "So that's a half pepperoni, half deluxe, large? What's the name?"

"Layla?"

A pause. "Yeah?"

"It's Sydney."

"Oh, hey!" She sounded so pleased to hear my voice that I almost burst into tears. "What's up? Regretting you only had one slice this afternoon?"

"Do you want to spend the night tonight?"

I literally blurted this; I doubted she'd even made it out. But again, she surprised me. "Sure. Let me just ask."

There was a clank as she put the phone down. As I sat there, listening to the register beep and some other muffled conversation, I realized I was holding my breath. When she came back, I still didn't exhale.

"I'm in," she said cheerfully. "Mac can bring me with the pizza. In, like, twenty minutes or so?"

"Great," I said, entirely too enthusiastically. "Thank you."

"Sure. Just give me your address and a phone number, okay?"

I did, and then we hung up. I went into the bathroom and washed my face, telling myself I could handle anything for twenty minutes. Then I went downstairs.

Ames was at the stove when I walked in, his back to me. "Ready to eat? I've got the table set."

I glanced into the dining room: sure enough, the candles were lit, two plates laid out with silverware and folded paper napkins. "I actually, um, have a friend coming over. She's bringing a pizza."

He didn't say anything for a moment. Then he turned around to face me. "I told you I was cooking."

"I know, but—"

"Your mom didn't mention anything to me about a friend visiting," he told me.

She also thought Marla was going to be here, I thought.

"It's not very polite, Sydney, to make other plans when a person has gone out of their way to do something for you."

I didn't ask you to do anything. "I'm sorry . . . I guess signals got crossed."

He looked at me for a long moment, not even trying to hide his irritation. Then, slowly, he turned back around. "You can at least have a taste. Since I've gone to all this trouble."

"Okay," I said. It was weird to see an adult pout. "Sure."

At the table, he served us both, then picked up his glass of cola, holding it up. "To good friends," he said.

I clinked my drink against his, then took an obligatory sip as he watched me over the rim of his glass. I glanced at my watch. It had been ten minutes.

"So I rented a couple of movies," he said, twirling some noodles around his fork. "Thought we'd settle in on the couch, have some popcorn. Hope you're a fan of heavy butter. Or else we can't be buds anymore."

If only it were that easy. "Yeah. Sure."

He smiled at me then, in a forgiving way. Like I'd earned another chance or something. Everything was wrong here.

Twelve minutes.

"This is good," I said, forcing myself to try the pasta. "Thanks for cooking."

"Of course." He smiled, clearly pleased. "It's the least I can do, since you're stuck with me all weekend. Speaking of which, what are you up to tomorrow? I'm heading to see Peyton in the morning, but I'll be free all afternoon. I was thinking we could hit a movie or go bowling, then have dinner out somewhere."

"I actually have a school thing," I said. "It's, um, kind of mandatory."

A pause. "On the weekend?"

I nodded. "Community service project. I'll be gone most of the day."

"Huh." One word, so many connotations. "Well, we'll see."

My stomach tightened, and for a beat or two, I was sure

the few bites I'd managed to get down were going to rejoin us. But then, thank God—thank everything in the world—the doorbell rang.

"I'll get it," I said, leaping up and tossing my napkin onto my seat. Starting for the door, I hit the edge of the table with my hip, causing something to clank loudly. I didn't slow down to see what it was.

In the foyer, I flipped the dead bolt, then yanked the door open hard, clearly startling Layla, who was standing right in front of it, holding a pizza box. I could see Mac in the truck, parked in the driveway.

"Hi," I said, breathless. "I'm so glad you're here."

"Well, it's nice to get such an enthusiastic welcome." She looked up at the tall windows on either side of the door, eyes widening. "Your house is gorgeous."

"Thanks. Come in. I'll, um, get the money for the pizza."

"Oh, don't worry about it," she said. "It's on the—"

She stopped talking suddenly, staring over my shoulder. Instantly, her expression went from open and friendly to guarded. Before I even glanced behind me, I knew Ames had appeared.

"This is the friend?" he said when I did look his way.

"Layla," I told him. To her, I added, "Come on in."

She didn't move. Instead, she turned her head toward Mac. I couldn't make out her expression, but a second later, he was getting out of the truck. When he joined her on the steps, she finally stepped inside.

"Ames Bentley," Ames said to them, extending a hand. "Close friend of the family."

"This is Mac," I said. They shook. I took the pizza from Layla. "Come on in the kitchen."

We went, with me leading, Ames right behind, and the Chathams bringing up the rear. Right away, I saw Layla surveying the scene in the dining room. When she saw the candles, she looked right at me.

"Pretty fancy," she said. "What's going on?"

"Just showing off my cooking skills for Sydney," Ames said. "Thought I'd wow her with my sauce, but she went and ordered a pizza. She's a heartbreaker, this one."

"Where's your mom, again?" Layla asked me, ignoring this.

"She and my dad are at a conference."

"All weekend?"

"Now, don't get any ideas about parties," Ames said, holding up his hands. "That's what I'm here to prevent."

"I wasn't going to have a party," I said quietly.

"Sure." He grinned, then looked at Mac. "You guys want some dinner? Or a drink? Nonalcoholic only. House rules."

"No, thanks," Mac said, just as his phone beeped. He pulled it out, glancing at the screen, then said to Layla, "Another order. I should get going."

"Lucky me," Ames said. "Spending the evening with two lovely ladies."

In response, Mac just looked at him, his expression flat and unsmiling. After a beat, he said to Layla, "You left your stuff in the truck."

"Oh," she said. "Right. I'll come out with you."

He turned to walk to the door. As she fell in behind him, she looked at me, clearly wanting me to follow. Before I could, I felt Ames put his hand on my shoulder. "Little help cleaning up, Sydney?"

I followed him back into the dining room, where he gathered up his plate. Lowering his voice, he said, "When your mom calls, you know I have to tell her about this."

"I'm not doing anything wrong," I said.

"She didn't expect you to have company, though." I looked at him, his head bent as he picked up his napkin, and felt a surge of anger bolt through me. Like my mom *was* anticipating what he'd intended for that evening. Turning toward the kitchen, he added, "Don't worry, I'll spin it the best I can. You just owe me."

To this, I said nothing, instead just standing there as, slowly, Mac's truck began backing down my driveway. When he reached the road, his headlights swept across the window, catching me in their sudden glow. He sat there for a beat. Another. Then, slowly, he drove away.

* * *

"Okay," Layla said, sitting down opposite me. "What the *hell* is the deal with that guy?"

I looked down at my hands. After an awkward conversation in the kitchen, with Ames hanging on our every word, she'd asked to see my room, giving us an excuse to go upstairs. I shut the door behind us; she went to lock it, only to find there was no way to do so. When Peyton first got into trouble, my mom had removed the locks from all the bedroom doors, implementing the policy of Knocks Not Locks.

It was, apparently, about respect and trust. Or so she said.

"He's my brother's best friend," I told her now. "And he creeps me out."

"Of course he does." She said this flatly: a fact. "He's creepy. He was with you that day, right? In the courthouse."

That explained the expression when she first saw him. Never forget a face. "Yeah. He, um, tends to stick pretty close."

She shuddered visibly. "What does your mom say?"

"She loves him. It's like he's filled the hole my brother left, or at least made it less empty."

"What about your dad?"

"He doesn't notice much of anything when it comes to me."

I'd never thought this before, actually, but as soon as I said it, I realized it was true. My mom's distraction was new, a result of cause and effect. My dad's had always been there. Before Peyton, it was work. Before work, who knew.

"Well, that sucks," she said. She looked around my room. "So he's here with you both nights?"

"I was supposed to go to a friend's. She got sick, so my dad asked him and his girlfriend to fill in last-minute."

"Girlfriend?"

"Stomach bug," I explained. "Apparently."

"I'm sure he wasn't exactly disappointed," she replied. "If he even invited her in the first place."

"You think?" I asked. She just looked at me. "The candles and dinner were a *bit* unexpected."

"Ugh." She shuddered. "I'm glad you called me."

"I'm glad you came."

She smiled. "We'll deal with tomorrow night later. For now, though, I need to get a peek inside your closet. It looks massive. It's a walk-in, right?"

What followed was an extended tour of not only my closet—which was a walk-in, not that you could tell with the door closed, as it had been—but the entire house, with me leading the way. As Ames stood outside, smoking in the overhang of the garage, Layla *ooh*ed over the sunken tub in my parents' bathroom ("Is that marble?"), *wow*ed about the War Room ("Your mom is so organized!"), and repeatedly admired all the environmentally friendly touches my super-green mom had implemented throughout ("I can barely get my parents to recycle"). It wasn't until I took her downstairs to see the workout room, though, that she really got impressed.

It wasn't the elliptical, weight set, treadmill, or mounted wide-screen TV on the wall that did it, but the door behind the stack of yoga mats, straps, and blocks. When I opened it, she let out a low whistle.

"Oh, my God. Is that . . . a recording studio?"

"A partial one," I replied, fumbling for the light switch. Once on, it illuminated the small booth, soundproofed, as well as the board of various switches and knobs. No one had been inside for a while; the air smelled stale, and there were a couple of to-go coffee cups, along with a guitar on the small couch, resting as if it had just been put there. "It's my brother's. They were just about to paint when everything happened."

"Okay if I go in?"

"Sure."

She stepped inside, and I followed, hitting another light switch, which brightened the booth and another row of bulbs overhead. I watched as she crossed over to the couch, where she picked up the guitar, admiring it.

"Les Paul Standard," she said, clearly impressed. "Wow."

I'd felt a little weird for this entire tour. It wasn't until this moment, though, as she examined one of Peyton's many expensive guitars, that I experienced something close to actual shame.

"What are you guys doing in here?"

I jumped, startled; I hadn't heard Ames come in. "Uh, nothing. Just showing Layla around."

He glanced at her, there on the couch, then stepped inside, brushing past me. "You like guitars?"

"Yeah," she replied, not looking at him.

Ames crossed over to the couch, which was small, squeezing in next to her. "Here," he said, reaching over her shoulders to take both her hands. "I'll show you some chords."

"I'm okay," she replied. By her voice, it was more like *Back off.*

Ames heard it, too, and did just that. Regrouping, he walked over to the opposite wall, where another guitar sat in a stand, and picked it up. Layla continued to ignore him, strumming, while he picked out a few chords, his brow furrowed.

"Needs tuning," he said after a moment. "But it'll do for a

quick lesson. Now, look. I'll show you the basic chords. This is an F . . ."

I watched as he demonstrated. Layla did not. When he noticed this, he moved on to actually playing, beginning a crude rendition of "Stairway to Heaven," one of the first songs Peyton had learned in rehab. And then, when I didn't think it could get any more awkward, he began to sing. His voice was thin and reedy, his eyes shut soulfully, as he teetered over the words of the first two lines. Sadly, we had to watch.

It was just so awful, and I hadn't thought anything could be worse than the dinner. I had the worst urge to just laugh out loud, but I knew I couldn't, so I bit my lip. Then Layla also began to play. First quietly, but as she kept on, it grew louder, her fingers moving faster. I didn't realize what was happening until she was suddenly playing right along with him. But she wasn't just picking it out, like he'd been; clearly, *she* knew what she was doing. Ames realized as soon as I did and abruptly fell silent. Only then did she begin to sing.

I remembered Layla telling me earlier that day, offhand, that Rosie was the one with the voice. If that was the case, she had to be at opera-like level, because Layla's singing was gorgeous. Suddenly the room was filled with the sound of her voice, melodic and pure, while her fingers moved so quickly over the guitar strings, they were blurring. I was pretty sure my mouth was hanging open. I know Ames's was. When she finished, it was like the air sucked right out from all around us. Silence.

"Wow," I finally managed. "That was *amazing*."

"You are pretty good," Ames added.

"It's 'Stairway to Heaven.' Everyone can play that." Layla put the guitar back where she'd found it, then looked at me. "Ready for pizza? I am."

We ended the night as Ames had planned, watching movies. He made his "famous" popcorn, drenched in melted butter, before settling smack in the middle of the couch facing the TV, so whoever else sat there had no choice but to be next to him. Layla chose the floor, then patted the carpet beside her. As I sat, Ames cut his eyes at me. He wasn't even trying not to look annoyed anymore.

The movies were romantic comedies, and Layla, the connoisseur, had already seen them both. She said we should go with the one that was funnier, rather than the one with the dreamy cover image of a couple in midkiss. Forgoing the popcorn, Layla opened her purse and pulled out a fistful of YumYum lollipops, then offered them to me. There was a root beer right in the middle, which I was sure was no accident. When she extended them to Ames, he shook his head.

"Don't like hard candy," he told her. "And all those flavors are always too sour anyway."

This Layla didn't even honor with a reply, instead just ripping a pink one open and sticking it in her mouth. I reached for some popcorn, starting to feel kind of bad for him. It was so buttery, it felt wet in my hand. I left it on my napkin.

About halfway into the movie, there was a burst of music,

and Ames pulled out his phone, glancing at it. "It's your mom," he said to me, then answered, putting on the speakerphone. "Julie, hey. How's the vacation?"

Layla was still sucking on her lollipop, her eyes on the TV, as my mom said the trip had been good, the flights easy, and they'd just had a great dinner. If Ames was going to tell her I'd invited someone she didn't know to spend the night, he was taking his time.

"Is Sydney there?" she asked finally.

"Sure," he replied. Then he handed the phone to me.

"Hi, Mom," I said. I wished I could take her off speaker, but it felt weird doing it on someone else's phone. Of course he wanted to hear everything that was said.

"Hi, honey!" My mom actually sounded happy, and for a moment I felt bad for not wanting her to go on the trip. "How are you doing? Having fun with Ames and Marla?"

"Marla's actually sick. Same bug as Jenn," I said. Ames was watching me still, eating a handful of popcorn.

"Poor thing! That's really going around." A pause. "Everything else okay, though? You had dinner?"

"Ames cooked." At this, he smiled mildly. "And now we're just watching a movie."

"Well, that sounds like fun. It's beautiful here. I haven't seen a beach so white since . . . well, ever. I might even get a suntan."

"That's great."

"Now, tomorrow, you know Ames will be leaving early to visit your brother. So you can go out for breakfast, or make your usual. I left money with him if you guys want to do dinner out or order in. Sound good?"

"Sure."

"We'll be back by dinnertime Sunday," she continued. "And tell Ames we'll stop and pick up something, so he should plan to stay. It's the least we can do for him helping us out on such short notice. And if Marla's better, tell him to invite her, too."

Beside me, Layla removed her lollipop and gave me a look. Then, clearly and audibly, she coughed. Twice.

On the couch, Ames shifted, putting down the popcorn bowl. The TV was on, dialogue still going, so I wasn't even sure my mom had heard until she said, "Sydney? Is . . . is someone else there?"

I looked at Layla, who gave me an almost imperceptible nod. Then I said, "Yeah. My friend I told you about, Layla? She came over with a pizza."

"Hi, Mrs. Stanford!" Layla called out. "It's nice to meet you!"

There was a slight pause as my mom, normally unflappable when it came to manners and civility, regrouped. "Hello there. I've heard a lot about you. I didn't realize—"

"Sydney's kind of saving my life right now," Layla told her. "We're remodeling, and they just started repainting my room today and got new carpet put in. Combined, the fumes are *awful*."

On the couch, Ames looked at her. "Don't worry, Julie," he called out. "I'll make sure she heads home soon so Sydney's not up late."

"Oh, yeah," Layla added, returning his stare. "It's been airing out for an hour by now, so it should be fine to sleep in."

Now I began to catch on.

"You're staying in that room *tonight*?" my mom asked.

"Um, yeah."

A pause. Then my mom said, "Layla, it's not my place to butt in, but it's really not safe to be exposed to carpet and latex fumes, especially when they're so fresh. Off-gassing is serious. Of course, ideally, you'd be using products that would not have chemicals, but I understand that's not always possible."

Layla widened her eyes, as if my mom could actually see her reaction. "So you're saying I shouldn't sleep there?"

"Well, ideally, no. Is there another room that uses a separate ventilation system?"

"Not that isn't already taken. But seriously, I'm sure it's fine. They're supposed to finish up the painting tomorrow, so . . ." She was still looking at Ames as she said this. The sight line between them was so strong, it was almost visible, if not vibrating.

A pause. Then my mom said, "Sydney? Could you take me off speaker, please?"

I did, then put the phone to my ear. "Okay. It's just me now."

There was a muffled noise: her hand was covering the phone, or she had it tucked against her. But I could still hear my dad saying something, and then her replying. After a moment, she came back on. "Honey? How well do you know this girl?"

I got to my feet and walked into the kitchen. "I told you. She's the only friend I've made at Jackson. She's been really nice to me."

"Hold on." More muffled conversation. Then she said, "If that's the case, I think, under the circumstances, she should stay over tonight. And honestly, if they're still doing work there, tomorrow as well. I'd just feel better, if she's your good friend, knowing what I do know about toxins."

"Really?" I asked. "Mom, that would be so awesome of you."

"Awesome?" She sounded surprised. And pleased. "Well, I think it's just common courtesy. Do you think I should call her parents and make sure it's okay?"

I walked back to the living room. Ames was still giving Layla the side-eye, but she'd resumed watching TV, the lollipop back in her mouth. "Hey. Do you want to stay for the weekend?"

She blinked at me, as if I hadn't already asked her this. "Are you sure it's okay?"

"Yeah. My mom just wants to know if she should talk to yours first."

"Oh, no," she said, clearly and loudly. "The new meds she's on make her really tired, so she's probably already in bed. I'll text my sister so she can tell her in the morning."

"Her mom has MS," I told my mom.

"Oh, what a horrible thing." She gave this a respectful silence. "All right, then. Make sure she has everything she needs, okay? The air mattress is in the guest room, and there are extra blankets in the linen closet, as well as a spare toothbrush."

"Okay." I turned my back, lowering my voice. "Thanks, Mom. Really."

"Oh . . . well, you're welcome." She sounded like she was smiling. "Now let me talk to Ames again, would you?"

I walked over, holding out his phone. He put down the popcorn bowl and wiped a greasy hand on his jeans before getting to his feet and taking it from me. Then he walked out of the room, waiting to talk until he was out of earshot.

From the floor, Layla said, "This movie's really good, isn't it?"

I looked at her: she was watching me, not the TV, and smiling wide.

"It's great. I think it might be my favorite."

To this she said nothing, just turned back to the screen. I sat down beside her, accepted another YumYum, and settled in.

For the next hour, on the screen, a couple fell hard for each other, were tested mightily, then were torn apart before rediscovering each other, and their love, at the last possible second. In the real world, Ames got off the phone, went to smoke, and made noises about how late it was getting until the final credits rolled. When Layla and I finally did go upstairs to go to sleep, I offered her the bed, but she declined, saying she was happy with the air mattress. I figured she was just being polite, a good guest. We set her up on the floor right next to me.

After the lights were off, we talked for a little while, and at some point I drifted off. When I next woke up, it was two a.m. When I rolled over to check on Layla, she wasn't there. Confused, I sat up on my elbow and rubbed my eyes, then spotted her. She'd moved her bed so it rested against the closed—but unlocked—door, and was curled up there. Keeping watch, keeping safe. I slept better than I had in months.

CHAPTER
8

MY MOM and I had not discussed Family Day at Lincoln since she'd brought it up the first time. I'd thought this was a good sign. Four days before it, I realized how wrong I was.

"So," she said from the stove, where she was stirring a pot of soup she'd made for dinner. "We should probably touch base about this weekend."

This was a typical conversation—she liked plans and schedules, and always made sure both were set days ahead—so I didn't realize what she was referring to. "I'm going over to Jenn's for her birthday on Friday. And Layla invited me over for dinner on Saturday, if that's okay."

She took a taste of the soup, her back still to me. Then she said, "Friday's fine. But we've got Family Day on Saturday. We might be back late, so it's probably not a good idea to have other plans."

I was silent for a minute, taking my time to figure out how to react. Finally I took a breath and said, "So Peyton said I could go with you guys?"

A pause. Then, "Your father's got a conference. So it'll

just be us. And he did submit a form for you, so I'm taking that as a yes."

Unlike my mom, my father did not visit Peyton that often. He'd made the first couple of trips with her, always returning looking haggard before disappearing into his office. For someone who made his living fixing things, seeing his only son in a situation for which this was not possible couldn't be easy. He did talk to Peyton and made sure he had everything he needed in terms of commissary money and other allowed incidentals. But I had a feeling that, for him, it was easier to think my brother was just away, and not know too much about the place where he actually was. Out of sight, pretending it was out of mind.

Clearly, I was not going to have this option, even if my brother and I both preferred it. When my mom was set on something, she rarely backed down. Like it or not, I was going on Saturday.

"Wow," Jenn said after I told her about this when we met to study at Frazier the next day after school. "I've never been to a prison."

"Most people haven't," I replied glumly, taking a sip of the complicated coffee drink Dave! had yet again talked me into. It was frozen and thick as mud, barely able to make it up the straw, but delicious. "Just us lucky folks."

Meredith, who was having a rare free afternoon, looked at me from across the table. "It's gotta be weird, right? Are you freaked out? Like, about the other people that will be there?"

This actually had not even occurred to me. Other convicted criminals I could handle; it was my own brother that made me uneasy. "I just really don't want to go. I wish I didn't have to."

They both looked at me, their faces sympathetic. Then Jenn reached over, squeezing my hand. "We'll have fun Friday night, though, okay? Margaret's coming, too, so you can finally meet her."

A couple of weeks earlier, Jenn had mentioned that she'd made friends with a new girl at school who'd just moved from Massachusetts. Since then, we'd hardly had a conversation where her name had not come up. Apparently, Margaret was incredibly funny, so cool, and even smarter than Jenn, something I wasn't even sure was possible. Even Meredith, who was impressed by very little except anyone who could vault better than she, had told me Margaret both spoke Mandarin and had once dated a guy who was a cousin of an actor on one of our favorite shows.

"Great," I said. "I'm looking forward to it."

"You will *love* her," Jenn said. "She's so funny."

"Oh, my God," Meredith chimed in. "The other day, during PE, when we were doing vinyasa? She fell sideways out of her tree pose and hit the floor. It was *hilarious*."

They both laughed at this, and I'm sure I would have, too, if I'd been there. But even after just a few weeks at Jackson, I couldn't imagine doing yoga for PE. The life I'd had at Perkins seemed so vastly different now. It didn't help that we weren't hanging out as much. With Jenn's tutoring job at the Kiger Center and Meredith's always-busy practice schedule, we were lucky to see one another at all. I hadn't thought our friendship was so based on school until we didn't have it in common anymore. The truth was, I'd changed.

Most of this—okay, probably all—was due to Layla. Since the weekend she'd stayed with me, we'd been in pretty much constant contact. It was like one day we weren't friends, and the next she was the closest I had. It seemed impossible that someone I'd not known at all six months earlier was now often the only person who understood me.

But that was the thing: Layla got it. Not just my uneasiness with Ames, but also how I felt about Peyton. Rosie might not have been in jail, but her problems had spilled over to affect all of the Chathams in one way or another. I knew Jenn and Meredith loved me and were always willing to listen. But there was an element of anger and shame involved they just could never understand. Now that I'd found someone who could, I realized how much I had needed it.

❧ ❧ ❧

"Ugh. These are so subpar. You can tell I'm in a bad state. Normally I wouldn't even *consider* them."

I looked at Layla, who, despite this statement, was still preparing the fries she'd gotten from the ice rink snack bar with her typical meticulousness. A double layer of paper napkins covered part of the bleacher between us, the fries arranged in a single row across them. Two ketchups had been mixed in a plastic cup. She hadn't bothered with her custom blend, which she treated like gold.

"The thing is," she continued, picking up a fry from the

center and dipping it, "nobody frustrates me like Rosie. If annoying people ~~were~~ was her sport, she *would* have made the Olympics. No question."

I smiled, then took a fry of my own when she offered it, pulling my sweater around me with my other hand. It had been years since I'd been to the Lakewood Rink, where my mom used to bring Peyton and me sometimes as kids. He went on to play hockey there a couple of seasons in middle school, but I myself had never graduated from the caved-in ankle stage. It was the last place I'd expected I'd end up when I'd gone to Seaside after the final bell, but I was learning that when it came to the Chathams, anything was possible.

That day, we'd put down our backpacks and were just about to order our customary slices when Layla's phone rang. She contemplated the screen for a moment before she answered.

"Hey." A pause. "At the shop, where else?"

Mac, who was studying behind the counter, a pencil tucked behind his ear, glanced up at her. By now, I was almost able to look right at him when I had his attention. Almost.

"Well, you should have thought about that when you said you'd be there." Layla listened for a moment, sighed, looking at the ceiling. "No, Dad's not here. He drove the Camry to Tioga's to talk to him about what's wrong with the truck."

"Other way around," Mac said quietly.

"What?"

"The Camry's the one in the shop," he told her. "Truck runs; the starter's just being wonky."

"Whatever," Layla said. This, too, I had gotten used to.

The Chathams had two vehicles, both of which were always breaking down. "The point is, we don't have a car right now."

Rosie clearly had something to say to this, because Layla didn't speak for a long time. Finally, in a way that made it clear she was having to interrupt, she said, "Rosie! You can talk all you want; I can't help you. Yeah, well, right back at you."

"Hey," Mac called out. "What's up?"

"She claims she needs a ride to the rink. It is apparently a skating emergency." Layla made a face, then held the phone away from her ear as Rosie responded loudly. To me she said, "When Rosie wants something, it's *always* an emergency."

"We can get her when Dad's back," Mac told her. "Half hour or so."

Layla relayed this, then reported, "No, that's unacceptable. And yes, that *is* a direct quote, in case you were wondering."

Mac shrugged, going back to his book. Rosie was still talking. "I can give her a ride," I offered. "I mean, if you want."

"You don't have to do that," she replied. Then, into the phone, she told Rosie, "Nothing. Sydney's just being entirely too nice to you."

"I really don't mind," I said. "I don't have to be home until six."

Layla looked at me, her expression caustic. "You do not have to do anything for my sister."

"I know. But I'm offering."

I felt it was the least I could do. Though I'd tried to buy Layla breakfast both mornings she slept over and pay for the movie we saw, she had refused. "I got to stay at your house instead of with my crazy family," she said. "I should be thanking you." If I couldn't repay her, this was the next closest thing.

Ten minutes later, we were turning onto a small residential street only a few blocks from Seaside. The houses were small, many of the yards cluttered with cars, swing sets, and lawn furniture. At the very end was a brick ranch with a detached garage. The grass was missing in huge patches, and at least four partial cars in various states of deterioration were parked in the side yard. A decorative flag by the door said HAPPY HOLIDAYS, even though it was September. And then there was the woods.

The trees behind their house were some of the tallest I'd ever seen. In the Arbors, the foliage varied: oaks, scrubby brush, some big cedars. Here, there were only tall, wide pines, close together. For the first time, I understood what it meant for a forest to be *thick*. As if the houses were laid out like bread crumbs along the road, leading you into the darkness beyond.

"Welcome to paradise," Layla said wryly as we parked by the curb. When we got out, I immediately looked up at the vast spread of greenery above us. "The woods are crazy, right? When I was a kid, I used to have nightmares about it. I still sleep with the shades pulled."

She climbed the short stairway that led to the front door and I followed. Up close, I saw the HAPPY HOLIDAYS flag was so old and weathered, it was translucent, the sun shining right through. She twisted the doorknob, pushing it open. "It's me," she called into the darkness beyond. "And Sydney. Rosie, you'd better be ready to go."

She was stepping inside, holding the door open for me. Once we were inside, it took a minute for the house to fall into place around me. When it did, I realized we were not in a foyer or entryway, but already in the living room.

It was very neat, but cluttered. Framed pictures crowded the mantle. Standing on the coffee table were little boxes of all varying sizes and materials: smooth wood, delicate mother-of-pearl, shiny chrome. A collection of beer steins lined a bookcase; a frame held nothing but aces from card decks. A large couch was covered with afghan blankets of varying patterns, while a smaller loveseat, stuffed with needle-point pillows, faced a flat-screen TV on the opposite wall. And then there was the chair.

It was a recliner, well-worn and flanked by two low tables. On one was a large insulated cup with a straw poking out of it, a jumbo-size can of mixed nuts, and a box of tissues. The other held a tall stack of magazines, two remotes, a phone, and a row of pill and vitamin bottles. While the chair itself was empty, it was obvious that whoever sat there owned that room, present or not.

Layla crossed the powder-blue carpet into the kitchen. Finding it empty, she sighed, coming back out and dropping her bag on the couch. "Typical," she told me. "Have a seat. I'll go find her."

As she disappeared down the hallway to my right, I moved to the couch, reaching down to push aside one of the blankets to make room so I could sit. As I did, my hand made contact not with mere fabric, but with something heavy and warm. With teeth.

I shrieked, drawing back my hand. I was still standing there, holding it to my chest, when Layla came back down the hallway.

"What's wrong?" she asked me.

I shook my head. "There's something . . . I moved a blanket. And then . . ."

She walked over, yanking the afghan off with one hard jerk, like a magician doing that trick with the tablecloth. Left exposed were three very small, very ugly little dogs, who looked none too pleased to see us.

"Sorry," she said to me. "Did they get you bad?"

I looked down at my hand. There was no blood, although the tip of my index finger was throbbing. "No."

"Such miserable, awful little animals," she said, reaching over and scooping the largest one up into her arms. It was very short-haired, with stubbly gray fur, a bald head, and little beady eyes, one of which it turned on me as she scratched behind its ears. The other two, still on the couch, were slinking under the remaining blanket, presumably to lie in wait for their next victim. "But we do love them, God help us."

"What kind are they?" I asked as the one she was holding let out a belch that seemed more appropriate for an animal twice its size.

"They don't really have a name. They're just desperately overbred freaks of nature." She gave it a kiss on its bald forehead. "This one's Ayre. The other two are Destiny and Russell."

I just looked at her. "Like . . . on *Big New York*?"

She cocked her head to the side. "Don't tell me you watch that show."

"I do," I admitted. Although "watch" was putting it mildly. Before her, it was the only thing I had in the afternoons. "I watch all of the Big franchise, actually."

"I knew there was a reason I liked this girl!" I turned to see Mrs. Chatham, in a red tracksuit, using a walker to make her way down the hall toward us. Rosie was behind her, carrying a Nike duffel bag and what I already recognized as her standard dissatisfied expression. "Are you Team Rosalie or Team Ayre?"

Sadly, I did not even have to think about my answer. "Team Ayre."

She smiled. "You can stay."

Layla rolled her eyes as her mother made her way over to the chair, easing herself down onto the seat. Rosie, meanwhile, fetched an afghan from the couch (I heard the dogs snap at her, then each other) while Layla picked up the insulated cup, carrying it into the kitchen. A moment later, she returned, twisting the top back on, and set it on the table.

"Thanks, sweetheart," Mrs. Chatham said as Rosie tucked the blanket over her. "Now, you two stop hovering, I'm fine. You don't want to be late for Arthur, since he fit you in last-minute."

"We'll be back after, just as soon as Mac can pick us up, okay?" Layla told her. "And I have my phone on."

"I am perfectly capable of spending a couple of hours alone. Now scoot, all of you."

She waved her hand and her daughters scattered, Rosie picking up her duffel bag while Layla moved to the TV, turning it on and cuing up an episode of *Big Chicago* I hadn't yet seen. Elena, the society wife, was crying, although her makeup remained perfect. Mrs. Chatham smiled, settling into her chair. The last thing I heard as we left was her cranking up the volume.

"Nice ride," Rosie observed as we got into my car. Just like her sister had upon getting in earlier, she ran a hand over the leather seat admiringly, then peered up through the sunroof. "Is it the sport package?"

"Nope," Layla said. "You can tell by the wheels."

"Sure beats our cars," Rosie replied, easing back against the seat. "I could get used to this."

"Don't," Layla told her. "Sydney's doing you a serious favor."

"And I appreciate it."

"Then maybe you should *say* so."

"It's really nothing," I said. "I hate being home after school anyway."

This got their attention: I could feel them both look at me, even though I had my eyes on the road. "Really?" Rosie said. "Why?"

"Mind your own business," Layla told her.

"What? You don't say something like that unless you want someone to ask about it."

"What are you, a psychologist now?"

I had a feeling this bickering was close to becoming a full-out argument, something I did not think the small space we were in could handle. So I said, "It's just sort of . . . weird. Since my brother's been gone. Lonely, I guess. Anyway, the point is I'm happy to have something to do. Really."

I could tell Rosie, behind me, wanted to ask more questions. But Layla pulled down the visor, ostensibly checking her face in the mirror there, and shot her a look. We drove the rest of the way, a short distance, without talking.

Once at the rink, Rosie went to the locker rooms while Layla made a beeline for the snack bar and the subpar fries. As the woman behind the counter scooped them into a paper cup, she sighed. "Sorry about all this. My sister makes me nuts."

"It's really okay," I said.

"She's just so . . ." She sighed again, picking through the basket of ketchup packets, as if one might be better than another. Knowing her, there *was* a way to tell. "Entitled. Like the world owes her. She's always been like that."

"My brother is kind of the same way," I told her. "I thought it was an only-son thing. But maybe it's a firstborn thing, too."

"I think, in this case, it's just a Rosie thing." She selected a second packet, then helped herself to some napkins. "At least when she was younger, she could blame the stress of skating, all that competition."

"She was good, huh?" I said.

"She was *great*." Layla slid a five-dollar bill across the counter. "It wasn't an excuse for being a bitch, of course. But knowing she was capable of something beautiful, as well as being wholly unpleasant? It somehow made it easier to take."

This made a weird kind of sense to me. Not that my brother had an impressive skill like skating, but he had gotten a long way on charm. Nobody was all bad, I was learning. Even the worst person had someone who cared about them at some point.

Now, back in the bleachers, I watched Layla drag another fry through her pepper ketchup (pepchup?), then take a halfhearted bite. Down on the ice, a middle-aged man with styled blond hair, wearing black Lycra pants and a bright blue fleece, was leading a girl who looked to be about twelve through some jumps. She had that consummate skater look I recognized from Saturday afternoon sports shows, small and lithe with a perky ponytail, and as she landed each jump, the man's face made it clear whether he was happy or not.

"That's Arthur," Layla said when she saw me watching him. "He's the reason I have crooked teeth and always will."

"Your teeth aren't crooked."

"They're not straight, either. Not like yours. You had braces, right?"

I nodded. "I hated them."

"Yes, but look at you now." She picked up another fry. "I needed them. The dentist said so. But private coaching at Arthur's level isn't cheap, so . . ."

Back on the ice, the girl had just landed and was circling around to try again. "Wow. Was she really aiming for the Olympics?"

"Yeah. But never got further than regionals. Then she took the job touring with Mariposa, which at least helped my parents out financially. I was so mad when she got busted and dropped from that show." She shook her head. "I'm all about taking one for the team. But her being so stupid . . . it stung. Like all those years, all that money, was for nothing."

As she said this, another girl skated onto the ice. It took me a minute to realize it was Rosie. Maybe it was the distance, or that she'd changed into skating gear, but she looked different. She began circling the outer edge of the ice, slowly picking up speed, and even with this most basic of moves, it was clear she was better than the girl we'd been watching. There was a simple, undiluted grace to her movements, something wholly in contrast to her normal, nose-wrinkled, complaining self. As if instead of shriveling in the cold like most people, she bloomed.

Layla was also watching as she passed by once, then twice. The third time, she turned, lifting her chin to acknowledge us, and Layla nodded back, giving her a smile. This surprised me, after all we'd been talking about. But then, a lot about Layla was a mystery.

"She's really nervous," she explained to me, as if sensing this. "She's been working out alone, but this is the first time he's agreed to see her since all this happened. That's why she was being such a bitch. Or one reason, anyway."

After a few words with Arthur, the younger girl left the ice and he waved Rosie over. They talked for a moment, and then he gestured for her to take another lap, turning to watch her as she began.

"Oh, God, I can't watch. Even at practice I get crazy nervous for her. I used to be such a mess during competitions. My mom would beg me to go get fries." She pulled out her phone, typing in her passcode, then opened her pictures. "When I did stay, though, I was always glad. Look at this."

She handed me the phone, where a video was now playing on the screen. It was of another rink, a fancier one, with Rosie twirling in its center. She started slowly, her arms spread wide, then began to speed up, pulling them in against her until she was almost a blur. Then, as the tinny distant music came to a sudden stop, she did as well, striking a pose with her head thrown back. As the crowd applauded and cheered, the sound a thunderous roar, she smiled.

"That was the last year she competed," Layla said. She flipped to the next shot, which showed Mrs. Chatham, clearly in better health, posing with Layla, Rosie (who held a bouquet of roses), and a huge trophy. Off to the side was a heavyset guy in a shapeless sweatshirt and jeans, half cut off by the camera. At first I assumed he'd just stumbled into the picture accidentally. Then I realized.

"Is that . . ." I stopped, then picked up the phone, narrowing my eyes at it.

"Mac," she finished for me. "Yeah. It is."

I reached down, using my thumb and forefinger to enlarge that part of the photo until his face filled the screen. With a much heftier frame and a bad case of acne, he looked so different, I couldn't quite believe it was the same person. But the eyes were identical, the hair with the lock tumbling over his forehead. "Wow. What did he—"

"Lost thirty pounds, for starters. And when he started eating better, his skin cleared up." She picked up another fry. "Crazy, right? Sometimes I still see him in the hallway at home and wonder who he is."

"I can't believe he looked like that."

"You would if you saw how he used to eat. The boy could *consume.* He was like Irv, but without the height, muscle, and football. And it was all junk."

"I can't even imagine that." I was still staring at his face, wider, pockmarked. "What made him want to change?"

"Wouldn't you?" she asked, nodding at the picture. She ate the fry. "Really, though, I think he finally just got sick of being the fat kid. It was what he'd been for as long as I can remember. Rosie was talented, I was cute. He was fat."

This wasn't news to me, how your entire life could come down to one word, and not of your choosing. I knew it better than anyone. Each time I was reminded, though, I wished that much harder it wasn't the case. I said, "So how did he lose the weight?"

"He started by hiking in the woods. Then he moved up to jogging, and finally outright running. He'd get up before school and just disappear back there for hours. Still does, every single morning."

"Really."

"Just hearing him *leave* at five thirty a.m. makes me tired," she said. "Plus he never eats, like, anything fun anymore. Just protein, veggies, and fruit. I wouldn't last a day. Or even an hour."

There was a shout from the ice, and we both looked back at Rosie, who had just landed a jump, apparently rather sloppily. Arthur shook his head, then barked something else, and she circled around, nodding, her hands on her hips.

"Ugh," Layla said, wiping her fingers with a napkin. "I can't take this, it's too stressful. Before I know it I'll be buying more of these awful fries just to cope."

I smiled, then looked at my watch. It was five forty-five; I had to be home in fifteen minutes, which meant even if I left right that second I'd be pushing it. I was not looking forward to dinner and more discussion of Lincoln's Family Day, however, so I stayed put long enough to see Rosie do a few spins, stumble once, and finally earn the slightest of approving smiles from Arthur, the sight of which caused Layla to audibly exhale.

"I'll see you tomorrow," I told her, gathering up my stuff. "Sorry I can't take you guys home."

"It's fine. Mac's always somewhere nearby. And you've done more than enough."

I smiled, then waved as I started down the steps to the exit. Before I pushed open the door to the lobby, I looked back just in time to catch Rosie doing her best jump yet, then sticking the landing and gliding on. It seemed like just the right note to depart upon, with everything perfect, at least for a second. I left before I could see anything else.

CHAPTER
9

"YOU'RE HERE!" Jenn reached forward, grabbing my wrist
and pulling me through the door with one big yank. "I am *so*,
so happy to see you! It's been *ages*!"

When she gave me a sloppy kiss on the cheek, though,
I knew something was up. Jenn was a lot of things, but ef-
fusive wasn't one of them.

"Hey," I said as she began pulling me down the hallway.
"What's going on?"

"We are having *so* much fun," she said. "Come on, you
have to meet Margaret."

Judging by the dragging, it was clear I didn't have a
choice in the matter, so I let her take me into the kitchen.
There, I saw Meredith at the island, looking uneasy, while a
dark-haired girl with her back to me dumped some ice in the
blender.

"Sydney's here!" Jenn, who also was not loud—ever—
shouted. "And she needs a drink."

"Of course she does," Margaret said, turning around. She
had long black hair tumbling over her shoulders, bright blue
eyes, and a sprinkling of freckles. A pretty girl, with a kind

of spark to her you saw right away. "And it's a fresh batch, to boot. Let me get you a glass."

It was when she moved aside, reaching up into a cabinet, that I saw the rum bottle. I looked back at Meredith, who had her own glass, which looked untouched. Two others on the island held only slushy dregs. "What are we drinking?"

"Piña coladas," Jenn announced. "Margaret's special recipe. And they are *delicious*."

"The ice is key," Margaret explained, pouring a glass, then topping off the two empty ones. "Most people don't realize that."

When she handed me my glass, I took it, but didn't drink. "So your parents aren't here?"

"No, they're in the living room," Jenn replied. I just looked at her. "I'm joking! Of course not. They're out for the night. I told them we were going to Antonella's for pizza and then watching movies."

"And we're not?" I asked.

"Is that what you want to do?" Margaret asked me.

"No," I said. There was something about her tone, the way she raised an eyebrow, that made me say this automatically. "I just didn't realize . . . Since when do you drink, Jenn?"

She put down her glass, then wiped a hand over her lips. "What do you mean? I've drank before."

"When?"

"All the time. You know that, Sydney."

Margaret was watching this exchange, an expression of

mild amusement on her face. Over at the island, Meredith picked up her glass and took a sip.

"Okay," I said, not wanting to point out that I'd known Jenn since preschool and never seen her do anything more than take a parent-approved sip of wine at Christmas dinner. I sniffed my drink. "What's in this?"

"Oh, just drink it," Margaret said, flipping her hand at me. "It'll help you relax."

I looked at her. "I don't need to relax."

She took a big gulp of her own drink. "All I'm saying is that this is a birthday celebration. So let's have fun, okay?"

"Seconded," Jenn said, holding out her glass. Margaret did the same before nodding at Meredith, who raised hers as well. Then they all looked at me.

I picked up my glass. "To Jenn. Happy birthday."

"Happy birthday!" everyone repeated. *Clink*. Jenn immediately took a big gulp, but Margaret kept her eyes on me, not drinking, as I raised my glass to my mouth, taking a sip. Then she did the same, still watching me.

"Okay," she said, and smiled. "Now it's a party."

* * *

"Just text him. Don't think about it. Just do it."

Jenn shook her head, blushing. "I can't! It's too weird."

"Oh, please." Margaret reached across the couch, grabbing the phone. "I'll do it, then."

"Don't!" Jenn shrieked, lunging at her to get it back. "Oh, my God, Margaret, if you do that I swear I'll—"

"—thank me forever for hooking you up with the guy you're crazy about? You're welcome." She started typing on the phone with one hand while batting Jenn away with the other. "There. It's done. Now we wait."

"I hate you," Jenn said, but she was grinning, her face flushed. She'd had two drinks, by my count, since I'd arrived.

"Maybe," Margaret told her. "But when he shows up, you'll love me."

The He in question was Chris McMichaels, who apparently my best friend had been madly in love with for ages, although she'd never mentioned it to me. Margaret, however, knew that he sat behind Jenn in World History, often asked her if she could spare paper or a pen, and had recently broken up with his longtime girlfriend, Hannah Riggsbee, leaving him, in Margaret's words, "ripe for the picking."

"He probably thinks I'm crazy," Jenn moaned, putting her head in her hands. "Texting him on a Friday night."

"If he didn't want to hear from you, he wouldn't have given you his number," Margaret said, topping off each of their glasses.

"That was for a group project!"

Margaret waved her hand. "Details."

Just then, the phone buzzed. Jenn went for it, but Margaret got there first, scanning the screen. "Well, look at this. He's around and says he'll stop by with some friends."

"*What?*" Jenn shrieked—the sound was shrill, grating—grabbing the phone. She read the text, then looked up, eyes wide. "You told him we were drinking?"

"*You* did," Margaret said. "It's a party, right?"

"Oh, my God." Jenn grabbed my arm. "Chris McMichaels may be coming over here? To *my house*? I don't know if I can handle this."

"Of course you can. I'll make another round."

With that, Margaret picked up the empty pitcher and turned on her heel, going back into the kitchen. Finally, it was just the three of us.

"Jenn," I said as she took another sip, "are you sure about this?"

"About what?"

I glanced at Meredith, who looked as hesitant as I felt. "I mean, come on. You don't drink. And now you have guys coming over?"

She turned to look at me, annoyed. "What is wrong with you tonight?"

"Me?" I said. "You're the one acting weird."

"I'm having *fun*, Sydney. It's my birthday."

"I know," I said. "I'm your best friend, remember?"

"Then why are you being such a buzzkill?" She shook her head, sighing. "Honestly, I'm shocked. With your history, I figured you'd be the last person to be so judgy."

Across the couch, Meredith's eyes widened. I forced myself to take a breath before I said, "My history?"

"Your brother," she said, her voice flat. From the kitchen, the blender began whirring. "I mean, I get it. Maybe you think that if I drink, I'll end up in jail, too? But I won't. So just calm down, okay? Have your drink. *Relax*."

I didn't even know what to say to this. She was like a stranger, but with the familiar features and mannerisms I knew as well as my own. I lowered my voice, then said, "I can't believe you just brought Peyton into this."

She rolled her eyes. "Oh, calm down. It's not like it's some big secret. Margaret already knows."

Margaret walked into the room, the blender pitcher in her hand. "Margaret knows what?"

"Nothing," I said, giving Jenn a hard look. "Never mind."

The next half hour was consumed by Margaret giving Jenn what she called "the express makeover," which consisted of putting on a more low-cut shirt, adding some jewelry, and layering on several coats of mascara. Margaret changed as well, into a dress she'd packed in her overnight bag. Clearly, she'd been anticipating a wardrobe transition, unlike the rest of us. Meanwhile, they both continued downing drinks, getting more and more sloppy. On the upside, neither noticed that Meredith and I had switched to water. At nine thirty, about when the guys were expected, Meredith bailed.

"Party pooper!" Margaret called out from the kitchen, where she was "giving needed volume" to Jenn's hair, a practice that apparently required clouds of hair spray.

"Buzzkill!" Jenn chimed in.

"I have a meet tomorrow afternoon," Meredith said quietly to me, like I was the one who needed a reason. "And this . . . is weird."

"Seconded," I said, holding up my water.

She held hers against it, then smiled. "Are you staying the night?"

"I don't really want to leave her here like this."

Meredith glanced back at the kitchen, where Jenn, I noticed, was suddenly looking a little queasy. Uh-oh. "You're a good friend, Sydney."

"So are you." I reached forward, giving her a hug. "Good luck tomorrow."

"Thanks."

She waved toward the kitchen, but only Margaret waved back. Once the door was shut behind her, I went to check on Jenn.

"You okay?" I asked her. "You don't look so good."

"She's fine. She just needs to eat something," Margaret said, although I saw Jenn wince, hearing this. "Let's order pizza. What's the number for that place you like, Jenn?"

"They don't deliver," Jenn mumbled, then got up off the bar stool, putting out a hand to steady herself. "I'm . . . I'm going to go to the bathroom."

She made her way across the room, using the wall for support. Margaret watched her go, then took a sip of her drink. "She'll be fine," she told me. "A quick puke is like hitting the reset button."

I watched as she picked up a compact, looking at her own face. Then I said, "She doesn't drink, just so you know."

"Her empty glass says otherwise," she replied, scooping out a bit of gloss on her fingertip. She ran it across her lips, then looked at me. "Look, when I showed up with the rum, she wasn't exactly protesting."

"She probably just wanted to impress you."

"You can read her mind now?"

"I'm her best friend. I've known her since we were in preschool."

"Well, then you're aware that she's a girl who can make her own choices," she said, shutting the compact with a click. "Go check on her, will you? I'm going to order some food so we have something here for the guys when they come."

She then picked up her phone, indicating the conversation was over. I could feel my temper rising as I walked down the hallway to the powder room, inside which I could hear Jenn retching. I knocked lightly on the door, then pushed it open. "Hey. It's me."

Jenn was huddled over the toilet, resting her head on one arm. She looked awfully pale, and the room smelled strongly of coconut. Ugh. "I'm dying," she moaned. "I'm going to die on my birthday. Which is really symmetrical, but unfortunate."

I smiled. This was my Jenn. "You're not dying. You're just drunk."

"I feel awful." She turned to look at me. Damp strands of hair stuck to her forehead. So much for the added volume. "Do you hate me?"

"Of course not." I picked up the hand towel from next to the sink, then soaked it in cold water. "Why would I?"

"Because I brought up Peyton. And made you drink."

"You didn't make me do anything." I handed her the towel. "Put this on your face. It'll help."

She did, and I slid down to sit against the door, my knees to my chest.

"You don't like Margaret," she said finally. It wasn't a question.

"I don't know her," I replied, sidestepping it anyway.

"She's really nice, Syd, I swear! And *so* funny! And, you know, not from here. She doesn't see me the way everyone else does. She thinks I *could* date Chris McMichaels. And drink piña coladas. And . . . be different. You know?"

I nodded. I did understand, in my own way. Not the boy or drinking part, but the clean slate that came with a new friend. "I miss you," I said, feeling bad about even thinking this while I was with her.

"I miss you, too." She looked at me again. "Will you stay tonight? I know you weren't planning to."

"Sure," I said. "Let me just make sure it's okay."

My mom answered on the second ring, and she sounded upset. At first, I thought this might be because I was calling so close to curfew and she assumed I was angling for an extension. But I found out soon enough that, once again, it had nothing to do with me.

"You may as well," she said, once I asked if I could stay. "Since we're not going to Lincoln tomorrow."

I blinked, surprised. "We're not?"

Silence. Then, "Your brother apparently has had his visiting privileges rescinded. Of course, I can't find out *why*, despite multiple efforts to contact the director of the prison."

She said this like prison was high school and contacting the office could fix anything. Not for the first time, I wondered if my mother really understood where Peyton was.

"I'm sorry, Mom," I said. "I know you were looking forward to that."

"I was." She sounded so defeated. I hadn't thought anything could be worse than her being sad. This whole experience: it just kept teaching. After a moment, she rallied, saying, "Tell Jenn happy birthday, and I'll see you in the morning. Love you."

"Love you, too."

Back in the bathroom, Jenn was looking slightly better, with a little color creeping into her cheeks. She still wasn't ready to be too far from the toilet, however, so I went to fill Margaret in on what was going on. I was almost to the kitchen when I heard voices and realized the guys had arrived. They were gathered around the island, and Margaret, as she poured them drinks. She'd taken off her shoes and added bright red lipstick since I'd seen her last. When she saw me, she smiled like we were best friends.

"Sydney," she called out, and the guys all looked at me. I knew them, of course, as we'd all been in school together since kindergarten. Besides Chris McMichaels, who had a sister in Peyton's grade, there was Charlie Jernigan, who also lived in the Arbors, and Huck Webster, captain of the Perkins Day soccer team. "How's the birthday girl?"

"Fine," I answered, walking up to them. Chris was already drinking from his glass, while Charlie and Huck were still sniffing theirs. "She'll be out in a sec."

"I poured you a fresh one." Margaret held out a glass to me. "You've got some catching up to do."

I took the drink without comment, then had a sip. In

truth, it smelled too much like the bathroom I'd just left, but I wasn't going to give her anything to comment on. "Thanks."

"How's the new school, Sydney?" Charlie asked me. "You liking it?"

I nodded. "It's good. Different."

"I hear you switched to Jackson High," Margaret said. "Why?"

"I was ready for a change," I replied.

"That's more a revolution than a change." She adjusted her dress. "I hear there are fights there every day. And that's with the *girls*. My friend who used to go there? She wouldn't even go in the bathroom."

"Not true," I told her.

"Anyway, Sydney's tough," Chris said, smiling at me. "No one's gonna mess with her."

"Exactly," I said. "They're all scared of me already."

The guys laughed. Margaret twisted a ring around her finger, then sighed. "I'm bored," she said. "Let's play a drinking game. Who's got a quarter?"

With this, she led them over to the kitchen table, bringing the pitcher with her. I went back to check on Jenn, only to find her asleep on the bathroom floor. So much for the birthday girl.

"Hey," I said, kneeling down beside her and shaking her arm. "Jenn. Wake up."

"It's not time to get up yet," she mumbled, rolling over and pressing her cheek into the tiles.

There was a sharp knock at the door. Instinctively, I knew

it was one of the boys. They even announced themselves differently. "Just a minute," I called out.

"Uh . . . okay." Then footsteps retreating. From the
kitchen, I could hear Margaret laughing.

"Jenn," I said, shaking her shoulder again. She squeezed
her eyes shut tightly into slits, as if this might actually make
me go away. "You have to get up. You don't want Chris to see
you like this, right?"

She groaned, clearly annoyed, but allowed me to get her
into a seated position. Then her eyes flew open. "Chris is
here? Are you serious?"

"He's in the kitchen. With Margaret."

Her head fell forward, hitting her chest. "Oh, God. This
is awful. It's not like I had a chance, but if he sees me all
pukey like this—"

"He won't," I told her. "Just focus on standing up. I'll get
you out of here."

She moaned again, but leaned back onto her hands,
pushing herself to her feet while I eased the door open and
peered down the hallway. The quarters game was still going
on in the kitchen, with Margaret at the head of the table,
Chris opposite her, and Charlie and Huck on either side. As
I watched, Chris bounced a coin into a cup, then pointed at
Margaret. She grinned, picking up her glass.

I looked back at Jenn, who was holding on to the sink for
support. "Come on. It's now or never."

She stepped forward, and I slid my arm over her shoulder, then flipped off the bathroom light before stepping into

the dark hallway. It was only about four feet to the living room, through which I planned to access the stairs to get her to her bedroom. After a few steps, though, there was a sharp, desperate squeeze of my hand. I stopped walking.

"Might puke," she whispered. I waited, holding my own breath. Then she exhaled. "Okay, let's keep going."

We continued like this past the sofa and coffee table, then the piano, stopping twice more. Just as we passed the front door, the bell sounded.

"Oh, God," Jenn moaned, squeezing my hand again. "I might—"

This time, I had a feeling she meant it. Without thinking, totally desperate, I threw the door open and pushed her out onto the front steps, where she grabbed the wrought-iron railing, leaned over it, and heaved into the bushes. On the steps beside her, holding a pizza box and wearing a SEASIDE PIZZA T-shirt, was Mac Chatham.

At first, this fact just did not compute. It was like I'd dreamed or conjured him, except for the throwing-up part. Gingerly, he stepped aside as Jenn puked again, then looked at me, raising his eyebrows.

"Hi," I managed to say over Jenn's retching. "What's up?"

He gave me a flat look. "You ordered pizza?"

"I didn't," I said. Now he looked confused. "I mean, they did. Or this girl here did. I didn't realize . . ."

"Sydney," Jenn moaned, then slid down into a heap on the steps by his feet. *"Help."*

"Excuse me," I said to Mac, shooting him an apologetic look

as I shut the door behind me, then came out and crouched down next to Jenn. I ran a hand over her matted hair, then explained, "It's her birthday."

"Oh." He cleared his throat. "Um, happy birthday."

At this, she slumped into me. Before I knew what was happening, her head was in my lap, legs curled up against the railing. I just sat there, not sure what to do. A moment later, she was snoring.

I looked up at Mac. "I'll . . . I've got money in my pocket. What do I owe you for the pizza?"

I figured he'd be more than relieved to tell me, get paid, and be on his way, as I could not imagine a more unpleasant scenario to stumble into. Instead, setting what I did not yet realize would be a precedent, Mac surprised me.

"Let's get her inside first," he said. "The last thing you want is neighbors seeing this."

He had a point. The houses on Jenn's street were close together, and all the ones across the way still had lights on. "You don't have to help me," I told him. "Really."

To this he said nothing, instead just holding out the pizza warmer to me. I took it, not sure what was happening until he bent down, scooping Jenn up in his arms. Her head flopped against his shoulder, and she stirred slightly, but then she was out again. "Lead the way," he said.

I did. Through the front door, where I put down the warmer on a side table, and then up the stairs and down the hall to Jenn's dark room. As I flicked on the light, stepping inside, it occurred to me that of all the ways I'd thought this night might end, me in a bedroom with Mac Chatham was the very last one of them.

He, however, seemed pretty much at ease, as if he dumped unconscious strange girls into their beds on a regular basis. Which I could only hope he did not. Once Jenn hit the mattress, she groaned and curled into a ball, pressing her face into her pillow. I went over and took off her shoes.

"You'll probably want to get her a glass of water," he told me. "And a trash can, if there is one around."

There was, and I got it, along with the water and a damp towel, which I put on her forehead. When all this was done, I stepped back beside Mac, who was just inside the doorway. "She never drinks," I told him. "I don't know what she was thinking."

"She probably wasn't," he replied. "It happens. Especially on birthdays."

"She'll be okay, right?"

"Just needs to sleep it off." I bit my lip, still worried. "Sydney. She's fine."

There was something in the way he said this, my name so familiar, the sentiment so confident and reassuring, that was more touching, actually, than anything else he'd done so far.

"Thank you," I said to him. "Seriously. I don't know what I would have done if you hadn't shown up."

"All pizza guys have this kind of training. It's required."

I felt myself smile, right at him, before realizing this was the first time I'd talked to him alone since the day we'd first met. And I *was* talking to him, not blushing or stammering, at least so far. Who knew a night could end so far from where it started, even when you stayed in?

"I should let you go," I said. "I'm sure they need you back for more deliveries, right?"

"This is the last one of the night, actually." He reached up, scratching his temple. "But I do need to get home. I'm supposed to bring burgers and fries from Webster's to Layla and my mom, and they're serious when it comes to their food."

"So I'm learning," I said.

We stepped out into the hallway and I turned off Jenn's light, easing the door shut behind us. Halfway down the stairs, we bumped into Margaret and Chris.

"Sydney?" she said, her eyes widening as she glimpsed Mac behind me. "What are you *doing*?"

Considering she was alone with the guy Jenn had clearly stated she was crushing on, in Jenn's house, on her way to where there were only bedrooms, I wanted to ask her the same thing. Instead I said, "This is Mac. He's a friend of mine from school."

"A *friend*," she repeated, drawing the word out. She looked at Chris. "And what were you two doing upstairs?"

"Checking on Jenn," I told her, narrowing my eyes at her. "Just like you are. Right?"

"Right," she said, not missing a beat. "Of course."

I stepped around her, brushing past as I went down the stairs with Mac behind me. As he passed her, she noticed his T-shirt.

"Wait," she said, turning around to look down at us. "Is this . . . Are you the *pizza guy*?"

She said this with a half laugh, her voice rising at the end. I'd already decided I disliked her, but it was only then that I felt a full-on bolt of rage. I was about to tell her where she could stick her pizza, in detail, but then Mac spoke first.

"Seventeen forty-two is your total," he told her. "Small bills appreciated."

Margaret just looked at him, her expression icy. He stared back, clearly unfazed. Finally, she turned to me. "Money's on the counter in an envelope. Don't overtip."

With this, she turned and began to climb the stairs again. Chris stayed where he was, his expression hesitant. "Hey," he said to me, his voice low. "I—"

"Come *on*," Margaret barked from the landing. There was a beat, and then he, too, turned and disappeared upstairs.

My face was hot as I walked down the hallway to the kitchen, embarrassed and pissed off all at once. "*She's* nice," Mac said. "Friend of yours?"

"No," I said flatly.

In the kitchen, we found Huck and Charlie still at the table, now taking plain shots and throwing cocktail peanuts into each other's mouths. They were drunk enough to not really notice us, but I saw Mac take them in as I found the envelope Jenn's mom had left, the words *For your birthday dinner!* in a flowery script on the front. If only she knew. I took out twenty-five, sliding it over to him. He handed the five back.

"Take it," I said, pushing it at him.

He moved it back toward me. "Sydney, come on."

My move. "Mac. It's the least I can do."

His. "I'm not taking your charity."

Me. "It's not my money."

Him. "I don't care."

I reached to push the bill again, and he did, too, our hands meeting right over Abe Lincoln's face. Neither of us moved. I could feel the warmth of his fingertips, barely tangible, against mine. We stayed there for one second. Two. Then, from somewhere, a buzzing sound.

Mac kept his hand on the five, reaching into a back pocket. He pulled out his phone and glanced at the screen, then showed it to me.

LAYLA, said the caller ID at the top. The message read only:

Where are my fries??????????

I smiled. "That's a lot of question marks."

"I told you. She's serious." He lifted his fingers away from mine, barely, and pushed the bill one last time in my direction. Then he glanced at Huck and Charlie, who were giggling like girls over something at the table. "You gonna be okay here?"

"Yeah," I said. "I've known them forever, they're fine."

He nodded, then put his phone back in his pocket and started for the door. I followed him, pulling it open as he took out the pizzas from the warmer and handed them to me. As he went outside, I said, "Thanks again. For everything."

"No problem. Like I told you, it's part of the job."

"Sure it is."

I stood there holding the boxes as he walked down the steps and to the truck, pulling open the driver's side door. Upstairs, Margaret was doing God knew what with Chris McMichaels, and I had two more drunk people to deal with once I returned to the kitchen. But Jenn was safe, so was I, and at least there was pizza. I waved at Mac as he backed down the driveway, and he blinked his brights at me before he drove away.

Back in the kitchen, the guys jumped on the pies, diving right in, but I went over to the counter. That five was still sitting there. Unlike some people, I wasn't one to take things that weren't mine, so I found one in my wallet and put it in the envelope before claiming the original bill as my own.

As I folded it carefully, I walked back to the front door, peering out at the empty street. *Mac's always somewhere nearby*, Layla had told me, but I hadn't realized how true it really was. That night, curled up on the other side of Jenn's bed, her soft breathing filling the room, I slept with one hand in my pocket, the bill between my fingers. Each time I woke up, I made sure it was still there.

CHAPTER

10

LOCAL TEEN FACES TRAGEDY, RISES ABOVE, the headline read. Just below it, there was a picture of David Ibarra in his wheelchair. He was smiling.

Suddenly it made sense. Why, when I'd come into the kitchen moments earlier, I'd found my dad standing over the newspaper, which was open on the table. His back was to me, but I could see he had one hand to his mouth. His shoulders were shaking.

"Dad?"

He put his other hand down on the table, sucking in a breath before turning around. "Hey," he said. "Ready for breakfast?"

I nodded as he shut the paper, then walked over to the stove, where a pan of scrambled eggs sat on the burner. My dad was a breakfast person: he started every day with a minimum of eggs, bacon or sausage, and toast. He was also an early riser, often gone by the time I came down for school, leaving just leftovers and the smell of pork products behind. Finding him still in the kitchen at seven a.m. was odd enough. Discovering him crying bordered on terrifying.

I'd eyed the paper as he prepared a huge plate for me, wondering what he'd been looking at. It wasn't until his phone rang that I got a chance to find out.

David Ibarra is having a good day. He's not in pain, he just hit a high score on his favorite video game, and he's about to dig into a deluxe pizza. For some, these things might be no big deal. But for David, who was hit by a drunk driver seven months ago and paralyzed, every day is a gift.

I felt my stomach twist. I could hear my dad talking out in the hallway. Quickly, I kept reading.

It was February fifteenth, and David was once again playing Warworld. "Competitive" doesn't do justice to how he and his cousin Ricardo were when it came to the popular video game. They could play for hours, and often did, staying up late That night, David says, was "especially epic, even for us. We played for so long, I could barely keep my eyes open. Eventually I did fall asleep. I woke up with the controller on my chest."

He knew he was already in trouble, but figured by waking up in his own bed he could maybe do some damage control. After all, his house was only two blocks away. It was about two a.m. when he climbed onto his bike and started the short trip through the dark streets. He was almost there when he saw the headlights.

"It was crazy," he remembers. "Like, there were no cars, nowhere. And then all of a sudden one was right in front of me. And they weren't stopping."

He has no recollection of the accident itself, something his mother considers a blessing. His first memory is coming to on the curb and realizing his legs were twisted up behind him. Then, the pain.

I could hear his footsteps: my dad was coming back. Quickly, I shut the paper, pushing it away from me just before he rounded the corner into sight.

"How's breakfast?" he asked.

I picked up my fork, forcing down a bite of eggs. "Good. Thanks. Where's Mom?"

"She's not feeling well," he said, refilling his mug from the coffeemaker. "Went back to bed."

My mom got up even earlier than my dad; she always brought the paper in and read it front to back. I could just see her, her own coffee at her elbow like always, turning the page to see that headline and picture. All over town, people were doing the same thing.

On my way to school, I was suddenly keenly aware of all the newspapers I saw in driveways and for sale by convenience stores and gas stations. Walking into school, I felt like everyone was staring at me, even though I had no idea if anyone at Jackson knew Peyton was my brother. During homeroom, while everyone chattered and laughed around me, ignoring the morning announcements, I pulled up the article on my phone.

TWO LIVES CONVERGE, the header for the next section read.

> *As far as anyone knew, Peyton Stanford was getting his life together. After a string of arrests for breaking and entering and drug possession, among other things, he'd completed a stay in rehab and had been sober for over a year. But on that February night, after an evening spent drinking and getting high, he climbed behind the wheel of his BMW sports car. Like David Ibarra, he was heading home.*

The bell rang, loud as always, and I closed my eyes, suddenly feeling sick. All around me, people were gathering up their stuff and pushing toward the door, but I just sat there, the words blurring before me. It wasn't until my teacher, Mrs. Sacher, said my name that I realized I was the only one left in the room.

"Sydney?" I looked up at her. She taught English and was young and nice, with a kind face and a tendency to belly laugh. "You okay?"

"Yeah," I said, putting my phone in my backpack. "Sorry."

For the rest of the morning, whenever I had a chance, I made myself read more of the article. During the few free minutes between the end of History and the bell. At my locker, when I had a short way to go from English to Calculus. By the time I got to lunch, I had only one paragraph to go.

*There are times David is angry about what hap-
pened to him. When he can't help but think how things
could have been different. If he'd just stayed at his
cousin's house. If he'd left ten minutes earlier. It's hard
not to follow this line of thinking, and all the dark
places it can lead him. But right now, he's not doing
that. Today is a good day.*

"Here you go," the guy behind the counter at the Great
Grillers food truck said. I looked up to see him holding the
bag with the sandwich I'd ordered. "Need anything else?"

I shook my head, suddenly sure that if I spoke, I might
burst into tears. So instead I just took some deep breaths and
walked over to where Layla and everyone else was sitting.
The topic of conversation was band names, one that came up
regularly during these discussions. Hey Dude's new concept,
Eric maintained, warranted a new moniker. But, of course, it
had to be perfect.

"What about the Logan Oxford Experience?" Irv asked.
"Like Hendrix, but not."

Eric just looked at him. "That is so far away from what
I'm talking about, I can't even justify it with a response."

Irv shrugged, hardly bothered. Layla said, "It should have
something to do with boy bands, though. But with a twist."

"No, no." Eric sighed, as if our collective ignorance literally pained him. "What I need is a name that works with
the wider concept, not a gimmick. Able to really explain the
meaning, the *irony*, because people are clearly not getting it.
I can't have people thinking we're just a retro cover band."

"Then maybe you shouldn't be playing covers of old songs," Layla pointed out.

"It's not about covers," he told her. "It's about the universal experience of mass consumption of music. How a song can remind you of something specific in your own life, like it belongs to you. But how personal can it really *be* if a million other people feel the same way about it? It's like a fake meaning, on top of a manufactured meaning, divided by a true meaning."

Silence. Then Irv said, "Dude. Did you take your Ritalin today?"

Over on his own bench, where he was cramming for a math test, Mac snorted and opened a stick of string cheese. Since the night he'd shown up at Jenn's a week earlier, I'd had trouble forgetting that moment we'd stood with both our hands on that five-dollar bill. It, however, was a memory I liked to relive. Unlike the one currently in my head, which was canceling out more than my appetite.

"You okay?" Layla asked me. She nodded at my lunch, still in the bag. "You're not eating."

"Not hungry," I told her.

"What's that like?" Irv asked, and everyone laughed. Layla, however, kept her eyes on me long enough that I picked up the bag and took out my sandwich. The fries that came with it I handed over to her without comment.

"Great Grillers?" she asked. I nodded, and she wrinkled her nose. "They're too skinny for my taste, usually. I don't like a spindly fry. But since you're offering . . ."

She started her typical extensive preparations. I took a

halfhearted bite of my sandwich, then put it down, over-
whelmed suddenly with the urge to call my mom. Since my
earlier efforts, when she'd shut me down with the party line,
we didn't talk about David Ibarra ever. But sitting there,
I suddenly felt so alone and craved someone, anyone, who
might understand.

"Hey," I heard a voice say. I looked up to see Mac, his
trash in hand, standing over me. "You sure you're okay?"

"Sydney?" Layla said. "What's wrong?"

I shook my head, quickly getting to my feet. The attention, added to the scrutiny I'd imagined all day, was suddenly
too much. "I . . . I need to go," I said. "I'll see you guys later."

No one said anything as I walked away. Nobody tried to
follow me. I went to the bathroom and locked myself in a
stall. Finally, I was alone, just like I'd wanted. It felt so awful.
Like it was just what I deserved.

* * *

By that evening, things were back to normal at home. The
paper was in the recycling, the news was moving on, and
we would as well. But while my mom puttered around the
kitchen making dinner and the usual conversation, I still felt
strange. Not only about the article, but the way I'd walked
away from Layla and everyone else. She knew Peyton's history; I could have told her about the story. And yet, I hadn't.
I still wasn't sure why.

It was just after dinner, while I was helping to load the
dishwasher, that my phone beeped. Layla.

My mom wants you to come for dinner
tomorrow. Y/N/MB?

I looked over to the counter, where my own mother
was making coffee for the next morning, as she did every
night right after dinner. I waited for the beans (fair trade
and organic, of course) to be done grinding before I said,
"Mom?"

"Yes?" she asked, walking over to the sink.

"I'm going to have dinner at Layla's tomorrow, okay?"

The first bad sign was when she put down the carafe,
only half-filled with water. The second was the look on her
face. "I need you here. Sawyer and that advocate, Michelle,
are coming over, remember?"

I hadn't, but now it all came back. After failing to find
out what Peyton had done to lose visiting privileges, my mom
had found a nonprofit that helped families of prisoners navigate the legal system. During the last week, she'd had two
meetings with a woman there named Michelle, reporting
back that she was "a lifesaver, so knowledgeable," and "just
the person we need in our corner."

"You guys will just be talking about Peyton, though," I
said. "Do I really need to be here?"

Her face tensed, that crease folding in between her eyebrows. "It's important that we present a united, supportive
front whenever possible. You are part of that."

She turned back to the sink. I bit my lip, looking at my
shoes as my dad came in and went to the freezer, pulling it

open. He stood there for a minute before saying, "Are we out of rocky road? Is that even possible?"

"Sydney doesn't want to come to dinner tomorrow," my mom replied, as if this had anything to do with his question. "Apparently, she'd rather eat over at her new friend's house."

"What happening tomorrow?" my dad asked, pushing aside a carton of vanilla and looking behind it.

My mom yanked up the top to the water chamber on the coffeemaker hard enough that it banged against the cabinet behind it. "Sawyer? The advocate? Dinner? Does *anyone* listen to anything I say?"

My dad, who had found his rocky road, turned, the carton in his hands. He looked so surprised, I felt bad for him. "Julie? What's wrong?"

"I'm just tired of being the only one who seems to care about Peyton." She shoved the carafe into its place. "I don't ask you both to visit with me, I don't ask you to keep track of all the dates and issues that must be kept up with. But I think I should be able to ask you to have dinner in your own house, *if* it's not too much trouble."

"Mom," I said, "I'll be here."

"Of course she will." My dad put down the ice cream and walked over, putting his hands on her shoulders. "Honey. It's okay. We'll do whatever you need."

"It's not for *me*," she said, her voice cracking. "That's the whole point."

No can do, I texted Layla later from my room. Family stuff. Wish I could.

Nothing for a few minutes. Finally, a beep.

You sure you're okay?

I hesitated, my finger over the keyboard. No, I wrote back. I'm not.

Another pause, shorter this time. Then: Sleep over Saturday. Y?

There was not a *No* or *Maybe* provided this time. Sometimes, fewer choices can be a good thing. Will try, I replied. And then, after a moment: Thank you.

XO, she wrote back. And then, as if I had already chosen after all: See you then.

❊ ❊ ❊

Sawyer Ambrose was a big, beefy guy with curly white hair whose cheeks were always red. He was like Santa, but in a business suit instead of a red, fur-trimmed one. When I opened the door the following evening right at six thirty, he was standing there with a bottle of wine, a cheesecake, and a smile.

"Sydney," he said. "How are you?"

"Good," I replied. "Come on in."

As I stepped aside to let him pass, Ames's red Lexus pulled into the driveway. He got out right away and waved at me, which meant unless I wanted to shut the door in his face I had no choice but to stand there as he came up the walk. He opened his arms, then said, "Hey. Long time, no see."

I hated the hugging. It was relatively new, having been instituted after the weekend he'd stayed with me. There was really no way to turn down a hug without looking like a bitch, and these were particularly squeezy and long. I let myself be drawn in and tried not to tense up totally as he slid his hands around me.

"Rough week, huh?" he said. "You doing okay?"

"Yeah," I said, managing to untangle myself. "Mom's inside."

"Great." He smiled at me, then headed down the hallway, where I heard him greet Sawyer and my parents with his usual loud familiarity. I stayed in the foyer, feeling like I needed a shower. When the doorbell sounded again, I opened it. A thin woman with her hair in a braid, wearing a flowing dress and leather clogs, was standing there. She looked very surprised to see me, as if she hadn't just pushed a button to summon someone.

"Hi," she stammered. "I'm, um, here to . . ."

"Michelle, right?" I asked. She nodded, blushing slightly. "I'm Sydney, Peyton's sister. Come on in."

She did, bringing the sweet smell of some kind of essential oil with her. "This is a lovely home," she told me as I led her down the hallway. "I've . . . I haven't been to this neighborhood before."

"We like it," I told her, because what do you even say to that? Thankfully, two more steps and we were in the kitchen. "Mom, Michelle's here."

"Hello!" my mother said. She was in her full-on gracious hostess mode, something I hadn't seen in a while. Before Peyton's problems, my parents had entertained a lot, both for my dad's work and within their own social circle. In the last year, though, the dinners and cocktails had gone from sporadic to nonexistent. No one was in the mood for a party these days. "Thank you so much for coming. It's an honor to have you."

"You have a lovely home," Michelle said again. There was a layer of pet hair—cat? dog? some other species?—on the back of her dress.

"This is Sawyer Ambrose, our family attorney," my mom continued. "And my husband, Peyton, and our friend Ames Bentley. You met Sydney?"

Michelle nodded. "Yes. She's . . . Yes, I did."

I was no expert, but it seemed that to be a professional advocate, you *sort* of had to be able to talk to people. Michelle, in contrast, seemed nervous whenever she was addressed during the wine and cheese my mother put out before dinner. Undeterred, my mother kept talking to her, catching my dad and Ames up on the various conversations they'd had in the last week about dealing with the warden, finding out information that wasn't being readily dispensed, and ways we could help Peyton from outside the prison.

"So," Sawyer said to me in the midst of all this, "I hear you're at Jackson High now. How are you liking it?"

"It's good," I said.

"My daughter Isley goes there," he told me, helping himself to a small cracker and a very big slice of Gouda. "The teachers are good. The boys, though, trouble. Although I guess that's the case wherever you are, am I right?"

"Um, yeah," I said. My mother had gotten her social skills

back, but mine were nowhere to be found. Apparently. "I guess."

"She was dating this musician over the summer," he continued. "Real blowhard. Walked around with a tuner in his pocket, yakking on about irony and nuance."

That sounded awfully familiar. "What was his name?"

"Eric." He sighed. "She came to her senses before it went too far, at least. If it was up to me, she wouldn't date until college. But it *isn't* up to me, of course."

"Sawyer," my mom interjected, putting a hand on his arm, "Michelle was just telling us about some really good opportunities for families to be involved at Lincoln."

"I'm in," said Ames right away. "Tell me more."

"I don't know," Sawyer said, taking a sip of his wine. "You have to be careful. It might be better for Peyton for there to be a clear line between his life there and this one."

"Well, of course Peyton's well-being is our top priority," my dad added, and Ames nodded.

Michelle cleared her throat. "It's been my experience that at Lincoln they are more progressive than some of the other institutions." A pause. A long one. Then, right when I could tell my mom was about to jump in, she continued. "Their warden is new and came from out of state—New York, I believe. He's got a reputation for being compassionate toward families."

"Well, I hope that is the case," my mom said. "But first I have to get him to return my phone calls."

"You called the warden?" Sawyer asked, surprised.

"Well . . ." My mom looked at my dad, then at Michelle. "Yes. I did. After this latest infraction, we couldn't get any information. And I felt that it was important—"

"Julie. This is prison, not PTA."

"I *know* that," she said, an edge of irritation creeping into her voice. She must have heard it, too, as she paused, gathering herself, before saying, "I just wanted to know what was going on."

"Which is your right," Ames told her. "They can't just keep information from you."

"Actually, they can," Sawyer said, wiping some crumbs from his mouth. "Really, the best thing you can do for Peyton is let him serve his sentence with as little interference as possible. He needs to keep his head down and do what he's told. It's the only way he has a chance of any time being shaved off."

"I'm not interfering," my mother said.

"Of course you aren't." God, Ames was such a suck-up.

"It's important for families to feel involved," Michelle added. When we all gave her our attention, she blushed. "It's better than helpless."

"No offense, miss, but I've been working in the law twenty years. I've seen a lot of clients in this situation. There are things that make it harder, and things that make it easier."

"I think we should have dinner," my mom announced, getting to her feet. "Just give me a minute. Sydney, a little help?"

I followed her into the kitchen, where she yanked open

the stove a *bit* harder than necessary. "You okay?" I asked.

"Of course." She took off her pot holder, picking up a spatula. "I just think we have to explore all options, in and out of the box. There's nothing wrong with that."

Sawyer, however, disagreed, and continued to do so throughout dinner. He sparred with my mom, Ames, and a flustered Michelle while my dad kept his head down, eating the biggest slice of lasagna I'd seen him consume in recent memory.

"The basic fact," Sawyer was saying at one point, long after I was done eating, "is that no matter what Peyton does, there's always the truth of his case. The facts. You saw the paper this week, I'm assuming?"

"Let's not—" my dad began.

"Totally biased piece," Ames said.

"Biased?" I said. Now everyone looked at me. "How can you . . . It was all about that boy."

"Yeah, but the way they wrote it." He waved his hand, as if somehow this completed the thought and sentence. "I'm just saying."

What *was* he saying? Never mind, I was sure I didn't want to hear it.

"Of course we feel awful for that boy and his family," my mom said. "But Peyton is our son. Our responsibility. We've got a duty to look out for him."

That sounded familiar.

"You can only do so much now, Julie," Sawyer said. "You need to accept that."

"Well, I think you're wrong," she said simply. My dad and I exchanged a look. "Who wants dessert?"

It was, in a word, excruciating. After dinner, Ames went out to smoke while my dad took Sawyer up to his office to show him some new computer he'd just gotten. My mom and Michelle camped at the kitchen table with their coffees.

"Everyone that's part of this process has a different viewpoint," Michelle said to her, patting her arm. She seemed more comfortable now, one-on-one. "That's why we need many voices. So we can have a conversation and keep it going."

My mom sighed, running a finger around the rim of her mug. "I just . . . This is so hard. I've never felt so out of control."

"It's normal. You're a mother. It's been your job to protect him. You can't just quit that, even when someone tells you to."

By nine p.m., both Sawyer and Michelle had left. Ames remained, sitting at the table having a conversation with my parents, although my mother was doing most of the talking. The irritation she'd barely managed to mask earlier had now blown up into a full-on rage, with Sawyer as the target.

"You'd think, with all the money we paid him, he'd be more supportive," she said at one point, taking a bite of the leftover cheesecake right out of the pan. "I mean, defending someone shouldn't end the second a trial does."

"Sawyer's done right by us," my dad said. "He just sees things differently."

"Well, then maybe it's time to look around for someone

with a fresh view. I've heard great things about Bill Thomas."

My dad sighed, clearly not convinced. Ames said, "The main focus has to be Peyton. We can't lose sight of that."

"Exactly," my mom said, pointing her fork at him. "Thank God someone agrees with me."

Not for the first time, I wondered if this was the reason I was so obsessed with David Ibarra and his aftermath and story. Someone had to carry the guilt. If my parents couldn't—or wouldn't—it was left to me.

"It's still early," Ames said to me, once my mom had gotten up to finish cleaning the kitchen and my dad disappeared upstairs. "Want to go out for some fro-yo? My treat."

"Oh, that's nice of you, Ames." My mom, drying her hands on a dish towel, smiled at him. "I know this was not exactly the way Sydney wanted to spend her evening."

In fact, she knew what my preference had been. I said, "Thanks, but I'm kind of tired."

"Come on," he said. "Are you really going to turn down a free hot-fudge sundae? Not to mention great company?"

"I'll tell you what," my mom said, reaching for her purse. "I'll treat you both."

"I'm really not in the mood," I told her. "Thanks, though."

My mom looked at me, raising an eyebrow. "You okay?"

"Fine. It's just . . . a long week."

She and Ames exchanged a knowing look. "It was," she agreed, walking over and smoothing a hand over my hair. "Not to mention a long night. Ames, take a rain check?"

"Of course," he said.

Sensing a chance to escape, I got to my feet. "I think I'll just go upstairs and get ready for bed."

My mom glanced at her watch. It was only nine thirty. As I started out of the room, she said, "Tomorrow is all yours, okay? Whatever you want to do."

I had a feeling that going to Layla's was not what she had in mind as she said this. But all I wanted was to get out of this house, be somewhere the ghost of my brother, not even dead, didn't haunt every corner.

Up in my room, I got into my pajamas, then brushed my teeth. I kept checking to see if Ames had left yet, wondering what else he could possibly have to say to my mother, but as a half hour passed, and then another, his car remained. Finally, I crept halfway down the stairs to listen.

"She's doing fine," he was saying. "It's a big adjustment. Imagine what it's like to be in high school and dealing with this."

"I just wish she'd stayed at Perkins. I feel like I'm losing touch with her, just because there's so much I don't know about her daily life."

"That sounds like a common feeling for you." I rolled my eyes.

"It is." A pause. "All I ever wanted was for them to be happy."

"Happy is a lot to ask for all the time."

"I don't want all the time," she replied. "Not anymore. I'd just take a little and be grateful for it."

She sounded so sad, so tired. At times like this it was hard to even remember the way my mom had once been, bubbling with energy and projects. Like the center of the wheel that was our family, she'd always held all our separate spokes together and kept them rolling. Now, though, more often than not, we were wobbling, lucky to be moving at all.

Before I turned out my light, I picked up my phone, glancing at the last text Layla had sent. I wished there was a way to catch her up all at once, so that she'd know what I was feeling right that moment and maybe understand. I flipped over to the article from the paper, still bookmarked, and copied the link, then pasted it into a fresh message. Then, before I could overthink it, I hit SEND. No explanation, no comment. Just the story as it was. I stayed awake for a while, wondering what she'd write back. When I woke up in the morning, I didn't know whether to be happy or sad that there was no reply from her at all.

CHAPTER

11

I WAS right. Despite her promises the night before, my mom was not exactly thrilled to discover that the one thing I wanted to do on Saturday was spend the night with Layla.

"Oh, honey," she'd said that morning when I brought it up. It was only nine a.m., but I'd already made her sound weary. "I don't think so. It's already been a long week, and I don't even know this girl."

"She spent the night here already, though," I pointed out, hoping to appeal to her sense of manners and social contracts. "Twice, actually."

"That was different," she replied, pouring herself more coffee. "You were here, and Ames was with you."

Which was so *much safer,* I thought. But of course she thought it was. I wondered if he actually looked different to her *physically,* his very features starkly different, since we saw him in such opposite ways. "I stayed home last night, like you asked me to. You said today was mine to do what I chose."

"I meant something like going to the movies, or out to lunch. Not disappearing for a full night to a strange place."

"Mom. It's across town, not Neverland."

She made a face at me, then looked at my dad, who was bent over his customary huge plate of bacon and eggs, reading the sports page. "Peyton? Could you weigh in here?"

"Sure." He sat back, wiping his hands on a napkin. "On what?"

"Sydney wants to spend the night at her friend Layla's house tonight."

My dad looked at me, then back at her, clearly trying to guess what the issue was. I marveled, as always, at his ability to be literally inside a conversation and yet miss it altogether. Slowly, he said, "And the problem is . . ."

"That we don't know her? Or her family?"

"Can we meet them?" he asked.

My mom looked at me, as if this prospect would dampen my drive to do this. "Sure," I said. "Her parents own a pizza place over by my school. I'm sure they're open for lunch. Her dad's usually there."

It was a tribute to how desperate I was that I was willing to bring my mom to Seaside. But this was not just me getting what I wanted. What I'd overheard her say to Ames the night before was still on my mind. There was nothing she could really do when it came to knowing more about Peyton's world. But maybe I could give her a wider glimpse into mine.

Three hours later, I was in the passenger seat of her hybrid SUV, directing her into a parking space. My dad had a racquetball game, so it was just us, and I was strangely nervous, as if this was some sort of test I needed to pass. She cut the engine, then flipped down her visor, checking her lipstick. "Hungry?" she asked me.

"Totally," I replied. "The pizza is great here."

Inside, I saw Mac first, in a SEASIDE T-shirt and jeans, behind the counter spreading sauce onto an uncooked pie. For the first time, the thin silver chain he wore was fully visible, and I saw that it had a charm on it, something circular that looked like a coin, although it was hard to tell from a distance. "Hey," he said. "Layla said you might be in."

"Is she around?"

"On her way. Five minutes or so."

I looked at my mom, who was silently taking in the dark décor, plastic tables, and black-and-white pictures lining the walls. "Mom, this is Mac," I told her. "Layla's brother."

"Nice to meet you," he said, wiping a hand on a nearby towel and extending it. My mom reached over the counter, and they shook. "Can I get you guys something?"

My mom squinted at the menu. "How are the salads?"

"Not as good as the pizza," he replied.

At this, she smiled. "They never are, are they?"

"Nope."

I shot him a grateful look, wondering how much Layla had told him. Is your dad at Seaside? I'd texted her earlier. Mom wants a face to the overnight.

Noon, she'd replied. Don't worry. We clean up well.

Texting was always weird when it came to tone, and seeing this, I wondered if I'd offended her. When she walked through the back door ten minutes later, though, I knew right off I shouldn't have worried.

"Hey," she said. She was in a wingy, patterned skirt and a white T-shirt, her hair pulled back in a ponytail, flip-flops on her feet. In her hand, glistening, was a cotton candy YumYum. Her dad was behind her, carrying a couple of shopping bags. She walked up to my mom and stuck out her hand. "Finally, we meet. I'm Layla."

"Well, hello," my mom said, shaking her hand. "I've heard a lot about you."

"Hopefully all good." Layla looked at me. "Although I bet it was mostly food-related."

"Layla loves French fries," I explained to my mom. "And lollipops."

"All the components of a healthy diet," Layla said cheerfully. As she turned, looking at her dad, I could see my mom sizing her up, and wondered how she saw her. No fancy labels on her clothes, a worn purse not from this season or probably even the last. That lollipop. "Hey, Dad. Come here a second."

Mr. Chatham emerged from behind the counter, tying an apron around his waist. "You must be Sydney's mother," he said to my mom. "Mac Chatham."

"Julie Stanford. You and your son have the same name?" my mom said, shaking his hand.

"Family tradition," he explained. "My dad was Macaulay as well."

"It's the same with my husband, his father, and Sydney's brother. Three Peytons. When they're all in the same room, confusion reigns."

"I can usually tell which one my wife is yelling at by her

tone," he told her. "I get a bit more leeway, due to the marriage factor. But not much."

"You have other children?"

"One. Rosie. She's two years older than this one," he said, cocking his thumb at Mac.

"She does competitive ice skating," I added. "She toured with the Mariposa show."

"Really?" my mother said. "How impressive. You must be so proud."

"Until the drug bust," Layla said. "Since then, not so much."

Mr. Chatham just looked at her, while my mom, clearly surprised, struggled to get her expression back under control. I closed my eyes.

"Anyway," Layla continued, "did you guys get everything you need? Drinks? Garlic knots?"

"We're fine," I told her. "I can't wait for Mom to try your pizza."

"I'll make sure you get an extra big piece," Mr. Chatham said, turning back to the counter. "Nice to meet you, Julie."

"And you as well!" she replied. She sat back down as Layla followed him back behind the counter, turning to look at me. When they were out of earshot, she said in a low voice, "Drugs?"

"Rosie had an injury that led to some legal issues with prescriptions," I explained, watching her face carefully. Before Peyton's troubles, the judgment would have been automatic, almost a reflex. Now, however, she didn't have that option unless she wanted to risk looking like a hypocrite. It was clever of Layla, I realized, to expose our common denominator right off the bat, letting her know that for all the differences, we did share something. "She's getting back into skating now. I watched her practice the other day."

"You did?" she said.

I nodded. "She was pretty amazing."

Mac appeared beside us, carrying two plates of pizza. "One pepperoni, one roma," he said, putting them down. "Anything else?"

"Not right now, I don't think," I told him. "Thanks."

He nodded, then returned to the register, where Layla was now leaning against the counter, YumYum in her mouth, watching us. Her dad said something and she nodded, then replied, tucking a piece of hair behind her ear.

"Wow," my mom said, dabbing at her mouth with a napkin. "That *is* good."

"Told you," I said.

She glanced up at the picture beside us, which was of a boardwalk lined with games of chance, the sea visible in the distance. "I'm curious about the name. Not much coast around here."

"I think it came from up north, from another place her granddad owned," I said.

She nodded, then stopped chewing, cocking her head to one side. "Is that a banjo I hear?"

"Bluegrass," I said. "It's all that's on the jukebox."

For a moment, we ate in silence. The phone rang behind the counter. Mac took an order. Mr. Chatham disappeared into the office. Meanwhile, the sun slanted in the front window, making little bits of dust on the table beside us dance.

"How did you meet Layla, again?" my mom finally asked me.

I swallowed the bite in my mouth. "Here. I came in for a slice after school. And we just started talking."

She looked back at Mac, who was pulling a pie out of the oven. "You said her mother was ill."

"She has MS. I think they trade off taking care of her."

"How awful." She wiped her mouth. "And where do they live?"

"About two blocks from here."

I could sense I was close to getting what I wanted, which was also near enough to worry about it slipping away. So I kept quiet and waited for her to speak again. Instead, the next sound that came was her phone.

She pulled it out of her bag. Upon seeing the screen, her eyes widened, and she quickly scrambled to hit the TALK button. "Hello?"

Distantly, I could hear the sound of an automated voice.

"Yes." Her voice was clear and loud enough that Layla and Mac both looked over at us. "I'll accept the charges."

It was Peyton. I could tell by her face, the way her eyes filled with tears when, after a beat, he began to speak. I couldn't hear what he was saying, but I didn't have to. I'd always had a sense when it came to my brother. And anyway, his voice had more presence than most people did face-to-face.

"Oh, honey," she said, putting her other hand to her face. "Hello. Hello! How *are* you? I've been so worried!"

As he replied, she got to her feet and headed for the door,

the phone clamped to her ear. Once outside, she began pacing on the sidewalk, her face all attention, listening hard.

"Looks like an important call."

I glanced up to see Layla standing beside me. "My brother," I said. "It's the first time he's had phone access in a while."

She was still watching my mom, moving back and forth in front of the window. "She sure looks happy."

"Yeah. She does."

Neither of us spoke for a second. Then, wordlessly, she put a root beer YumYum beside my plate. Compensation? A gesture of sympathy? It could have been both these things, or neither of them. It really didn't matter. I was grateful for it.

❧ ❧ ❧

When I got to Layla's later that afternoon, I was surprised to see several cars parked in the driveway and along the curb. Clearly, I was not the only one who had been invited over.

No matter, though. I was just glad to be there, even if it did take my brother to make it happen. After hanging up with him, my mom was so over the moon, I probably could have gotten anything I asked for. This, though, was all I wanted.

I parked behind a minivan that I recognized as belonging to Ford, the bass player in Eric and Mac's band, the name of which was still in flux. Before Hey Dude, they'd been known as Hog Dog Water, both names Eric felt did not "do their art justice." This had been the subject of another extended discussion at lunch on Friday, during which Layla said he should pick a name and stick with it, for recognition if nothing else. He, however, maintained that a band's identity was not something to be decided lightly: whatever they became next was important. Unlike, say, Hot Dog Water.

From there, the conversation had gone about how they all did, segueing from a somewhat civilized discussion to Eric performing a loud monologue that no one else could interrupt. I often left lunch feeling exhausted, and that day I'd almost fallen asleep in my ecology class afterward.

The band might have been nameless, but this didn't prevent them from practicing, if the noise I heard as I walked up to the house was any indication. The music was coming from around the side of the house, so I followed it, coming upon an outbuilding that sat between a truck up on blocks and a large sedan with a sunken-in roof. Smaller than a garage, but bigger than a shed, it had two wooden doors that were open, revealing Mac at his drum set, Eric behind a microphone, and Ford, who was fiddling with an amplifier. In front of them was Layla, in a lawn chair. She was wearing sunglasses.

"Verdict?" she was saying as I came up behind her. "Too loud. Not good."

Eric just looked at her. "Don't feel the need to candy-coat, Chatham."

"Don't worry. I won't."

"We're supposed to be loud, though," Ford said, unplugging something, then plugging it back in. "That's part of the whole ethos, right? That this music was, in its original form, so highly controlled and conducted, even computerized. Making it raw and rough turns it on its head."

Mac, drumsticks in hand, raised his eyebrows. "Dude,"

he said. "You've been hanging out with Eric *way* too much."

"On the contrary, I think someone is finally talking sense around here," Eric said. "Now we just need to get our drummer on board with the message and we'll be all set."

"Forget your message," Layla told him. "Concentrate on playing well."

"Nobody asked you," he said. "Don't you have special ketchup to formulate or something?"

"Nope." She sat back, crossing one leg over the other. "Right now, I have all the time in the *world*."

"Lucky us," Eric grumbled, turning back to the other guys. "Okay, let's try 'Prom Queen' again, from the top."

Mac counted to four, and then they began playing again, sounding a bit disjointed at first before gelling, somewhat, by the end of the first verse. Despite Layla's ongoing commentary, I saw her tapping her foot as I came up beside her.

"Front-row seat, huh?"

"Hi!" She looked genuinely happy to see me. "Well, it's hardly the real Logan Oxford. But at least we don't have to go far. Here, let me get you a chair."

"Oh," I said. "You don't . . ."

But she was already going into the shed, squeezing past Ford and his bass to retrieve a battered pink lawn chair patterned with palm trees. As she plunked it down in front of me, a couple of dead spiders fell off it. She ignored this, wiping it clean with her hands before presenting it to me. "Best seat in the house. Or this house."

I sat. The band was still playing, although Eric had

stopped singing and turned around, his back now to us. I said, "So this is where they practice?"

"Sometimes," she replied, plopping back into her own seat. "There's also Ford's basement, but there's always laundry going down there and Eric claims the smell of fabric softener gives him a headache."

"Rock star problems."

"*Eric* problems." She sighed. "They're like first world, but even more privileged."

I looked at the man in question, who had now stopped playing altogether and was tuning his guitar, a frustrated look on his face. As Mac and Ford moved alone into the chorus, I realized they actually sounded better without him. Maybe this was why I said, "You're tough on him."

"Eric?" I nodded. "Yeah, I guess. But it's from a good place, I swear. Before he met Mac and started coming around, he was *such* a freaking jerk. Just a total know-it-all blowhard. But the thing was . . . it wasn't really his fault."

"No?"

She shook her head. "His parents, they tried to have kids for, like, ever. All these fertility problems, miscarriages. They'd basically been told there was no way it was ever going to happen for them. So when his mom got pregnant without even trying, it was like . . . a miracle. And when Eric arrived, they treated him accordingly."

"Like a miracle?"

"Like God's gift. Which was what they thought he was." She shifted in her seat. "The problem was when it became how *he* saw himself, and there was no one there to tell him otherwise. Then he met Mac."

"And Mac did?"

"In his way," she replied. "That's the thing about my brother. He's subtle, you know? And a good guy, a guy you *want* to like you."

I cleared my throat, concerned I might be blushing.

"So he just told Eric that he didn't have to try so hard. Win every discussion, talk louder than everyone else. That kind of thing. And Eric, to his credit, listened. Now he's not so bad, although he has his lapses. And when he does, I feel it's my duty to speak up. We all do."

"For the common good," I said.

"Well, it takes a village," she replied. "Or a city, really, in his case. A big one. Many citizens."

I laughed as there was a blast of feedback, followed by Eric shouting something. Layla winced. "Okay, I need a break. Let's go get something to eat."

She got up, and I followed her across the muddy backyard to the house, where a mossy line of paving stones led up to the back door. It creaked when she pulled it open, a sound that appeared to summon the dogs, which swarmed our ankles, barking wildly, as we went inside.

"Sydney's here," she called out as the door swung shut behind us. It took a second to adjust from the brightness outside. But then, yet again, it was all in place: the couch, the huge TV, the two cluttered tables flanking the recliner, in which Mrs. Chatham was seated, wearing a sweatshirt that said MIAMI and scrub pants. As I watched, the dogs, having lost interest in us, jumped up and burrowed under the blanket spread across her lap.

"Welcome," she said to me. "I hear you're spending the night."

"Yeah," I replied. "Thanks for having me."

"Don't thank us yet," Layla said. "You may change your mind once the music starts."

"The music?" I repeated. I looked out the window. "They're already playing, though."

"Not that music. My dad's. As it turns out, he also invited a bunch of people over tonight. Not that anyone told me."

"I bet Sydney will love it," her mother said.

"It's bluegrass," Layla told me. "Nothing *but* bluegrass. All night long. If you don't like mandolin, you're in trouble."

"You have a door on your room; feel free to use it," Mrs. Chatham said, in a tone that, while cheerful, made it clear it was the end of the discussion. "Now, go make some popcorn, would you, honey? I want to talk to Sydney a second."

Layla glanced at me, then turned, walking into the kitchen. For a minute, I felt like I might be in trouble, although I couldn't imagine what for. When I looked at Mrs. Chatham, though, she was smiling at me. I sat down in a nearby chair just as Layla turned on the microwave.

"So," she said as one of the dogs shifted position on her lap. "I saw the article in the paper."

Over the last few months, I'd realized that there was really no ideal way for anyone to talk to me about Peyton. If they avoided the subject, but it was clearly on their minds, things felt awkward. Addressing it head-on, however, was often worse, like a train coming toward me I was helpless to stop. Really, nothing felt right, yet this gentle inquiry was the closest I'd gotten. An acknowledgment and sympathy, while still respecting the facts. It took me by such surprise, I couldn't speak at first. So I was glad when she continued.

"That must have been so hard for you, and your family," she said. "I can't even imagine."

"It is," I finally managed. "Hard, I mean. Mostly for my mom. I hate what it's done to her."

"She's suffering." It was a statement, not a question.

"Yeah." I looked down at my hands. "But . . . so is that boy. David Ibarra. I mean, he really is."

"Of course." Again, no judgment, just a prod to keep going. So I did.

"I think . . ." I began, but then suddenly it was too big to say or even exist outside of my own head. It was one thing to let these thoughts haunt the dark spaces of my mind, but another entirely to put them into the light, making them real. She was looking at me so intently, though, and this place was so new, with no semblance of the world before except for the fact that I was in it. "I think my parents see Peyton as the victim, in some ways. And I hate that. It makes me sick. It's just so . . . It's wrong."

"You feel guilty."

"Yes," I said, the vehemence of this one word surprising me. Like simply concurring made my soul rush out, gone. "I do. So much. Every single day."

"Oh, honey." She reached out, putting her hand over mine. In the next room, the popcorn was popping, producing the buttery smell I associated with movies and after school, all those lonely afternoons. "Why do you feel like you have to shoulder your brother's responsibility?"

"Because someone has to," I said. I looked into her eyes, green flecked with brown, just like Layla's. "That's why."

Instead of replying, she squeezed my hand. I knew I could pull away and it would still be all right. But when Layla came in a few minutes later with the popcorn, that was how she found us. I'd let so much go, finally. It made sense, I suppose, that right then I would maybe just want to hold on.

CHAPTER
12

"HOW MUCH farther?"

"You always ask that."

"And I always mean it." A pause. Then, "Seriously, how much?"

Up ahead, Mac turned around, shining the flashlight back at Layla. "If you're angling for a ride, you should just ask."

She smiled. "I wouldn't want to impose . . ."

In response, Irv, who was walking alongside Mac, dropped back so we could catch up with him. "Hop on," he said, crouching down, and Layla climbed onto his immense shoulders, piggyback-style. Then we continued on into the darkness.

I'd felt so shaken after my talk with Mrs. Chatham that I was grateful, actually, for the chaos that followed. After we had polished off the popcorn and watched one episode of *Big Los Angeles* (one catfight, two breakdowns, too many gorgeous outfits to count), Mac, Eric, and Ford had come inside to raid the fridge. Then Rosie showed up with a couple of her Mariposa friends, who were in town doing a week of performances at the Lakeview Center. The house already felt packed, even before Mr. Chatham came home and *his* friends arrived, instruments in hand. After the constant quiet of my own house since Peyton had been gone, I expected the contrast to be overwhelming. Instead, I found that I liked the constant hum and noise, the fullness of many people and much energy in a small space. I could hang back and just watch, yet still feel involved. It was nice.

Dinner was a huge amount of pizza, salads, and garlic knots from Seaside, which we ate in the outbuilding while Layla's parents and their friends filled the living room and kitchen. It was just starting to get dark when I heard the first strains of music coming from the house through the open back door. It sounded like the jukebox at Seaside, but more real. Alive.

I'd assumed we'd head inside for the music, but everyone else had other plans. After checking in with Mrs. Chatham to see if she needed anything, Mac returned with a duffel bag, which he took into the garage. A moment later, with the bag visibly fuller, he returned and hoisted it over his shoulder. Layla pulled a flashlight from a nearby cabinet, while Irv, who had arrived post-popcorn and pre-dinner, grabbed the backpack he'd brought with him. Eric packed up his guitar, and then they all headed outside in silent consensus. I followed, the only one who had no idea where we were going.

As it turned out, it was into the woods. They all started toward it, as if entering a huge swath of dark forest at night made total sense. I guess to them, it did.

"Hey," Layla said, looking over at me. "It's okay. Come on."

When Peyton and I went into the trees behind our house,

it took a few minutes to leave our yard and the neighbor-hood behind. Here, though, it was different. We'd no sooner stepped in than we were swallowed up, lights from the Cha-thams' house dimming, then disappearing altogether. I was grateful for Mac's white shirt, which seemed to almost glow as he led us deeper and deeper into the trees. We'd been walking almost twenty minutes when Layla first complained. Once she was on Irv's back, we easily doubled that time.

"I always forget how freaking long this takes," Eric com-plained, his guitar case bumping against his leg.

"Do you want Irv to carry you, too?" Layla asked him.

I was somewhat out of breath, both from Mac's fast pace and the distance. Irv, however, hardly seemed winded, even with an additional hundred-plus pounds on his back. We kept walking.

And then, right when I was sure someone—maybe even me—was about to voice more displeasure, I saw a clearing ahead. The trees thinned, then disappeared altogether, leav-ing us facing a large metal structure, plopped down in the middle of all that forest like God himself had dropped it there.

"Finally," Layla said, as if she had walked the whole way. Irv slid her off his back. "Beer me, someone."

Mac had already put down the bag he'd been carrying and unzipped it. As I watched, he tossed a can to her, which she caught with one hand, then passed one to Eric as he set his guitar down. Then he held one up to me. I looked at Irv, as he was closer and, as far as I was concerned, had seniority. But he shook his head.

"Don't drink," he explained. "No point."

"He can't get drunk," Layla told me. "Too big."

"That's why we call him HW," Mac said. "Heavyweight. As opposed to . . ."

"Don't say it," Eric warned him, popping the tab on his beer.

"LW," Layla finished. "Another one of Eric's many nicknames."

"I am *not* a lightweight." As if to prove it, Eric sucked down a bunch of his beer, then belched, loudly. Then he looked at me. "Want one?"

I was not much of a drinker, especially after Jenn's piña colada disaster. But I wasn't driving, and we were in the moonlight. So I nodded. Mac went to throw one to me, but Eric took it first, then opened it before bringing it over.

"Thanks," I said. It was cold in my hand.

"My pleasure." He held out his can. "To you."

Layla rolled her eyes but withheld comment, letting her civic duty slide as she walked over to sit down on the edge of the structure I'd seen earlier. I'd thought it was a vehicle, maybe an old truck, parked off what I now could see was a logging road that twisted into the trees. Looking closer, I saw it was something else entirely: an old metal carousel, so corroded it almost blended into the dark. I stood there a minute, taking it in. If I'd had more than one sip of beer, I would have assumed I was imagining it.

"Cool, right?" Layla said. She was perched at the base of one of the horses. "Mac found it, during his weight-loss wanderings."

"They're called runs," Mac said.

"Whatever. The point is, someone left this here at some point. But why? And how? Did they bring it on a truck and plan to come back for it? Or build it here?"

I walked around the front part of the carousel, taking in several more horses and a rickety-looking chariot with grass growing up through a hole in the seat. "It's amazing," I said. "You really don't know who it belongs to?"

"There aren't any houses for miles."

"What about this road?" I asked, nodding toward it.

"If you follow it, it just ends, long before the woods does." Layla took a sip of her beer, swinging her legs. "It's so creepy."

But it wasn't scary to me. Instead, it felt magical, like the kind of thing Peyton and I could only have dreamed of discovering during our own explorations. The chance of finding something like this was what brought you into a woods in the first place.

Thinking this, I looked over at Mac. I was surprised to find he was watching me over the rim of the can as he drank, and I returned his gaze, remembering that five-dollar bill tucked safely away in my wallet. Unspent.

"You should check out the other side," Eric said, appearing suddenly beside me. I heard a pop: he was moving on to his next beer. "That's where the ring is. Come on, I'll show you."

I followed him around, past the chariot, to where a large horse was rearing up, head thrown back, mouth open. Whoever had made this had taken their time.

"You kind of have to get in the right place to see it," Eric said, climbing up beside the horse. He held out his free hand. "I'll pull you up."

I looked back at Layla, who I could now barely make out in the dark. Mac I'd lost sight off entirely. Only Irv remained fully visible, but it wasn't like he was one to blend in. I gave Eric my hand, feeling his fingers tighten around mine as he lifted me up next to him. Beneath our feet, the carousel creaked.

"Okay," he said, putting his hands on my shoulders and gesturing for me to look up at the roof of the carousel above us. "Now, see where the pole meets the metal up there?"

I nodded. "Yeah."

"Then look right to the left of it." He pointed. "It's sort of small, but it's there."

It took a minute, but then I made it out: a simple ring, hanging above us, close enough that if you were on the horse as it rose to its highest point, you could grab it. "I'm surprised no one's pulled it down," I said.

"Oh, believe me, we've tried." He took another drink. "It's stuck in there good. Whoever made this didn't want anyone to take it."

I could see how it would be tempting. Who doesn't try for the prize if it's that close? "How do you get up there, though?"

"When it's moving."

I turned around, only to realize we were *really* close, practically face-to-face. Eric, for his part, did not seem startled by this, and I suddenly had the feeling, if not the certainty, that he had done this—all of this—before. "It *moves*?"

"Only when someone's pushing it," I heard Mac say.

Somehow, he'd approached without us hearing him and was now standing just in front of the horse. In the moonlight, I noticed again the coin hanging from the chain around his neck. Instinctively, I stepped out from beneath Eric's hands, which were still on my shoulders. "How is that even possible? Isn't it, like, crazy heavy?"

"Not as long as you don't load it up with too many people," he said. "We've gotten it going at a decent clip before. Especially if Irv's here."

"Can't get drunk, have to push the merry-go-round," Irv's baritone came from the darkness. "Don't know why I even hang out with you guys."

"Because you love us," Layla, who had also now walked over, called out to him. She looked up at Eric. "Your phone's beeping, just FYI."

"Oh, that might be about this gig next weekend. I should take it." Eric patted my shoulder. "Back in a sec."

Layla watched as he went around to the other side. Then, without comment, she followed, leaving me and Mac alone. We were quiet for a moment. I could hear Layla talking to Irv and another beer popping. Finally I said, "I wish I'd found something like this when I used to walk in the woods."

He looked up at it. "Yeah?"

I nodded. "The coolest thing I ever found was an arrowhead. Oh, and a bat skull."

"Sounds like you were out there a lot."

"My brother and I were. When we were kids." I looked up at the ring again. In the right light, with the moon hitting a rust hole just near it, you could see it perfectly. I took a drink. "He was the explorer, really. I just tagged along. I wanted to do everything he did."

Another silence. I heard Layla laugh. Then Mac said, "I heard about what happened to your brother. I'm sorry."

"It didn't happen to him," I said. "He did something. There's a difference."

As soon as I said this, I realized how angry it sounded. He said, "I didn't—"

"No, you're fine," I said quickly. "It's just . . . a tender spot. I guess."

Immediately, I was horrified. What possessed me to use the word *tender* in any context around a cute guy I barely knew, I had no idea. I took a big gulp of my beer, then another.

"Well," he said after a moment, "everyone has one."

He was looking up at the trees as he said this, his face brightened by the moonlight. Maybe it was the beer, or the fact I'd already said the wrong thing twice. But I figured I had little left to lose. So I said, "Even you, huh?"

Now he did look at me. "I was the fat, pimply kid up until pretty recently. You don't just forget."

I shook my head. "I still can't believe that."

"It's documented." Another sip. "Despite my best efforts to destroy any and all evidence."

Distantly, I heard Layla laugh. "I would think you'd want the proof. That maybe it might, you know, make you proud. Seeing where you came from."

"I'd be prouder if I had never let myself get to that point," he said.

"Can't change the past."

He reached up, sliding his finger under the chain around his neck. "Doesn't mean you should dwell on it."

Eric wasn't the only lightweight: the beer was hitting me now. I finished it off, then put it down beside me. "What's the story with that coin?"

"Coin?" I nodded at it, and he looked down. "Oh. It's actually a pendant of a saint. My mom gave them to all of us when we were kids."

"A saint?"

"Yep." He pulled it out, angling it to the moonlight. "Bathilde. Patron saint of children. I guess she figured we'd need all the help we could get."

I moved closer, barely able to make out a figure and some tiny words on the pendant. "It's nice."

"Yeah. But it's also a reminder."

"Of what?"

"When I was at my heaviest, this thing choked me. I mean, seriously. It left welts. I didn't want to take it off. I wouldn't. I needed all the help *I* could get."

"Protection," I said.

"Something like that." He let it drop. "Now I keep it on so I don't forget what I lost."

It was weird, hearing this. Like no longer having something could be a *good* thing, and the proof of it as well. I was used to the opposite, when absence equaled heartbreak. Suddenly, I had a million questions, and between the beer and the dark, I felt like I could ask them. But then Eric came around the corner, his guitar in hand.

"Sorry to interrupt," he said. I heard a slur in his voice. "But you're *kind* of being impolite all sequestered over here."

"How many beers have you had?" Mac asked him as I slid off the carousel, taking my can with me.

"An infinitesimal amount," Eric replied. But I noticed, as we fell in behind him, that his steps were anything but sure.

"Eric's using his big words," Mac reported to Layla and Irv, who were now sitting opposite each other in a chariot. She had plenty of room next to her; he barely fit, as if the metal might give way at any moment.

"Dead giveaway," Layla said. "No more beer for you, Bates."

"He gets super verbose when he's buzzed," Irv explained to me. "One of his many tells."

"I am perfectly compos mentis," Eric protested, sitting down a bit bumpily on the grass. He strummed his guitar. "I'll prove it by entertaining you with a musical interlude. Sydney, come join me here on the terra firma and tell me what you want to hear."

"Oh, for God's sake." Layla held up a hand. "Please stop before you embarrass yourself."

"Too late," Irv said.

Eric, undeterred, patted the grass beside him. "Come. Enjoy my aural stylings."

I felt so bad for him that I actually went. As soon as I sat down, he leaned into me, strumming the guitar. "I once knew a girl, Sydney was her name . . . She was so pretty, she drove me insane . . ."

"Can I have another beer?" I asked. Irv snorted. Mac tossed me one.

"Met her at school, there on the wall," he crooned. "Sat down beside her, gave it my all . . ."

"O-kay," Layla said, getting up from the chariot. "I think it's time we head back. Mom's going to be wondering where we are."

"I'm in the middle of an original composition," Eric protested.

"You'll thank me later," she told him as Mac picked up the duffel bag, filling it with our empty cans. Irv stepped off the carousel, and it made a sound like a sigh of relief. Beside me, Eric had thankfully stopped singing, although he was still picking out a few sloppy chords. "Before we go, though, one ride?"

"One ride," Eric mumbled. "On the inside. Be my bride and let it ride . . ."

Irv looked at Mac, who shrugged. "Okay," he said. "Climb on."

Layla clapped her hands, then got back on the carousel, hoisting herself up onto one of the horses. "Come on," she said to me. "You have to try this."

I was buzzed now, feeling the beer and a half as I walked over and joined her. My horse was a small one, and I felt unsteady as I got on, trying to remember the last time I'd ridden a merry-go-round.

"Ready?" Irv said.

"Ready," Layla shouted, turning around to grin at me. I felt myself smile back, even though nothing had even happened yet.

Mac and Irv got on opposite sides of the carousel and

began pushing. It turned slowly at first, with a fair amount of creaking, but within a minute or so we were moving at a good clip. As my horse rose, I could feel the wind in my hair; up ahead, Layla reared back, laughing. We moved quickly, then faster still, the night and woods big and wide all around us. It was one of those moments that, even while it was happening, I knew I would remember forever, even before the ring came into view and my grasp. I didn't reach for it, though; I didn't need to. I felt like I'd already won.

*   *   *

We could hear the music before the house even came into view. One moment, the only sound was our footsteps, crunching across the leaves. Then we heard instruments and a single, haunting voice.

Layla stopped just at the edge of the tree line, listening. "Rosie's singing. Wow. Wonder how they swung that."

Up ahead, the house was all lit up, and through the open back door I could see the living room was crowded with people. Meanwhile, the voice continued, high and sweet. I couldn't make out the words, but it still gave me chills.

"Okay," Mac said. "What's the plan here?"

Layla looked at Irv, who was carrying a now-asleep Eric on his back. Halfway through our return journey, he'd started to really stumble, then announced he needed to rest before lying down on a bed of pine needles. Apparently, like the verbosity, this was not an unusual occurrence, so Irv scooped him onto his back without comment and we carried on. Now, his face against Irv's sweatshirt, Eric looked almost sweet, like the miracle baby he'd once been.

"He can sleep it off," Layla said. "He'll come find us when he's up."

I followed her as she walked toward the shed they'd rehearsed in earlier, clearing some papers and a pair of drumsticks off a rumpled sofa there. Irv deposited Eric onto it, and she covered him with a sleeping bag. As she tucked it around him, he mumbled something in his sleep. The others were already heading to the house, so I was the only one who saw her smooth his forehead with her hand, lingering there as she shushed him.

The house wasn't just crowded: it was packed. We had to squeeze in, then apologize and avoid feet and elbows all the way to the kitchen, where there was more breathing room. Once there, I looked back to see Mrs. Chatham in her recliner, her husband on the couch, head ducked down, a banjo in his lap. He was flanked by two other men, also playing, and a redheaded woman sat in a nearby chair, a violin on her shoulder. But it was Rosie everyone was watching.

She was standing at the edge of the couch, wearing jeans and a tank top, sporting her trademark ponytail. Her eyes were closed. I didn't know the song she was singing, as I knew none of the ones I'd heard on the Seaside jukebox. But it was haunting, about a girl and a mountain and a memory, and it wasn't until it was over that I realized I'd been holding my breath.

"Wow," I said to Layla as everyone applauded. Rosie, her cheeks pink, gave a rare smile, then leaned against the wall, crossing her arms over her chest. "You weren't kidding. She's amazing."

"I know," she said. "She doesn't agree to sing much. But when she does, she blows me away."

Behind us, the guys were more focused on food, busy rifling through the cabinets. "I need something good," Irv said. "And a lot of it."

"Carrot sticks?" Mac said. "Vegetarian jerky?"

Irv, staring into a collection of spice jars, turned his head slowly, looking at him. "Are you serious right now? Do I *look* like a vegetarian to you?"

"How do vegetarians look?"

"Not like me." He shut the cabinet, then opened another one, revealing a box of Pop-Tarts. "Okay. *Now* we're talking."

"I want one!" Layla called out. "Let me see if we have any frosting to put on them."

Irv snapped his fingers, pointing at her. "I like the way you think."

Mac, over at the sink, sighed. I watched him open a smaller cabinet, up high. Taped inside was a handwritten sign: MAC'S FOOD. DO NOT EAT!

"As if anyone would want to," Layla, now eating strawberry frosting from a container with a spoon, said as she came over to stand beside me. Irv was at the toaster oven, laying out rows of Pop-Tarts on the rack inside. "We have mice, and *they* don't even touch what's up there."

Mac, ignoring this, pulled out a box of crackers, then walked to the fridge, where he dug around for a minute before producing some kind of spread. He got a knife and took a seat at the kitchen table just as the music began again. When Layla went over to consult with Irv about toaster settings, I slid into a seat opposite him. He angled the now-open box in my direction.

"You don't want that," Layla called out. "Trust me. Hold out for the tarts with frosting."

It seemed rude, however, to say no, so I reached in, pulling a cracker out. It was octagonal-shaped and dotted with seeds and grains. Mac watched me as I took a bite. It was so thick, my teeth barely cut through it. And dry. Very, very dry.

"Thanks," I said, managing to get half the word out before being overcome by a coughing fit. In response, Layla plunked a glass of water by my elbow. The girl thought of everything.

"They're better with hummus," Mac told me as I tried to catch my breath. It was like that one piece of cracker was clinging to my esophagus with a death grip. He pushed the spread toward me, the knife balanced on top. "Here."

I smiled, sucking down a sip of the water. Across the room, the toaster pinged. "Saved!" Irv said, opening the door. He reached in, immediately burning his fingers. "Shit, that's hot."

"You never learn, do you?" Layla grabbed a wooden spoon, then used it to pull the tarts out, piling them on a plate. "Grab the frosting. It's go time."

They settled at the table on either side of me. Layla tore off two paper towels, giving one to Irv, and then distributed a Pop-Tart to each of them, along with a healthy dollop of frosting. They each dipped, then toasted each other. I looked down at the remains of my cracker. Then, purely out of loyalty, I plunged it into the hummus.

It was better. Not good, mind you. But better. I only coughed a little. "What are these, again?" I asked Mac.

"Kwackers," he told me, turning the box so I could read the label. "They're sugar-free, low-carb, and fortified by additional Kwist Seeds, which are like soy, but healthier."

"Yum." Layla fixed me a paper towel plate and a tart, then pushed it toward me. "Don't be a martyr, Sydney. Even for Mac."

"Are those my Pop-Tarts?"

I looked up to see Rosie squeezing her way into the kitchen, two girls of her same build and size—one dark-haired, one white-blonde—following. The brunette had on leggings and a Mariposa sweatshirt, featuring the trademark pink butterfly character I remembered from the Saturday morning cartoons of my childhood. The blonde was in shorts and a crop top, displaying one of the most perfect sets of abs I'd ever seen.

"They didn't have your name on them," Layla replied. "But help yourself."

Rosie walked over and took one, holding it out to her friends. When both of them shook their heads, she tore off a piece and dunked it in Mac's hummus, then took a bite.

"Ugh," Irv said.

"It's actually not so bad," Layla told him.

"You've tried that?"

"Desperate times, desperate measures."

The brunette stepped out from behind Rosie, sticking her hand out to Mac. "I'm Lucy. And you are?"

"My brother," Rosie said flatly as they shook. "He's seventeen."

"I love seventeen," Lucy said, smiling.

"I'm Layla," Layla said, offering her own hand. "I'm sixteen."

Lucy shook, with visibly less enthusiasm. "Hi."

The girl with the abs, for whatever reason, was not introduced, nor were the rest of us. I reached over to the box of Kwackers Mac was holding to take another one, and he moved it closer to me. This time, I was well aware that Layla, and everyone else, was watching.

"So we're in your room tonight, just so you know," Rosie told Layla, dipping the other half of her Pop-Tart in the frosting.

"What?" Layla asked.

"Mom said it was okay," Rosie told her as the song wound down in the other room. There was a burst of laughter, some scattered applause.

"It's not her room. And I have Sydney here."

"You know I basically sleep in a closet. There's not enough space for all three of us."

"Where are we supposed to sleep?"

"The couch? I don't know."

"They'll be out here all night, though."

"Rosie!" Mr. Chatham called out from the living room. "Come back in here, gal, and sing us another one. For your dear old dad."

Mac sighed. Irv said, "How many beers has *he* had?"

"Not as many as he will." He got up, then held the box out to me one last time. I shook my head as Rosie turned, leaving the room with the blonde following. Lucy, however, lingered in the doorway, watching Mac as he reached up to put the Kwackers back in his cabinet. It was a stretch, and his shirt inched up, exposing his belt and a strip of his stomach. "You guys can take my room. I'll sleep on the couch."

"And he's a gentleman, too," Lucy said.

"Down, girl," Layla said. Lucy, either not hearing this or ignoring it, finally left. She was walking entirely too slowly, as far as I was concerned.

"Ugh," Layla said as Rosie began singing again. "Those Mariposa girls are all *so* gross, I swear. If all those little girls who buy tickets only knew."

"They're not all bad," Mac said, shutting the cabinet.

Layla rolled her eyes, but said nothing as Rosie's voice, which had been quiet at first, began to soar, filling the living room and then our ears. This song had a quicker pace, more of something you'd dance to. Mrs. Chatham, in her chair, was flushed and smiling, tapping her foot, as the woman playing the violin closed her eyes, the bow slashing back and forth across the strings. It seemed amazing to me that one night could hold so much, from a merry-go-round to a Pop-Tart with frosting to the most beautiful singing I'd ever heard. I thought of my own house, across town. Perched on a hill, all lights off except those in use, with just my parents and myself bumping around its large space.

Rosie's voice was rising now, the violin player going even

faster. Someone was stamping his feet, and my own cheeks felt hot. It was amazing to feel so at home in a place I'd only just come to. The night was not even close to over yet. Still, I could think of nothing but how I so very much did not want it to end.

＊ ＊ ＊

"Just so you know," Layla said, stretching a sheet across the bed, "this was *not* what I had in mind when I invited you over."

It was about two hours later, and we were in Mac's room. After listening to the music for a while, we'd gone out to the garage, where Layla had roused Eric, then made him walk a few laps around the house to sober up before Irv drove him home.

"It's been great," I told her.

"I don't know about *that*." She slid the pillow into a fresh case, then plumped it. "It's so typical that Rosie just takes over my room. She gets whatever she wants."

"I really don't mind sleeping on the couch," I said.

"No way. You are a guest. Mac will be fine there." She turned, picking up one of the two sleeping bags we'd brought in from the garage and shaking it out of its sack.

I sat down on the bed—Mac's bed, I realized belatedly, which made it feel different suddenly. As she spread a blanket over the sleeping bag, I looked around the room. It was small, with a twin bed and bureau, both made of the same well-worn yellow wood. Two car posters—one Audi, one BMW—were up on the wall, along with a map of what looked like Lakeview, dotted with pencil marks. On a metal desk, dinged with dents, there sat a computer, speakers, and a row of books, mostly about running and exercise. At the far end, there were several clock radios, all in different stages of disrepair: some were missing knobs, another the glass screen, and one had several springs poking out of it, as if it had exploded.

"He's kind of a mad scientist," Layla said. I looked at her, and she nodded at the desk. "Or maybe not mad. Just curious. He likes to see how things work."

"Where did he get all the radios?'

"Yard sales," she replied, plumping her pillow. "Thrift stores. The same places my mom gets all the stuff she collects. Get dragged along enough and you'll find something you're into. It's inevitable. With Mac, it's Frankenstuff."

"Frankenwhat?"

"That's my word for it," she explained. "He calls it improving on design. Like you can take anything and make it work better. You just have to figure out what it needs and add it on. See that clock?"

I looked where she was pointing, on the bedside table by my elbow. There sat a clock radio that, at first glance, I'd assumed was totally normal. Now that I looked more closely, though, I saw it had been retrofitted with a large circular lens that pointed straight upward, as well as a small keypad attached to the back. "Yeah," I said slowly.

"It was great, except it always reset itself, and he wanted to have it reflect the time on the ceiling. He had another one that did *that*, but never brightly enough to see. So he combined them, added a custom time-setting apparatus—"

"A what?"

"His words," she explained. "Anyway, that's the final result. Time always right and bright as hell overhead. I told you—he's a freak."

I looked back at the clock, taking in the careful, neat attachment of the keypad, how the projection lens looked like it belonged there. "He's good at it, though."

"I know. He should totally be an engineer or build airplanes or something," she replied. "Too bad he has a pizza future instead."

I blinked, surprised. "What do you mean?"

"Seaside." She adjusted the blanket, pulling it a bit to the right. "As far as my dad's concerned, Mac will take it over, just like Dad did from my grandpa. Don't need college to toss dough."

"So he won't go?"

"Doubt it." She looked over at the desk again, all those broken pieces. "It stinks, right? That's why I'm always telling him *I* should take over the business. I'm the logical choice, you know? Rosie will hopefully have her skating thing, and I'll be *thrilled* when school is over. But Mac's different. He's always been the smart one."

I thought of Mac, always with a textbook beside him at lunch, or while he—yes—tossed dough at Seaside. It seemed crazy to me that someone curious and driven enough to vastly improve on basic alarm clock design wouldn't have a chance to go to college and learn how to do it on a bigger, better scale. From the start, I'd known the Chathams were different from my family. But the proof just kept coming.

Outside in the living room, it was quiet: most of the guests had left. Layla's mom had gone to her room even earlier, about the same time Rosie and her Mariposa friends disappeared. Now I could only hear one person playing a banjo, the sound distant and plaintive.

"So, speaking of brothers . . . I read that article you sent," she said suddenly. "About that kid. I showed it to Mac, too."

I looked down at my hands, then said, "I was worried, sending it to you."

"You were?"

I nodded. "I thought you guys might judge."

"Why?"

"I don't know." I shrugged. "Everyone else did."

"Sydney." She said this in a way that made it clear I should look at her, so I did. "We're not like everyone else. Haven't you figured that out yet?"

I smiled. "I'm getting an idea."

"If it were me," she said, shifting on the sleeping bag, "I'd want to talk to that kid. Apologize."

"I do," I said, surprised she'd nailed it so quickly. "But it feels selfish. Like what good could it possibly do for him? My 'I'm sorry' won't bring back his legs."

"If it were a movie," Layla mulled, looking up at the ceiling, "you guys would become best friends, bond over some shared hobby, like, say, competitive eating, and you'd help him learn to walk again. Cue the happy ending."

I just looked at her. "Competitive eating?"

"I only just started thinking about this movie!" she said, and I laughed. "Cut me some slack."

We sat there for a second, the banjo outside still playing. I said, "It's not a movie, though. And there is no happy ending. Just . . . an ending, I guess."

Layla tucked a piece of hair behind her ear. "I hate when that happens," she said softly. "Don't you?"

Before I could answer, there was a light rapping noise on the door, and then Mac stuck his head in. "Mom's calling for you," he told Layla.

She immediately got to her feet. "Everything okay?"

Instead of answering, he opened the door wide and she slipped through, quickly turning down the hallway. In the living room, I could see Mr. Chatham was standing now, holding his banjo by the neck. His face was flushed, and when he saw me, I could tell for a second he had no idea who I was.

"You want some water?" Mac asked him, and he started, pulling his gaze from me.

"I can get it," Mr. Chatham told him. He put the banjo down slowly, then took a step back from the couch. Mac glanced at me, then eased the door shut.

It felt like I sat there a long time by myself. But that alarm clock beside me only marked two full minutes before Layla returned. "Just the woozies. Nothing to worry about."

"The woozies?"

She nodded, resuming her cross-legged position. "My mom's on a lot of meds. It takes, like, all of us to keep track of them and how often she takes them. Sometimes when she gets overtired or has too big a night, they make her dizzy and she wakes up confused. Sometimes she calls Rosie. But tonight it was me."

She'd left the door open behind her; the living room was empty, the coffee table cluttered with beer cans and food wrappers. "How long has she been sick?"

"Since I was in sixth grade." She laced her fingers together, examining her nails. "It wasn't so bad at first. She was still walking the same, bossy as ever, hitting every yard sale every Saturday morning. But it's a progressive disease. This last year has been really hard, and it's only going to get worse."

"There's not a cure?"

"Nope." She let her hands drop. "Drugs can do a lot, but eventually it will just break her body down to the point where she can't function. Hopefully not for a while, though."

I'd only known this family a short time, and it was a testament to the power of Mrs. Chatham's personality that I couldn't imagine them without her. Like my mom, she was that center of the wheel, with everyone connected drawing strength from her. She needed a saint of her own.

"I'm sorry," I said.

"Yeah," she replied, with the sad solidness of tone that came with the acceptance of an unpleasant fact. Even if it was just one word, you knew a million thoughts followed that were not said aloud. "Me too."

The house was quieting now. Layla went down to her room to change into pajamas and brush her teeth, pointing me to the small bathroom where I could do the same. When

I came out, there was no one around but Mac, at the coffee table with an open garbage bag, cleaning up.

"You need help?" I asked him.

"You don't have to," he replied.

I picked up some crumpled napkins and a couple of half-full plastic cups from a nearby end table anyway, sliding them into the bag. "Quite a party."

"It'll reek in the morning if I leave it like this," he replied, tossing in a handful of bottle caps. "Plus it'll feel like I slept in the recycling bin."

"Sticky."

"And stinky." He picked up a heap of blanket, exposing one of the dogs, who snapped at him. Unfazed, he scooped it up and put it on the floor, and it slunk under the couch, glaring at us.

"Sorry about taking over your room," I said to him.

"Not your fault." He grabbed a stack of wet napkins, making a face. "Rosie's always had a bit of an entitlement complex. Funny, *she* never ends up on the couch."

"I told Layla I can sleep out here," I told him. "I really don't mind."

"The dogs would eat you alive," he replied.

"What?"

He smiled at the look on my face. He had a nice smile. Seeing it, I felt like I'd won a prize, because he was so sparing with them. "I'm speaking metaphorically. Although their gas does feel deadly at times."

"Who's got gas?" Layla asked, returning from the bathroom.

"The dogs," I told her.

"Oh, God, no kidding." She shuddered. "Don't ever think of letting them under your covers. You'll dream you're suffocating. True story. You need another garbage bag?"

Mac nodded, and she padded off to the kitchen to get one. He and I kept cleaning in companionable silence until she returned, and then we all finished the job together. By the time Mac took the other sleeping bag and pillow out to the couch and we turned out the light, it was after one a.m.

Layla insisted I sleep in the bed, even though I told her I was fine on the floor. I knew she was just being a good host. Still, knowing that this was where Mac slept was both weird and thrilling. God, I was such a nerd.

Once the lights were out, she fidgeted around, getting comfortable. "I'm a thrasher," she'd explained to me at my house before beginning these same adjustments. "But once I'm out, I am *out*. If you need me for anything, kick me. Hard. Okay?"

"Will do," I'd said. In contrast, I was lying very still, my hands crossed over my chest. I tried to picture Mac in this same place each night, looking at this same ceiling, where his hybrid alarm clock was projecting the current time very brightly onto the ceiling above us: 1:22 a.m.

"God, I *hate* that thing," Layla said. By her voice, I was guessing she was already drifting off. "The last thing I want to be reminded of every single time I wake up is how much longer I have to sleep."

"Tomorrow's Sunday, though," I pointed out.

"Yeah, but I take care of my mom in the mornings." She

yawned outright. "So I'm always up at six, when she is."

"Oh. Right."

A silence. Then she said, in a flat monotone, "One twenty-three a.m. Get to sleep, you loser. You're already going to feel terrible tomorrow."

I laughed, and she moved around a bit more, then told me good night. Moments afterward—but really, three minutes, at 1:26—I heard her breathing go deep and steady.

I, however, felt very awake. So at one forty-five, when someone started talking out in the living room, I heard it right away.

It was a girl's voice first. I could tell by the tone, although I wasn't able to make out what she was saying. Then, after a pause, a lower timbre. I rolled over, looking down at Layla, who was sound asleep, knees pulled to her chest.

At 1:50, things had gone quiet, and I was suddenly aware that I really, truly had to pee. It was always weird to navigate someone else's house, especially at such a late hour. By 1:59, I knew I didn't have a choice. I slid out of bed, stepping carefully over Layla, and walked to the door, turning the knob as quietly as possible.

The first thing I saw was Lucy, Rosie's Mariposa friend, sitting on the couch. She was in a tank top and pajama shorts, her hair loose over her shoulders. Mac was beside her, his eyes on the TV, which was showing an infomercial I'd actually seen before, for a product that cut fruit into fun and jazzy shapes. By the intense, focused way he was watching it, though, you would have thought it was breaking news.

They both turned toward me as I stepped out into the hallway. Mac said, "Everything okay?"

"Yeah. Just, um . . ." I nodded to the bathroom, then started toward it, feeling hopelessly awkward. As I shut the door behind me, I heard Lucy say something, then laugh. There was no way of knowing if it had anything to do with me, but still, I felt my face flush.

I did my business, washed my hands, and ran a hand through my hair, which, considering I'd not yet slept, was sporting a serious case of bedhead. Then I opened the door as loudly as I could, announcing myself. I wanted them to know I was coming.

The infomercial was still on—"BUT THERE'S MORE!"— and Mac continued to give it his full attention. Lucy, however, had moved closer to him, and was now resting her head on his shoulder. This time, she didn't look at me.

"Good night," I said to Mac, then pushed the bedroom door open. I was just about to slip inside when he spoke.

"Is that bothering you?"

I turned around. "What?"

"The clock," he said, nodding toward the room. "It's kind of bright. I can turn it off, if you want."

Lucy shifted, pressing herself against him. On the TV, a woman was entirely too excited about the prospect of making star-shaped watermelon pieces. I looked at Mac, who was holding my gaze in such a way that I knew, somehow, I should say yes.

"Actually," I told him, "I was kind of wondering how to—"

Before I could even finish, he was on his feet, startling Lucy, who now did turn, clearly irritated. I stepped back as Mac came into the bedroom. Then, with her still watching me, I slowly shut the door.

It felt very dark, and I stood still for a moment, letting my eyes adjust. Mac, however, walked right over to sit on the bed, pulling the clock toward him. As he hit a button, turning off the projected time, he said, "Thanks. For the save."

"She's pretty . . ." I trailed off, not sure what adjective I was going for. "Intense."

"That's one word for it." He put the clock back down, then got to his feet. "You have everything you need?"

"Yeah," I said. "Thanks."

He nodded, stepping carefully over Layla, who was now snoring slightly. As he put his hand on the knob, I heard myself say, "You can stay, if you want. Until she goes to bed. It is your room, after all. I'm fine on the floor."

I realized, too late, how this might sound: now I was the girl making the strong move. When Mac turned, though, he looked relieved. "I'll take the floor."

As he grabbed a blanket from the closet and spread it out on the carpet, I got back into the bed, pulling up the covers. With Layla smack in the middle of the room, there was no real space other than parallel to where I was. Still, he left as big a gap as he could, even though it meant basically resting his head against the desk.

"You want this pillow?" I asked him as he shifted, trying to get some headroom.

"No, you keep it."

"I don't need it. And you are on the floor."

"I'm fine." He shifted again, and I heard a clunk. "Ouch."

I snorted, and then laughed outright.

"Oh, that's nice," he said. "Mock my pain."

"I'm trying to give you your pillow."

"I don't need it." Another clunk. "Crap."

I sat up, grabbing his pillow and launching it at him. It hit him right in the face. Whoops. "Sorry," I said. "I—"

Before I could finish, it was coming right at me, at twice the speed I'd thrown it. I ducked, and it bounced off the wall, hitting the clock, which immediately projected the time back on the ceiling, bright as day.

"See what you did?" he said.

"It's two fifteen a.m.," I replied, launching it back at his head. "Time to take your pillow."

Suddenly, there was a soft knock on the door, and we both went silent. A moment later, it opened, a slant of light spilling in. "Mac?" a voice said. Lucy. "Hello?"

I closed my eyes. For a moment, all I could hear was Layla breathing. Then the door shut with a click.

Still, we were silent for a full two minutes, according to the clock. I was beginning to think that maybe he was asleep, somehow, when the pillow hit me square in the face.

"I'm not throwing it back," I whispered. "You've officially forfeited it now."

"I never wanted it in the first place."

"Just go to sleep before she comes back," I told him.

"You're the one talking."

I felt myself smile widely in the dark. It was 2:22 a.m. "Good night, Mac."

"Good night, Sydney. Sleep well."

This, however, seemed impossible at that moment, with him only an arm's length or so away. So I was surprised when I jerked awake at 4:32 from a deep, thick dream, the details of which disappeared the moment I opened my eyes. I blinked, then rolled over, taking in Layla, still curled up, and then Mac, who'd shifted away from the desk and now lay on his side, one hand stretched in my direction. He was sound asleep, I knew, and not at all aware of this. What you do in your dreams is never your choice. But it made me happy anyway.

CHAPTER
13
~⤳⤶~

I THOUGHT I'd dodged the bullet of Family Day at Lincoln. A couple of weeks later, however, another issue arose. Just my luck.

"I have *great* news," my mother announced at dinner one evening. Suddenly, it all made sense: the way she'd been humming to herself while she set the table, the extra cheerful manner in which she questioned me about my day at school. "We're going to get to see Peyton. All of us, together."

"Really?" my dad said.

She nodded. Clearly, she wanted to draw this out: it was that good. "I got a call today. He's finished his first course, and there's going to be a graduation ceremony, with all family invited."

From the way she said it, so proud, you would have thought he was getting an Ivy League diploma, not a certificate from a prison program that was, in fact, mandatory. But that was my mom. When it came to Peyton, all she needed was a glimmer of good to extrapolate to outstanding.

"This is the civics course?" my dad asked, helping himself to more bread.

"Civics and Law." She took a sip of her wine. "It's such a great thing. He's really learned a lot, and now that he's done, he can pick other classes. There's quite a variety, actually. Michelle says Lincoln is good that way. The warden really believes in the importance of on-site learning."

"When is this happening?" my dad asked.

"The end of November," she replied. "I'm thinking we'll drive up the night before and stay at that hotel that's right nearby. That way we won't have to leave at the crack of dawn."

"But I have school," I said automatically.

For the first time all day, my mother's cheeriness waned. "You can miss one day. This is important, Sydney."

End of discussion. My father glanced at me, as if maybe he might speak up, but then returned to eating. And so the countdown began.

Plans were made, two hotel rooms booked. One for me and my mom, and one for my dad and Ames, who was of course coming along. My mother, in her networking mode, reached out to some other Lincoln families with "graduates" (as she insisted on calling them) to coordinate a potluck of desserts and coffee for after the ceremony. Just like that, she was back in her comfort zone. She was so busy, in fact, that she hardly noticed that I was spending just about every afternoon at Seaside. Which was fine with me.

"So it's a class he took?" Layla asked me as we sat doing homework there one day. "I didn't know there was school in prison. Seems like being locked up would be punishment enough."

Unlike Jenn and Meredith, with whom I'd always shared a drive to succeed academically, Layla basically spent the school day counting down to the final bell. Even homework made her uncharacteristically grumpy, and she usually needed two or three YumYums to get it done.

"It's a class everyone there has to take, about the law." I flipped a page in my calculus book. "I guess to remind you not to break it?"

"I thought that's what the whole being-behind-bars thing was for." She put her lollipop in her mouth, then took it out. "Actually, though, I can see the point. If going to school was the only activity I was allowed, I'd probably love it."

I raised an eyebrow at her. We'd been sitting there a full hour, and all she'd done was doodle her name and some hearts on the page in front of her.

"Okay, maybe not." She sighed. "I think it's time for a break. Want to hit SuperThrift?"

"Layla."

"Fifteen minutes."

"No."

"Ten. I swear I'll go when you tell me to." I looked at her, making my doubt clear. "I will! Come on."

Against my better judgment, I packed up my books, then stored my backpack behind the counter, where Mac was prepping vegetables, his chem textbook propped up against the counter in front of him.

"Where are you two going?" he asked.

"Nowhere," Layla replied.

"SuperThrift," I said at the same time.

He shook his head, then looked at me. "She won't leave when you want her to, even if she says otherwise."

"We'll be back in ten minutes," Layla sang out over him. I sighed, then followed her out the door.

SuperThrift was housed in a small, nondescript building just around the corner from Seaside. I'd driven past it a million times in my life and never given it a second look, as my family didn't do much secondhand shopping. We donated—my mom was forever picking through my closet, a bag in hand, demanding if I'd worn this or that in the last year—but more to Goodwill or other charities. SuperThrift was a business.

The first thing you smelled when you walked in was a strong, pungent cranberry air freshener. It was like a wall of scent, stretched across the entrance area. Once you passed through it, you realized why: the next thing you breathed in was mothballs and mildew.

"I love the smell of bargains in the afternoon," Layla said. This transition always made my nose itch, but it seemed to energize her: I had to quicken my step to keep up. "Ooh! Look at this!"

The first time I saw the racks of clothes stretching all the way to the back wall, I just felt tired. There was just so much, and arranged in a way that it was work to browse through it, with no set categories or sections. You'd see a thick winter coat, smashed up against a cheap rayon shirt with shoulder pads, bracketed by two hideous prom dresses. And that was just one inch of what was there.

Layla, however, had a gift. Somehow, she was able to spot the good stuff, as haphazardly as it might have been presented. I'd still be bogged down trying to get past a pair of extra-long men's tweed trousers from circa 1950, but she'd already have found a cropped leather jacket and a white dress shirt that only needed a good ironing to look like something my friends at Perkins would wear.

"It's just practice," she explained to me the first time I complained about this. "My mom is a serious bargain hunter. We used to hit this place, all the other thrift shops, *and* yard sales every weekend. She always says you have to look and move fast. Do it enough and it becomes second nature. Like Mac with his clocks."

I hadn't realized, when we first met, how much of Layla's stuff was secondhand. It was only when Rosie and her friends finally relinquished her room the morning after I stayed over that I got my first glimpse of her closet. While a small space, it was packed, as well as meticulously organized. When she saw me notice, it became clear it was a source of pride.

"These," she said during the ensuing tour, as she pulled out a pair of jeans folded neatly over a hanger, "I found at Thrift World. They're Courtney Amandas! Barely worn, and all I had to do was hem them. That was a good day."

I soon realized that all of Layla's clothes had a similar origin story. I couldn't remember where I'd even gotten the shirt I had on, but she knew the background of every single thing she owned. It made me ashamed, even more than the fact I didn't own anything I hadn't gotten brand-new. But

Layla didn't seem bothered at all by the differences between us. It was just . . . well, how it was. One more way I aspired to be like her.

Whenever we were at SuperThrift, Layla always pulled stuff for me as well as herself. I'd still be trying to get past a slew of housecoats in various patterns, holding back the inevitable sneeze, when she'd appear beside me and toss a vintage dress, a barely worn pair of boots my size, or a cashmere sweater "just my color" at me before disappearing again. After the first couple of trips, I'd stopped looking for myself altogether and just killed time wandering around, knowing if there were things that were right for me, she'd find them.

Today, this was a pair of black capri pants and a shoulder bag made from a feed sack, both of which she brought to me just after we arrived. "Six minutes," I reminded her. She acted like she didn't hear me.

By now, my nose was running. After digging for a tissue, I wandered to the back of the store. The shoes, unlike the clothes, were arranged by gender and size, although who did this it was hard to say. I'd never seen anyone actually working at SuperThrift, other than the women who, when you rang the ASSISTANCE button at the register, emerged from a glass-walled back room where they were watching TV. Even then, they acted like their true job was to show how much they disliked having to help you.

Kids' and ladies' shoes were on the left, and men's were on the right (there were fewer of them, and a lot of bowling shoes, for some reason). Then there was a final section that simply said ETC. Today, it was filled with galoshes.

That was the thing about SuperThrift. Usually, Layla had explained to me, its inventory was made up of donations, castoffs from yard sales, and things other secondhand stores couldn't get rid of. Occasionally, though, they were given collections, either from places going out of business or estates of people who had passed. This explained why, on one of my first visits, there had been an entire rack of old big-and-tall three-piece suits in varying patterns and colors. It was also probably the reason a box of unworn gas station coveralls, unused, appeared one day.

The galoshes, however, were harder to figure out. They were in bright colors and children's sizes: small, and green, yellow, red, and polka-dotted. Clearly they'd been worn (I saw fade marks and scuffs), but who had *that* many kids? I'd counted at least ten pairs and was still going when I heard a voice behind me.

"Man," it said. "That's a lot of boots, huh?"

If you had asked me, as I faced the SuperThrift footwear collection, who I would see when I turned around, the last person who would have come to mind was David Ibarra. And yet there he was, in jeans and a red sweatshirt, in his wheelchair. Smiling at me.

I went deaf for a second. Then I stood there, staring at him openmouthed. All those months of studying his face, absorbing every detail I could get about him, and now here he was, real and in the flesh. It seemed like he should know who I was, my association with my brother like a pervasive smell, warning him away.

"Man. What's with all the boots?"

It was Layla, now coming toward me, her arms full of clothes. She peered at the boots, then looked at David Ibarra. Immediately, her own eyes widened. She'd read that article; never forget a face.

"That's what I was saying," he said, moving the controller on his wheelchair so he could get closer to the bin. "Guess it means there's a bunch of kids out there who are gonna have wet feet next time it rains."

"When I see stuff like this here," Layla said slowly, glancing at me, "I want to buy it just *for* the story."

"Not me," he replied, backing up again. "Just because someone gave up all those bathrobes behind us doesn't mean I necessarily want to know why."

"Brother?" I heard a voice say from behind a rack of dresses. "Where are you?"

"Coming," he replied, turning himself around. I still hadn't said a word; I couldn't. But maybe he was used to people staring at him, mute, because he just gave us a friendly wave and then drove off.

"Hey," Layla said, dropping her stuff on the floor and coming over to me. "Sydney. You look sick."

"That . . . He was—"

She put a hand on my shoulder. "I know. Seriously, take a breath. You're scaring me."

I did as I was told, sucking in that awful smell. Distantly, I could hear a whirring noise as David Ibarra and whoever he was with made their way up to the front of the store. After a moment, Layla stepped away from me, leaning into the aisle to look at them. I made her swear on her mom, twice, that they were gone not just from the store but the parking lot as well before I would move.

When I finally got outside, I leaned against the glass window, closing my eyes. Layla paid for her stuff, and then we walked back to Seaside, where we settled into our booth and continued our homework. This time, though, Layla was the only one who got anything done. I just sat there, my textbook open in front of me. Whenever I tried to focus, I saw not the words or even David Ibarra's face. Instead, it was that rainbow of galoshes, mismatched and displaced.

It wasn't until I was leaving and Layla handed me a bag that I realized that not only had I dropped the stuff she'd picked out for me at SuperThrift, but she'd collected it, adding it to her own purchases. I didn't want to be rude, so I took the things, pushing them deep into my closet once I was home. I knew my mom, in her donating mode, would eventually find them and ask if they were important. I'd have to tell her yes. Like so much else, even if I wanted to be rid of them, they were now with me for good.

❧ ❧ ❧

For obvious reasons, I was not in the mood to shop in the week that followed. Layla, however, had her eye on some stuff at her favorite consignment store. Which meant she also had a plan.

"Girls delivering pizzas in pairs," she announced to her dad one afternoon. She'd asked him to take a seat so she could present what she'd referred to as "an important business proposal." "Just picture it: a market niche. We'll establish a specific, visual brand of customer service."

I raised my eyebrows. She'd recently found a how-to book on small-business marketing at the annual library sale. Despite her dislike of school, she'd devour any instruction manual or romance novel in hours.

"Bad idea," said Mac, who had not been invited to the table but was listening, as always.

"Nobody asked you," Layla told him.

"Doesn't matter. It's not safe," he replied. "You'll be walking up to people's houses, strange apartments . . ."

"But Sydney and I will be together," she told him. I blinked—I had not realized I was involved. "And we'll leave you the runs to sketchy neighborhoods."

"What if *all* the calls are from bad neighborhoods?"

"Then we probably need to rethink our marketing, wouldn't you say?" She turned back to her dad. "You said yourself deliveries are up, especially on the weekends with game days. We can help. Keep it in the family. And I need to start getting more experience here at the shop if I'm going to do it full-time after I graduate."

Hearing this, Mac looked up. "Nobody's talking about that happening, as far as I know."

"Which is exactly why we *should* be," Layla replied without missing a beat. "It's pretty sexist to just assume a girl can't move into a leadership position, don't you think?"

"Leadership?" Mr. Chatham said. "I thought we were talking about delivering pizzas."

"We were talking about the business." Layla sighed. "The bottom line is, you need more delivery help. I need hands-on experience. It's a win-win."

Mr. Chatham rubbed a hand over his face. He hadn't said no yet, but he was clearly a ways from agreeing. "If I were to consider the delivery thing—"

"You shouldn't," Mac said.

"—there would have to be some rules, for sure."

Layla, sensing victory anyway, shot me a grin. "Like I said, we'd always be together. And we'd both go up to the door, every time."

Her dad mulled this over as Mac, shaking his head, spread some sauce on an empty crust. "I could see offices," Mr. Chatham said finally. "And maybe *some* residential areas on weekends, during the daytime. But not evenings, and no apartment complexes."

"Oh, Daddy, that's great! Thank you!"

"But," he said loudly, holding up a hand, "Mac trains you first, and we have a trial run on Saturday, during the game, with no promise of a commitment on my part. Understood?"

"Yes," Layla told him solidly. Then she kicked me under the table so I'd say it, too.

And so it was decided. Our training happened two days later, on Thursday evening. I told my mom I was going over to Jenn's, assuming she might not be thrilled to know I was taking on a job, much less this one. I'd really only agreed for Layla's sake, so I was surprised to discover how much I enjoyed it.

I couldn't say why, exactly. We *were* with Mac: there was

nothing not to like about that, at least for me. Since the night I'd stayed over, we'd definitely been more friendly with each other, although I could sense he felt it important to keep our distance when we were around Layla. I had not forgotten the way she'd talked so angrily about Kimmie Crandall dating, then dumping him. I didn't want to break any rules, although it was difficult when you weren't certain what they were.

It wasn't just Mac, though. As he went over the various rules and procedures in substantial detail, Layla—despite her leadership aspirations—got bored immediately. I, however, was intrigued by the whole idea of the delivery business. There was something about going up to strangers' houses, getting a glimpse of another place and the lives within it, that appealed to me. Maybe it was because I felt that for so long, people had been outside my family, peering in. It was nice, for once, to be on the other end of things.

At our first stop, the guy answered the door in his bathrobe. It was dark in the living room behind him, the only light coming from two TVs set to the same channel and a row of laptops lined up on the coffee table. He squinted at us and the light like a mole, as if it hurt him, before paying and taking the pie wordlessly, then shutting the door in our faces.

At the next stop, we interrupted a teenage Bible study and were greeted at the door by a beaming girl with braces, who invited us in for a slice and some testimony. Even though we declined, she tipped generously. Jesus would have approved.

Then it was on to the Walker Hotel, where we sat out

front with three large pies until the guest who'd made the order came down to retrieve them. (Mac explained that, because of its own room-service business, the Walker frowned on deliveries to the rooms themselves.) While we waited, he joked around with the red-shirted valets who were hanging around a key cabinet, shooting the breeze.

In just an hour, we'd seen all these little pieces of various lives, like a collage of Lakeview itself. Layla, still bored, spent most of the time on her phone, although she perked up at the hotel because the valets were cute. But when it was eight o'clock and she had to get back to help with Mrs. Chatham, I sort of wished I could stick around.

Mac must have put a good spin on this experience, because we were allowed to go ahead with our trial run that weekend. On Saturday, just after eleven thirty a.m., Layla and I stood in the parking lot, waiting for him to bring out a magnetic sign for my car from the office. Ten minutes later, he still had not emerged.

"I swear, it's like he'll do anything to keep me from cutting into his tip profits," Layla complained, adjusting her outfit— SEASIDE T-shirt, jeans, black motorcycle boots—for the umpteenth time. Thanks to her small-business book, she'd emphasized the importance of our "brand look." As I did not have any motorcycle boots, I was wearing a pair of Rosie's, which were easily a size too small. My brand, apparently, involved limping. "I'm trying to help him out in the long run, too, as far as college goes. You'd think he'd be happy to share the wealth."

"I think it's more of a protective thing," I told her. "He's worried about you."

"Well, he shouldn't be. It's delivering pizza, not going into warfare."

I laughed, but once Mac had arrived, I kind of had to wonder if she wasn't sort of right. First, he repeated what he'd already told us about handling the money and keeping the car locked even if you were only out of it for a second. Then he moved on to the importance of stepping far enough back from the door after knocking that no one could touch you when it opened. He was just segueing into a few cautionary tales from his own experience to emphasize these points when Layla looked at her wrist and said, "Can we start now?"

He made a face at her. "You're not wearing a watch."

"True. But if I were, it would say you've been talking too long." She turned on her heel, starting back to Seaside. "I'm going to get our first order, Sydney. Warm up the car!"

We both watched her go, her steps light. She was more excited than she'd been at any point during the training. "Don't let her go to a door alone even if she insists she's fine," he said as she disappeared inside. "And if she starts talking too much to customers, cut her off. Get the money, give the pie, and go. Should take no more than five minutes."

"Right," I said, again feeling like I was being prepped to infiltrate enemy lines.

"And only take the cash you'll need to the door with you. If you have to make change, turn your back."

"Got it."

"If you're ever in doubt or feel weird, just leave the pizza. It's not worth it."

I nodded just as Layla emerged from Seaside's door, carrying a warmer in her hands. She was beaming as she approached. "It's our maiden voyage! And in your neighborhood, Sydney."

"Really?" She held out the slip: sure enough, it was an Arbors address, although not one I recognized.

"We need to be careful, though," she said, shooting Mac a serious look. "You know how dangerous those rich people can be."

"Ha-ha," he said as she opened the back door, putting the pizza on the floor as he'd taught us. (There was less risk there of cheese slide, apparently a cardinal sin in the delivery business.) Then, to me, he said, "Drive safe."

"I will."

The ride over was uneventful, marked mostly by Layla making grand plans for what we would do with all our tip money once it started rolling in. By the time we pulled up to a large Colonial in my neighborhood, she'd spent more than I figured we'd ever make, unless we planned to do this into our thirties. Little did I know that as soon as the door opened, our new endeavor would pretty much be over before it even began.

"Pizza's here!" a voice called, and then there were footsteps, followed by the sound of a lock flipping. We both stepped back—Mac would have been proud—as the door opened, revealing a guy about our age, blond, with blue eyes and broad shoulders, wearing a U football jersey. When he saw us, he smiled.

"Do you need me to come pay?" a woman's voice, older, called from down the hallway behind him.

"No, I've got it," he replied, then stepped outside, shutting the door behind him. I took another step back, but Layla stayed where she was.

"Extra large half cheese, half ham-pineapple," I said. "That's fifteen-oh-nine with tax." ("Recite the order and price first thing, even if they've already paid over the phone. It's like a verbal contract they can't renege on, plus they'll know how much they should tip.")

Although I'd spoken, it was Layla he was looking at as he pulled out some bills. "How much for the delivery?"

"For you, it's free," she told him.

"It's my lucky day, then," he said, peeling off a twenty and handing it to her. "Keep the change."

"Thank you!" she said cheerfully, pocketing it as I opened the warmer and handed him the pie. "I hope you enjoy your lunch."

"I would, if it meant you weren't leaving," he told her.

"Duty calls," she replied. But I was pretty sure I saw her blush. "Pies to deliver, money to make."

I turned around, hoping to give the signal that she should do the same. But of course, she was lingering, following me down one step but not the next.

"If I were to order another," he said, his hand now on the knob, "would you deliver it?"

"Maybe." She tucked a piece of hair behind her ear. "Or it might be my big brother."

"Fifty-fifty chance?" He smiled. "I'll take those odds."

To this, Layla said nothing, instead just following me back to the car. Once safely inside, engine on, I said, "You do realize you just broke, like, every one of Mac's rules."

"Do you know him?" she replied. "Like, from the neighborhood?"

"No," I said flatly. He was still on the steps, watching us, as if he thought maybe she might get out of the car. I backed out of the driveway, quick. "Never seen him in my life."

When we got back to Seaside, another order had been placed from the same address. So we doubled back across town, this time with Layla primping the entire way. More flirting ensued and another five was tipped, while I stood by feeling awkward, to say the least. This time, when we returned, Mac was waiting, the warmer in hand.

"Same address?" he asked. "Three pizzas?"

"They're *very* hungry," she said, reaching for it.

He pulled it back, out of her reach. "We're running a restaurant here, not a dating service."

"It's an order, and I'm a professional. It needs to be delivered!"

He just looked at her. "Then I'll do it. You're done for the day."

"Mac," she protested, but I could tell he wasn't budging. "We'll see what Dad says."

With that, she went inside. Mac said, "At least tell me the guy is her age."

"He is," I told him. I glanced at my watch. "You know, I can deliver that on my way home. Save you a trip."

"No," he said.

"It's my neighborhood," I said. "And he's already had two chances to kill us, if that's what he really wanted."

He raised his eyebrows. "That's how you're selling it? Really?"

"Just give me the pizza."

After hesitating another moment, he pulled a pen from his back pocket, then scribbled something on the back of the ticket. "My number," he said. "You text when you're leaving. Got it?"

"Got it."

He handed me the warmer and watched as I put it on the floor in the backseat. Then I went in to say good-bye to Layla, who was pouting at a table, a strawberry YumYum in her mouth. She cheered up a bit when I handed over her half of the tips.

"We'll really hit it hard next time," I told her. "Big money."

"Yeah, yeah," she said, waving her lollipop at me. "Whatever."

Back in the Arbors, I rang the bell, then waited for the door to open. When it did, it was the same guy, although he'd changed his shirt into a nicer button-down and put on shoes. When he saw me, he made no effort to hide his disappointment.

"Fifteen-oh-nine with tax," I said, keeping my voice cheerful anyway. "Thanks for your business."

He glanced at me, then pulled yet another twenty from

his pocket. "Your friend," he said. "What's her name?"

I shook my head. "I can't."

He thought for a minute. "Okay. But if she wonders if I was asking about her"—he scribbled a number on the flap of the box, a name beneath it, then ripped it off—"give her this."

I didn't agree or say no outright. I just took it and went back to my car, where I texted Mac.

Leaving now, I told him. Alive and well.

I was pulling up to my own house when he replied. She wants to know if he asked for her number.

I thought for a second, trying to figure out where my loyalties lay in this situation. Then I typed No, which was not a lie. And waited. My phone beeped. This time, it was Layla.

Did he give you his for me?

I smiled. As tricky as I thought I was, she was again one step ahead. If I had to be behind, though, there was no one else I'd rather follow.

Yes.

A beep. A row of smiley faces filled my screen, then another. But it was Mac's text I was focused on as I cut my engine. ADD TO CONTACTS? my phone was asking, as it did whenever an unknown number came in. It felt like a leap of faith, or even an assumption. But as I typed in his name and hit SAVE, I looked back at those rows of faces and smiled, too.

CHAPTER
14

⤳ ⤶

HIS NAME was Mason Albert Spencer, but everyone called him Spence. He'd just moved to Lakeview and went to W. Hunt Academy, the military school just outside town. When he officially became Layla's boyfriend, everything began to change.

Well, not everything. We still hung out at lunch every day, as well as at Seaside after school. Spence had a packed extracurricular schedule in the afternoon, so he could only see Layla on weekends, and even then he had a tight curfew. At first, I'd just assumed he was like so many other kids in the Arbors, where the number of activities you participated in reflected the money available to do them. And Spence's stepfather, a plastic surgeon, could afford just about anything. Pretty soon, though, I began to recognize certain aspects of Spence that gave me pause. I didn't want to say anything to Layla, though. She was just so happy.

"He's just the *sweetest*," she told me one day as we sat in our customary booth, only crusts left of our pizza slices between us. Her phone, which had always been close at hand, was now our permanent third. She checked it constantly, hopeful for even the smallest missive. "I mean, he's, like, chivalrous. Who's like that? And did I tell you the way he eats his French fries?"

She had: with mustard, using a knife and fork. Based on that alone, they were clearly meant for each other. Unfortunately, there were other facts, too.

Like that W. Hunt was his third school in three years. He'd ended up there only after leaving two separate boarding schools. He told Layla that things "just hadn't worked out," but it sounded a bit too much like Peyton's history for my comfort. Plus, he volunteered several hours a week—at the senior center, an animal shelter, and a local after-school program—more than even Jenn, the most altruistic person I knew. Sure, maybe he had a big heart and wanted to give back. But I knew mandatory community service when I saw it.

And then there was his charm. I'd seen a glimpse of it that first day on his doorstep, but the second time we crossed paths, when he met us at Frazier Bakery one afternoon, it was in full force. Anyone else seeing him arrive wearing a big smile and carrying flowers would have probably been just as tickled as Layla was. But I knew what that mix of confidence and entitlement looked like.

"You," she said as he slid in beside her, handing over the flowers with a flourish, "are crazy."

"Crazy for you," he replied, then leaned in, giving her a kiss on the lips. When they separated—about two beats longer than I was comfortable with—he turned his attention to me. "Sydney. Hey."

"Hi," I said.

This courtesy done, he turned back to Layla, who flushed happily. It had been her idea to pick Frazier and not Seaside, as she maintained that both her dad and Mac hated everyone she dated on sight. I seemed to remember Mac saying this was not true of her last boyfriend, even if Mr. Chatham hadn't wanted to admit it. This was just a small detail. But the secrecy didn't help with my suspicion.

It soon became clear that Spence felt about as enthusiastic about me. At first, he seemed fine that I was always tagging along to their various meetings. After a couple of weeks, though, I could tell that the little time they did get between his busy schedule and the fact that Layla was always working they wanted to spend alone. Maybe I should have taken this hint and left them to do just that. Instead, I made her spell it out for me.

"It's just," she said one day at lunch, while Eric, Mac, and Irv were having yet another loud debate about possible band names, "Spence really likes you. I mean, he thinks you're so funny and smart. Because, you know, you are."

I raised an eyebrow. This kind of kiss-up always led to a rug being yanked out from beneath you.

"But," she continued, looking down at her hands, "we both want to, you know, have a chance to get to know each other. Alone."

I glanced at Mac, but he was eating a handful of sunflower seeds, listening to Eric defend the name Cro-Magnon as a reference to the "evolutionary" nature of the band's direction. "How are you going to do that, though?"

"Well." She cleared her throat. "If I went home with you once in a while . . ."

"You want to hook up at my house?" I asked.

"No!" Now she looked at the boys, then lowered her voice even further. "He could meet me there, get me. And then I could come back. Later."

"You want me to lie to Mac, too?"

"Sydney, it's not lying." I gave her a look. "It's not! I'll be at your house. Just . . . not the entire time."

I knew I should say no: this sort of thing never ended well. But it was Layla asking, and she'd done so much for me. So I agreed.

The first time, everything went according to plan. We went to my house after school, where my mom immediately fell back into her snack-and-school-day-summary mode. When she went to the War Room to do some stuff for the Lincoln graduation, we took a walk, ostensibly to the convenience store just outside the neighborhood for Slurpees. Two blocks from my house, Spence was waiting.

"We meet in one hour," I told her as she climbed happily into the passenger seat of his huge Chevy Suburban. "Right here. Yes?"

"Yes!" she said. He already had his hand on her knee. "Thank you!"

And they had showed up right on time, parting with a kiss so long, I had to distract myself by studying the topiary in a nearby yard. As we walked the two blocks back, she was happier than I'd ever seen her. That was enough to make me feel like whatever this was we were doing couldn't be all bad.

We tried again the following week, with these same steps. This time, though, two things happened: Layla was late, and Mac showed up unexpectedly.

I was sitting on the curb when I saw him coming. At first, I felt the same burst of nervousness and happiness that I always did in his presence. The latter waned, then disappeared altogether, when I realized not only that his sister was nowhere in sight or nearby, but that I didn't even know where she was.

It was too late to try to dodge him. So I just sat there as he pulled up beside me. He had on a blue long-sleeve T-shirt, and as he leaned out the window, looking at me, his Saint Bathilde pendant slid down the chain into view. Every time I saw it, I tried to imagine his neck so thick it was tight there. I still hadn't been able to.

"Hey," he said. "What are you doing?"

This was a fair question. Unfortunately, I did not have an answer. "Um, just sitting," I said. "Waiting."

"For?"

He didn't say this in an accusing way. His voice was not pointed nor his tone suspicious. But I caved, immediately and totally, anyway. "Layla."

Somehow, he did not look surprised to hear this. He cut the engine, then sat back. "She's with that guy, huh? The three-pizza eater."

Now I was taken aback. "You know about him?"

He just looked at me. "Sydney, please. You guys are not that stealth."

"Hey!" I protested.

"What, you want to be a good liar?"

He had a point. "She does seem to really like him."

"She must, if she's leaving you sitting here alone." I looked down at my hands, not sure what to say to this. "I've got to run a delivery. Want to come?"

"Really?" I asked.

In response, he cranked the engine, then reached over, clearing a spot on the seat next to him. I walked around, pulling open the door, and got in.

Mac showed up, I texted Layla as he turned around and we headed out of the neighborhood.

A moment later, she responded. Shit.

We're doing a delivery, I typed. Same spot in 20?

OK. Then, just as I was about to put my phone away, one more message. Sorry.

I wasn't. In fact, as Mac and I pulled out of the Arbors, I was happier than I'd been in a while. And, weirdly enough, not nervous. As if where I was—riding beside him in the dusty truck, the radio on low—was not a new place, but one altogether familiar that I'd returned to after a long absence.

It was a testament to how being with Mac pretty much made me oblivious to everything else that I didn't notice the situation with the ignition at first. As we turned onto a side road, though, something hit my leg. When I looked down, I was surprised to see a pair of pliers dangling from some coiled wires, just hanging there.

"Um," I said, in a voice I hoped didn't sound as panicked

as I was starting to feel, "I think your truck is falling apart?"

Mac looked at me, then the pliers. "Nope," he replied. "That's the starter."

Granted, I was no expert on cars. But I felt relatively confident as I said, "I thought that was in the ignition?"

"In a perfect world, yes," he said, putting on his turn signal and slowing down. "But this is an old truck. Sometimes it has to be modified to, you know, actually run."

I had a flash of all those clock radios on his desk, the protruding springs. "Layla said you liked to tinker with stuff."

"I don't *tinker*," he replied, sounding offended. "Tinkering is for grandfathers in shop aprons."

Whoops. "Sorry," I said.

He looked at me again. "It's okay. Tender spot."

I smiled. "Everyone has one."

"So I hear." He sat back. "Layla has a tendency to make everything I do sound kind of twee. My 'woods wandering.' My 'tinkering.' It's like I'm her own personal gnome or something."

This was so far from how I saw him, I almost laughed out loud. Thank God I managed to resist, saying instead, "For what it's worth, I was impressed by your alarm clock. And if my starter were busted, I'd be walking. End of story."

"Well, thanks." He slowed for another turn. "There's no shame in trying to make stuff work, is how I see it. It's better than just accepting the broken."

I wanted to say he was lucky he even had a choice. That for most of us, once something was busted, it was game over. I would have loved to know how it felt, just once, to have something fall apart and see options instead of endings.

The order had been called in from a gymnastics school, and it was a big one: seven pizzas, four salads, and enough garlic knots that I could smell them through the plastic. I took the cold stuff and one pizza, he got the rest, and then I followed him up to the building. Inside, there was a window that looked into the gym itself, a huge room lined with mats featuring a balance beam, uneven bars, and a vault. There were girls of all ages milling around in brightly colored leotards and sporting ponytails, like an army of Merediths.

"Just put that here," Mac said, walking to a nearby counter and sliding his warmer onto it. I put down my pizza, then the bags of salads as he began to unload. He was almost done when I heard the first shriek.

It was sharp, yelp-like, and startled me. When I turned toward the sound, which had come from the big window, I saw there were now about four girls, a couple very small, the other two a bit taller, all skinny, looking at us. One of them—I was guessing the shrieker?—was blushing fiercely.

"Hi, Mac," two of them sang out through the glass, and then they all dissolved into giggles. Mac, who was still stacking pizzas, nodded at them.

"Coach Washington!" one of the smaller girls called out. "Mac is here!"

More giggles. A few other gymnasts now ran over, while the blusher was turning red enough to make me wonder if they had a defibrillator.

"Okay, girls, clear the way, please," I heard a voice say, and then the assembled ogling crowd was parting to let a woman with short, spiky blonde hair, wearing sweatpants and a tank top, come through. She had a whistle around her neck, but even without it you would have known she was in charge. She pushed open the door from the gym and began to walk toward us, a couple of the girls spilling out behind her. "Well, if it isn't our favorite pizza guy, triggering the usual hormone rush."

Mac, clearly uncomfortable, put the last pizza on the counter. "Big order today."

"Scrimmage meet with Beam Dreams," the woman told him, stopping in front of us. She put her hands on her hips, her posture perfect. I stood up straighter. "And who's this?"

"Do you have a *girlfriend?*" one of the girls called out. More giggles.

"Employee in training, actually," I said to the coach. "Just started."

"About time he had some help," she replied. "Let me get some money for you guys."

As she disappeared into a back office, the girls were still at the window, clearly discussing us. I turned my back, then said, "It's always like this?"

"No," he said, so curtly that I immediately knew it was.

The coach returned, giving Mac a tip and a thank-you, and we headed for the exit. As he pushed open the door for me, a chorus of voices rose up behind us

"*Good-BYE, Mac!*" This time, the giggles were thunderous.

I bit my lip, trying not to laugh as we walked to the truck. I could so remember that feeling as a tween, when just being in proximity to a good-looking older boy could make you feel like you might explode. If all you knew was going crazy over someone famous on TV, like Logan Oxford, meeting the real-life equivalent was almost too much to take.

Mac started the truck and we backed out, still not talking. Finally he said, "It's the only time I wish we actually did have another driver. When I see an order come in from here."

"You're pretty popular," I agreed. From his expression, this was not the adjective he would have chosen. "What? Some people would be flattered to be so admired."

"Would you?"

I thought about it for a second. "Probably not, actually."

He nodded, as if this was what he'd thought I would say.

"But I'm kind of used to being invisible," I continued. "So any kind of attention makes me nervous."

This was something I thought a lot but had never said aloud. It was the first time, but far from the last, that I understood being with Mac had this particular effect on me. Before I could regroup, he spoke.

"You? Invisible?" He glanced at me, then turned on his blinker. "Seriously?"

"What?" I asked.

"I just . . . I never would have thought of you that way, is all."

As he said this, I caught a glimpse of myself in the side mirror and wondered how, exactly, I did appear to him. "Well," I said, "you don't know my brother."

We were at a light now, slowing to a stop. "Big personality, huh?"

I looked out the window, this time making a point not to see my own face. "He just . . . When he's around, he fills the view. You can't look anywhere else. I feel that way about him, too."

"Sometimes it's preferable to not be seen, though," he said. "Before I lost the weight, people either stared or made a concentrated effort *not* to look at me. I preferred the second option. Still do."

I thought of all those girls at the gym window watching him. How strange it must be to go from looking one way to such a vastly different other. For the attention to change and still not feel better. Maybe the invisible place wasn't all bad, all the time.

"I think," I said, "that the best would be somewhere in between. You know, to be acknowledged without feeling targeted."

"Yeah," he said as the light changed. "I'd take that."

A car pulled suddenly in front of us, and Mac hit the horn. The lady behind the wheel shot us the finger. Nice.

"I still can't believe that was you in the pictures I saw," I said. "Did you really just lose the weight with diet and exercise?"

"A *strict* diet," he said. "You tried those Kwackers. They were my *dessert*. And lots of exercise."

"Like wandering in the woods."

He shot me a look, then smiled, stretching his fingers over the wheel. "It was a free workout and right outside the back door. No excuses. Whenever I had time, I just went into the woods. I brought my GPS and tracked the route, so I knew how far I'd gone."

I thought of the map I'd seen on his bedroom wall, the pencil marks. Tracing his way, out and back. "And you found the carousel."

"*That* was a good day. I just rounded a corner, and there it was. For a long time I didn't tell anyone about it, not even Layla. But eventually, it was too good a secret to keep."

Good secrets, I thought. *What a novel idea.* "I miss exploring the woods. My brother and I used to do it so much."

"It's not like it's gone anywhere," he pointed out.

"True." I thought of Peyton, ahead of me, leaves crunching beneath our feet. "It just feels different now. Scarier."

"Really?"

I nodded, then looked at his pendant. "Maybe I need a patron saint. Of wanderers. Or woods."

"I'm sure they exist," he told me. "They have them for everything. Boilermakers, accountants. Divorce. You name it."

"You're an expert, huh?"

"My mom is." He sat back as we hit another light. "She always liked the idea of protection, but especially since she got sick. I'm not wholly convinced. But I figure it can't hurt, you know?"

Sometimes, this was the best you could hope for. Not an advantage or a penalty, but the space between. "Yeah," I said. "I do."

Back at our meeting spot, Layla had still not shown up, so we parked by the curb to wait, Mac undoing the pliers to kill the engine.

"Thanks, by the way," I said to him after a minute. "For bringing me along."

"You like running deliveries?"

I turned to face him. "I do, actually."

"Yeah?"

"Yeah." I paused, looking down at my hands. "It's something about seeing all these people in their separate places. Like little snapshots of the whole world as it's happening, simultaneously. Is that weird, to think of it like that?"

Straight-faced, he said, "Yes. Very."

"Nice," I told him.

"I'm kidding, I'm kidding." He reached over, touching my wrist, his fingers the slightest weight there. "I get what you're saying."

"But you think it's crazy, drawing some deep symbolism from pizza delivery."

"A little," he admitted. I made a face. "But I kind of like it. Makes the job seem more noble, or important, or something."

"I'm such a moron," I said, yet again speaking aloud a thought I had so much, it had worn a groove in my brain.

"Nah," he said, tightening his fingers on my wrist. "You're not."

For a moment, we just looked at each other. It was late afternoon in the fall, the sky the pretty pink you only see right before sunset, like the day is taking a bow. I was in a new place, with someone I didn't know that well, and yet it felt like the most natural thing in the world, another groove already worn, to lean forward as he did until we were face to face, his fingers still gripping my arm. Then Spence and Layla pulled up beside us.

We jerked back from each other, just as she lowered her window. Immediately, I felt guilty, not knowing what she'd seen. But it was Layla who said, "Hey. I'm sorry."

Spence smiled. "You must be Mac."

"Yep."

Silence. Except for my heart, which was pounding in my chest and ears. But nobody else could hear that. I hoped.

"Isn't his car awesome? It's just like that one you've had your eye on," Layla said to Mac, a bit too eagerly. When he didn't reply, she sighed. "Look, it's not his fault I didn't tell you about him. I was just worried about how Daddy would react."

"To keeping secrets and lying?" Mac asked. "I'm guessing not well."

"Fine," she said, throwing up her hands. "I'll bring him to Seaside tomorrow, okay? Will that make you happy?"

"It's not about me," Mac said. Then, "We should go. Mom's waiting."

Layla looked back at Spence, then at us. "Let me just say good-bye, okay?"

Before he could respond, they'd pulled up and parked alongside the curb in front of us. As time passed, I could only imagine what was happening behind the tinted windows. Mac, looking equally uncomfortable, picked at a loose stitch on the steering wheel. Had I really just almost kissed him? It seemed unreal now, like something I'd dreamed. Or, if not, the best secret of all.

"Well," I said finally, "I should get home, too, I guess."

"You want a ride?"

"Nah. It's only a block or so." I opened the door. "Thanks for taking me along, seriously. It was fun."

"Anytime," he said. I smiled, then hopped out. As I shut the door and started to walk away, I heard him say, "Hey. Sydney."

"Yeah?"

"You had on a shirt with mushrooms on it, and your hair was pulled back. Silver earrings. Pepperoni slice. No lollipop."

I just looked at him, confused. Layla was walking toward us now.

"The first time you came into Seaside," he said. "You weren't invisible, not to me. Just so you know."

I didn't know what to say. I just stood there as Spence drove off, beeping the horn, and Layla climbed in where I'd been sitting. "Let's go," she told Mac, then looked at me. "See you tomorrow?"

Mac cranked the engine, and our eyes met again. Layla was digging in her bag, already distracted, so she didn't notice that it was to him, and really only him, that I replied. "Yeah. See you then."

CHAPTER
15
～つ♡～

I TRIED to stay away from Mac. I really did. But it was hard when Layla was always pushing us together.

"I just feel *bad*," she said at Seaside one afternoon about a week after she'd brought Spence to meet her dad and, in doing so, made their relationship official. He wasn't volunteering in the afternoons as much anymore—Layla claimed he'd overcommitted and decided to ease back, but I wondered if he'd just served out his hours—so I saw her only on days he had other obligations. "I never wanted to be the girl who dumps her best friend for her boyfriend."

"You haven't dumped me," I said. "We're here now, aren't we?"

She nodded, then picked up a piece of her pizza crust, considering it for a moment before returning it to her plate. "But when I'm not, you can ride along with Mac. He said you liked doing that."

"Layla." I put down my pencil. "You don't have to arrange babysitting for me. I'm fine."

"I know, I know," she said, putting her hands up. "I just—"

There was a beep as her phone lit up. She scanned the

screen, smiling, then typed a response. Funny how just a couple of words from someone could make you so happy. But I got it, especially lately.

Since Mac had told me he remembered seeing me for the first time, something was different. Before, the thought that we might get together was a far-fetched fantasy, the most ludicrous of daydreams. But now, with Layla immersed in Spence, us hanging out more, and what had almost happened in the truck, there was a sense of inevitability about it. No longer if, just when.

❊ ❊ ❊

"That's twenty-six forty-two, charged to your card," I said to the frazzled-looking woman in the doorway wearing sweatpants and a rumpled cardigan. Behind her, several children were jumping on the couch in front of a TV showing cartoons.

Wordlessly she reached out for the two pizzas I was holding. As I gave them to her and she tipped me, one of the kids tumbled off the couch, hitting the carpet with a thud. There was a pause. When the wailing began, she shut the door.

"Five bucks," I said to Mac as I climbed into the truck. "And I was right: only cheese pizzas means kids, and lots of them. You missed one doing a face-plant into the carpet."

"Bummer," he replied. He shifted into reverse. As I went to slide the bill into the plastic cup that sat in the console, he said, "You keep that. You did the work."

I just looked at him. "I walked to the door."

"It counts," he told me. I put it with the rest anyway.

After a few days of delivering together, we had worked out a system: Mac drove and kept up with the orders waiting at Seaside, and I did the legwork, running in to get the food and taking it to customers. He claimed this was efficient, that his time was better spent coordinating the next stop and our return trips to pick up more orders. But I was pretty sure he was just indulging my interest in seeing what was behind each door.

"Sorority girls," I reported from the next stop, at a big yellow house right across the street from the U. "Should have known it from all the salads."

"Look at you. You're like the order whisperer."

"There is a science to it," I agreed, sliding the tip in the cup. As I sat back, I realized he was looking at me. "What?"

"Nothing," he said, smiling and shaking his head.

It was only a couple of hours every other afternoon or so, but no matter: this time had quickly become the best part of my week. Layla might have felt she needed to apologize for falling so hard, so quickly. She didn't realize I was doing the same thing.

Just then, my phone beeped. It was the latest text from Jenn, one of several we'd exchanged while trying to work out a time to get together. With her after-school job tutoring and activities and my new routine with Mac, we'd gone from seeing each other at least once a week to hardly at all.

Frazier at 5? she wrote now. Off at 4:30. Mer can come late.

I looked at my watch. It was four p.m., which left me with another two hours with Mac before I was due home.

I thought of Layla, all her apologies, and felt my own guilt for putting my friends second to a boy, especially one who wasn't really mine. But then I did it anyway.

No can do. Tomorrow?

Gone till Monday, she replied. Next week for sure.

Which meant two more full afternoons without any other obligations. Jenn was a good friend, even when she didn't realize it.

Definitely, I wrote. XXOO.

The last delivery of the day was in the Arbors, right inside the front entrance. It was for two extra-large pepperoni and sausage pies with extra cheese, and I'd had it pegged as guys for sure, probably ones drinking beer. Instead, the door was answered by a small, very tan woman in tennis whites who called me "hon" and tipped me ten bucks. I was thinking I'd lost my touch until I was heading down the driveway and noticed a sign on the truck we'd parked behind. BASSETT CARPENTRY, it said. DECKS OUR SPECIALTY. When I glanced into the backyard, I saw a group of guys digging into the pizzas. They were drinking beer.

"You're like Layla with her face thing," Mac told me when I relayed this to him. "Just be sure you use your powers for good, not evil."

"I'll try," I replied as we pulled out of the driveway. We'd only gone a short way when I saw something. "Hey. Stop for a second."

He did, and I turned to my window, peering closer. There,

just across the street and beyond the sidewalk, was a small opening in the brush.

"What is it?" Mac asked.

"See that clearing? Between the skinny tree and the stump?"

He leaned across me. "Yeah."

"That used to be the best path into the woods from this neighborhood. You could get on it right here, where the houses begin, and follow it all the way back to where I live. It went for miles. We always wondered who put it there."

"Probably some kids, just like you."

"There was this one part," I continued as a car slowed, then passed us, "where there was a giant sinkhole. Huge. Somebody had managed to pull this fallen tree across it, and everyone always dared each other to walk across."

"Did you?"

"No way," I said, shuddering. "But Peyton did. He was the only one I ever saw do it."

Just saying this, I could see it all so clearly in my head. The bareness of the trees in late fall. Broad blue sky. And me and those older kids we'd come across in the woods that day watching as my brother put one foot in front of the other, slow and steady, all the way across.

"We can go, if you want," Mac said now. I turned, distracted, to face him. "We've got time. You can show me."

I looked back at the path, barely visible. Who knew how it looked now, what was back there. Part of me wanted to see, especially if I wasn't going to be alone. But another part, heavier, wasn't ready. Yet.

"Maybe another time," I said.

At six p.m., like always, we returned to Seaside so I could head home, while Mac kept delivering until close. Usually, for the rest of the evening I'd wonder what he was doing. It hadn't occurred to me that he might do the same about me. But that night, when I was sitting on my bed doing some reading for English, my phone beeped.

3 deluxe, 2 pepperoni mushroom. 6 orders garlic knots. Go.

I smiled. Has to be a team. All men.

A pause. I tried to go back to my book. Finally, a response: a picture of the sign in front of 7-10 Bowling Center. Impressive, it said below it.

I do my best, I replied.

Will stump you eventually, he wrote back.

I laughed out loud, alone in my room. Bring it.

That was how the texting started. No longer was Layla the only one who kept her phone within easy reach at all times. At night while I was eating dinner and doing homework, Mac crossing town, then back again, we kept in touch. It was the next best thing to being there. Or maybe the best thing, period.

❋   ❋   ❋

"This is a collect call from an inmate at Lincoln Correctional Facility. Do you accept the charges?"

I could hear the garage door opening as my mom idled in

the driveway. In just five minutes, she'd be inside. But Peyton was calling now.

"Yes," I said.

There was a click, and then I heard my brother's voice. "Hello?"

"Hey. It's Sydney."

"Oh. Hey." He cleared his throat. "How are you?"

"Good," I replied. "Mom's just getting home. She'll be here in a second."

"Okay."

We sat there for a moment, the only sound the empty buzzing of the line. Finally he said, "So, how's school? I hear you're at Jackson now."

"It's okay," I replied. "Different. But I've made some friends."

"That's about all I can say about this place." He laughed softly. "Although I'd pick high school over it any day of the week. And I hated high school."

"You did?" I was genuinely surprised. For all that had happened, I'd never doubted that Peyton had enjoyed himself, at least when he wasn't in trouble.

"Oh, yeah," he said. "It was probably why I was such an idiot. Misery makes people do stupid things."

It was so weird, talking like this. Like he was someone else I didn't know at all. "Why was it so bad?"

He was quiet a moment. "I don't know. The regular reasons. Bad grades, pressure from Mom and Dad. You know."

But I didn't, not really. I'd just assumed being the firstborn meant all the privilege; it hadn't occurred to me that another level came with it, one of responsibility, everything happening to you first.

Thinking this, I said, "I saw that path the other day, the one we used to take into the woods here. Remember?"

He was quiet for a second. "Yeah. With the sinkhole."

"Yeah," I repeated. "You walked across it that time, on a dare." As I said this, I realized how much I really did want him to remember.

After a pause, he said, "Not my brightest moment."

Again, I was surprised. How much else did we see differently? "But you did it," I said.

"Yeah." He sighed. "Like I said, I did a lot of stupid things."

Neither of us spoke for what felt like a long time. It was so awkward that I finally said, "So I'm looking forward to our visit. We all are."

"Your visit?" he asked.

"The graduation. From your class," I told him. "Mom's been talking about it for ages."

"You're coming?" He sounded surprised.

"Yeah."

"Oh." A pause. "You don't need to."

"It's okay. Mom said you'd filled out a form for me," I told him.

"I did. But that was just for . . ." He trailed off. "It's really not a big deal. I doubt anyone else's family is coming."

"Mom's planning this whole thing, though."

"She is?"

"Yeah." I could hear my mom putting her keys in the

door. "I'm, um . . . It'll be good to see you. Finally."

Silence, but a different sort. The kind that means not only that no one's talking, but that something very specific is not being said. My mom came in carrying two bags of groceries, her purse over her shoulder. "Sydney. You're home already."

"Is that Mom?" Peyton asked.

"Yeah."

"Can I talk to her?"

"Sure." I walked over to where she was beginning to unload her bags. "Mom. It's Peyton."

"Oh!" She turned, smiling, and took the phone from me. "Hey, honey. What a nice surprise. How are you?"

I went back over to the kitchen table, where I picked up the plate, now empty, I'd used for the slice I'd brought home with me from Seaside. I'd only stopped in, as Layla was with Spence and Mac was at band practice. My after-school piece of pizza had become enough of a habit, however, that I found I couldn't miss it, even when I was missing them.

"Well, I told you. I heard about it from Michelle." My mom reached up to put a can of soup in the cabinet in front of her. "The family liaison I've been meeting with, who's helping me communicate better with the administration at Lincoln."

I was putting my plate in the dishwasher. Something in her voice, suddenly defensive, made me shut it slowly, quietly.

"Yes, I did, Peyton. Several times, in fact." She took out another can, but this one she just held. "No, I do remember that discussion. But you said you would be ready, eventually, which is why you did the form. And I thought this would be a great opportunity—"

Distantly, I could hear my brother talking. A lot.

"I'm fully aware of that," she said after a moment, so abruptly it was obvious she was having to interrupt. Then, "Because I don't agree that it means we should abandon you, or not acknowledge your accomplishments. And—"

I picked up my backpack, pretty sure it was time to make my exit.

"Well, that's not what Michelle thinks. And it's not what I believe, either." She put the can down on the counter with a thunk. "Well, I hope that you do. I think that if you really take the time to look at it—"

Another interruption from Peyton, louder this time.

"I think maybe we should table this for now. You're clearly upset, and—" I watched as she reached up, putting a hand to her face. "Okay. Yes. Fine. Talk to you later."

The phone beeped off, and I heard her exhale. Not sure what to do, I turned to the window, slipping my backpack over my shoulders, then looked out at the street. A beat passed. Another. Then she left the room, her footsteps padding upstairs.

For all I knew, this was how many of their exchanges ended, as I usually made myself scarce when they talked. But it had been a while since I'd heard my mom upset, and I wondered if I should go to her. I didn't have the right words or even know what those might be. So instead, I put away the rest of the groceries. That way, when she came back down, at least one thing would be just how she wanted it.

"Listen up," Eric announced. "I have *big* news."

I was the only one who looked at him. Eric was a fan of both announcements and pronouncements: never just information, always an exclusive. Everyone else had been around long enough to know not to fall for his conversational hype.

"Is this about the señorita?" Irv asked.

Eric looked at him. "Who?"

Mac, on the bench eating a Kwacker and doing his history homework, swallowed. "The girl from your Spanish group? The one you're sure is obsessed with you?"

"Oh, no." Eric flipped his hand: señorita, forgotten. "Bigger. This is about the *band*."

Now, at least, he had Mac's attention, if not everyone else's. "The band?"

Eric, smiling, slid onto the end of the bench where I was sitting. "Well, it's kind of about Layla. But also the band."

"Huh?" Layla asked from my other side. As always, she had her phone in her hand, determined not to miss a possible midday texting opportunity with Spence. Cell phones were banned on the W. Hunt campus, and yet more days than not at this time he still managed to contact her. "What about me?"

Now that Eric had the floor, he was determined to keep it as long as possible. So we all had to watch as he pulled a paper flyer from his pocket, then unfolded it slowly before holding it up. "We're going to enter this. And you're going to help us."

LOCAL YOKELS: A SHOWCASE, it said in large black type. FIVE BANDS, ONE PRIZE. ACCEPTING ACTS NOW. BENDOVENUE .COM/LOCALS FOR DETAILS.

"That's the big news?" Mac asked. "We've done show-cases before."

"This isn't *just* a showcase," Eric told him. "It's a competi-tion, with a record demo deal as a prize."

"What does that have to do with me, though?" Layla asked.

"I'll tell you." A pause. Mac looked at me, then sighed, as we waited for him to do just that. Finally: "You're our secret weapon."

"Since when?" she said.

"Since I did my research and realized how few of the groups around here have girl singers, or girls at all, for that matter. Everyone's like us, totally dude-centric. With you up front, we'll stand out. Better our chances."

"Wait a second." Layla put down her phone, which meant she was serious. "Are you saying that you're going to let *me* sing lead? Because that does *not* sound like you. Unless you have a head injury I missed."

"I resent that implication," Eric protested. "I am a team player, all the way."

Irv laughed out loud at this. Mac said, "What's the catch?"

"There isn't one. I want to win," Eric said. "Anyway, Layla wouldn't be singing lead. She'd solo on one new song, in between two of our standards."

"So I'm a guest vocalist?"

"You're a member of the band! Just like everyone else!"

"Except that I'm not," she told him.

"But they," Eric said, shaking the paper at her, "don't know that. Nor do they need to. We win this, get the deal, and then record what we want."

"I don't know," she said, picking up her phone again. "I'm not much into the singing thing lately."

Eric just looked at her. "You have to help us."

"Actually, I don't." She scrolled down, tapping her finger on the screen. "Ask Rosie. She's got the voice, anyway."

"I don't want Rosie. I want *you.*"

Now he had all of our attention. It didn't matter that he was, ostensibly, still talking about the band. The fact that Eric still pined for her months after their short relationship and ensuing breakup was as much known to the rest of us as his ego and penchant for showboating. This was the first time I was aware of, though, that he'd said anything close to it aloud. He realized it, too: color was already flooding his face.

"You're assuming we'll be ready," Mac said, breaking the awkward silence that followed. "We only just got back to a regular practice schedule. We don't even have a name."

"It's three songs," Eric said. "And only one new one."

"When's the tryout?"

"No tryout. They want a recording."

"What?" Mac shook his head. "Then this is a moot point anyway."

"Why?"

"Because we don't have one? Or any way of paying to produce one?"

"It can't cost that much."

"It's not cheap."

"Well, I've got some birthday money. You work. And I bet Ford's parents might chip in . . ."

He trailed off, though, obviously less sure of this aspect of the plan. Layla, who had gone back to her phone, gave him a sympathetic look.

The bell rang then, and we all started gathering our stuff together. Eric remained on the bench, glum, as everyone else got up to head off in their different directions. "There'll be another showcase," Irv said, clapping him on the shoulder. "With an audition. I promise."

"Yeah, yeah," Eric said, shrugging.

I grabbed my bag, then started—slowly—toward the steps that led up to the arts building, where my next class was. Mac's sixth period was in the same direction, so he joined me and we started climbing the stairs. Eric, who had a free sixth, was still on the bench, his guitar case at his feet.

"Poor guy," I said. "He's like a kid who just dropped his ice-cream cone."

"He'll survive," he replied. "And maybe it will inspire him to get a job, too. Then we'd have money for a demo."

"They're really that expensive?"

He shifted his bag up his shoulder. "The demo itself isn't. Studio time is where it gets pricey."

All through the ecology lecture that followed, and the calc test after that, I forgot about this entire exchange. In my final period, my English teacher, Ms. Feldman, was saying something about metaphors when a thought occurred to me. Some way that I might actually be able to help *them* for once.

That afternoon, when I got to Seaside after the final bell, I was the one with a plan.

"Hold on," Mac said. "You have a recording studio in your *house*?"

"A partial one," I told him. "My parents were building it for my brother."

"Oh, my God, that's *right*," Layla said, turning away from the front window, where she was in her customary spot, waiting for Spence to pull up. "And I've been there! How did I forget that?"

"Well," I told her, "it was kind of a weird night."

She thought for a second. Then: "Oh, right. Yeah. I blocked it out, for sure."

Mac looked at me. "What, it's haunted or something?"

"Not exactly," she said. "That guy was there, her brother's friend. Remember?"

"Oh." He looked at me. "Right. The creeper."

I hadn't thought it was possible to like him more. I was wrong. I said, "I'm sure it would be okay. It's not like anyone ever uses it."

"We'd still need someone to engineer the demo, though," Mac said.

"Isn't that what Eric spent the whole summer doing last year, at that camp?" Layla said. "He certainly came back seeming like he could do it."

"We're talking about Eric here. He acts like he can do everything."

"Just text him and ask."

Mac pulled out his phone, then looked at me. "You sure

this is okay? Because if I mention it to him, he'll be like a dog with a bone. He will not let go of things, even when he should."

Just then, a big black SUV pulled up at the curb. "Spence is here!" Layla called out to us and her dad, who was in the kitchen. "I'm going!"

"Back by five thirty," said Mr. Chatham.

"Six at the latest!" she replied, then darted out before he could object. Mac watched her climb into the passenger seat, an expression of suspicion on his face. According to Layla, he was like this with *all* her boyfriends, way too overprotective and biased from first glance. I could see that. But she had been pushing limits a bit since Spence was around more after school: showing up late, then a bit later. Being evasive, even to me, about where they'd gone or what they'd done. If I was noticing it, I knew Mac had, too.

"I'll ask my parents, but I'm sure it will be fine," I said to him as they pulled away. "And I want to help you guys out."

"You don't have to," he told me.

"I know." I nodded at his phone. "Just text him. Give the dog a bone."

Of course, Eric maintained he could handle everything if he had a studio and suggested we try for the next day or, barring that, the coming weekend. All that was left was getting official permission. And how hard could that be?

I walked into the kitchen two hours later. Usually, by six, my mom had her customary one glass of wine poured, dinner well under way, and her typical questions about my day ready. Today, she was nowhere in sight. I put down my bag, then headed upstairs to the War Room. The door was half shut, and I could hear her talking.

"I just feel like something else is going on," she was saying. "He's been so easily upset the last few times we've talked, and he doesn't want to discuss anything. And then there's the graduation . . ."

She fell silent as whoever was on the other end of the line spoke. Downstairs, my dad was coming in the front door.

"I did read that the three-month mark can be a transitional one. Something about the newness wearing off with so much sentence left to do." Another pause. "Well, that does make sense. Peyton was never good at discussing his feelings. I blame that, in fact, for a lot of his troubles. If he'd only been able to be honest about the pain he was in . . ."

"Julie?" My dad's voice came up the stairs. "Are you up there?"

I walked over to the landing. "She's on the phone."

"Oh." He looked back at the kitchen, clearly wondering about dinner, too. "Okay."

"Goodness, is that the time?" my mom said as she came out of the room. Spotting me, she gave a tired smile. "I don't know where the afternoon went. I guess we'd better try to pull together something to eat, huh?"

I nodded, then followed her down to the kitchen, where my dad was uncapping a beer. "Long day?" he asked her.

"Epic," she replied, walking to the fridge and opening it. "Now, let's see. I was going to make a pork shoulder before I got distracted. I think I have some chicken in here . . ."

"Or we could do delivery," my dad, who never met a takeout box he didn't like, suggested.

"We could," she agreed. She shut the door, then looked at me. "What about pizza? The place Sydney took me was delicious. They deliver, yes?"

"Yeah," I said, surprised. "Sure."

"Perfect. What do you think, Peyton? One large, half deluxe, half roma?"

"How about one large deluxe and one large roma," my dad suggested. "I'll take the leftovers for lunch tomorrow."

This was hardly a surprise. My dad would eat pizza at any time of day or night, and had a seemingly endless appetite when it came to doing so. Leftover slices never lasted in our fridge, even if you set them aside especially, *with* your name on them. I knew this from experience.

"Fine," my mom said. "Make the call."

I did, and Mr. Chatham answered. "Sydney! Long time, no see. If you're calling for Layla, she's not here. Half hour late and counting. Again."

Uh-oh, I thought. "I actually need to place an order."

"Yeah?" He sounded pleased. "Great. What can I get you?"

I told him what we wanted. He took my mom's card number, then said he'd throw in some garlic knots—even when I told him it wasn't necessary—and that I'd see Mac in twenty minutes.

After we hung up, I went and brushed my hair, changed my shirt, and put on some lip gloss. When I came back downstairs, my dad looked at me. "What's the occasion?"

"Nothing," I said as my mom looked over as well. "I just felt gross from school."

"Pretty fancy for pizza," he observed, picking up the paper from that morning and flipping through it.

"I think she looks nice," my mom said, and smiled at me.

I rolled my eyes. It was a small moment, but right then it felt so wonderfully normal that I wished I could tuck it away in my pocket. Me and my parents, pizza on a weeknight, just your typical family. At least for a few minutes.

Maybe it was because of this that I decided, right then, to bring up using the recording studio. "So, Mom. I have a favor to ask."

"Okay," she said. "What is it?"

"Well, Layla's brother, Mac? You met him, at the pizza place."

"Yes. I remember."

"He's in this band. And they need to record a demo tape for this showcase they're hoping to get. I was wondering if they could maybe use the studio downstairs."

She looked at my dad, who was now scanning the sports page. "I don't see why not."

"Really?" I said.

"For all we put into it, seems like someone should use it, don't you think, Peyton?"

"Absolutely," my dad replied, in such a way that I knew, right off, he hadn't been listening.

"Oh, that's great," I said. "Thank you. Seriously."

She looked at me, surprised, and smiled. "You're welcome."

Just then, the phone rang. Thinking it might be Seaside,

calling back with a question about the order, I grabbed it right up. "Hello?"

"This is a collect call from an inmate at Lincoln Correctional Facility. Do you accept the charges?"

"Yes," I said, then waited for the buzz and the click. "Peyton?"

At his name, my mom looked over, immediately alert, invested. "Hi," my brother said. "What's going on?"

"Not much," I told him. "Dinner."

"Is Mom around?"

"Yeah. Hold on."

She was already beside me, her hand ready to take the phone. When I gave it to her, she ran a hand over my hair before putting it to her ear. "Hey there! How are you? Getting excited for graduation?"

As she walked across the room, my dad opened the fridge, scanning the contents, and took a sip of his beer. I glanced at my watch: it had been ten minutes. Soon, Mac would arrive and I could not only tell him about the studio but also introduce him to my dad. After so long feeling disjointed and out of step, things seemed to be falling into place. Once, I might have taken this for granted. But now, I knew to not only notice but savor it. Which was probably a mistake.

"Honestly, I just don't know where this is coming from," my mom said. It had only been a moment since I'd last heard her voice, but in that time it had gone from easygoing to tight, high. My dad, hearing it, too, looked at her. "I thought we already discussed this."

A pause as Peyton spoke.

"Because it's an accomplishment, and it should be rec-ognized. And all the liaisons and literature say that—" She stopped short—now she was interrupted. "Well, I disagree. And I think the other families would, as well."

"Julie," my dad said. "What's going on?"

She put up her hand, palm out. "I just don't understand why you're doing this to us. What? I disagree. I'm an in-volved parent, Peyton. And all I want—"

Out of the corner of my eye, I saw a blur outside. When I turned to the window, Mac was pulling into the driveway.

"Well, I can't talk to you when you're like this," my mom said, shaking her head. "You won't even let me—"

My dad walked over, putting out his hand. "Give me the phone."

She shook her head. Outside, Mac was getting out of the truck.

"Julie." My dad put a hand on her shoulder. Then, gently, he reached over, taking the receiver away from her. He put it to his ear, then said, "Peyton. It's me. What's this all about?"

My mom had tears in her eyes as she leaned against the counter, watching him as my brother responded. When the doorbell rang a moment later, I was pretty sure I was the only one who heard it.

Minutes earlier, all I'd wanted was to bring Mac inside and introduce him. Now, though, seeing him standing there with the warmer in one hand and a paper bag in the other, I wished I could step out and leave with him.

"Hey," he said. He held up the bag. "Hope you're in the mood for garlic knots. My dad sent, like, an entire batch."

Before I could answer, his eyes shifted, following something behind me. I turned just in time to see my mom taking the stairs two at a time.

"Great," I said, stepping back. "Come on in."

He did, following me into the kitchen, where my dad was just then hanging up the phone. His back was to me as he said, "Your mother is, um, upset. She—"

"Pizza's here," I said quickly.

My dad turned and saw us. "Oh. Right."

"Dad, this is Mac," I said. "He's a friend of mine from school."

"Nice to meet you," Mac told him, putting down the warmer on the table and offering his hand.

"And you as well," my dad said. They shook. "I hear this pizza's pretty great."

"It is," I said. "You're going to love it."

Upstairs, a door shut. It wasn't *quite* a slam, but we could hear it. "So," my dad said, pulling out his wallet. "What do I owe you?"

"I put it on the card," I told him. "The total was twenty-three forty-two."

He took out a five and a couple of ones, handing them to Mac. "For you, then."

"Thank you."

"So my parents said it was okay," I said, glancing at my dad, "for you guys to use the studio."

"Really?" Mac said. "Wow. That's awesome. Eric's going to go bananas."

"Eric's the lead singer," I explained to my dad. "Mac plays drums."

"Great," my dad replied, clearly distracted. "I'm, um, going to check on your mom. Set the table, okay? Nice to meet you, Mac."

"You too."

As he went upstairs, I walked over to the cabinet and took down some plates, even though I was pretty sure we wouldn't be having a typical family sit-down. "My brother just called," I said. "He's mad about something. That's why my mom's upset."

"Oh," he said. "Sorry."

"It's not like it's that big a deal. But we were having a good night, you know? For once."

He said nothing to this as I put the plates on the counter. Upstairs, I heard another door shut.

"I asked them about the studio, and they were great about it, and you were coming over . . ." I swallowed, opening the napkin drawer. "I'm just so tired of this. Of him being everything."

Mac just watched me as I moved to the silverware. As I counted out three forks, I felt like I was going to cry. And then, just like that, I was.

Not just tears pricking my eyes, or that slow throb in your throat that gives you enough warning to breathe and, maybe, get under control. Instead, instantly, I just found myself sobbing: chest heaving, nose running, making noises that sounded almost primal. I gripped the edge of the countertop, dropping my head, and tried to suck in some air and calm down. It was just occurring to me that I should be embarrassed when I felt Mac's hands on my shoulders.

"Hey," he said. His palms were warm. "It's okay. It's okay, Sydney."

But it wasn't. Nothing had been okay, not for a long time. And every moment that I thought I was getting close, like the one I'd had earlier, seemed to remind the universe that I didn't deserve that, not yet.

What *was* due me, then? Only tiny seconds where things felt right, just fleeting enough to make me crave more? Was that it? I was beginning to think so, that I just couldn't get what I wanted, that maybe I didn't even have any idea what that was. But as Mac turned me to face him and I looked up into his eyes, I realized I was wrong. So I took a single step—one foot, then the other—and then his arms wrapped around me, pulling me in the rest of the way.

CHAPTER
16

~

PEYTON DIDN'T want me at his graduation. Actually, he didn't want any of us there. But my mom was only willing to compromise so much.

"It's not that he doesn't want to see you, or that he doesn't miss you," she'd explained the next morning. "He'd just prefer that you not interact with him in that setting yet. I thought that might have changed by now . . . but it hasn't. It's actually a very common sentiment among the incarcerated when it comes to family, children in particular."

She was speaking slowly, carefully picking her words. What a difference twelve hours made. The last time I'd seen her, she'd been disappearing upstairs in tears; this morning, she was at the coffeepot calm, rested, and capable. She was also clearly concerned about how I'd take this news, somehow having forgotten that I'd never wanted to go in the first place.

"I understand," I said. "It's fine."

She was still watching me as I took a bite of my breakfast. Suddenly, my welfare was very important, which would have been nice had I not known the real reason she was suddenly so invested. By focusing on Peyton's not wanting me to go, she could skirt the wider truth of how he really felt about having her there. My mom had always been good at narrowing an issue.

"As I told you," she continued, "Peyton's time at Lincoln will be marked by a series of transitions. It's very possible that his emotional need for us will at some point manifest itself in his feeling like he has to pull away. So the key is that we allow him to do what he thinks is necessary, while at the same time making clear that we *are* here and not going anywhere."

My dad, who was getting a rare late start to the office, walked into the kitchen, adjusting his tie. He'd already eaten, but still stopped by the eggs on the stove, picking out a bite with his fingers.

"So you're all still going?" I asked. "To the graduation?"

"Your father and I will go. We'll ask Ames and Marla to stay here with you. That's probably the best plan."

"I don't need anyone here with me, though," I said quickly. "I mean, it's only one night."

"It's already arranged," she told me, glancing at my dad. "Right?"

"I mentioned it to him last night." He wiped his hand on a dish towel. "Apparently things with Marla have . . . cooled. But he's happy to do it."

"Really?" My mom looked at him. "I had no idea! He hasn't said a thing to me about their breaking up."

Considering how much he and my mom talked, this was

kind of surprising. But I had learned not to put much past Ames.

"He didn't sound too upset about it," my dad said now, eating another piece of egg. "Anyway, he's got to work that night, but he's going to try to get off early."

"He shouldn't do that," I said, apparently too adamantly, as they both looked at me, surprised. "I'll be fine."

"Sydney, we've had this conversation before. I don't want you here alone," my mom said. "Ames stayed with you last time, and it worked out well, didn't it?"

"I'll stay at Layla's," I said, instead of answering her.

"On a school night? No." She sat back. "Frankly, with all the time you've been over there and at their pizza place, I worry we've overimposed as it is."

"Let me invite her here, then." I thought for a second. "Actually, we could use the studio that evening. That way, you guys wouldn't even be bothered with it."

She blinked at me. "The studio? Peyton's studio?"

"Yeah," I said as she looked at my dad, who shrugged. "You said that Mac's band could use it, to record."

"Mac," she repeated, like she was trying to jog a distant, faded memory. "I don't—"

"Layla's brother. My friend." I turned to my dad. "You met him last night. I asked if his band could use the studio to record this demo, and you guys said yes."

"Oh, Sydney, I don't know," my mom said. "Even if Peyton *was* okay with that—and really, we'd have to ask him—it couldn't happen with us out of town."

"But you said—"

"Then I spoke without thinking," she told me, looking at my dad again. "Or we did. The bottom line is, until this graduation thing is over, I really can't focus on anything else."

"It's not just anything," I said. "It's *my* thing. My friends."

I could tell I'd surprised them. I'd always accepted being second in importance; it was my place in the pecking order. But when it came to this—to Mac—I was ready to fight. Like finally I felt I had a real reason. It would have been better if it had been for me, myself. But I'd still take it.

"You didn't even *know* these people three months ago," my mom said. "I find it hard to believe they're suddenly more important than family."

"Mom—"

"We're not talking about this anymore," she said, rising from her seat and pushing her chair in. "We will go support your brother because he needs us, whether he's choosing at this moment to admit it or not. After that, we can talk about everything else."

She walked to the coffeemaker, her back to me as she re-filled her mug. My dad watched her go, then gave me a sympathetic look. But once again, he didn't do anything. Like this was her job, it was decided, and he couldn't go over her head, as much as I wished he would.

Even though this was the way it always went, I felt a flush of anger rise in me, unexpected and unprecedented. Something had changed. Before, she'd grouped me within "anything else." Now, "everything." I'd always been the other, the one not Peyton; I'd come to accept it. But finally, I'd met people who saw me differently. Now that I'd been real and first to someone, I never wanted to be invisible again.

* * *

"So what I'm thinking," Eric said, "is that we start strong with a Logan Oxford, end big with that 'Six of One' with my solo. We'll put Layla doing vocals on another one in the middle to shake things up."

"Yeah, but which one?" Mac asked, peeling another clementine. He had Irv's phone disassembled in front of him, replacing the shattered screen, a result of its being sat on. Just looking at all the tiny screws made my head hurt. "It's not like we have anything rehearsed with her."

"It's not complicated, it's pop music," Eric told him. "And she knows all these songs already. It's just a matter of picking one with the perfect meaning."

"You just said it's simple, though," said Irv, who was finishing off what was by my count his third chicken leg. "So how can it have meaning?"

"That's where the *irony* comes in." Eric sighed: yet again, none of us were keeping up. "I'm going to pick a song that is clearly from a guy's point of view, then turn it on its head both with the original arrangement—I'm thinking acoustic, maybe—and having a girl singer."

"We," Mac said quietly, picking up another screw. "*We* will pick a song."

"Right, right," Eric replied, flipping his hand. "Consensus rules. But let's be honest: I'm the one who's really driving the depth of our message."

"'Depth of your message'?" Irv repeated, then laughed out loud. "Man. You're outdoing even *yourself* right now."

Beside me, Mac laughed, too, and I forced a smile, trying to join in. I hadn't yet figured out how, exactly, to break the news that my parents were not actually okay with the band using the studio. So I hadn't, instead just sitting there getting more and more anxious as they made their plans to do just that.

I wasn't the only one out of sorts. Even though she was partly the subject of this conversation, Layla wasn't paying attention. Instead, she was focused on her phone. It was clear enough by her face she wasn't happy, but the fact that her lunch was untouched just sealed it.

"You okay?" I asked her for the second time that day. I'd bumped into her in the hallway after homeroom, just in time to see her hanging up, looking irritated. We'd both been running late and headed in opposite directions, so when she said she was fine, I'd taken her at her word.

"Yeah," she said, not looking at me. "Just . . . Spence stuff. It's stupid."

I hesitated, not sure how much to push this issue. Since she and Spence had been spending more and more time together, I'd only gotten bits and pieces from her about their relationship. I had noticed that the swooning, "He's so great and sweet!" phase had waned. Apparently I hadn't been wrong about her perfect boyfriend having his own complicated history. After some prodding, she'd admitted to me that not only was it mandatory community service he'd recently completed, he'd been expelled from *three* schools be-

fore landing at W. Hunt. At the time they'd met, he was
keeping in line and on the upswing. With people like that,
though, there was always a down waiting.

"So what I'm leaning toward," Eric continued, "is going
with a Paulie Prescott for Layla's song."

"Paulie Prescott? Was that the guy with the hair?" Irv
asked.

"You're going to have to be more specific," Mac told him.

"*The* hair." Irv reached up one hand, swooping it over his
head. "Remember? Dude looked like he'd been in an air tun-
nel, all the time."

"No, that was someone else," Eric said. "The other guy,
with the really high voice."

"Abe Rabe," Layla and I said at the same time. She didn't
even look up.

Mac raised his eyebrows, the new screen in his hand.
"Wow. That wasn't weird or anything."

I smiled at him, thinking again of what had happened
the night before. Despite my initial nervousness around him,
when he pulled me close it felt familiar, like we'd done it
a million times. No awkwardness, no adjustments needed.
I'd just pressed myself against his chest, the pendant on his
chain against my cheek, and breathed in his smell. I knew
very little for certain, but I was sure that if my father had
not come back down the stairs moments later, I would have
kissed him. So sure that now, sitting close but not too close,
him smiling at me, it felt like I had.

"Paulie Prescott was the fake gangster," Eric said. "Rich
kid from the suburbs who sang about his past being street.

He had that whole bad-boy-trying-to-be-good thing going on. Girls ate it *up*."

"Oh, right," Irv said, wrinkling his nose. "I *hated* that guy."

"Everyone did." Eric had no problem speaking for the world. "But that's why it's intriguing to have Layla do one of his songs. Take away the production, the facade, and shift the braggadocio to a female point of view? That's going to be deep. Epic."

"Did you just use the word *braggadocio*?" Mac asked him. "Are you drunk?"

Layla suddenly got to her feet, grabbed her bag, and started walking quickly toward the main building. We all just watched her go in silence. Then Irv said, "God, what'd you do, Eric?"

"Me?"

Mac was watching me as I stood up. "You know what that was about?"

"No," I said, picking up my backpack. "But I have a hunch."

I checked the girls' bathroom first, as it was my go-to place for taking refuge, but the only people there were a group of dance team members busy doing a makeup tutorial. Out in the hallway, I thought for a second, then headed to Layla's locker, my next best bet. On the way there, I found her sitting on the stairs. When she saw me, she bit her lip.

"Okay," I said, joining her. "What's going on?"

She sighed, stretching her legs out in front of her. "Spence has just been . . . into some stuff lately. That he shouldn't be doing, with his history. Basically."

"Drugs?"

A slight nod. "Just pot. Some pills. They make him different. But when I nag him, he gets mad, then doesn't answer my texts. Then I don't *know* what he's doing, which is worse."

"You're not going to be able to fix him," I told her.

"I know, I know." She pulled her knees to her chest. "It sucks, because if I say something, he disappears. If I don't, I have to watch him sabotage himself. It's like I can't win."

A couple of guys carrying instrument cases pushed past us on their way up the stairs. I said, "I hate that feeling."

This wasn't particularly wise of me, or enlightening, at least as far as I was concerned. But hearing it, Layla exhaled, then leaned her head on my shoulder, closing her eyes. I tried so hard, so often, to say just the right thing, only to come up short. It felt good to get it right for once, even if it was by accident.

❦ ❦ ❦

"Okay," Mac said as I climbed back into the truck. "Work your magic."

I looked down at the order in my hand. Four fettuccine alfredos, four salads. "Someone's pretending they're cooking dinner. Five dollars says they already have serving dishes ready to dump this stuff into."

"You're on," he said, cranking the engine.

Usually, I was confident enough about my predictions that they were accompanied by trash talk. Today, though, I just wasn't in the mood. Between knowing I'd have to tell Mac (who'd have to tell Eric, who would be crushed) about the studio being a no-go and Layla's confession earlier (which she'd sworn me to secrecy about), there was a lot I was having to keep in. That this meant holding back from Mac just made it worse.

When the door at the house was answered by a young woman in a dress and pearls and heavy makeup, wearing a shiny diamond ring and a new-looking gold band, I could barely muster a pat on my own back. Even though it was pretty cool.

"Oh, thank goodness," she said, untying the apron she was wearing, which said KISS THE COOK (still sporting crease marks—its first use, I guessed). "My in-laws will be here in twenty minutes."

"Enjoy your meal," I told her, handing off the food. She gave me a grateful look and a big tip before shutting the door.

Mac, who had been watching from the truck, just looked at me as I returned. "Okay, I used to think this was impressive. Now it's getting sort of creepy."

I managed a smile as I got in the cab. "Leave me alone. I have few talents."

"Oh, I don't think that's true," he replied, shifting into reverse. "You manage to get Layla to talk to you."

I knew he'd been waiting for me to tell him what had upset her at lunch. Because I'd made a promise, though, I only said, "That's relationship stuff. All girls have a knack for that. It's part of our genetic code."

"Really."

"Yep."

It was obvious I was dodging the issue, but thankfully,

he let it go, instead handing over the next order. "Good luck with this. It's a real doozy."

I took it, glancing at the ticket. "Two large cheeses, four garlic knots? What's complicated about that?"

"Read what it says at the bottom."

"*ALLCOUP?*" I asked. The word was underlined. Twice. "What does that mean?"

He put on his turn signal, switching lanes as we approached a light. "All coupon. That means they have enough discounts that it's free."

"Free?" I looked at the ticket again. "How is that possible?"

"It's not supposed to be," he told me. "We run a special on Thursdays. The ad's *supposed* to say if you buy a cheese pizza and knots, you get a pizza and order of knots for free. But about a year ago, the copy for the ad got messed up. Badly."

"Meaning?"

"Meaning," he continued, turning onto a side road, "they left off the first part and only printed the second."

I had to think for a minute. "So it said you could get a large pizza and a side of knots for free? No purchase required?"

"Yup."

That was a lot of dough. Literally and figuratively. "How many were given out?"

"They were sent in the mail," he replied. "To every listed address in city limits."

"Oh, my God," I said. "Your dad must have been freaking."

"He was." He sat back, running a hand over the wheel. "Most people would have just copped to the error and not accepted them. But he's not like that, so he still honors them. Although it makes him really grumpy."

That explained why the underlining for *ALLCOUP* was several shades darker than the word above it. "So this has been going on for a year?"

"We don't get many anymore. But there are a few people who, once they realized the error, made a point of collecting as many as they could get their hands on."

"And they fit a type," I said, finally getting it.

He nodded. Then he waited.

I thought for a moment. "They're smart. Resourceful. Plus, they had time to collect coupons and could keep them organized. That's a *lot* to do for free pizza, though, so they're either broke or young. Most likely both."

We were approaching a street of apartment complexes now. "Anything else?" Mac asked me.

"Boys," I told him.

"What's your reasoning there?"

"I don't have any. It's just a hunch."

My second of the day, so far. But this one I felt less confident about than guessing the source of Layla's issue. When Mac got out with me, I assumed it was not only because this was an apartment, to which we always went together, but also because he wanted to see me get one wrong for once.

We walked up two flights to a door with music thumping behind it, and he knocked. A moment later it was opened by a skinny guy, a college student most likely, wearing a plaid shirt, jeans, and a headset.

"Seaside Pizza," Mac said, his voice flat. "You placed an order?"

"We did," the guy said. He glanced over his shoulder to the room behind him, where I could see two other guys on a couch, also in headsets, video game controllers in their hands. "And what was the total on that?"

"You have coupons?"

The guy's smile broadened. "You need to see them?"

"Yeah," Mac said. "I do."

He turned, walking over to a table that was piled with books, takeout containers, and chargers plugged in but not charging anything. After moving a few things around, he returned.

"Here you go." He smiled. "I think you'll see that says we can get two pizzas and two garlic knots for free from your fine establishment."

"Pizza," one of the guys, still focused on the TV, said in a robotic voice.

"*Free* pizza," his friend in front of us said. Then he looked at me. "It just tastes better, you know?"

I didn't say anything, just stood there as Mac examined the coupons—back and front—and then pocketed them. When he nodded at me, I handed over the food. "That's twenty-four seventy-two at full price," I told him, hoping at least he would tip.

"I know!" he said gleefully. "It's *great*. Thanks!"

And then he shut the door. I was so surprised, I just stood there looking at the 2B on it, but Mac was already walking away. As I caught up with him, I said, "I amend my earlier assessment. They are also assholes."

"Agreed." He looked so annoyed, I knew to stay quiet as we started across the lot toward the truck. He pulled out his phone, glancing at it. "No deliveries on deck. I need a break. Let's do something."

"What did you have in mind?" I asked, pulling my door open.

"We're near your neighborhood," he replied. "Want to show me that sinkhole?"

I thought of my brother on the phone, how he'd surprised me by his reaction when I'd brought this up. Like the fact that he saw the story differently—him as stupid, not superhuman—made it seem like maybe it hadn't happened at all. "Sure," I said. "Let's go."

The path was more narrow than I recalled, and overgrown enough in a few places that I had to stop and bend branches back to get through. It was weird to be in the lead, as I'd always followed Peyton. After about a quarter mile, though, the woods opened up, and Mac fell in beside me. As we climbed a ridge, a hawk soaring over us, he took my hand.

His palm was warm, and my own felt small within it. Protected. We didn't talk, the only sounds our footsteps as they crunched over leaves and the occasional whisper of trees, swaying in the breeze. I thought of all those other afternoons, walking this same path, and how different it felt now, for so many reasons.

"It should be up here somewhere," I told him as we

climbed another hill. "I remember this clear-cut."

"Looks like they were going to build here."

"Maybe. Or just cut them for logging." We navigated around a bunch of stumps covered with moss and lichen. A couple of beer bottles, half-filled with dirty rainwater, sat against one of them. And then, just when I was wondering if I truly had imagined everything, I saw it, just ahead: a place where the ground opened up, wide like a mouth. We walked right up to the edge.

It wasn't as vast as I remembered, and no log lay across it. But there *was* something familiar, in the exposed roots, the layer of red clay halfway down, the suddenness of its appearance, so unexpected.

"I guess it's not that impressive," I said to Mac. "Not like the carousel."

"I wouldn't want to walk across it, though."

I smiled. "When Peyton did that, my heart was in my throat. I was sure he was going to fall and die and I'd have to go home and tell my mom."

Mac leaned over a bit more, peering down. "But he didn't."

"Nope." I looked up at the blue sky over our heads. "I think he had his own saint protecting him back then. Is there one for morons taking stupid risks in the woods?"

"I don't think so. But there are a few that can be applied pretty broadly. Like the saint of wanderers, travelers, the lost. Or whatever." He reached up, taking out his own pendant and glancing at it. "My mom's favorite is Saint Anthony, the finder of lost things. She has this rhyme she says when anything's missing: 'Tony, Tony, turn around. Something's lost that must be found.'"

"Does it work?" I asked.

"Sometimes," he replied, sliding the pendant back under his shirt. As always, I noticed the give in the chain, the empty length now there. "Doesn't hurt."

We stood there a moment, everything silent except the breeze blowing overhead. Looking across the hole, I had a flash of Peyton's rigid shoulders as he walked over that tree. For once he was focused not on finding the invisible place, but on having everyone's attention; it was just the beginning of that.

Remember? I'd asked him on the phone that night when I'd mentioned this.

Not my brightest moment.

All this time, I'd thought Peyton saw himself the same way I did, the way we all did. Invincible. Otherworldly. But he'd known he was human, long before I did. Or maybe all along.

Mac turned, looking down at me. "What is it?"

I knew he was asking because I'd made a noise, or a face, thinking this. Or even just gone visibly still. But I took this inquiry wider, stretching it to include everything that had changed since that first day I walked into Seaside. The changes in me.

What is it? Maybe the lives I'd glimpsed in the last hour: the sneaky geeks eating pizza while savoring their resourcefulness, the new bride serving bought fettuccine on her wedding china. Or this place, so strong in my memory, even as I made another memory right now. All I could think was that here, finally, for once, I wasn't only watching and reporting but part of this moving, changing world as well.

I took my hand from Mac's, then reached up to touch his cheek. When I did, his fingers moved to my waist, pulling me in closer. It was fluid and easy, like everything had been since we'd met, as I stood on my tiptoes and finally, finally kissed him. There, in the woods, on a late fall Thursday afternoon, it was perfect. I'd had no way of knowing this when I did it, of course. It was just a hunch.

CHAPTER
17

"WAIT. SO we *can't* use the studio?"

"No, you can," I said. "It's just going to be a little more complicated than I thought."

I was leaning against Mac in the truck, his arms around me so I couldn't see his face. When I twisted, he was giving me a look I already recognized: wary, waiting. Classic Mac. "Complicated," he repeated. "*That* sounds promising."

"It's fine." I turned back around. "Just trust me. Okay?"

He didn't reply as I rested the back of my head against his chest, folding my legs up against me. The cab of his truck was cramped and smelled of garlic knots, hardly the ideal place to be together. But I'd learned not to even expect perfection in any form. And actually, this was pretty close.

It had been less than a week since the afternoon in the woods. Since then, one unbelievable thing had happened after another. Us saying good-bye a half hour later, and lingering, the way I'd only seen others do, before I finally made myself drive away. Texts all through the evening and one final call, so his voice was the last I heard before going to bed.

Then there was the first day back at school, everything so different, if only to us. Again, I was a girl with a secret. This time, though, it was a good one.

I felt bad keeping anything from Layla, especially something so big as me actually, maybe, falling in love for the first time. This, though, was complicated. Kimmie Crandall, the cautionary tale, was always in the back of my mind. As much as she liked me, Mac was her brother. Better to keep things quiet, for now, anyway.

So we'd done our best to proceed as normal. At school during lunch, we stayed on our separate benches. At Seaside, he remained behind the counter with his textbooks while Layla and I took our normal table to do homework. Nothing was different, except when we were alone.

Like now, pulled over in a neighborhood playground called Commons Park. No deliveries waiting, nowhere to be. The engine was off but the truck's cab still warm as I curled up against him; outside, red and yellow leaves kicked up by a breeze swirled across the windshield. In a twist I never would have expected, these hours between school and dinner I'd once dreaded were now the ones I most looked forward to.

I was learning new things about him all the time. Not just that he was a good kisser (very good, actually) and had the tightest set of abs I'd ever seen or touched (Kwackers, maybe?). There was also the way his hair was just long enough in front to always need to be brushed aside, something he did with a slight jerk of his head, something I now considered a signature move. The way that when he talked about a topic that troubled him—his dad expecting him to take over Seaside, for instance—he automatically lowered his voice, so you wanted to lean in deeper, listen harder.

"As far as my dad's concerned, it's just how it is," he'd told me a few days earlier when this came up. "Business *is* family, and vice versa. Nothing trumps them."

"You going to school would be *good* for the family, though," I pointed out. "More education, more earning potential. And Layla wants to take it over."

"Layla *says* she wants to take it over," he corrected me. "There's a difference."

"And there's Rosie, too," I said. "It shouldn't be just about you because you're the boy."

"Not how he sees it," he said. He shook his hair out of his face again. "I'm still going to apply to the U and a few other schools, though. I can't not try. That's like quitting."

I thought of our talk, weeks earlier, about broken things and how he didn't accept there wasn't a fix for everything, somehow. It wasn't just about clocks and starters. Like so much with Mac, what he felt strongly about was wide and vast. I felt so lucky to be included in it.

For as long as I could remember, other people had either overshadowed me or left me out in the open, alone. But Mac, as Layla had said all those weeks ago, was always somewhere nearby. He left me enough space to stand alone, but stood at the ready for the moment that I didn't want to. It was the perfect medium, I was learning. Like he was *my* saint, the one I'd been waiting for.

This was never more evident than when I talked to him about Ames. One day, when we were out delivering, a red Lexus had pulled up beside us. I'd frozen, he'd noticed, and the next thing I knew I was telling him everything.

"I can't believe your parents aren't aware of any of this," he said when I finally finished talking. "The dude's got a bad vibe."

"Not to them," I said.

"They should be able to tell if *you* seem weird."

I shrugged. "I told you. They don't look too closely at me."

"Then make them," he said. "If you told them what you just told me, they'd pay attention."

I knew he was probably right. But just the thought of bringing this up with my mom made me nervous, like I didn't have even a foot to stand on, much less a leg.

"Just think about it," he said, clearly sensing my hesitation. "Okay?"

"Yeah," I said. "Okay."

In response, he turned to face me. When he leaned in, kissing me once on the lips, then on the forehead, I felt safe enough to close my eyes.

At home, however, things were getting more and more strained. On Thursday, my parents would leave to spend the night at a hotel in Lincoln so they could attend Peyton's ceremony the following morning. My mom was in overdrive, fielding phone calls and sending e-mails as she organized the reception she and a couple of the other family members had put together.

"I was thinking we could have dinner with the Biscoes

the night before," she'd told us one evening. "You know, Rog-
erson's parents? I told you about him, he's on Peyton's hall? It
might be really helpful to share our stories, get to know one
another. I've found a good place that takes reservations—"

"Julie." My father's voice was gentle, even though it was
obvious he was cutting her off. "Maybe we should hold off
on that."

She put down her fork. "Why?"

My dad looked so uncomfortable, I found myself shifting
in my chair in sympathy, like it was me who'd chosen to walk
out on this particular plank. "We're going to an event at a
prison," he said finally. "Not a preschool."

Instantly, her smile vanished. "You really think it's necessary to point that out to me?"

"I didn't before. But from the way you're talking—"

"I," she said, her voice wavering, rising, "am putting a
positive spin on a bad situation. When life gets dark, you
celebrate any light. This is my light. Let me enjoy it."

It was a testimony to how black things had gotten that
this event signified brightness. I was always aware of how
things had changed. Times like this, though, it surprised me
all over again.

I couldn't talk to her about this, of course, or to my dad,
either. But there was someone who did understand, or at
least listen. Thank goodness.

"So, Sydney," Mrs. Chatham said. "How are things at
home?"

We were in their living room, with her in her chair, me

on the couch, keeping my distance from the dogs. Mac was taking a break from deliveries to tinker with the truck's still-stubborn starter, as he often had to, and I'd taken to visiting with his mom until he was finished or another order came in.

"The same," I told her as the engine gurgled to life outside, then quickly died. "My parents are going to a graduation thing at the prison, and my mom's completely obsessed with it. You'd think he was getting a diploma from Harvard, the way she's acting."

She smiled. "I felt the same way when Rosie finished her rehab. You take what you can get, I guess."

We were both quiet a moment. Outside, I was pretty sure I heard Mac cursing.

"Layla tells me you bumped into that boy," she said. "At SuperThrift."

Just hearing this, I had a flash of those galoshes. "Yeah. It was the first time I'd seen him face-to-face."

"And?"

"I freaked." At the other end of the couch, one of the dogs sighed loudly. "I couldn't even speak."

"Oh, honey." She was quiet for a moment. "It's not like it's going to come easy, if it ever comes at all. You know that, right?"

"I just don't know what I could say that would even make a difference. An apology won't change anything."

"Maybe you shouldn't expect it to. For him, anyway." She looked at me, her gaze kind as always. "But that doesn't mean it wouldn't help in some way for you. It could, you know, lift some of the weight."

Again, she'd hit it dead-on. How the guilt felt so heavy on me, like ten of those drapes they put on you at the dentist before they take X-rays. More than enough to hold you down, no matter how you struggle to rise up.

"I don't know," I said.

"You don't have to right now," she told me. "You're doing just fine."

I wasn't so sure about this. But hearing it was a comfort anyway. As was the sound of the truck starting up again outside, the engine revving a few times. Making stuff work. Somehow.

That afternoon I came home to find the house empty and the phone ringing. It was five forty-five, a time that Peyton often called. This time, though, I didn't have that familiar sense of dread when the recording announced it was a call from Lincoln.

"Hey," I said, once he was on the line. "How are you?"

"Okay." A pause, voices in the background. "What's up with you?"

I paused, wondering what I should tell him. It seemed weird to mention Mac or the Chathams, to talk about a world he was no part of, all my own. But then I remembered that day in the woods.

"I went out to the sinkhole with a friend of mine," I said. "It had changed."

"Yeah?"

I nodded, even though he couldn't see me. "I mean, it was the same, I guess. But the perspective was different. I remember it being so wide. Huge."

"It looked even bigger when you were halfway across it," he said.

"I bet."

We were both quiet a moment. Then he said, "So, it's funny. That show you love, the one with those crazy women? I've been . . . watching it."

I blinked, surprised. "You're watching *Big New York*?"

He laughed. "And *Los Angeles*. Although I can't believe I'm admitting it."

"I thought you hated those shows," I said, still in shock.

"I did." He sighed. "But this friend of mine here . . . he's totally into them. He's a doctor, a shrink. He claims for him it's about the personality disorders, all that narcissism. But I think he just likes the drama."

"He's your doctor?"

Another laugh. "No. He's an inmate, an addict. Got busted for selling prescriptions. We call him MD. He's a nice guy. Even if he has bad taste in TV shows."

"Hey, now," I said. "Remember who you're talking to."

"Like I could forget," he said. And then the recorded voice came on, warning us time was about up. For the first time, I wished it weren't.

I didn't mention any of this to my mom, even when I told her he'd called. After all the pushing for us to talk, now that we were, I wanted to keep it to myself. Peyton

302   SARAH DESSEN

didn't tell her, either. Another secret, all our own.

The truth was, Mom was so immersed in her plans, she wasn't noticing much of anything. The upside was she hadn't said more about Ames staying with me. It was foolish, I knew, to think I'd dodged this particular bullet because it hadn't been fired just yet. But everything else had been going so well. I should have known better.

"So," she'd said that morning when I came down for breakfast. "Tomorrow, your father and I are leaving at around three. Ames will be here by ten at the latest. It's not ideal, but with Marla out of the picture and his valet job, it's the best we can do."

She had her back to me as she spoke, busy checking things off another list. Piled on the counter were all the baked goods she'd gotten at Big Club, the bulk store, for the ceremony: danishes, cookies, cupcakes. The whole room smelled like sugar.

"I really think I can stay alone," I said. "By the time he gets here, I'll almost be in bed anyway."

She picked up a box of mini cupcakes, moving it to the top of another stack. "It's all set. Now get your cereal together, you're going to be late."

End of conversation. Once again, I was an item on a list, crossed off and archived. When I left twenty minutes later, I couldn't help it: I slammed the door behind me.

Now, in the truck, Mac's phone buzzed. He shifted behind me, pulling it from his pocket. "Delivery up. Back to work."

I glanced at my watch. It was five fifteen, and I'd told my mom I'd be home before six, but all I wanted to do was stay in this safe, easy place, with Mac's arms around me. But he was already starting to sit up as I said, "Five more minutes?"

"Two." He kissed the top of my head, easing back. A moment passed, and then he said, "You know, we don't have to record at your place if it's a problem. Eric will find another way. He always does."

"It's not a problem," I told him. "It's going to be perfect."

This was not a word I used much, if ever. But sometimes, lately, I'd allowed myself to think that things actually could work out. After all, I was here now, with him, and who would have ever expected *that*?

He drove me back to Seaside, pulling up to my car before heading in to grab the delivery. We said our good-byes, the careful way we always did, and I got out, shutting the door behind me. But as I started to walk away, I looked up at that setting sun, the sky blue, dappled with pink. *Perfect*, I risked thinking again, if only for a moment. I turned around and went up to Mac's open window.

"Forget something?" he asked.

"Yeah," I told him. "This."

I stood on my tiptoes, leaned in, and gave him a kiss. I could feel his surprise, then hesitation, before he eased into it. It was a risk, being public like this, but I was already tired of hiding. Anyway, Layla, my only true concern, was with Spence; it didn't occur to me to think of anyone else. At least, not then.

❀ ❀ ❀

"Wow," Eric said when I opened the door. "Nice digs."

"Did you just say 'digs'?" Irv asked from behind him, where he was filling the rest of the door frame. "Really?"

"What? It's actually a quite common term."

"And these are actually quite heavy. So would you enter the digs, please?"

Eric rolled his eyes, and I stepped aside to let him in. He was carrying his guitar, his backpack over one shoulder. Following behind and carrying all the rest of the equipment were Irv, Ford, and finally Mac.

The fact that I'd noticed this inequity must have been obvious, as Mac explained, "Eric's got a bad back."

"Eric," Irv added, huffing slightly as he lifted a black case about half my size over the threshold, "*claims* he has a bad back. I've never seen evidence of it, except when we have something heavy to move."

"It's my L3 and L4 disc," Eric replied in a tired voice. "It's agitated."

"*I'm* agitated. This shit is heavy." Irv put down the case with a thunk, rattling the glass table beneath my brother's portrait. "Where are we taking it?"

"Downstairs," I told him. "Follow me."

I led them through the door past the kitchen, down the winding stairs (more huffing, more comments about Eric's disc), and finally, into the workout room and then the studio. As I flipped on the light, Eric stood back, taking an appreciative look around while the others carried in the stuff. "Wow. This was all for your brother?"

"Was supposed to be," I said. "He kind of got, um, preoccupied before he could use it much."

"Is that what we're calling prison now?" Irv asked. "A preoccupation?"

Mac poked him, hard. "Hey. Watch it."

"What?" Irv looked at him, then at me. "Oh. Sorry, Sydney. I'm just talking, being stupid."

"It's fine," I said, and smiled at him.

Still, Mac came over as Ford and Eric began unpacking instruments. "Sorry about that. Irv's kind of a straight shooter, especially about certain things."

"He's right," I told him. "My brother is in prison. It's kind of refreshing, actually, to be around someone who calls it that."

"Yeah?"

I nodded, and then Ford was calling his name, asking him something. As he went over, then bent down to unpack a case, I watched the Saint Bathilde pendant around his neck slide into sight before he reached up, tucking it back under his collar. Yesterday, I'd held it in my own hand, between my fingers, twisting it in the dappled light at Commons Park. Just remembering made me flush.

"So, Sydney," Eric said, jerking me abruptly away from this thought, "I hear we're on a time constraint here. How long do we actually have?"

I looked at my watch. It was six thirty. "About three hours."

"Not long to get down these songs." He lifted his guitar and backpack onto the nearby couch—an action that apparently did not require his agitated disc—then rubbed his hands together. "When did you say Layla was coming?"

"Seven at the latest," Mac told him.

"Okay. Then I'd better get acquainted with this equipment." Eric walked over to the board of switches and buttons, taking a seat in the rolling chair there. "Man. This is nicer than the setup we had at VAMP."

"VAMP?"

He sat back, twisting a knob. "Vintage Acoustic Musical Performance Camp. It's where I spent last summer. Music and production classes during the day, serious jam sessions at night."

"Wow. Sounds great."

"Life-changing," he corrected me. "I mean, it was for me, anyway. Spending eight weeks with people who actually care about the music the way I do? Like an oasis in the ongoing creative desert that is my life here."

There was a rap on the glass separating us from the booth. When I looked up, Mac was standing there. "We can hear you, you know."

Eric flipped his hand, hardly bothered. But I noticed he did unpress the only button whose function I knew—the intercom—before saying, "Look, don't get me wrong. These guys like to play. But they're not *passionate*. Once high school is over, they'll tell stories about how they were once in a band. I want more than that. You know?"

I nodded as Irv helped Ford stack one amp onto another. Mac was back at his drum set, twisting clamps onto cymbals. I was watching his face, so focused, as Eric said, "So, um. There's been something I've been wanting to ask you."

"Me?"

"Yeah, you." He smiled at me. "It's not a secret I think you're cool, Sydney. I want to take you out. What do you think?"

I honestly did not know what to say. This was such a direct question, there was really no way to circumvent or dodge it. Still, I was trying to think of a way to do just that when I heard the doorbell ring. Saved.

"Shoot," I said, as if I weren't insanely grateful for this interruption. "I'll be right back, okay?"

Although I had the entire way across the workout room, up the stairs, and through the foyer to consider what to say when I returned, I made little progress. When I opened the door to find Layla supporting a red-faced, mud-streaked, damp Spence, though, all thoughts of Eric vanished.

"A little help?" she said, dragging him into the foyer. As they passed, I got a strong whiff of alcohol. And, strangely, fertilizer. "Do you have a towel or something?"

"Hey, Sydney," Spence slurred at me cheerfully. "What's up?"

"Stop moving, would you please?" Layla said to him. "Just stay there. And take off your shoes."

With that, she disappeared into the powder room, leaving us alone. Weaving slightly, Spence kicked off his Nikes, first one, then the other, before reaching into his back pants pocket to pull out a slim glass bottle. He uncapped it, took a big swig, then held it out to me. "Vodka?"

"No, thanks," I said. "Is it raining or something?"

He shook his head, taking another sip. "Sprinklers. Came on when I was crossing your neighbor's backyard. Serious water pressure. Apparently. Sure you don't want a drink?"

"She doesn't," Layla replied, emerging from the bathroom. She was holding one of our hand towels, which she held up to me, raising her eyebrows. I nodded, and she tossed it to him. "Dry off and put that away, would you? They're not going to be happy I brought you in the first place."

"Nonsense." Spence slid the bottle back into his pocket, then stepped closer to her, sliding his arms around her waist. "I told you, baby. You won't even know I'm here."

While Layla clearly doubted this, she allowed herself to be pulled in for a kiss. To her surprise, not to mention mine, it quickly became openmouthed and full-on tongue. Luckily, just then, the phone rang.

I ducked into the kitchen, grabbing the handset. "Hello?"

"This is a collect call from an inmate at Lincoln Correctional Facility," began the familiar robotic voice. "Do you accept—"

"Yes," I said, taking a few steps toward the front window.

"Are they downstairs?" Layla called out from behind me. When I turned to look at her, Spence was nuzzling her neck. I nodded. "Did they start already?"

There was a buzz, then a click. "Sydney?"

"Yeah, one second," I told my brother. To Layla I said, "Yes and I don't know. I'll be there in a sec, okay?"

She nodded, pulling away from Spence, and disappeared down the hallway. He followed, removing the bottle from his pocket again. Great.

"Sorry about that," I told Peyton. "I have some friends over. How's everything?"

"Okay," he said. "Considering that I've actually picked a team on that stupid show you like so much."

"Let me guess," I said. "You're Team Ayre."

"Nope," he replied. "MD is, though. I'm solidly Rosalie."

"What?" I said. "That's crazy. She's insane."

"Oh, and Ayre isn't? Did you not see that dinner party where she pushed Delilah in the pool?"

"She was *provoked*," I said defensively.

"Yeah, whatever." He snorted. "Well, I don't want to hold you up if you have people over. Is Mom around?"

I blinked, surprised. "No. She's already headed there."

"What?"

"She and Dad left this afternoon. For the ceremony?"

"It's not until tomorrow," he said.

"Yeah, but I guess she had a lot of stuff to do for it or something?" He said nothing. "They're staying at a hotel, meeting some of the other families, I think."

There's a difference between quiet on a phone line and angry silence. One is light, the other heavy. Right then, I pictured the connection between us sagging, almost to a breaking point.

"I can't believe this," he said finally. Behind him, the noise I knew from our few conversations was typical: raised voices, banging, intercoms. Prison was even louder than Jackson. "I told her I didn't want her to do all that. I didn't want them here at all, actually. I'm in *prison*, not school. I don't get why she can't understand that."

Wow, I thought. I'd been waiting so long for someone else to feel this way. I'd just never expected it to be Peyton. As I wondered how to reply, I heard a thump from beneath me in the studio. "I guess . . ." I began, then found myself hesitating. The line buzzed. "She's just hanging on to anything she can make feel normal."

"But this isn't normal," he replied. "I screwed up, I hurt someone, and I'm doing time for it. When she tries to make it anything else, it just . . . it makes me *nuts*. This needs to be different, you know? To be hard. Everyone else understands that. But she just doesn't *get* it."

Even with our recent talks, this was the most my brother had said to me in months, if not years. It was so unexpected, not to mention emotional, that I realized I was holding my breath. For so long, I'd seen him and my parents as one unit, sharing the same party line. But Peyton was his own person and carried his own weight. How could I not have understood that?

"I'm sorry," I said. Two words, but they felt heavy, too.

"Yeah." A pause. His voice sounded tight. I thought of him walking across that sinkhole: I saw bravery, him something else. "I'm, um . . . I'll try her on her cell."

"Okay. Take care, Peyton."

"Bye, Syd."

Another click, and he was gone. I hung up the phone, feeling a pang as I remembered my mom organizing her Big Club baked goods the previous morning, not to mention all the other work she'd done. She could tell us and everyone else it was for Peyton, and maybe she really believed that. I wasn't so sure. I hadn't thought I could feel more ashamed about the entire situation. Wrong again.

CHAPTER

18

〜⁓

"WAIT," ERIC said. "I didn't like that intro. Let's try it again."

Ford groaned, while Mac sat back behind the drum kit, rolling his eyes.

"Dude," Irv said from beside me, "it's a demo for a showcase, not your first album."

"That doesn't mean it has to suck," Eric said.

"It's not going to *exist* if you don't ease up, though," Irv replied. "We've been here for . . . how long, Sydney?"

"Hour and a half," I told him.

"Hour and a half," he repeated, emphasizing the words, "and you've got nothing down. It's time to get serious."

"I *am* being serious," Eric said.

"Then get less serious," Mac told him. "Let's just get this done."

Eric, his expression darkening, turned his back to the glass between us, adjusting something on his guitar. I looked at my watch: Ames would be showing up at ten, at which point they and all their equipment needed to be long gone. At the beginning of the evening, this had seemed entirely doable. Now I was beginning to have my doubts.

Eric's perfectionism was one problem. Another was Spence, who, after arriving and immediately knocking over two amps (that was the thump I'd heard), had been told by Layla to sit on the couch, out of the way. There he proceeded to drink most of his bottle of vodka, providing a stream of not-helpful commentary ("Are you sure you're in tune?" "More cowbell!") as he did so. I had no idea why Layla had brought him.

"I didn't," she told me out in the workout room, where we'd slipped away during yet another complicated skirmish about verse transitions. "I told him I was coming here and that your parents were gone. All he heard was 'party,' so he grabbed a bottle and headed over. When Rosie dropped me off, he was in the driveway waiting."

I thought of earlier, when I'd opened the door to see him standing on the porch, slumped against her. "Does he drink like this a lot?"

"No," she said, her voice clipped. She added, "I mean, some, sure, but it's not usually like this. Anyway, it's not his fault they're not recording. It's Eric's."

I glanced back at the open studio door, where Irv was now sitting back in the chair by the control board, his hands over his face. I could relate.

"Lay-la," Spence called out, then leaned forward on the couch, peering at us. "Come here. I miss you."

"One sec," she said, pulling her phone out of her pocket. She glanced at the screen. "Crap."

"What is it?" I asked.

"My mom." She turned, walking back into the studio,

leaning over Irv to hit the intercom button. "Mac. Rosie just texted. She thinks Mom might need to go in."

He was on his feet immediately, coming out the door. "What happened?"

"I don't know; I'll call right now." She put her phone to her ear, walking over to lean against the wall. Spence, on the couch, offered her the now-almost-empty bottle, but she waved him off. "Hey, it's me. What's going on?"

As Rosie replied and she listened, we were all silent. I glanced at Mac, but he was watching Layla.

"Okay," she said finally. "Yeah. Well, keep me posted. If you decide to take her, we'll meet you there. What? We were planning ten thirty, but we can come now if she wants us to."

Someone exhaled, frustrated. Eric, I assumed.

"All right. Yeah, do that. Thanks, Ro." She hung up, then looked at Mac. "Just the usual. Dizzy, shortness of breath. She got super light-headed and Rosie panicked, but Mom says she's fine now. She's going to keep an eye on her."

"Could be those new meds," he said. It was like the rest of us weren't there. "They said the side effects could be more pronounced, even with the smaller dosage."

"Which sucks, because they're working." Layla slid her phone back in her pocket. "Whatever, let's just try to get this done. I want to get home."

"Seconded," Mac said, turning back to the recording room. Once inside, he said to Eric, "This take is the last one for this song. Then we move on. Okay?"

Eric did not look happy about this. Still, he nodded, adjusting his guitar strap as Irv got everything on the board set up again. Mac counted them off and they began playing. I held my breath as they passed the intro into the first verse and then the chorus, the farthest they'd gotten so far.

"Sit down and relax. Have a drink," Spence said to Layla, pulling her down beside him. She sighed, then, to my surprise, reached for the bottle and took a swig. "That's my girl. Better, right?"

She swallowed, wincing, then wiped a hand over her mouth. "I swear, I don't see how this night could get any worse."

I could. Because right at that moment, Ames appeared in the open doorway. I was so startled by the sight of him, I thought for a minute I had to be imagining it. When he spoke, I knew it was for real.

"Well, look at this. It's a party."

I opened my mouth to respond, but, unfortunately, Spence spoke first.

"Now we're talking!" He turned, looking at Ames, and held out the bottle to him. "Welcome, comrade. Drink?"

"No," I said, answering for him. Still regrouping, or trying to, I said, "It's not a party. They're just recording a demo."

Ames made a point of looking at the bottle, as well as Spence slumped against Layla, before turning his attention back to me. "Your mom didn't say anything about this."

"She's been distracted," I replied. "And anyway, they're almost done."

"I wish," Irv said. The guys were wrapping up the song now, having actually made it through the entire thing. "Although we're further along than we were, I'll give you that."

I didn't like the way Ames was surveying the room, taking it all in: Layla on the couch, the guys on the other side of the glass, Irv in his seat at the controls. Then, finally, me. "Let's talk outside," he said. "Okay?"

Layla was watching me as I followed him out into the workout room, where he gestured for me to take a seat on my dad's workout bench.

"So," he said, crossing his arms over his chest. "Want to tell me what's going on here?"

"I did. They're recording a demo."

"And drinking," he added.

"Spence is drinking," I corrected him. "I don't even really know him."

"And yet he's here, in the house, while Peyton and Julie are gone." He cocked his head to the side. "I have to say, Sydney, I'm surprised. This is not like you."

"They're my friends; they needed a studio. It's not that complicated."

"And that guy playing drums? Who's he?"

I blinked, caught off guard. "Why?"

He shrugged, then leaned back against the wall, studying my face. "Just curious. I saw you with him the other day, in the parking lot of that strip mall off Mason. You seemed pretty close. *Very* close, actually."

It took me a moment to catch up. In the lag, he was watching me, the slightest of smiles on his face. "Are you going to tell my mom about this?"

Instead of answering, he looked back into the studio, where Spence was now stretched out across the couch, eyes closed, the bottle on the floor beside him. Layla was nowhere in sight, which I assumed meant they had indeed moved on to her song.

"I don't know," Ames said finally. "We'll talk about it later."

I wanted to know now. Then I could accept my sentence and the reality of the repercussions. But I knew Ames. Now he finally had the upper hand, and he wasn't going to relinquish it any earlier than necessary.

"Sydney."

Glancing at the studio, I saw Irv filling the doorway, looking out at us. "Yeah?"

"We need you."

I looked at Ames. "Go ahead," he said. "I'm right behind you."

I went back in to find Layla on the other side of the glass, headphones on, a microphone in front of her. Eric was at the board, getting things set up so that Irv could record again. Behind me, I could hear Spence snoring.

"What's going on?" I asked.

"We need backup vocals," Eric told me, still futzing around with some dials. "No time to layer them in. So you're up."

"Me?" I said. "I don't sing."

"Everyone can sing."

"Let me rephrase that," I told him. "I don't sing well."

"It's not opera," he replied. "We just need to fill out the sound. You know the song, right? Paulie Prescott, 'Four A.M.'?"

Of course I did. After I finished swooning over the safe boy-next-door Logan Oxford, Paulie Prescott was my first bad-boy crush, or as bad as you could be wearing eyeliner while performing concerts at malls. "Four A.M." was his biggest hit, a half-rap, half-sung description of driving home after a night of partying and fighting and wanting to call a girl, but deciding she deserved better. It was just the kind of thing that, at thirteen, you wanted some lovesick rebel to sing about you. I'd had it on repeat for weeks.

"I think I remember it," I said.

"Great." Eric stood up, turning to face me. "Now, we're doing it acoustic, very quiet, in contrast to the original production. Remember all those big guitars? It was all swagger, or fake swagger, actually. So for this, we're turning it on its head, going light, ballad-esque, more of a love song than the original ego-driven recitation of various acts of valor that may or may not have actually happened."

Beside me, Ames blinked. "Whoa."

"Exactly," Eric told him. "So we'll just have you come in during the chorus, behind Layla, to convey the *routine* aspect of this, that it's not just one girl who's felt it, but many. But just for two lines: 'You're sleeping only a mile from here/But it feels so far away.' The two following—"

"'While I want to see you, touch you, feel you/In my dreams I'll let you stay'?" So much for pretending I didn't know it by heart.

"Right. For those, I want only Layla, for contrast. See, your lines are about the truth of this situation: the wanting. The other are the ideal, the way girls *wish* guys really felt. Okay?"

It was a testament to how familiar I'd become with Eric and his music discussions that none of this seemed over the top to me. Ames, however, exhaled as Eric went back into the recording room, then said, "Man. I've heard that song a million times. Never thought of it that way."

"Nobody does," Irv told him, adjusting something on the board.

I turned back to the glass, looking in at Layla, who was nodding as Eric talked to her, explaining all this again. Mac was back on the drums, saying something to Ford, when I felt Ames move closer, putting his hands on my shoulders. He gave a light squeeze, then left them there while saying, "So you're singing? I can't wait to see this. Nervous?"

"No," I said, although I was. I shifted slightly, trying to get out from under him, but he was too close, and now squeezing again.

"You'll be great. Just relax."

I swallowed, doing the exact opposite and tensing up, hoping he'd take the hint and back off. But no. He was still right there, his fingers lightly on my shoulders, when Mac looked up and saw us.

Seeing his face, I had a flash of Layla's, all those weeks ago at the courthouse. But while her expression, as a stranger, had been a question—*You okay?*—Mac's was different. Like he knew I was not, and because of that, he wasn't, either. He was just getting to his feet when Eric spoke.

"Okay, Sydney. You ready?"

I pulled away quickly, then walked into the recording

room, where Eric was setting up a microphone. As he waved me behind it, Layla leaned into my ear.

"What's he doing here?"

"He's staying tonight. But he wasn't supposed to come until ten."

"Huh." She adjusted her headphones. "What are the chances. Is he going to tell your mom?"

"He says we'll talk about it."

She made another pointed look as Ames gave us a thumbs-up. "I'd stay if I could, I swear. But I've got to get home to my mom."

"It's fine," I said. Then I turned, glancing behind me at Mac, who, as I expected, was watching me. I only had a second to try to convey that he shouldn't worry, I was all right. But just in case, I said it, too. "It'll be okay."

At that point, despite everything, I still believed this. This confidence stayed with me as we ran through a quick rehearsal, then started to record. I could almost forget about Ames on the other side of the glass and whatever might happen later; right then, there was only the music. Eric's guitar, and Ford behind it. The haunting sweetness of Layla's voice moving over the words I knew so well, and then my own, blending with it if only for a moment. Through it all, Mac was behind me, keeping the beat, holding it all together. Later, I'd look back at this as the last time things felt perfect, and be so grateful for it. Some people never get that at all.

❧ ❧ ❧

"Do we have it?"

We all waited, silent, as Eric punched a few buttons, his brow furrowed. Then, finally: "Yep. We've got it."

"*Hallelujah*," Irv said, speaking for everyone. "Can we go eat now?"

"You've been eating the whole time," Layla pointed out.

"I've been *snacking*," he corrected her. "It's mealtime."

"Actually, it's go time," she said. "Rosie's waiting for us. Let's get packed up, okay?"

Mac nodded, then headed back into the recording room, where he, Irv, and Ford began dismantling the instruments and equipment. Upstairs, I could hear Ames moving around as Layla turned her attention to Spence, still crashed out on the couch. He hadn't budged since falling asleep.

"Luckily, he sobers up fast," she told me, walking over and shaking his shoulder. "Spence. Wake up. Time to go."

"Just five more minutes," he mumbled into the cushions.

Layla shook her head, then picked up the vodka bottle from the floor. She began to twist the top on, but then changed her mind, opening it and taking a swig. Then she handed it out to me.

I'd go over this moment again and again in the coming weeks. It was just such a stupid thing, a handful of seconds. And yet it was a pivotal point, the shift between before and after. I don't know why I took the bottle, tipping it up to my mouth. Maybe it was the long night. Or what still might lie ahead, with Ames. Whatever the reason, I did it, taking one big gulp and closing my eyes, tight, as I swallowed.

When I opened them, my mother was in the doorway.

Like Ames, she'd just appeared. As I looked at her face, everything crystallized: the smooth glass of the bottle in my hand; Spence's foot, hanging off the couch; the guys moving in my peripheral vision, talking amongst themselves; Layla beside me, equally surprised. That bottle, again, in my hand.

"Sydney?" Like she wasn't sure it was me, either. The crease between her brows was deeper than I'd ever seen it. "What is going on here?"

"Mom," I said quickly, putting down the bottle. This seemed important, although I already knew it wasn't going to make any difference. "It's not . . . They were just using the studio."

"You're drinking." A statement, although she sounded so incredulous, it might as well have been a question.

"I wasn't, actually." She shifted her gaze to the vodka, then to Spence, snoring softly on the couch. "I mean, I just took that sip. Just now."

"You're drinking," she repeated. She looking into the recording room. "Who are these people in Peyton's studio?"

"My brother's band," Layla said. My mom looked at her. "Mac. You met him at the pizza place? They needed to record a demo, and Sydney—"

"I told you, remember?" I cut in.

"And I said no." Her voice was clipped, each syllable sharp. She looked at me. "You deliberately disobeyed me, Sydney. And you have alcohol here in our house, not to mention people I do not know."

"Mom—"

She raised a hand. *Stop.* "I don't want to hear it. It's been a long, bad night. Just get these people out of here. Now."

Layla was instantly in motion, going over and giving Spence a hard enough shake to finally wake him up. "Wha—" he mumbled.

"Come *on*," she told him. Then she walked over to the board, hitting the intercom. "Speed it up, fellas. Time to go."

Eric, his back to us, sighed. "We're moving as quickly as we can. This is delicate equipment."

"Go faster," she snapped, then dropped her hand. Hearing this, they all stopped what they were doing and looked at us, finally seeing my mom. Mac's eyes went wide. It was strange to see him surprised. The next thing I knew, he was heading our way.

Oh, God, I thought, both grateful and terrified as he came through the door. Layla was busy with Spence, so it was just me there with my mom when he joined us. "Mrs. Stanford," he said. "This isn't . . . Sydney was just doing me a favor. I shouldn't have put her in this position. It's my fault, totally. I'm sorry."

He said this so genuinely, so truthfully, that I felt something inside my heart shift. Each time I thought I'd felt all I could for him, there was more.

I slid my hand down his arm, wrapping my fingers around his. "You don't have to say that," I told him.

"I want to," he replied.

"I'm sorry, but who are you?" my mom snapped.

"*Mac*," I said. "Layla's brother. My friend."

"Boyfriend," another voice said, from outside the door. Ames. "Either that or just a guy she makes out with in parking lots."

"*What?*"

I turned, slowly, to see Layla frozen behind me. She was looking at our still-joined hands the same way my mom had the bottle, as if she couldn't quite believe her eyes.

"I saw them," Ames said to my mom. "I wasn't going to tell you, figured Sydney would. But I guess now you know."

"Now I know," my mom repeated. To Mac, she said, "Is that your alcohol?"

"No," he replied. "It's not."

She looked at me. "I want these people out of here, Sydney. Do you understand me?"

"Mrs. Stanford—" Mac said.

"*Do not talk to me.*" She kept her eyes level, dark and furious and solidly on mine. "Just get out of my house, and take your friends with you. *Now.*"

Mac kept my hand in his a moment longer. Then he unfolded his fingers and let me go.

As they'd come in and set up, there'd been constant conversation: directions of equipment placement, discussion of Eric's agitated disc, all the back and forth of a group of people trying to get something done together. While they packed up, no one spoke. I knew, because I was listening as I stared into my mom's eyes, still focused on mine. After so long in my own invisible place, I was squarely in her sights. Just not the way I'd wanted to be.

Distantly, I was aware of everything else that was happening: Layla brushing past me without a word, tugging a stumbling, sleepy Spence behind her. Eric's and Ford's quick, cautious looks. How surprisingly light Irv's large hand felt as it touched my shoulder briefly. And, finally, Mac, the last one to leave us. Only then did my mom look away from me, her eyes following him, but I couldn't bring myself to do the same. I was not punished yet, had no idea what would happen next. But already all that space left in my heart, open after being clenched tight for so long, was narrowing. When the door shut behind them, I felt it close.

CHAPTER
19

WE WEREN'T in a courtroom, and nobody asked me to rise. But I still knew a sentencing when I saw it.

My mom, sitting across the table, cleared her throat, then looked at my dad. It was seven a.m. the next morning; a half hour earlier, he'd come into my room and told me to wake up, get showered, and come downstairs. The first part was easy, as I hadn't slept all night. This, though, was going to be hard.

"Sydney," he began as I crossed my legs tightly under the table, "I don't think we have to tell you that we are very, *very* disappointed in you right now."

I said nothing. I knew I wasn't to speak yet.

"Your mother specifically told you that your friends could not use the studio," he continued. "Still, you invited them to do so. You are underage and know the rules of this house. Yet there was alcohol here, and you were drinking."

I couldn't help it. "I only—"

He held up his hand, but it was my mom's glare that stopped me midsentence.

"You know how concerned and worried we both are

about your brother and his situation. It's frankly unfathom-
able to us that you would choose to add to our burden, to
this *family's* burden, with this kind of behavior."

"I wasn't trying to burden anyone," I said quietly, studying the tabletop. "I just wanted to help a friend."

"This is Mac?" my mom said, enunciating his name like
you might the word *herpes* or *molestation*. "Ames tells us he's
your boyfriend."

I felt my face flush, angry now. "Ames doesn't know anything about me."

"Clearly. He came over expecting to watch a movie with
you and found a party instead."

"It wasn't a party!"

"Sydney! There was a drunk boy here!"

"That's Layla's boyfriend, and I didn't invite him. I hardly
know him!"

"Well, *that's* reassuring," my mom said.

"That's not . . ." I stopped, forcing myself to take a breath.
"Mac and Layla are my friends. Mac's band had a chance to
enter a showcase and needed a demo. We have a studio."

"A studio," my mom added, "that we said they could not
use."

"But at first, you did!" I pointed out. "That night we
ordered the pizza. You were open to it. And then Peyton
called, and he got angry with you, and just like that, everything changed."

"This is not about your brother," my dad said to me.

"For once!" I said. They both looked surprised: my voice
was higher, louder than I'd realized. "Everything is about

Peyton, all the time. And that's okay, I get it. But this was one thing, for me, that I wanted."

"You wanted to have your friends over, drinking, unsupervised, in our home," my mom said. "Well, that's great. Just wonderful."

"No," I said, again loudly enough to get shot a look from my dad. I lowered my voice. "I wanted to do something to thank my friends for being so good to me. To repay a bit of the debt I owe them for taking me in. That's all. That's *it*."

My mom sighed, taking a sip of her coffee as my father leaned forward. "You can understand, I'm sure," he said, "that it's surprising for us that you're close enough with people we barely know to break our rules and trust this way."

"I *wanted* you to know them," I said. "I still do. I invited Mac in that night, when we first talked about the studio. You met him, Dad. I wasn't keeping him a secret."

"Oh, well, good," my mom said. "Because I was beginning to think you lied about everything."

"Why are you *being* like this?" I asked her. "I'm not a bad kid, and you know it. This was one night, one thing. One mistake. And I'm sorry. But you can't—"

"Your brother started with one mistake as well," she replied. "Which led to another. And another."

"I'm *not* Peyton," I said. It seemed crazy I'd have to say this, as all my life they'd made it clear it was the one thing they knew for sure.

"You're damn right you're not. And you won't be, as long as I have anything to say about it." She pushed back her chair, getting to her feet. "First thing Monday, we go meet with

Perkins Day about transferring you. In the meantime, you go to school and nowhere else. I want you home by three thirty every day until we get this sorted out."

"Sorted out?" My voice and panic were both rising. "You can't make me switch schools."

Suddenly, she was pouncing, lunging across the table at me, slapping her hands on the surface. "I," she said, right into my face as I drew back, startled, "can do whatever I want. I am your mother, and I make the rules. From now on you follow them. We're done here."

She pulled back, straightening up, but I stayed where I was. I was still gripping the chair arms when she left the room.

For a moment, my dad sat there, not saying anything. We both knew he'd follow her, the way he always did. But it was the pause before that I'd recall later. Like if my parents were finally going to shift from their respective, decided responsibilities, this was when it could happen. Maybe he might have listened, if I tried to explain. It couldn't have made things worse. I'd never know, though, because then he was getting to his feet, wearily, and pushing the chair in behind him. Court adjourned.

* * *

I had Peyton to thank for everything that happened that night. After our conversation, he had indeed reached my mom on her cell, just as my parents were checking in to the hotel. I could picture the moment of her answering, her face brightening as it always did at his voice. And then her smile wavering, followed by confusion as he told her, now adamant, that he *did not* want her there. I imagined her resisting, explaining, tears audible in her voice before filling her eyes. Then silence as Peyton told her he wouldn't be attending the ceremony, even if she was, and hanging up on her.

All of this was so easy to imagine, as was the drive back home and the moment she came in and Ames told her what was happening downstairs. The weird thing was that even though what followed I *had* seen, with my own eyes, it was the part that still felt like a dream.

By Sunday morning, my mom was rested and ready to focus on a new project: me. It was obvious the moment I came down to breakfast and found her at the table with a shiny new folder, a stack of papers, and her coffee.

"So I've been in touch with Headmaster Florence," she said, skipping a salutation, "and she's of the mind that a midsemester switch is not in your best interest."

I paused, right where I was, to give Mrs. Florence—a tall woman with birdlike features who had never been particularly fond of me—my eternal gratitude. "So I get to stay at Jackson?"

My mom picked up her coffee cup, taking a sip. "Until the end of the marking period, yes. After that, we'll revisit the issue. In the meantime, there will be some modifications."

That didn't sound promising. I went over to the fridge, taking out the milk, then gathered my cereal and a bowl. She was waiting for me to ask her what was in store, I knew, and the only power I had was not doing so. So I didn't.

"Starting tomorrow," she said, "I've signed you up for tutoring and SAT prep at the Kiger Center. Monday through Friday, three thirty to five."

The Kiger Center was where Jenn worked, in the strip mall just across the street from the Arbors guardhouse. "My grades are good, though. So are my prep test scores."

"There's always room for improvement," she replied. "Additionally, there's a Kiger study group that meets at Jackson each day at lunchtime. I've signed you up for that, as well."

"I have to study at lunch?"

She leveled her gaze at me. "You're a junior now. SAT prep is crucial. You need all the practice you can get."

"But," I said, realizing even as I spoke that arguing was probably futile, "all I'll be *doing* is studying."

She opened the folder, jotting something down on a sheet of paper inside. "Well, then you'll be more than prepared to transfer back to Perkins, or to one of the other schools I'm considering, after the break."

"Other schools?" This just kept getting worse.

"There are actually quite a few options since I last did this kind of research," she said. She took out a sheet of paper, putting it in front of me. "Kiffney-Brown is my first choice, but you'll need to really work to pass their entrance exam. There's also a charter school that just opened with a focus on math and science that's intriguing. But I'm just beginning to read up on it."

I'd thought the dread I'd been feeling since Thursday

night had already hit its maximum. Seeing the printed spreadsheet of schools—each listed with its average SAT score, tuition (if applicable), and requirements for enrollment—proved me wrong. I knew my mother in this mode. Peyton had finally succeeded in stopping her from organizing his life. Now she had her full arsenal of resources, not to mention all the time in the world, to focus on mine.

"She's just reacting still," Mac told me when I reported all this. My parents hadn't taken my phone as part of my punishment—yet—so I was calling and texting him as much as I could while I still had the chance. "It freaked her out, seeing you with the bottle and all of us there. Too much like your brother."

"She wants to send me to Kiffney-Brown," I said. "That's, like, the genius school. She's delusional. Even with all this studying she's signed me up for, I'd never have a chance."

"It would probably still be better than that charter, though," he replied. "Irv has a bunch of friends there. Says it's like college."

There was that dread again. Not about the academics, although that wasn't exactly calming. Worse, though, was the thought of being away from him, from Layla, from this world in which I'd somehow managed to find a place. That was assuming, however, they still wanted me.

"Has she said anything?" I asked him again. I'd texted Layla multiple times, even gone so far as to leave a voice mail, but had heard nothing in return. To be fair, she'd been clear about her rule concerning dating Mac. But I was hoping for forgiveness, and if not that, a chance to explain.

"She's been caught up with Spence," he replied. "Total drama. You know how they are."

It was kind of him to sidestep the question, but it just made me feel worse. To me, the Chathams were like that merry-go-round out in the middle of nowhere in the woods. I hadn't been aware they'd existed; it was pure luck to have stumbled upon them. Now that I had, I couldn't forget and go back to the way I'd been before. Just knowing they were out there changed everything. Especially me.

Monday morning, my mom sent me off to school with my own folder, containing the information about the Kiger lunchtime study group (*Attendance taken daily*, she'd highlighted in bright yellow), as well as a packet with the details of the after-school program. When I got to my locker before the first bell, Mac was waiting for me. The only upside of all this—and it was a big one—was that we had no reason to hide anymore.

"Hey," he said. "Long time, no see."

I smiled, or tried to, and then he was wrapping his arms around me, pulling me close. Despite all of the typical loud noise of Jackson around us, it was like everything went quiet as I pressed my face into his shirt, feeling his pendant against my forehead. He smelled like soap and coffee, and I just wanted to stay there, breathing nothing but him, for as long as possible. But the bell was already ringing, so he walked me to homeroom, kissed me, and disappeared into the crowd.

I looked for him everywhere, though, and for Layla. Jackson, which had seemed so vast and infinite when I first arrived, had become manageable, even familiar, once I had friends there. With no contact at lunch, my chances of seeing any of them were left up to fate. Between second and third, over the heads of several people, I caught a glimpse of Eric. I rerouted every chance I had to pass by Layla's locker; she was never there. At lunch, rushing to the Kiger group, I craned my neck at a window, trying to see the benches where I knew they gathered, but had no luck. My mother's plan was working. I was alone again. It was so much harder this time.

"It's going to be okay," Mac told me that first afternoon as we grabbed a fleeting few minutes at his truck before I had to leave for the Kiger Center. Already my mom had texted me twice, reminding me to be there at three thirty sharp to meet her for an overview of the program. "It's just the first day. We'll work it out, I promise."

I wanted to believe this, and him. But I knew my mom. Once she had a project in her grasp, her grip only tightened. I didn't say this, though, as he leaned down, putting his lips on mine. When we finally pulled apart, I opened my eyes to see Layla across the parking lot. She had on her army jacket, her hair loose over her shoulders, and when she saw us, she stopped walking. We looked at each other for a moment, Mac there unaware between us. Then she turned around and went back the way she'd come.

* * *

"Okay," Jenn said later that afternoon, when my mom had finally left the Kiger Center after exhausting everyone with all her questions and concerns. It was four forty-five, so I had no time to actually get anything started, but she insisted I stay the full time, anyway. "What is going *on*?"

We were in the front lobby. Her PSAT cram class, made up mostly of Arbors kids, was taking a practice test down the hall.

"The short version is that she caught me with friends over when she was out of town, and I was drinking."

Her eyes widened. I could always count on Jenn for a reaction. "Seriously?"

I nodded. "The longer version involves me trying to help out my friends, Ames being typically creepy, and my mom happening to walk in at the exact moment that I took my only sip of alcohol."

"Long version sounds more complicated."

"That's why it's longer." I sat back in the uncomfortable chair I'd chosen; it was clearly meant for people to only alight on for short periods, not actually settle in. "My parents were supposed to be at Lincoln for something of Peyton's. But he told her he didn't want her there. She came home, walked in on me, and has basically had me on lockdown ever since."

"Except for daily tutoring and SAT prep class here," she replied. She looked around, then lowered her voice before adding, "Nobody does that, by the way. Even the people who need it. And you don't."

"She has me at the daily Kiger lunch study hall at school, too."

"What?" Bigger eyes. God, I loved Jenn. "What's she trying to do, make you skip next year or something?"

"She's got her eye on Kiffney-Brown. Or that new charter."

"Oh, man. You don't want either of those. The kids at Kiffney are competitive to the point of bloodthirsty. And Marks Charter is so hard to get into, I know people who went on Xanax just to apply there." This was her area of expertise. "Anyway, everyone knows continuity of education is something admissions officers look at. Does she really want you to have to explain three schools in two years?"

"I think right now she just wants to keep me away from Mac and Layla. Everything else is secondary, as much as she's trying to pretend otherwise."

Down the hall, there was a burst of giggling. "I hear you!" Jenn called out, and quickly, it got quiet again. She sighed, shaking her head, then said, "I know about Layla. Who's Mac?"

"Her brother," I replied. "The pizza guy, from your party? Do you even remember?"

"I've tried to block out what little does remain." She cleared her throat. "What's her problem with him?"

I looked down at my hands, trying to think of a way to explain whatever it was that was going on between me and Mac. I was still grappling when I heard her laugh. With old friends, sometimes it's what you don't say that speaks volumes.

"Sydney," she said, reaching out and slapping my leg. "Oh, my God. Why didn't you *tell* me?"

"It's really—"

"You're blushing!" She hooted. "No wonder you haven't wanted to hang out lately."

I looked at her. "I'm sorry I've been kind of a lousy friend. I got . . . kind of caught up, I guess."

She didn't say anything for a minute, acknowledging this truth and the apology for it. Then she smiled. "It's okay. But seriously, back up and tell me everything. Also, I want to see a picture. Do you have one?"

I did. Several, in fact: some from that night at the merry-go-round, a few I'd snapped from the passenger seat as we drove around together. But only one of both of us, taken in the cab of the truck at Commons Park. I'd held my phone out at arm's length as I leaned back into him, and he'd rested his chin on the top of my head. You could see the leaves falling out the window behind us. *Click.*

"Wow," she said when I'd scrolled past this one. "I must have been really drunk. Because him I would remember."

I smiled, looking down at it as well. "He's a really nice guy. And all of this just really happened, like, recently. Now with this, and Layla finding out . . ."

"Finding out?" she repeated. "What, it was a secret?"

"Sort of. Yes." I shut off my phone. "The last friend of hers who dated him left him kind of wrecked."

"You wouldn't do that, though," she said with such surety, it was like she was reciting a theorem or historical fact. "She knows that, right?"

"I hope so," I said. "Right now she's not exactly talking to me."

Jenn sat back, crossing her legs. "Wow. I don't talk to you for a week or two and everything in your life changes. All that's different with me is my ringtone."

"Stop it," I said, smiling.

"It's true!" She looked out the front window at the traffic passing by. "Maybe *I* should transfer to Jackson."

"Please do. You can go to Kiger study hall with me."

She snorted, then looked at her watch. "I better get back to my morons."

"Jenn," I said, surprised.

"Oh, please. It's no secret, trust me. Most of them are taking this class for the third time." She leaned over, giving me a quick hug. "I hate how you ended up here, but I'm happy to see you. Is that bad?"

I shook my head. "No. Just don't get sick of me. I'll be here a lot, if my mom has her way."

"Not gonna happen." She got to her feet. "See you tomorrow?"

"Yep."

And with that, she headed down the hall, ducking into a door off to the left. I sat there until the clock over the front desk hit five o'clock exactly, then went out to my car. I was just getting in when my phone beeped. It was my mom.

Heading home?

I actually glanced around, thinking she might be watching me from somewhere nearby. I would not have put it past her.

Right now, I replied.

A pause while I cranked my engine and backed out of the

space. Over at the Kiger Center, some of Jenn's morons—students—were filing out, chattering with one another.

See you in five, my mom responded. For some, this was a figure of speech, casual. But I knew she was watching her own clock. I drove home as slowly as I could, like doing so might change what was waiting there for me. As I pulled into the driveway, I could see the afternoons following this one laid out in front of me one after another, neat little squares filling the calendar. It made me want to speed away as fast as I could and not look back. But I was a good kid, despite what my parents thought. I went inside.

CHAPTER
20

2 XTRA lg veggie, 2 xtra lg roma. Greek salad. Onion rings. Go.

I picked up my phone from beside my calculus book, smiling.

Girls, **I wrote back.** Unhealthy vegetarians. The one with the salad also got the onion rings.

I hit SEND, then waited. It was a Thursday night, and I'd been on my new schedule for almost two weeks. It felt like longer—like years, to be honest—even though I'd figured out how to see Mac for a few minutes before school, after, and sometimes en route to study group at lunch. At night, in my room doing even more homework, I kept my phone close at hand so we could be in constant touch. It wasn't the same as riding along with him, but I'd take it.

A few days into all this, when we met at my locker before the early bell, Mac told me to close my eyes and hold out my hand. When I did, he dropped something into it.

"Okay. You can look now."

I opened my eyes to see a silver chain, like his but thinner, longer, with a saint pendant on it. It wasn't the same as his, though; the image was a man's profile, his eyes turned upward.

"Who is it?" I asked.

"No idea. I found it in a jar my mom has full of them," he said. "I was looking for one like mine, then just someone I recognized. But then I thought maybe it was cooler to have it be a mystery, you know? So it's not just about one thing, but anything. That way, it can be about what you want it to be."

I turned it over in my hand. Like the image on the front, the back was well-worn, the few words there unreadable. "Saint Anything." I looked up at him. "I love it. Thank you."

"You're welcome."

He picked it up, undoing the clasp, and I turned around and lifted up my hair. When he draped it over me and fastened it, the pendant hung low, against my heart. This seemed fitting, as it was where I kept Mac now, as well. From that point on, it was a solid, daily reminder that even though I was by myself a lot, I wasn't alone. Not anymore.

Even though I continued to do everything my mom asked of me, she had not let up one bit. I remained on the tightest of timetables, my days consisting solely of school and studying. I'd become such a presence at the Kiger Center that they'd offered me a job working the front desk, which was allowed only because it kept me close to home and would look good on my applications. So now, instead of the study sessions Jenn had assured my mom I did not need, I answered phones, fielded questions, and helped oversee practice tests. It wasn't nearly as much fun as delivering pizzas. But at least I was out of the house.

Right again, Mac texted me a few minutes later. Apartment full of estrogen.

Did you doubt me?

A pause. Then: Nope.

Most nights, it was these exchanges that got me through, along with the short conversations between deliveries and longer ones once he was home and doing his homework before bed. My phone, which I'd always viewed as necessary, was now the only evidence I had of my life before that night in the studio. School and home were so different, but in my pictures, my text messages, and the ringtone I'd programmed just for Mac (bells, like a merry-go-round), I had proof that I had lived another life. Even if it was on pause, for now.

"You're seriously not missing much," he reported to me one night. "Irv is still eating everything in sight. Eric's obsessed with coming up with the perfect band name before the showcase. Same old, same old."

"What about your mom?"

Mrs. Chatham had been to the ER twice in recent days due to blood pressure issues related to another new medication she was on. Both times she'd been released relatively quickly, but I could tell when he was concerned, that natural wariness turning to all-out worry. "Better," he said. "I'll tell her you asked about her."

We were both quiet a moment. Then, finally, I said it. "And Layla?"

"She's coming around," he told me. "Just give her some more time."

I could do that; time *was* all I had, even if I didn't have a say in how it was spent. But in those afternoon hours, as I sat at Kiger or at our kitchen table with homework in front of me, I missed her. Not in the concentrated, aching way I did Mac, but something broader. I'd think of our time together at Seaside, pizza crusts between us, her tapping her pencil and staring out the window while bluegrass played on the jukebox behind us. The complicated fry preparation at lunch. Her voice, singing high and light, or laughing as she ribbed Eric. It was like Dorothy in *The Wizard of Oz*, going from black-and-white to color, then back again. You first had to have something—change, light, friendship—to understand the loss of it. And I did.

I was also very aware of the fact that Peyton was not calling. A month or two earlier, I probably wouldn't even have noticed, and if I had, I'd have been relieved. Now, though, on the days I was home, I put on *Big New York* or *Los Angeles* and tried to focus on it, thinking of him and his friend maybe doing the same. Instead of feeling better, though, it made me miss him in a way I couldn't quite explain. Everything was different now.

The following Saturday, I was at work, trying to help an

Arbors ninth grader in a field hockey uniform download our app. I couldn't figure out if the problem was her phone or our Internet, so I'd ducked under the front desk to reset the connection. When I came back up, Spence was right in front of me.

"Hey," he said, flashing me that same million-dollar smile I remembered from the Day of Three Pizzas. "Look at you."

"Look at me," I repeated, gesturing for the girl to try the download again. "What are you doing here?"

"SAT test tutoring session," he replied, sliding his hands in his pockets. "Need to juice my scores. Hear the tutors are hot. That true?"

The ninth grader inched down the counter, putting space between them. Smart girl. I said, "How's Layla?"

A shrug. "She's okay. Haven't gotten to see much of her lately. Shit kind of hit the fan at home."

"Really."

"Yeah." He flipped his hand, this one gesture encompassing the entire story. "No biggie. I show up to this enough, I'll be golden."

Just then, Jenn came down the hallway, following her two o'clock study group. As they bunched around the doorway, heading out, she plopped into the chair beside mine. "Is it five yet?" she asked.

"It is somewhere," Spence told her, leaning forward on his elbows. "That's what I always say."

Jenn gave him a polite smile. I looked at my computer, pulling up the Kiger schedule. "This is Spence," I told her. "Your three o'clock."

"No shit." He grinned at me, then her. "My day just got better."

And yours got worse, I wrote on a piece of paper, sliding it over to Jenn under the counter. She raised her eyebrows. *Layla's boyfriend,* I added. By this point I'd told her enough of the long story to make it unnecessary to provide more details.

"O-kay," she said, getting to her feet. To Spence she said, "Did you bring your study materials?"

"My what?"

"The list you were e-mailed? With what you'd need for each session?"

Spence looked at me. "My mom set this up. No hablo any list. Sorry."

Jenn sighed, coming out from behind the counter. "Follow me."

He did, and thus ensued the first of several, in Jenn's words, "excruciatingly painful" tutoring sessions.

"It's not *just* that he thinks he's so charming," she said to me later, as we were packing up. "Although that's a lot of it. He's also just really, really stupid. It's not a flattering combination. I'm surprised Layla can stand him."

"She'd be the first to tell you she does not have the best taste in guys," I replied. "And I don't even know if they're still together, anyway."

"For her sake, I hope not." She zipped up her bag. "I don't even know that girl and I'm sure she can do better."

Apparently, Layla had, in fact, not yet realized this. The next Saturday, I looked out to see Rosie pulling up in front of Kiger's front window, Mrs. Chatham riding shotgun. As she turned toward the backseat, I saw Layla there, gathering her purse into her lap. Her hair was falling across her face, so she didn't spot me as she replied, then got out of the car. It was only when they drove off and she peered in the window that our eyes met.

I never forget a face, she'd said all those weeks ago, but I wondered what she thought now, seeing mine. She had on a black sweater, jeans, and motorcycle boots, her bag slung over one shoulder, and like every other time I'd caught a glimpse of her since that night, I realized how much I missed her. On the counter in front of me, my phone lit up as a text came in, Mac's icon popping up on the screen. For once, though, I didn't grab it. Then, like a reward, she was coming in.

The tone sounded over the door—*beep!*—but neither of us said hello. She didn't approach the counter, either, stopping instead by one of our uncomfortable foyer chairs. Still, this was progress, so I did my part and spoke first.

"Hey. You here to meet Spence?"

She looked at me. "Yeah. He said you were working here."

So she had known and came here anyway. Another good sign. "Just for a couple of weeks now."

"You like it?"

"No," I said. For this, I got a mild smile, encouragement enough to add, "My mom signed me up to be here every day. I might as well get paid for it."

Layla sat down on the chair arm, pulling her bag into her lap. "Mac said she's keeping you on a pretty tight leash."

"More like a choke collar." Saying this, I realized I'd been holding my breath. She'd mentioned Mac, though—that had to be good, right? God, I hoped so. "How have you been?"

She shrugged, playing with a bit of fringe on her purse. "All right. Busy. My mom's been sick some. I guess you knew that, though."

Up until this point, the whole conversation had felt like a house of cards, liable to collapse at any moment. But this was Layla. I'd always spoken straight with her. It felt wrong to do otherwise, even if it was safer. "Look," I said, "I should have told you about Mac, how I felt. I'm sorry."

She bit her lip, still fiddling with her purse. Then she looked at me. "I just couldn't believe you kept it a secret. I thought we told each other everything."

"We did," I replied. She raised an eyebrow. "Okay, okay. But you'd been so clear that you did not want any of your friends ever liking him. And I did. I . . . I do. I didn't want to have to choose between you. But then everything happened, and now you hate me anyway."

"Sydney." She cocked her head to the side. "I don't hate you."

"You're not happy."

"Because you guys snuck around behind my back!"

"How was I supposed to tell you? You said you never wanted to have a friend date him again."

"No, what I *said*," she told me, "was that I'd never again be responsible for bringing someone into Mac's life who would hurt him. Are you planning to do that?"

I shook my head. "No."

"Good. Then there's no problem here, other than you guys made me feel stupid. And I *hate* feeling stupid. You know that."

"I'm sorry," I said, meaning it.

"Okay." She took a deep breath, then let it out. "But if you do hurt him, I don't care if you are my best friend, I'll kick your ass. Are we clear?"

"Crystal," I replied.

Now I got a real smile, and then she was coming over to the counter across from me. "So tell me about this tutor of Spence's. He claims she's got the hots for him. True or not?"

For the next ten minutes, until Jenn and Spence emerged from their study room, we talked nonstop. About Mrs. Chatham's visits to the ER and yet another new medication she was on. How Rosie's return to training was going, and her hopes of returning to the Mariposa tour. The latest on Eric's submitting the demo to the showcase—no word yet, but he was wholly confident, as always—and the ongoing band name debate. Then, finally, how Spence's grounding after getting busted for breaking into his stepdad's liquor cabinet had made their meetings practically impossible.

"But you're here," I pointed out.

"Only after much strategizing, and just for an hour," she said. "He told his mom he was taking an extra session, so he's not expected back until five. But he got his car taken away, and I never have any of ours, so we're at Rosie's mercy."

"Or Mac's," I said.

She shook her head. "He was never a fan of Spence's. But after what happened that night at your house, and to you? He's not doing *anything* to help him out. Even if it means helping me, too."

Hearing this, I felt touched and guilty all at once. "Sorry."

"It's okay. I understand." She tucked a piece of hair behind her ear. "But like you were saying, when you really care about someone, you can't just stop. Even if you have a good reason. You know?"

I nodded, and then Jenn was coming down the hallway, a tired expression on her face. Behind her I could hear Spence saying, "Lighten up! I didn't mean it as an insult. I was just saying if you smiled more, you'd be a pretty girl."

"Just stop talking," Jenn told him. "Please."

"Prettier! I meant prettier!" he added, just as he rounded the corner. "Oh! Hey! Baby! You're here."

Layla just looked at him, a flat expression on her face. I said, "Um, Jenn, this is Layla. Layla, this is my friend Jenn, from Perkins Day."

Jenn, ever friendly, stuck out her hand. "Nice to meet you finally. I've heard a lot about you."

"Same here," Layla replied. They shook. "So. Is he a genius yet?"

"Not quite," Jenn told her, sitting down behind the counter. "But we have made some progress on vocabulary."

"Abscond," Spence said to Layla, sliding an arm around her waist. "That means run away with. You impressed?"

"No," she said, pulling back.

"What if I buy some fries?" he asked.

"It's a start." She sighed, pulling her bag over her shoulder, then said to me, "See you Monday?"

I nodded. "See you then."

Jenn and I watched them leave, the door buzzing as they did so. They started across the lot to CrashBurger, whose fries I knew Layla rated a seven on her ten-point scale. Good news for Spence. He needed all the help he could get.

At five o'clock, Jenn and I shut down the computers, locked up, and said good-bye. I was standing by my car, digging for my keys, when I heard a horn beep. I turned and there was Rosie, pulling into a spot nearby. When I waved, Mrs. Chatham gestured for me to come over.

"Hi," I said as she rolled down the window, smiling at me.

"Hi yourself!" she replied as Rosie put the car in park. "What are you doing here?"

"I work at the tutoring center," I told her.

"Mom, I'm running in the drugstore. You need anything?" Rosie asked.

"Nope. I'll just stay here and catch up with Sydney." Rosie climbed out of the car, shutting the door with a bang behind her. "So. How are things at home?"

I wasn't sure how much she'd been told. My guess, however, was enough so it would make sense as I said, "Complicated."

"Ah," she said, nodding. "How's your brother?"

"He's . . ." I trailed off, for once not sure what word to use to describe Peyton. "We were actually talking a little bit. About my mom, and kind of about what happened, as well as some other stuff. Not much, but a little."

"That's good to hear." She smiled at me. "Slow progress is still progress."

"I'm realizing . . ." I began, then stopped, taking a breath. "Maybe I didn't know exactly how he was feeling. I assumed a lot. I feel kind of bad about it."

"You shouldn't," she said. "Relationships evolve, just like people do. Just because you know someone doesn't mean you know everything about them. Even your brother."

"It's just weird. Like, I got used to talking with him, but he's not speaking to my mom and not calling." I looked down at my keys. "He got upset with her about being so involved in his life, even in prison. So now I'm her main project."

"I did hear," she said, "that you've been otherwise occupied."

I glanced over at CrashBurger: there was no sign of Layla. According to the sign outside the bank, it was now 5:04. My mom was waiting. But I didn't want to leave, not yet. "The thing is, I can admit I did something I shouldn't have. Broke her trust. But it was the only time I ever did, the only time I've done *anything* wrong. By the way she's punished me, you'd think I was the one who almost killed someone."

A car drove by, the music loud and all bass, in that way that makes your teeth hurt. Mrs. Chatham waited until they passed us, then said, "She's scared, Sydney. She doesn't want to lose you, too."

"It's not fair, though. I'm paying for what Peyton did. Again. I'm sick of it."

She gave me a sympathetic look. "Remember how you

told me how often you think about that boy? The one your brother hurt?"

"David Ibarra," I said.

She nodded. "If you feel that way, that strongly, that *guilty*, can you even imagine how it is for her? You were just a bystander. But your brother, that's her *child*. Her responsibility. Whatever he does is part of her. Always."

I thought of Rosie. With her bust, she'd only really hurt herself. Or so I'd thought.

"What I'm saying is that she can't take back what he did, or even begin to fix it," she continued. "But she *can* try to make sure, with you, that it never happens again on her watch. It's all about regret and how you deal with it. That's something you two have in common. Maybe you should talk to her about it."

"She doesn't discuss David Ibarra, ever," I told her. "As far as she's concerned, it's all about Peyton."

"Just because a person isn't talking about something doesn't mean it's not on their mind. Often, in fact, it's *why* they won't speak of it."

I was quiet a moment, thinking about how Peyton had surprised me. Then I said, "Because it makes it real."

"Exactly."

A breeze blew up behind me, kicking some leaves into the air. I wished, in that moment, that I was at Commons Park with Mac, not thinking about any of this. It was easier to just be mad at my mom; sympathy and empathy are complicated things. But nothing had been simple, not for a long time. I looked at the clock. 5:10.

"I should go," I said as Rosie came out of the pharmacy, a bag in her hand. Still no sign of Layla. "She freaks out if I'm unaccounted for."

Mrs. Chatham nodded, then slid a hand out the window toward me, palm up, fingers spread. I gave her my own hand, and she squeezed it tight. "Just think about what I said, yes? About talking to her."

"I will," I replied. "And thanks."

She winked at me, then released my hand, just as Rosie got in, climbing back behind the wheel. Once in my car, I looked over at them, sitting there together. They were talking, Rosie drinking a soda while her mom ate from a bag of potato chips. I watched her pop one in her mouth, then offer the bag over. Rosie took one, then handed her the soda to take a sip. All wordless, so natural, a sync long established. It was such a little thing, hardly important, but it stayed with me all the way home.

* * *

"Well, that's just ridiculous. I've never even heard of such a thing." I'd come home with Mrs. Chatham still on my mind. When I pulled up to the house and saw Ames's Lexus in the driveway, however, any possibility of bridging the topic of David Ibarra with my mom was shot. Inside, I found him at the kitchen table, while she stood at the stove, stirring a risotto.

"I've only been late one month before this," Ames was saying. "One! I think they just wanted me out so they could jack up the rent for some other sucker."

"You need to look at your lease," my mom told him, glancing at me as I put my backpack on the counter. "See if they're actually allowed to do this. I could call Sawyer, if you like."

"No, I don't want you to go to any trouble," Ames replied. Then he looked at me. "Sydney! I was wondering when you'd show up."

"Work ran late?" my mom asked. Of course she'd noticed.

"Just a little," I said. "Can I help with anything?"

"You could set the table. Put a place for Ames; he's staying."

"Oh, Julie," he said, as if he didn't know being over at this hour meant an automatic invitation, "you don't have to take pity on me. I'm a big boy."

"You're practically homeless," she replied. "The least I can do is feed you."

I walked over to the silverware drawer behind the kitchen table, making a concentrated point not to look at Ames. "My crooked landlord kicked me out today," he explained anyway. "Add that to being laid off last week and I'm batting a thousand."

"Ridiculous," my mom said again. "When it rains, it pours."

"I'm in a monsoon, then," Ames replied. He was still talking directly to me. "But I've got a couple of leads on jobs, and some friends with open couches. I'll be okay."

My dad was pulling into the driveway, the garage door opening. "You don't have to resort to that when we have a free bedroom just sitting there," my mom said. "You'll stay with us until you find a new place."

I froze, my fist full of forks.

"Julie, no," Ames told her, a fake firmness in his voice. "I can't impose on you like that."

"You're not imposing," she replied. "After all you've done for Peyton, and us, it's the very least we can do."

Somehow, I managed to set the table, then sit through dinner. Ames was there in my brother's traditional seat, to my dad's left and across from me, and now he'd be moving into his room, as well. He continued to pretend to resist, while my mom assured him it was just until he was "back on his feet." After we ate, I took as long as I could to load the dishwasher and clean up before I went upstairs to do homework. Even so, I had a front-row seat as Ames unloaded his stuff—*such* a coincidence, he happened to have it all in the car—load by load into the room next to mine. Each time he passed, he glanced in at me. Finally, I shut the door.

CHAPTER

21

"WE'RE IN!"

I'd never seen Eric run before, but in the seconds preceding this announcement, he'd covered the school parking lot in the blink of an eye. Now, panting, he stood before us, eyes wide.

"In . . ." Mac repeated, prompting him.

"The showcase! We made it!" He bent over, hands on his knees, then sucked in a breath and straightened up. "I just got the text."

"Seriously?" Layla said.

Eric nodded, still breathing hard. "It's three weeks from this Friday, at Bendo. Five bands, all ages. Holy crap, I think I'm having a heart attack."

"Dude," said Irv, who was leaning against the truck, eating a bag of pretzels, "you seriously need to work out more."

"Three weeks," Mac said. "Not much time to practice."

"Which is why," Eric told him, "we need to go hardcore. Clear the schedule, pedal to the metal. This takes top priority, starting now."

"Some of us have jobs," Mac pointed out.

"And lives," Layla added.

Eric just looked at them. "Are you serious? This is our shot. Our big chance! Winner gets to record a real demo with Hambone Records. That's where Truth Squad and Spinner-bait started out."

"Hate Spinnerbait," Mac said.

"True. But the point is," Eric continued, "nothing is more important than this."

"Except my post-school meal," Irv said. "So if you want a ride, you're buying at DoubleBurger."

"I can't believe you go there," Layla told him, shaking her head. "Their fries are greasy. And mushy."

"Just how I like 'em," Irv replied, and she rolled her eyes. "Come on, Bates. My stomach's grumbling."

As he said this, he was still eating pretzels. Irv's appetite always surprised me, but at times like this, I was almost scared.

"Practice," Eric said. "Tomorrow, right after school. Yes? I'll tell Ford."

"I'll see what I can do," Mac said.

"Do what you have to. This is serious. There's no gray area here. We win or lose. Triumph or go down in flames. Succeed or—"

"Why is there never a gray area with you?" Irv said. "Everything's always brilliant or catastrophic."

"Because," Eric replied, "that's the way true artists—"

"*That* should be your band name," Layla, studying her phone, said.

Irv said, "True Artists?"

"No. Brilliant or Catastrophic."

Silence. Due to experience, I was expecting immediate rejection of this from someone (probably Eric), followed by the debate beginning all over again. But then Mac said, "I like it."

"It *is* intriguing," Eric agreed. He thought for a moment. "Also, it fits the idea of our ironic take on the songs we're doing as well as what they did for the larger community of music. So pop, total earworms: you have to give the song-writers credit. Even while acknowledging the damage they caused not just to the integrity of the music industry, but society as a whole."

"Society?" I asked.

"I just like how it sounds," Irv said, starting to walk away.

"I'll sit with it awhile. Let you know what I think," Eric told us, falling in behind him. Watching them go, all I could think was that they were the oddest of pairings.

"Huge Guy and Hipster Guy," Layla observed, once again reading my mind. "They're like superheroes. Without the, um, super part."

I snorted, then looked at my watch. I was doing that these days. "It's getting late. I better go."

Mac looked down at me. "Already?"

The fifteen minutes or so I had here in the parking lot before I had to leave for Kiger always went too quickly. "I left my computer charger at home, and my mom's bringing it to me. I need to be on time today."

"Okay," he said. But his arm stayed around me, and I didn't budge. This usually took a couple of tries. As I thought this, I felt his phone, in his pocket, buzz against my leg. I extracted myself as he reached for it, glancing at the screen. "Shit."

"What is it?" I asked.

"My mom."

On my other side, Layla, studying her own phone, looked up. "What's going on?"

Mac was already typing something. "Shortness of breath, and she started to pass out. They called the doc. Meeting him at the hospital."

"Crap," Layla said. "Let's go."

She pulled open the truck's passenger door, throwing her bag on the floorboard. Mac, however, stayed where he was, again scanning his phone's screen. "We're supposed to go to Seaside and stay there."

"What? I want to go to the hospital."

"Dad says no. He wants us to man the shop." Mac started around the truck. "Rosie will keep us posted."

"You know she's terrible at that," Layla said. "We're lucky she even told us they were en route. I need to be there."

"Are you not listening to me? I can't take you. Now get in, we've got to go."

"I'll take her." I said this without thinking. It was only in the next beat that I remembered I was already late leaving for where I had to be.

"You sure?" Mac asked me, climbing behind the wheel. "What about your mom?"

"It's an emergency. She'll understand." I hoped.

"Keep me posted?"

"Yeah." Layla grabbed her bag while he cranked the engine. "Thanks, Sydney."

"Sure."

He backed out of the spot, kicking up a cloud of gravel
dust all around us, and started driving out of the lot, dodging
the familiar potholes. At the stop sign by the guardhouse he
barely paused, prompting a shouted warning from the security officer there. And then he was gone.

"Which hospital?" I asked Layla once we, too, were on
our way out.

"U General."

That was all the way across town. "Are you sure?"

"It's the only place that takes our insurance," she replied.
"Sorry."

"No, it's okay," I assured her. I glanced at my dashboard
clock. Three thirty already, and we hadn't even left yet.

I tried not to think of the time, even as we hit every red
light along the way. I'd never been to U General—everyone
at the Arbors used Lakeview Methodist, which was brand-
new and only a mile away—and the signs were hard to follow, especially in a distant part of town I didn't know well.

Finally, after winding our way through a construction
zone and two more red lights, I was pulling up to the emergency room entrance.

"This is good," Layla said, gathering up her stuff as I
slowed to a stop behind an ambulance, its back doors flung
open. No one was inside.

"Do you want me to go in with you?" I asked her.

"No, I'm fine. Thanks. I'll call you, okay?"

She got out, shutting the door behind her, and slung her bag over her shoulder before walking quickly through a set of automatic doors. I felt guilty for not going with her, balanced by a sense of relief as I pulled away, finally heading in the right direction. On my way around the traffic circle, I passed a city bus stop, the bench packed with people. A little boy with his arm in a sling, his face solemn, watched me as I went by.

By now, I was a full half hour late for my shift at Kiger. I'd already texted Jenn that I'd had an emergency and would be there as soon as I could, but she wasn't the one I was worried about. All the way to the hospital and back, through traffic and more red lights, I kept waiting for my phone to buzz. Where are you? my mom would ask, and I didn't even know how to tell her in a simple text. I was just hoping for mercy once we were face-to-face. When I pulled into the Kiger lot, I found Ames instead.

"Sydney, Sydney," he said as I walked up to where he was standing. He had my computer charger coiled neatly—I recognized my mom's handiwork at a glance—in his hands. "You were supposed to be here forty-five minutes ago."

"I had something to do," I told him, reaching for the charger.

He pulled it back, just out of my reach. "Funny, Julie didn't say anything about you having plans. Did she know?"

I felt my jaw clench. Inside, Jenn was behind the counter, watching us. "I needed to give a friend a ride to the hospital."

"Oh." He still hadn't handed over my charger. "Everybody okay?"

"Hope so. May I please have that now?"

Finally, slowly, he relinquished it. "You know, you're putting me in a bad spot again. Your mom's done a lot for me. I don't feel right lying to her."

"I'm not asking you to," I said.

"But if I *do* tell her about this," he continued, as if I hadn't spoken, "I have a feeling she'll tighten your restrictions even more. And I don't want to be responsible for that."

This time, I said nothing. I was trying to figure out what angle he was working.

"Let's say this," he continued. "We keep this between us. But you owe me one."

"You can tell her," I said. "I don't care."

"Nope." He held up his hands. "Don't want to be that guy. It's our secret. Agreed?"

I didn't like the sound of that. But before I could say anything, my phone buzzed. It was a message from Mac.

Just a scare. Everything fine, he'd typed.

"I need to go in," I said to Ames, grabbing the door handle and pulling it open. "They're waiting for me."

"Sure thing," he replied cheerfully, stepping aside. "See you at dinner."

I walked into the lobby and behind the desk, dropping my bag at my feet. Jenn, in the other chair, was watching Ames, now heading to his car. "What was that all about?"

"Nothing," I told her. "Just him being his creepy self."

She picked up a folder. "I'm going to check in on the morons. You sure you're okay?"

I nodded, and then she was disappearing down the hallway. I picked up my phone to reply to Mac.

Glad to hear it. Was worried.

Don't be. All okay.

I looked outside, where it was starting to get dark; winter
was coming. On my phone screen, these words remained,
awaiting a response. Or maybe not. "All okay" was a good
stopping point, after all, a place to stay while I could. As long
as you stretched out a moment, it couldn't end; if I didn't
write back, there'd be no further conversation, good or bad.
I sat there for an hour. I never wrote anything.

* * *

For a good five minutes, I kept thinking I was hearing crunching. Finally, I was sure.

"Are you eating something?"

Silence. Then, a beat later: "Potato chips."

I was shocked. In the entire time I'd known him, I'd never
seen Mac consume anything unhealthy. This was a guy
whose typical lunch consisted of lean turkey rolled up with
lowfat cheese, a handful of almonds, and two tangerines. It
was hard to picture him eating anything with trans fats,
much less from a vending machine. I couldn't even speak.

"Whatever you're thinking," he said finally, "I've already
thought it. With paralyzing guilt added."

"Since when do you eat potato chips?"

"Birth, basically." Another crunch. "Until the March before last. After that, I was off them like a junkie kicking dope."

"Until . . ."

"Yesterday." Crunch. "I guess things are kind of getting to me."

Again, I wasn't sure what to say. Mac was naturally guarded; it wasn't like he walked around bursting with sunshiny optimism on his best day. Selfishly, though—now I was the one adding guilt—I worried it might have something to do with me. "What kind of things?"

"My mom," he replied. A sigh, then I heard what I was pretty sure was the sound of an empty chip bag being balled up. Oh, dear. "The showcase. And, you know, us."

Outside my room, someone walked down the hallway, slowing their steps as they approached. Instinctively, I looked at the door at the precise spot where a lock *would* be, if I'd had one. I lowered my voice. "Us?"

"Yeah," he replied, his voice casual. "I mean, don't get me wrong, I'll take what I can get when it comes to seeing you. But this situation . . . it's not exactly ideal."

I felt myself smile. "I know. I'm sorry."

"Not your fault. It's Spence's." He shifted, the phone muffled for a second. "I mean, it would have been bad for your mom to walk in and find us there, I'm sure. But not bad like this."

"Layla said you were still mad."

"She's right."

We were quiet a moment. I couldn't tell if whoever was in the hallway had moved on or was standing there, silent, on the other side of the door. A week into his stay, I'd known Ames to do both.

I'd thought it was bad before, his being around. But the weird long looks, the way his eyes followed me around the room—none of it compared to suddenly having him in the house. Though he'd arrived with only a suitcase, a duffel bag, a few boxes, and a computer, he'd already managed to fill much of our shared living space. What began as a pack of cigarettes by the garage door became a damp U basketball towel I had to step over on our shared bathroom floor. That, then, morphed into the sound of talk radio flowing constantly from Peyton's speakers right on the other side of my wall. Voices, all day and into the night. I dreamed of round-tables and panels, when I wasn't having nightmares.

Then there were the constant drop-ins: Did I have a spare tube of toothpaste? Where were the lightbulbs kept? Did I feel like it was too warm up here, too? And that was just in the first thirty-six hours. It seemed like he was always passing by my door, peering in at me, stopping to chat while leaning against the door frame. When I started shutting it regularly, he knocked: a soft three raps, one slow, two fast. If I opened it, he always came inside.

"Serious cram time, huh?" he'd said to me the previous evening as I was finishing up an essay for English on *Wuthering Heights*. I was at my desk, and he on my bed, flipping through a magazine I'd left open there. Normally by this point, I'd have put on my pajamas, but I'd taken to doing that at the last minute. "I should have been more like you in high school. Could have avoided a lot of trouble."

As was my way, I responded to this with a single nod, pretending to be laser-focused on my closing paragraph.

"Peyton used to say the same thing," he continued, turning another page. "How you were so different from him, and he was glad of it."

It had always made me uncomfortable when he talked to me like this about my brother. For my mother, though, this had always been the main reason to keep him around, especially with Peyton's ongoing silence toward her.

She'd tried to reach out, every way she could, since the debacle of the ceremony. Calling was impossible, so she wrote daily, and enlisted the connections she'd established—the liaison, the family outreach officer—to pass her pleadings along. The only response she ever got was from Ames, whom my brother still contacted.

"He just needs some space," I'd heard him tell her in yet another of their coffee-fueled discussions at the kitchen table. "He'll reach out when he's ready."

"I just feel like if I could explain myself he'd understand," my mom replied. "If only he would call you when I'm nearby, I might be able to talk him around."

"I want that, too," Ames told her. "And it very well may happen. But for now, you've got to respect his wishes. You know?"

At this, my mom had only looked glum. It struck me as odd, since Ames was at the house constantly—he claimed to be "on the job market," not that I saw him doing anything about it—that one of these many calls from Peyton he reported *hadn't* occurred with my mom nearby. Apparently, though, I was the only one to wonder about this.

Now, with Mac on the other end of the line, I got up and walked to the door, opening it. The hallway was empty, but the door to my brother's room was ajar, light and the sound of talking spilling out from it. Looking the other way, I could just see my mom in the War Room on her computer.

"I'm hoping," I said, shutting the door again, "that all this good behavior might make my mom ease up a bit. I really want to go to the showcase."

"If I were you, I'd lower my expectations," he replied. "Maybe aim for, you know, getting to choose where you eat lunch once in a while."

"That will come, too," I said, more confident than I felt. "But this is a special occasion, a one-time thing. It's an early show, and I'm doing everything I can to stockpile points."

"I just don't want you to be disappointed if it doesn't happen," he said. "I mean, I want you there. You know that. But it's not everything."

That was just the issue. I knew not to expect everything; I never had. All I wanted was *this* thing. Even if it was a long shot, at least it gave me something to aim for during all those long afternoons at Kiger, or here in my room at night, staring at my unlocked door with only my Saint Anything for welcome company.

"Just think a good thought for me, okay?" I asked him. "And step away from the chips."

He exhaled; I'd made him smile. "I'll do my best."

When we hung up, I looked at the calendar I kept on my desk. On it were my school and work obligations—my personal stuff I kept on my phone—and I scanned the various items: SAT practice test, college night, Kiger payday. Then I picked up a pen, moved to the date of the showcase, and drew a circle around it, then another. I didn't write anything, as that did seem too confident. But just putting it in there made it seem possible, and anyway, I knew what it was.

CHAPTER

22

MY DAD cleared his throat. Because I knew from experience this meant a subject change, announcement, or important remark was to follow, I gave him my full attention. So did my mom. Ames, however, kept eating.

"So. What's the latest on the job front?"

My mother picked up her wineglass, taking a sip. From the way she was watching my father, it was clear this query was not spontaneous. A discussion had preceded it: there was a plan here.

Ames swallowed. "I've got a few leads. One of my friends at the Walker has a call in to that new Valley Inn about a front desk position. It's really competitive, though, so I'm not sure of my chances."

"I'm sure there are other opportunities besides hospitality," my dad said. "I've seen a lot of Help Wanted signs lately."

"Maybe," Ames replied, picking up his water glass. "But I'd prefer to hold out for something in my field."

My parents exchanged a look. Then my dad said, "A paycheck's a paycheck, though."

"True," Ames agreed. "But I have a feeling this Valley Inn thing is going to happen."

The silence that followed this was so awkward, I felt it in my stomach. Finally, something was shifting here. I just didn't know what it was yet.

After dinner, I went up to my room and settled in at my desk, my phone nearby in case Mac had a few minutes between deliveries to talk. I was just starting my ecology homework when I heard someone come up the stairs. A beat, and then: *rap, rap-rap.*

I walked over, opening the door. "Yeah?"

"Question," he said, stepping forward so I had no choice but to move out of the way and let him in. "Got a phone charger you can spare? I can't find mine."

Already, he was sitting on my bed, grabbing one of my magazines off the bedside table. I pulled open my desk drawer, retrieving my charger, then held it out to him. "Here."

He flipped a page, then glanced up at me, but didn't reach for it. "Oh. Great, thanks."

I dropped it on the bed beside him, then went back to my desk. He didn't budge, even as I returned to my homework. Every minute or so, I'd hear him turn a page.

My phone beeped, and I glanced at it. It was a text from Mac.

6 orders garlic knots. Nothing else. Ideas?

I smiled. Spaghetti dinner? Carb addicts meeting?

Will let you know.

"So," Ames said. "What are you working on over there?"

I put my phone down. "Ecology."

"Ugh." He made a face. "Just the word sounds hard."

To this, I said nothing, going back to my work and hoping he'd take the hint. No luck. I was wondering if I'd actually have to ask him to leave when my mom came down the hallway.

"Sydney, I forgot to mention that—" she was saying, but stopped suddenly when she spotted Ames on my bed. "Oh. I thought you were studying."

"I am," I said.

"I'm distracting her," Ames said cheerfully, shutting the magazine.

As the crease between my mom's eyes deepened, I knew I hadn't been wrong earlier at dinner: whatever pull Ames had once had over her, it was waning, if not gone altogether. And he didn't even know it. "Better let her get back to it," she said, her voice clipped. "Okay?"

Now he looked up. "Oh. Sure."

My mom stepped back from the door, clearing the way for him to leave. A beat passed, though, then another, before he took the hint and got to his feet. "Thanks for the charger," he said to me, then squeezed my shoulder as he passed. "You're the best."

I said nothing, my eyes on my mom as she watched him take his time leaving the room. As he passed her, he said, "You want some coffee? I'm thinking about making a pot."

"No, I'm fine," she replied. "I have work to do."

"Okay," he said, turning toward Peyton's room. "If you change your mind, just let me know."

My mom watched him walk away. When she looked at me, I went back to my book, quickly.

"You want this open or closed?" she asked, nodding at the door.

We looked at each other for a long moment. *She gets it*, I thought. Not all of it, but some, finally. *Finally.*

"Closed," I said. She nodded and shut the door.

※ ※ ※

The next afternoon, I was sitting behind the counter at Kiger listening to Jenn lecture her morons about quadratic equations when Mac's truck pulled up right outside the door. I blinked, not quite believing my eyes. But when Layla climbed out and came in the door, I knew it was for real.

"Is he here?" she asked. Her face was red, eyes swollen.

"Spence?" I asked, although I knew. She nodded. "No."

She bit her lip, then pulled out her phone, handing it to me. There was a text exchange on the screen, first her asking if they could at least meet and talk. Then his reply.

Have tutoring. Sorry.

"He dumped me," she said. I looked up at her: now she was outright crying. "Over the goddamn *phone*."

"Oh, Layla," I said. Outside, Mac was still behind the wheel. As much as I wanted to see him—I always wanted to see him—I understood why he was keeping his distance. This was about her, not us. "I'm so sorry. That sucks."

"He's an asshole." She wiped her eyes with the back of her hand, sniffling. "I *knew* something was going on. He was suddenly so busy, not replying to my messages . . . so I called today and asked him, flat-out. He didn't even try to deny it." She cleared her throat, sticking her phone back in her pocket. I glanced out at Mac again: he was still looking in at us. "I don't know why this keeps happening to me. I'm a good person. I mean, I try to be, and—"

"You are," I said, standing up and walking around the counter.

"All I want is someone decent." She sniffled again, her eyes filling with tears. "You know? Kind. Good. Like in all those love stories I'm such an expert on. It can't just be fiction. It can't. Those guys are out there, I *know* it. I just can't find them."

With this, her voice broke. I put my arms around her, pulling her in close as she buried her head in my shoulder. I knew whatever I said right then she wouldn't hear; with that kind of pain, a deafness comes. But if she had been able to listen, I would have told her she was right. Those guys *were* out there. In fact, one was watching us right now, somewhere nearby. Keeping his distance, knowing she needed me to herself right then, but still, just outside the door.

≈ ≈ ≈

"I don't even see why you need me," Layla said glumly as we sat on the hood of my car after school a couple of days later. "I thought I was just helping with the demo."

There was now less than two weeks until the show-case, and clearly, Mac was not the only one getting nervous. Eric, high-strung even under the best of circumstances, had switched into maniacal preparation mode, demanding constant practice and focus. The fact that Mac had to work, Ford was more interested in getting high, and Layla's heart was broken did not deter him.

"That was the plan," Eric told her, pacing in the short space between my car and the one beside it. "But their feedback was that they especially liked that song. We can't leave it out now."

"I didn't sign on for anything public, though. I can barely even deal with my own face in the mirror right now."

I looked at Mac, who was leaning back on the bumper beside me. Although Layla had been freshly dumped when we first met at Seaside, this was my first time seeing this total loss of confidence. For such a bold girl, it was like she'd wilted. Only time, Mac said, would bring her back to us, although fries did help some.

Now Eric walked over, putting his hands on her shoulders. I expected Layla to at least flinch if not swat him away totally, but instead, she just looked to the side as he said, "*You* are going to be great. In fact, this might be just what you need."

"To sing a song about a busted relationship in front of a huge crowd of people?" she said. She sighed. "I don't think so."

"To sing a song about *strength* and *fierceness* in the face of *heartbreak* in front of a huge crowd of people," he corrected her. "Just trust me, okay?"

She didn't look convinced. But she still didn't push him away, either. And when he leaned forward, kissing the top of her head, she closed her eyes.

I looked at Mac, then leaned close to his ear. "What was *that?*"

"Temporary insanity," he replied into mine. "I told you, she's not herself."

"What are you two whispering about over there?" Layla demanded.

"Nothing," Mac told her.

"Me going to the showcase," I said at the same time. Whoops. She gave me a look, not amused. "I'm going to ask my mom about it tonight. Wish me luck?"

"Good luck." She pulled her knees up to her chest, turning her face into the sun. "Somebody's due some."

When I left Kiger later that afternoon and headed home for dinner, I was ready, with my proposal memorized and precrafted responses to all expected objections. Even if she said no—and I so hoped she wouldn't—she would have to be impressed with my prep work.

When I came in the house, my mom was in the kitchen, stirring something on the stove. "What are you making?" I asked, putting my bag on a chair.

"Pepper tempeh stir-fry," she replied, adding something to the pan that sizzled. There was a cookbook open on her left. "I figured it was time to try some new recipes, shake things up."

"Really," I said. "Any particular reason?"

"No." A handful of green things hit the pan; a beat later,

I smelled onions. "Just in the mood to make some changes."

This was either the best moment or the worst. Since I was feeling optimistic, I said, "Actually, I kind of wanted to talk to you about something related to that."

She poked at the pan, steam rising. "Related to . . ."

"Changes. Or discussions about them."

A pause. More sizzling. Then, "I'm listening."

Okay. I took in a breath. "So, I know I screwed up having my friends here that night. And Layla's boyfriend drinking—"

"You were drinking, as I remember."

One sip, I thought, then reminded myself to stay focused. "Right. What I did was wrong. But since then, I feel like I've done everything you and Dad have asked me to. The study group at lunch, Kiger anytime I'm not at school, then home-work here afterward. I haven't been anywhere else, nor have I asked to do so."

She still had her back to me, so I couldn't see how I was doing. I took it as promising, however, when she said, "I'm with you so far."

Headlights were turning into our driveway, which meant either my dad or Ames would be walking in soon. One-on-one was better; I needed to keep going. "My friends' band got a spot in a showcase. The winner gets a real demo from an actual label. The show's early, at seven, next Friday. All ages. I really want to go."

She lowered the heat on the burner and put the spoon down. Then she turned and looked at me. "These are the same friends who were here?"

I nodded. "Yes."

"Oh, Sydney." She sighed, running a hand through her hair. "I wish you would have asked about anything else."

My heart sank. "But this is what I want."

"To go to a club? With people that I know drink?"

"It was just Layla's boyfriend. They're not together anymore."

"That's not the point," she replied. "What you're asking is a big leap for your father and me. We'd prefer to return your privileges gradually, based on how things go."

Which was just what Mac had said. "It's just one night," I said, not ready to cave yet. "Then we can go right back to how it is now."

"You say that like it's a bad thing. You've been doing very well lately." She turned back to the stove. "To be honest, I'm hesitant to change anything."

"You just said you were in the mood for it, though."

She laughed. "I was talking about *dinner.*"

The garage door was creaking open now. I had a minute, maybe two, before I was facing a united front. "Please just think about it. That's all I'm asking. Not a no, not yet. Please?"

I'd laid out my case, presented points to her counterpoints. There was nothing else I could do but ask and hope that the luck Layla had talked about might find me.

"All right," she said as the door from the garage opened. "I'll think about it. Now will you please get me the curry powder and cumin from the cupboard? My sauce is thickening."

I walked over, taking down the bottles she needed and bringing them to her. The contents of the large frying pan

looked unlike anything she'd ever prepared before. I didn't
even know what tempeh was, but it didn't seem very appe-
tizing. I kept that thought to myself, however, as I handed
her the spices. She squinted at the open cookbook, then
twisted the top off the cumin.

"Here goes nothing," she said, shaking some in. More
steam rose up, followed by another blast as the curry powder hit. She poked at the vegetables with her spoon, folding
them over once, then again. "What do you think?"

"That it is." She tossed in some more cumin, then leaned
in close, taking a long sniff, then gestured for me to do the
same. Hesitantly, I did. It didn't smell bad or good. Just new.
Different.

CHAPTER

23

IT WAS Saturday morning, and I was just getting out of the shower. The first voice I heard when I opened the bathroom door was Ames's.

"Julie? Got a minute?"

He stepped out into the hallway, his phone in his hand. Instinctively, I pulled my towel more tightly around me.

"Not really," my mom called back from the War Room. "I'm kind of in the middle of something."

"I have a feeling you're not going to mind this particular interruption." He smiled at me, broadly, as he walked to her open doorway. Then he held the phone out to her.

I had to give the guy credit. Presented with the possibility of being evicted from our house and daily life, he'd worked the only miracle he was capable of. I knew it the minute she said hello.

Peyton, he mouthed at me anyway, still smiling.

Suddenly, my mom was breathless, laughing, her words coming quickly and close together. Even from another room, I could feel her mood brighten, picture her face, flushed and happy. Just like that, everything changes.

But not completely. Despite the fact that they talked for a full half hour—my mom not budging once from the War Room, as if taking a single step might break this spell— Peyton wanted to take things slowly. When she asked if she could visit, he told her no, not yet; the phone was all he was ready for. Later, I wondered how Ames had talked him around, what he'd said to break this stalemate. If mothers could lift cars off their babies when necessary, it made sense that a person could go even further for their own self-preservation.

I'd gotten so used to Peyton's not calling that I was actually surprised when the phone rang one afternoon a couple of days later. After the recorded voice finished, I took a breath.

"Hey," I said. "Long time."

There was a pause; I heard voices in the background. "Yeah. Things got kind of . . . tense. It had nothing to do with you."

Now I was quiet for a moment. Then I said, "It's been tense here, too. Mom busted me with my friends over, and I was drinking. She freaked and has had me on lockdown since."

"What? You were *drinking*?"

He sounded so surprised, outright shocked, that I wondered if he'd actually forgotten where he was calling from. "It was a sip," I told him. "And—"

"Sydney, don't get caught up in that stuff. You're way too smart."

"It was a *sip*," I said again. "And she basically took everything away from me. It's not fair."

In the silence that followed, I realized that this was the

closest I'd come to telling Peyton how I felt about what he'd done and how it affected all of us. Immediately, I felt I should backtrack, cover my steps. Like it was too much, too soon, but at the same time long overdue. I opened my mouth, but then he was talking.

"You're right," he said. A pause. "It's not fair. It sucks. I'm so sorry."

I was not prepared for what I would feel, hearing these three words. All this time I'd wanted something just like this from Peyton. But now that I had it, it kind of broke my heart.

"It's all right," I told him. And that was how we left it. All right, or the closest we could get. Still, I'd replay this conversation in my head again and again, trying to get used to how it made me feel. Like my Saint Anything, it was a comfort I hadn't known I needed until it was finally in my grasp.

As the days passed and my mom's mood steadily improved, I let myself get a little hopeful. The showcase was so close, and her being again distracted by Peyton could only work in my favor. I was biding my time before I mentioned it again: I went to school, to Kiger, and to my room, hoping my good behavior was noticed. The times I did have with Mac, plus the promise of more to come, were the only thing that got me through. From the minute I saw him before the first bell to the last kiss as I got into my car to leave for Kiger, the day was just better.

A couple times he called me up when the band gathered in the outbuilding behind his house so I could listen in while Brilliant or Catastrophic—the official name, for now anyway—practiced. I'd put my phone on speaker next to me as I sat at

Kiger or in my room at my desk. Listening, I'd imagine the scene: Eric posturing at the microphone, Ford in his typical daze, Mac keeping the beat behind them. There were the sudden stops and starts, occasional blasts of feedback, and routine disagreements. Each time Layla sang, though, I got chills. I could only imagine what it would be like to hear her at Bendo in person. If I got to go.

When he wasn't at practice, Mac was working. If he had deliveries near my neighborhood, he'd swing by Kiger just long enough for me to catch a glimpse and say hello. More often, though, we were texting. That Tuesday, I was shutting down my computer at Kiger when he wrote this:

Just had a weird delivery.

This was different, as he normally started with the order, daring me to guess who'd placed it.

What was it?

Large pepperoni. Garlic knots.

Even I knew this was the most generic of tickets; it could be anyone. Or everyone. I was about to text back that I needed more details when the phone pinged again.

I think it was that kid.

I raised my eyebrows, confused. What kid?

A pause. Jenn came out of the conference room, shutting the hallway light off behind her. "You ready to get out of here?"

"Yeah," I said. "One second."

Ibarra?

I stared at this word, the letters at first not coming together. Like when you've looked at something so much, it starts to feel like a different language. Jenn was by the door now, pulling her backpack over one shoulder. I came from behind the counter, following her out, then stood there as she typed in the security code and locked the door behind us.

"See you tomorrow?" she asked me. I nodded, and she started across the lot toward her car. As I walked to mine, I pulled up Mac's name from the top of my Favorites and hit CALL.

"How did you know it was him?" I asked as soon as he picked up.

"I didn't, not at first," he replied. Clearly, he was not surprised I'd skipped a hello. "I've actually delivered there before. It's a ranch, over off—"

"Pike Avenue." Of course I knew.

"Yeah." He was driving: I could hear his turn signal clicking. "For some reason, today, I put it together. He's a nice kid."

Of course he was. And now, even though I'd seen him at SuperThrift with my own eyes not too long ago, he was more real to me than ever before. That's what a random connection can do, that moment when separate things suddenly come together. Like fate tapping you on the shoulder so you'll pay attention.

"I should go," I said. "The last thing I need right now is to be late."

A pause. Then: "You okay, Sydney?"

Was I? I couldn't say for sure. After so long just paddling along, trying to keep my head above water, I felt like the tide was turning, sweeping me along with it. The showcase was in three days. David Ibarra was now not only a face, or a Ume.com page, but a place, one I could get to if I chose. For so long, I'd been waiting for something to happen, a change to come. Now that I could sense it getting ever closer, however, it was all I could do not to step back.

※ ※ ※

It was time.

"Mom?"

My mother looked up from her desk in the War Room. "Yes?"

"Can we talk for a second?"

Instead of responding, she shut the open folder in front of her. It was Wednesday evening, a time I'd chosen after deciding it was not *too* far ahead of Friday, while at the same time not the last minute. I'd also waited until after the nightly call from Peyton, when I knew I had the best chance of catching her in a good mood. Clinching the deal, both my dad and Ames were out. It was now or never.

"I wanted to talk to you about Friday," I began, "and the showcase I told you about."

The crease appeared between her eyebrows: not a good sign. "Showcase?"

"Mac and Layla's band?" *Don't panic,* I told myself. *This might work in your favor.* "It's an all-ages show? You said you'd think about it?"

It was not good to be speaking only in questions; confidence was key. Time to regroup.

"It starts at seven," I told her, as if she'd already agreed and we were just hashing out details. "They're second on the bill. So I'd be home by ten at the latest."

The crease deepened. I wished I hadn't noticed. "I thought we said we'd start a bit more slowly than a night at a club, Sydney."

"I haven't done anything or been anywhere for weeks, Mom."

She sighed, already tired of this conversation. "I just don't think it's a good idea. Why don't you call Jenn and Meredith, see if they want to do something?"

"It's not the same," I replied, although I knew that was exactly why she'd suggested it. "Mom. *Please* say I can go. Please?"

Already I'd arrived at the last resort of the truly desperate: begging. Next time, I thought, no planning, no strategy. Just the fact I was already thinking of next time only confirmed the obvious: I was done here. Still, I stood there and made her say it to my face.

"Honey, no," she told me. Then she gave me a sad smile, which just made it worse. "I'm sorry."

And that was that. My Hail Mary, the field goal kick that could win the game but instead went so wide you felt stupid for expecting anything different. I could have stood there and pleaded more, circled back to all the bullet points and arguments I'd compiled. But there was no use. My mom was a lot of things, but a waffler wasn't one of them. Once a no, it stayed that way.

"It's okay," Mac said to me the next morning, when I told him about this at my locker before the first bell. I'd actually started crying, which was so humiliating, not to mention unattractive. "It's one show. There will be others."

"What did you *do?*"

I turned, and there was Layla, glaring at him.

"Nothing," Mac said.

"The girl is crying, Macaulay." She dug in her purse, pulling out a pack of Kleenex and holding it out to me. "You guys better not be breaking up right now. If I can't be in a happy couple, I at least need proximity to one."

"It's not him," I told her, taking a couple of tissues. "It's my mom."

Just saying this set me off again, so I busied myself trying to get cleaned up. Mac said, "She said no about the showcase."

"You're crying about *that?*" Layla sighed. "Please. I wish someone would tell me I couldn't go. Eric's already so bossy and insufferable. It's only going to get worse. Did Mac tell you that he wants us all to meditate before the show now?"

I was touched: I knew she was humoring me. "What?"

"Apparently," she said, leaning against the locker beside mine so we were shoulder to shoulder, "that's what serious bands do before big gigs. Meditate and visualize. He claims it will get us on the same mental plane, 'in spiritual harmony before we make actual harmony.'"

I sniffled. "That sounds like a direct quote."

"Of course it is!" She put her head on my shoulder. "You'll be missed. But it's just one stupid night. Sadly, there will probably be others."

The bell rang then: time for class. The clock was never in my favor. Mac slid his arm around me, pulling me closer to him. "You going to be okay?"

"Yeah," I told him, reaching for his hand. He gave mine a squeeze, then held on for a beat longer before pulling away. As he walked down the hallway to his class, I started crying again.

"Young love," Layla said, handing me another tissue. I wiped my eyes, embarrassed. They were right: it was just one night, one show. But I wasn't a big crier; my emotions, so sudden and fierce, had surprised me. So much, in fact, that it wasn't until later in the day that I realized the most shocking thing at all. It wasn't that I'd broken down, but that I hadn't been alone when I did so. You only really fall apart in front of the people you know can piece you back together. Mac and Layla were there for me. Even if, and especially when, I couldn't do the same for them.

CHAPTER
24

"DID YOU make plans with Jenn?"

My mom felt bad about saying no to the showcase. Not enough to change her mind, of course. But if I'd asked for just about anything else, I had a feeling my chances were good. Too bad it was the only thing I'd wanted.

"No," I replied, shutting the dishwasher.

I could feel her watching me as I picked up a dish sponge and wiped down the counters. In the dining room, my father and Ames were still at the table, continuing a discussion that had begun over dinner about movement on the job/ housing front. When this came up, it was obvious Ames was surprised. Clearly, he'd assumed that reconnecting my mom and Peyton had bought him more than just a few days. I could have told him that my parents never forgot anything. Once they brought something up, it was always still on the table, even if you chose not to see it.

"Well," he'd said to them, reaching for another piece of bread, "my lead at the Valley Inn didn't pan out. But I've got applications in at a few other places."

"And apartments?"

Ames looked at my mom. "Is it a problem, my being here?"

"We've talked about this," my dad told him. "This stay was meant to be temporary, as well as dependent on you actively seeking alternative arrangements."

"There's nothing out there," Ames told him, buttering his bread. He had a lot to learn. At the very least, he should stop eating. "The job market . . . it's tough right now."

My dad looked at my mom, who reached down to the empty chair beside her and pulled out a folder, putting it on the table. Uh-oh.

"I took the liberty of examining the classifieds today. I found six positions you're qualified for. And too many roommate want ads to count."

Ames was chewing, staring at her, as she slid the folder across to him. Finally, he swallowed. "If you guys want me out, I'm out," he said.

Silence. This was *his* Hail Mary. "I think that's best," my mom told him. "Peyton?"

"I agree." My dad picked up his napkin and wiped his mouth. "We appreciate all you've done for us. But this is better for everyone."

I was in shock. Funny how the world works. You don't get the something you really covet, but then the universe provides unexpected compensation. Here I thought you had to make a wish for it to come true.

Ames, true to form, was not going down easy. First, he tried to negotiate for another month. Then a week, followed by the rest of this one. As his offers got lower and lower, it became that much harder to watch, which was why my mom and I had gone into the kitchen. My dad, however, was in his element. He could go all night, and I had a feeling he might have to.

They were still there when I went up to my room at seven thirty. The showcase had started at seven, and Irv had promised me he'd message me on HiThere! when they went on at seven forty-five so I could watch on my phone. In the meantime, I was with them in spirit, via dueling text message exchanges with Mac and Layla.

Layla: Eric just informed me that my outfit isn't meta enough. What the hell does that mean?

Not enough black? I wrote her back.

Mac: Our sound check sucked and everyone's fighting about clothes. Kill me now.

You'll be great, I replied to him.

There was a sound out in the hallway, past my half-open door. I paused, listening. A moment later, I heard my mom moving around the War Room and went back to my phone.

Lot of people here, Layla had written in the interim.

Nervous?

No. A pause. Then: Yes.

Another beep. Mac: Might have to smack Eric. For common good.

Try to resist, I wrote him back. Hear you have a big crowd.

Showcase does. Not us.

Typical, I thought. Back to Layla.

Not right w/out you. Wish you were here.

Beep. Mac. I flipped back to his screen. Rather be at Commons Park with you.

It was dizzying, carrying on both of these conversations at once. So I was grateful that I could give them each the same answer.

Me too.

It was seven forty-five when Irv sent the HiThere! invite. I hit ACCEPT and then he appeared, his face taking up the entire screen. I could barely hear him, the noise of the crowd was so loud.

"They are taking the stage," he reported, as a girl with platinum hair bumped him from behind.

"How was the first band?"

"Awful. Basically amplified screaming. We're lucky there's anyone still here." He shifted, letting a guy in a leather jacket pass. "Everyone's in place but Eric. He's . . . Oh, here he comes. He's making his entrance through the crowd."

I lay back on my bed, smiling. "Of course he is."

Some music was beginning, just a couple of chords, a bit of drumming. "Okay," Irv yelled. "You ready?"

Outside my doorway, someone was passing by. But for once, I didn't care. "Yes," I said. "Show me."

I turned my phone sideways just as the picture changed.

Thanks to Irv's perfect vantage point and massive reach, I could see the entire stage, as well as the first row of the crowd pressed up against it. There was Eric in his fedora, angling himself at the microphone. To his right was Ford, shuffling his big feet. And on the other side, Layla, in her cowboy boots and a red dress, hair pulled back loosely at her neck. Eric glanced at her, smiled, and began to play.

Nervous for them, I touched my Saint Anything pendant, then turned up my phone volume as loud as I could. As Eric launched into the lyrics of the Logan Oxford song I knew by heart, I reached to the picture, pinching it further open, closer in. A moment to focus, and I found what I wanted. He was bent over his drums, playing hard, his hair hanging in his face. Maybe I was the only one looking closely. I'd never know. But he wasn't invisible, not to me. *There you are*, I thought. *There you are.*

※ ※ ※

Any word?

Not yet.

It was after midnight, and all the bands had performed. Now it was just up to the judges and showcase sponsors to pick a winner. Meanwhile, we waited, everyone else at the club and me in my room. I was trying to study, but couldn't focus, distracted by Mac and Layla's collective nervousness (I had never texted this much in one short period, which was really saying something) as well as the noise I kept hearing from the room next door. Not just talk radio this time, but the sound of packing. *Angry* packing.

I hadn't realized it was happening until after their set was over. They'd played well, with Layla's song a highlight, and although the final chorus from the last number got a bit bungled, I was pretty sure nobody else noticed. Throughout, the music was loud, even through my phone speaker, as was the applause and cheering that followed it. Once Irv and I hung up, it was suddenly very quiet. That's when I heard the first thump, followed shortly after by the knock of a drawer being slammed shut. By the time the closet door slammed, my parents were outside my door.

"Ames is leaving in the morning," my mom told me when I opened it. "We just wanted to let you know."

Another bang. My dad raised his eyebrows. I said, "Is everything okay?"

"Yes," he told me. "It was a mutual decision."

The continuing racket of the next hour said otherwise. Every drawer opened was closed with emphasis, the closet door rattling its frame after each use. It was concerning enough that, in the sudden quiet during one of Ames's smoke breaks, I went over, poking the door open and peering in. I glanced over my shoulder, then went to the bed, where a row of boxes sat waiting. One was filled with books, paperback novels and a couple of titles about recovery and addiction. Another held some linens and towels, a few balled-up socks. The last was odds and ends: coffee cups, lighters, charging cords. In one corner was tucked a stack of pictures.

The one on top was of him and Peyton, standing on a sandy beach, probably during their Jacksonville trip. They had their arms around each other's shoulders and were smiling. I flipped to the next: my brother again, this time at our kitchen table, a coffee drink at his elbow. He had one eyebrow raised, half-annoyed, waiting for the shutter to click. A shot of Ames and Marla standing in front of a Christmas tree. The last, at the bottom, was from Peyton's graduation dinner at Luna Blu. I remembered my mom handing the waitress her phone so we could all be in it. My brother was in the middle in a crisp white shirt, my parents on either side of him. I was next to my mom, with Ames beside me, Marla on his other side. We were all smiling, the twinkling lights above us blurring as the flash popped.

Distantly, I heard my phone beep. I dropped the picture back into the box with the others, then went back to my room, where I walked over to my bed to see if the text I'd gotten was the one I'd been waiting for, about the showcase outcome. It wasn't.

On way to hospital. This time, Mac had written for both of them. My mom. It's bad.

*　*　*

There's a lot you can do with a phone. Send a message or a picture. Get the weather, news, or horoscope. See and talk to someone in real time, play games, pay for parking. One thing technology still hadn't mastered, though, was the ac-

tual act of being there. I'd been all right with settling for
distance with the showcase. But not this.

It didn't even occur to me to ask permission to go to the
hospital. It was well past midnight and I'd had enough nega-
tive responses to more reasonable requests. Instead, in those
panicked minutes after getting that three-sentence text, I
put my phone aside, sat down at my desk, and wrote a note.

I wasn't kidding myself. I knew my mom would probably
only get to the second sentence before coming after me, dis-
regarding the rest. It seemed important, though, that for this
last argument, I get to have my say. If I was to be sentenced,
I wanted the details of my crime, too, to be clear.

> Mom,
> I've gone to U General. Layla and Mac's mother
> is there, and I want to be there for them. I never
> wanted to disobey you, that night in the studio or
> now. I'm not Peyton. I'm doing this because I'm a
> good friend, not a bad daughter. I know you might not
> understand, but I hope you will try.

I left it on the keyboard of my open computer. Then I
got my purse and jacket and left, shutting my door behind
me. After all these months of watching the clock and biding
my time, I knew I only had so long before being found out.
I wasn't the only one who could always hear the garage door
opening.

Downstairs, the house was dark, except for one light on

in the kitchen. I glanced in: it was empty. But then, when I put my hand on the door to the garage, someone was right behind me.

I felt a presence first, the heaviness of a body. Then heat. Finally, breath, right on the back of my neck. I froze, and a hand appeared right in front of my face, fingers spread across the door.

"And where are you going?"

Instinctively, I gripped the knob, turning it, and pulled hard. The door didn't budge. I closed my eyes, willing myself to turn around, even though I knew it would mean us being face-to-face, if not nose to nose.

"Leave me alone," I said to Ames, struggling to keep my voice both low and firm.

"Sydney, it's midnight." His voice was high, mocking. Clearly audible. Shit. "I don't think your parents would like this."

I turned around. All I could smell was cigarette smoke. We were uncomfortably close. I couldn't step back, as I was against the door. He chose not to.

"Leave me alone," I repeated. Instead, he moved in. When I lifted my hands, palms out, to push him back, he grabbed my wrists.

I surprised myself with the sound I made, a gasp, almost a shout. All this time, with him first just around, then living under our roof, I'd considered myself trapped. But I hadn't been. I saw it clearly, now that I really was.

"Ames," I said, but now my voice was wavering, "back off."

Hearing this, he smiled, then tightened his grip on my

wrists, pushing them back, back, against my ears. That was when I got scared.

But as he leaned in, closing his eyes, I knew I had to act. I'd been passive for so long. Watching TV all those long, lonely afternoons. At the nearby table, not telling my parents the things that scared me. All around, in this house, there were evidence and symbols of the girl I'd been but no longer wanted to be. Peyton wasn't the only one locked up inside something.

I tried to turn my head as he put his lips on mine, squeezing my eyes shut, but he grabbed my face, jerking me back to face him. I could feel his fingers digging into my chin. "I want you to look at me," he said.

I kept my eyes closed. "No."

"Sydney." The grip tightened. "Look at me."

"No." My voice came out tight, like a scream. It was only when I heard it that I realized my right hand was free.

"Just—" he began, but then my palm was connecting with his face, the sound of skin to skin loud, a smack, and he stumbled backward, bumping into the wall behind him. I reached down for the doorknob, now pressed into my spine, my fingers grappling and sliding, trying to get a grip on it. I'd just twisted it open and turned around, almost free, when he grabbed me around the waist. This time I *did* scream, and pulled as hard as I could away from him, throwing every bit of my weight in the opposite direction. I wasn't budging, totally stuck, and then suddenly, in a snap of a moment, I was stumbling forward, loose, down the steps to the garage.

I put out my hand, touching the front fender of my mom's

car to steady myself. Then I turned, expecting him to come at me again. Instead, I saw my dad.

He had one arm hooked around Ames's neck, tight, the fist clenched, and was pulling him backward down the hall-way, away from me. It was all so crazy and quick, and the only thing I could concentrate on was the sound of Ames's feet jerking across the floor. My father had a look on his face I'd never seen before. I almost didn't recognize him.

"What were you going to do?" he was saying, the words punctuated with deep, jagged breaths. "What were you go-ing to do?"

"Hey," Ames squeaked, reaching up to try to free him-self. "I can't—"

"Are you okay?" my dad asked me, ignoring him.

I nodded, mute. Then a light came on behind them, and I heard my mother's voice. "Peyton? What's going on down there?"

I looked back at my dad, at Ames's face, now bright red. There was no way to explain this quickly, and I had little, if any, time left. So as my father pushed Ames into a chair in the kitchen, and my mother's shadow grew visible, then larger, as she came down the stairs, I slipped into my car.

My wrists ached, and I could still feel his fingers, press-ing hard on my chin. But shaken as I was, I knew there were people who needed me, and whatever else happened here would have to wait. As I reached up, hitting the button for the garage door on my visor, it seemed fitting that the same familiar creaking and grinding—just like my father leaving the night of Peyton's arrest and my mom arriving home those lonely afternoons—would signal the start to whatever this was, as well. It had become the sound at which our lives in this house briefly revealed themselves to the world before going hidden again. When I backed down the driveway, I didn't even look to see if anyone had come out to try to stop me—I didn't want to know. I left the door open behind me.

※ ※ ※

At every stoplight on the way across town to the hospital, even as my head swam with everything that had happened, I checked my phone. I knew Mac: he'd tell me not to worry as soon as there was no reason to. No messages.

U General was all lit up and busy. I parked in a nearby lot, then hurried over to the emergency room, which was crowded and loud, like Jackson but with more adults and crying babies. After I waited for a long fifteen minutes, a nurse informed me that Mrs. Chatham had been admitted and wrote a room number on a scrap of paper: 919. In the elevator going up, I kept looking down at it, like it might carry some hint of what I'd find once I got there. Magical thinking, in the most real of times. When the doors slid open, I stuffed it in my pocket.

With each thing I did—pushing the button for nine, watching the floor numbers climb, taking those first steps down the scuffed, worn linoleum of the hallway—I imagined another action happening as well. My mom awakened by the sound of the scuffle downstairs, or our voices. Seeing my father and Ames in the kitchen before spinning to look for me. Going to my room, finding the note. Scrambling into her clothes, then getting in the car to follow me. Two lives moving separately, but about to intersect soon, not unlike Peyton and David Ibarra on another night. In any moment, there were so many chances for paths to cross and people to clash, come together, or do any number of things in between. It was amazing we could live at all, knowing all that could occur purely by chance. But what was the alternative?

It—not living—was close here at the hospital. I could see it in the rooms I passed, with beeping machines, curtains pulled or open, sighs and moans. At the end of a hallway, I saw a sign: FAMILY WAITING. The room, which was filled with couches and recliners, a TV playing on mute in one corner, was empty. But there was a guitar case leaning against one wall, a duffel bag beside it. And on the lone table, a purse I recognized on a pulled-out chair and a bubble gum YumYum, already licked, on a napkin. They had been here, recently. And left in a hurry.

919, I thought, going back out into the hallway. The rooms blurred as I passed them, focused only on the numbers, always the numbers. 927. I pictured my mom at the wheel, driving in the dark. 925. The hospital finally appearing in the distance. 923. That same bright, busy lobby. 921. So little time. And then I was there.

The door was open. I stopped outside, breathing hard. Just over the threshold, his huge, broad back to me, was Irv. Rosie, in a Mariposa jacket and her ponytail, seemed tiny

next to him, holding his hand. Grasping her other one was
Eric, hat off, his face looking young and scared. Then Layla,
hair loose over her shoulders and staring straight ahead, and
Mac beside her. Together, they circled the bed where Mrs.
Chatham lay, oxygen mask on, eyes closed. Mr. Chatham sat
in the only chair, his head in his hands.

In my pocket, my phone buzzed. I knew who it was, and
that it would be the first call of many. But I didn't budge. Instead, it was Mr. Chatham who moved, somehow prompted
to spot me, and then Layla turned as well.

As our eyes met, I thought again of that long-ago afternoon in the courthouse. When faced with the scariest of
things, all you want is to turn away, hide in your own invisible place. But you can't. That's why it's not only important
for us to be seen, but to have someone to look *for* us, as well.

Layla let go of Mac's hand, then held her own out to me.
As I went to stand between them, closing the circle, I could
feel Mac looking at me. But my eyes were only on her. Then
I kept them open, wide, as she closed her own.

CHAPTER
25

"FOR YOU."

Layla sat up in the recliner, wiping a hand across her mouth. Her hair was sticking up on one side, creases from the chair's corded fabric on one cheek. "What is it?"

"Just look."

She took the bag from me carefully, so as not to wake her mom, who was sleeping. It was pretty much all she'd done while recovering from the mild heart attack to which the other recent episodes had been leading. During her few waking moments, she asked after Mr. Chatham, whichever of her children weren't present and accounted for, and occasionally updates from *Big New York* and *Los Angeles*. Then, tiring quickly, she'd again drift off, leaving us to wait for the next time to ask our own questions, or be left to pose them to each other.

I sat down in the other chair. The seat was warm, recently vacated by Rosie, who'd gone to get some fresh air and some coffee. Outside, the sun was just setting. It was hard to believe it had been less than a full day since we'd all gathered here on a different night, in another darkness. You always lost track of time in places like this, or so I'd heard. But it wasn't just the hospital that had made the recent hours seem to me like the longest in a while.

Layla opened the bag, stifling a yawn with her free hand. Seeing the contents, her eyes widened. She looked up at me. "Did you . . . ? You didn't."

I smiled. "Special occasion."

"Are you *serious* right now?"

"Shhhhhhh!" hissed a passing nurse in the hallway. They moved so quietly, until they were reprimanding you.

Sorry, Layla mouthed, clapping a hand over her mouth. Then, grinning, she dug into the bag, pulling out a box of fries from Littles and putting it on the tray table beside her. She removed a layer of napkins—nodding approvingly at my effort to prevent cross-contamination—then took out one from Bradbury Burger, followed by more napkins and a final order of Pamlico Grill's, lining them up neatly. Then she sat back, taking them in. "The Trifecta. It's amazing."

"I thought you might like it."

"I'm *honored* by it." She sighed happily, then looked into the bag again. "Did you happen to—"

I dug into my purse for the other bag, this one full of ketchups from all three places. Of course there were tiny taste variations. Didn't you know? "Here."

She grinned, taking it as well, then pulled her feet up under her as she began her ministrations. As I watched her,

Mrs. Chatham sighed in her sleep, shifting her feet one way, then the other.

I was tired, too, more so than I could remember ever being. With everything that had happened in the last twenty-four hours, I'd barely slept, other than a couple of hours grabbed that morning between a talk with my parents and returning to the hospital. During that short time, however, I'd still managed to miss the removal of Ames's belongings from our house. Dozing off, I heard my mom and dad conferring with Sawyer in the War Room while one of his employees took the boxes away. When I awoke, there was only silence. I still went to Peyton's room, though, to see it empty for myself. The bed was stripped, the windows cracked, the carpet already vacuumed. He was really gone.

In time, I'd have to make some decisions about whether to press charges, as well as see the psychologist my mom insisted I visit, both with her and my dad and alone. It was just the first step in dealing with what had happened that night and the months leading up to it. Because I'd fled to be with Layla and Mac, I'd never know the words that were said once my mom came downstairs, or the exact blows that caused the injuries Ames's lawyer would later try to get him compensated for. Whatever had occurred, it had not only allowed me to get to Mrs. Chatham's bedside, but also be there long enough to stay with Mac and Layla until she finally opened her eyes. For once, time was on my side.

I wasn't aware of any of this then, though. Instead, I focused only on Mac's hand in mine, Layla leaning into my shoulder on the other side. Even though there were a full eight of us in that small space, it was so quiet, the only sound the beeping of the heart monitor. It was scary, this quiet vigil, like something I'd never before experienced. But I wouldn't have wanted to be anywhere else. Whatever it would cost me—and I didn't know the entirety of that sum yet—I already knew it was worth it.

It was somewhere around two a.m. when I started worrying about my mom. I'd been expecting her to turn up at any moment, and as more time passed without that happening—not to mention another text or call—I started to wonder why. I couldn't imagine what would keep her from coming after me, much less prevent the inevitable confrontation that would follow. By three, though, I was outright concerned. So while everyone was talking at once, relieved that Mrs. Chatham had come to and was able to speak, I whispered to Mac that I was going to make a quick call. When I stepped into the hallway, I saw her.

She was right outside the door, in a metal chair against the wall. So close that if I'd been looking, I might have glimpsed her from inside. Like me, she'd arrived at U General, asked after Mrs. Chatham, and gotten the room number. Although she was shaken by what had happened with Ames—and finally understood my protests about being alone with him— she'd still been upset with me for leaving the house. All she wanted was to get me out of there.

"But you didn't," I said the next morning, when we finally

sat down with my dad to talk about this. "You didn't even come in."

My mom rubbed her eyes; she looked as tired as I felt. "I was going to. I had every intention of dragging you out of there by your hair, if it came to that."

"So what happened?" I asked.

She looked up at me, her expression so similar to the one I'd seen on her face in the hallway the night before. Tired, sad. "I saw you," she said simply.

Me, surrounded by people I cared about. Me, being a good person, a good friend, all the things she prided herself on having taught me. After so many months of looking at me only in the context of my brother, finally, in that bright institutional light, my mother had glimpsed me simply as Sydney, with no precedent or comparison.

Peyton had always been there, coloring the view. Big, vibrant colors first, then the grays and darkness of the last couple of years. But in that moment, surrounded by people she didn't know in a strange room and place, I was the opposite of invisible, the sole thing she recognized. And with that came an understanding of what I'd been trying to tell her for so long: I was different from my brother. And maybe that meant that she, now, could be different, too.

I didn't know this when I went out and found her in the hallway. I just stopped short, so surprised at the sight of her, I couldn't speak.

"Is she okay?" she asked finally, nodding at the open door to 919.

"She will be," I replied.

As she reached up, running a hand over her face, I waited: for directions, admonishment, something. The end of a chase meant someone was caught. Now it was just about details.

And later, they would come. Our conversation at the table the following morning would be the first of many about the last few months. We didn't just talk about that one night, but everything, all the way back to before Peyton had ever gotten into trouble. The walks in the woods. Those long, lonely afternoons. My choice of switching to Jackson. Mac and Layla. David Ibarra. Ames. After holding it in for so long, I sometimes felt like I didn't even have enough breath to say everything I needed to. But somehow, it came.

When the talking got hard—and it did—I'd think back to that one moment in the hospital hallway. I was used to my mother always having a plan. This time was different.

As I watched, she leaned forward, elbows on knees, and rested her head in her hands. A nurse was coming down the hall toward us, her shoes squeaking softly. She barely glanced at us. She was accustomed to anguish.

You get used to people being a certain way; you depend on it. And when they surprise you, for better or worse, it can shake you to your core. My mother had always been tough, so fierce and protective. I would never have thought seeing her fall apart would be anything but devastating. Little did I know that it was just what would give me the chance, finally, to be the strong one.

I knelt down by her chair, sliding my arms around her. At first, she stiffened slightly, surprised. Then, slowly, I felt her weight soften against me, human and living and warm. Our embrace was awkward—her hair in my face, one of my ankles slightly twisted—the way the most vulnerable and precious of things can be. But we were there, together, and in the next room I could hear that monitor beeping. Keeping track of another heart's beat and giving enduring, solid proof of our own.

CHAPTER
26

"READY?"

I looked at Mac behind the wheel of the truck. "As I'll ever be."

He smiled, then reached over, squeezing my hand. Then we pulled out from the curb in front of Seaside and were on our way.

It had been two months since the night of the showcase, a new year begun. Already, I knew it would be better than the last one.

Mrs. Chatham was home and recuperating, her children and husband rallying around her more than ever. Brilliant or Catastrophic did not win the showcase—apparently, the judges were more fans of screaming than Irv—but had attracted the interest of a local studio owner, who was recording a real demo in exchange for Eric doing grunt work for him. With an actual music-related job, his ego was bigger than ever, something I hadn't even thought possible.

Layla, however, clearly saw things differently, or so I'd realized one afternoon at the hospital two days after the showcase. I'd had my usual provisions—fries, magazines,

YumYums—and come into the room expecting to find her in the customary spot, the recliner next to her mom's bed. She was there, but not alone. Eric was lying back, stretched out, with her curled up tight against him, her arms around his neck. I'd stepped back, surprised, and didn't mention it when we met a few minutes later in the hallway. A couple of weeks later, when they officially announced they were a couple, I made it a point to act surprised.

As for me and Mac, we were solid, helped by the fact that my mom had eased her grip on my schedule. I didn't have total free reign—this was Julie Stanford, after all—but we'd worked out a compromise. I had my lunches free, but still worked three days a week at Kiger with Jenn. It kept us in contact, and often Meredith joined us for lunch as well (it went unsaid that Margaret, while still in the picture, was not invited). Layla and I had at least one afternoon a week to hit SuperThrift and to seek out great fries when I wasn't teaching her to drive, a process that was both terrifying and hilarious, often at the same time. Whatever time remained, I was with Mac, either at his house, Seaside, or in the truck, running deliveries. My pizza whispering continued to be spot-on, if I did say so myself. Mr. Chatham said I had a knack for the business. I'd honestly never been more flattered.

After I'd decided not to press charges against Ames, his lawyer had stopped contacting my father about his injuries, and we heard nothing else from either of them. My brother, however, was now calling me regularly on my phone, so we could talk away from my house and parents. We had a lot

to cover, with what had happened with Ames and everything else, and sometimes the pauses and silences felt heavy
enough to break me. When all else failed, we had *Big New
York* to fall back on. I'd even talked him around to Team
Ayre, or close to it. Progress.

Peyton had been increasingly in touch with my parents,
too, calling more regularly. He'd started running on the track
every day during the time he was allowed outside, and he
was working on his speed, reading everything he could get
his hands on about training. My mom, who had run cross-
country in college, was somewhat of an expert, and with this
new topic came a new, hesitant phase of their relationship.
Eventually, Peyton asked her to come to visit. At first, hearing this, I'd been apprehensive, wondering if we'd go back
down the same path where her involvement became more
like an obsession. But my mother surprised me. She did visit,
and enjoyed the calls, especially the running discussions. But
she gave Peyton the space he needed and let him come to her
once in a while, instead of chasing him down.

It helped that she'd found a new cause to busy herself
with. After that night at U General, she'd returned to visit
with Mrs. Chatham. They ended up talking about insurance
issues, as well as the lack of outreach at U General for pa-
tients and their families. What began as her offering to meet
with some administrators on the Chathams' behalf to do a
little fact-finding had, over the ensuing weeks, led not only
to her volunteering in patient relations, but to the prospect
of a paid position. She claimed to still be mulling it over,

that she was too busy with everything else, but my dad and I knew she'd eventually agree. My mom loved a worthy cause, and at U General, she'd never again have a shortage of them.

Peyton had ten more months at Lincoln, his sentence having been cut down a bit due to good behavior. Once released, he'd move to a halfway house for six weeks, where he'd be expected to find a job and housing while also training for his first 10K. For all her progress, I could tell it was making my mom nuts not to help with this, and more than once I'd walked up on her computer to find rental info or classifieds pulled up on the screen. Old habits are hard to break. But I knew she was trying.

I was, too. Another Family Day was coming up at Lincoln in February, and I'd decided to attend. My mom was thrilled—naturally—but less so when I told her that he and I had decided I'd go on my own. We'd come this small distance alone, with so much more to go, and I didn't want to change anything for fear of losing ground. What I was sure of was that whatever relationship my brother and I would have once he was out would be different from our lives as kids. We'd both grown up, in vastly different ways. But I was looking forward, now, to getting to know him. I hoped he felt the same way.

Meanwhile, at home, we were learning, too, finding a new way to be together without Peyton always present in spirit, if not person. My mom and I were talking about colleges and making plans to visit campuses. Thinking about a different future now. Mine. And after not a little pressure from me, Mac had finally talked to his dad about his hopes for going to the U for engineering, or even elsewhere. Mr. Chatham had been dubious, which we'd all expected. But he didn't say no. Now, in the afternoons at Seaside, Mac and I spent time researching schools in between homework assignments, finding out everything we could about the application process. Meanwhile, Layla—who had shown a new interest in the business after finding some books on corporate management at the library—was busy overhauling the Seaside register system and trying to convince her dad to make other changes. He was hesitant about this as well, but listening. After all, she was a connoisseur. And who knew? Maybe even with Mac away at college and beyond, Seaside would stay in the family after all.

That was just it. You never knew what lay ahead; the future was one thing that could never be broken, because it had not yet had the chance to be anything. One minute you're walking through a dark woods, alone, and then the landscape shifts, and you see it. Something wondrous and unexpected, almost magical, that you never would have found had you not kept going. Like a new friend who feels like an old one, or a memory you'll never forget. Maybe even a carousel.

As for me, I had some old business to tie up. It was Mrs. Chatham, actually, who put the idea in my head, during one of my shifts keeping her company in the cardiac rehab wing. They'd had her walking the hallways, getting her strength back, and she'd returned to her room exhausted, getting into bed and immediately closing her eyes. I'd thought she was sleeping and was starting on some calculus homework when she spoke.

"You should talk to him, you know."

We'd been discussing Peyton during our walk together, how he and I were slowly working through things, even though it was sometimes hard. This happened often in her recovery, a sort of elasticity of time and conversation that led her to circle back to something I'd already forgotten. The doctors said it was partly meds, partly exhaustion.

"I'm trying," I said. "But a lot of the time, even now, I don't know what to say."

"Yes, you do." She yawned, turning her face into the pillow. "Start with 'I'm sorry.'"

"Sorry?" I repeated.

She sighed, clearly drifting off. "Then just go from there."

I sat there, confused, as a man passed outside the open door, carrying flowers and a big bouquet of balloons. I watched them bob past, bright and shiny, wondering what I was supposed to apologize to Peyton for. It was not until the next day that I realized maybe she hadn't been talking about him at all.

Now, in the truck, my phone buzzed in my pocket. I pulled it out, glancing at the screen.

At studio with Eric. He is literally strutting, showing me around. Oh my god.

I smiled. You love it.

I swear I do not.

Another beep. My mom, this time.

Bring a pizza home for dinner? And your father
is requesting garlic knots.

Done, I replied. There by six.

OK.

"Everything good?" Mac asked.

"Yeah," I told him. "Everything's fine."

I was getting more nervous, though, the closer we got.
While these were streets I knew well, having driven them
myself more than once, it had been a while since I'd seen
this turn, that intersection. By the time he pulled up in front
of a small brick ranch with black trim, I could feel my heart
beating in my chest.

Mac cut the engine, then turned to look at me. Wary as
always, waiting for my okay. I reached for the door handle,
opened it, and slid out. As I walked around to the curb, he
reached behind him for the warmer. When I got to his window, he had it waiting.

"I can go with you," he said. "If it would make it easier."

"It would," I told him. "But I think I need it to be difficult."

Instead of replying, he reached out, cupping my face in his
hands, and kissed me. Like always, I wanted it to last forever.

I knew we had plenty of time now, though, so I made myself pull away.

And then, somehow, I was going up the walk. The closer I got to the door, the tighter my focus became. It was like I could see and feel everything, crystal clear and right up close. A yellow tabby, licking a paw by the steps. The slight incline of the ramp as I climbed it. Sound of a TV or music from inside. Someone laughing. As I got to the door, I glanced back at Mac. Being with him hadn't fixed everything in my life; no one person could do that. But it was okay. Anyway, it was unrealistic to expect to be constantly in the happiest place. In real life, you're lucky just to be always somewhere nearby.

I shifted the warmer, then reached up and knocked. There's always that lag between when you announce yourself and a door opens, while you wait to see what's on the other side. Working with Mac like this, I'd caught brief glimpses of so many lives, tiny bits of a million stories. This one, though, was mine.

"Coming," a voice called out, and then I heard a whirring sound, growing louder as it approached. I reached up, cupping my hand over the pendant Mac had given me, the way I now found myself doing often. My Saint Anything. I liked the thought of someone looking out for me, whoever it might be. We all need protecting, even if we don't always know what from.

A lock clicked, and I watched the knob twist and the door open. And then David Ibarra was looking up at me, his face surprised. "Did we order a pizza?"

"Not exactly," I replied.

I had no idea what would happen from here, if there were even words to say everything I was feeling. He might slam the door in my face. Ask what good I thought I'd do, coming here. I had imagined all these scenarios, and every possible variation thereof. Only now, though, showing myself, would I find out what was meant to be.

Start with "I'm sorry," Mrs. Chatham had told me. Standing there facing him, all I could think of was another beginning, in that courtroom so many months ago. The judge had asked something—*Would the defendant please rise*—and what followed was for me, Peyton, my parents, Mac, Layla, all of us, one long, still ongoing answer. It seemed only right that now, here, I'd pose a question of my own.

"I'm Sydney Stanford," I said. "Can I come in?"